AROUND THE SOLAR SYSTEM IN 80 DAYS

Jonathan Ammon

Los Angeles, California

For more information:
atssi80d@gmail.com

Follow on Twitter:
@ATSSI80D

Edited by Ben Way
http://benjaminway.co.uk/

Cover art by Ron Miller
www.black-cat-studios.com

Cover ship model and interior illustrations by Jonathan Ammon
Juno Image Credit: NASA/JPL-Caltech/SwRI/MSSS
Cassini Image Credit: NASA/JPL/Space Science Institute

Library of Congress Control Number: 2020910676

ISBN: 978-1-7345362-2-5

Printed in the United States of America

First Edition 2020 – UK Version 1.2

To the scientists and engineers
whose curiosity and ingenuity revealed
faraway worlds to human eyes.

PROLOGUE

A GENTLEMAN'S GENTLEMAN

DAY 1—April 15, 2078

The gaslights along Savile Row flickered valiantly, despite being outshone by the rising sun as it cast its golden rays over the cobblestone street. The historic avenue appeared largely unchanged since the days of Queen Victoria, but in fact it had evolved quite a bit over the centuries. As recently as the 2050s, it had been a bustling metropolitan thoroughfare, drawing the stylish to its legendary bespoke tailors, but the neighbourhood's shops had languished and eventually shuttered with the advent of home fabric printers. Extensive renovations in recent decades had seen it restored to the idyllic state of yesteryear in which it had persisted in the public mind for so long, largely in a failed attempt to attract tourists. Thus Savile Row had become a novelty, home to a few affluent residents willing to pay a premium to live immersed in a quaint fantasy of a bygone era.

Yet it was still obvious upon more than a casual glance that Queen Victoria was long in her tomb and the larger world around the corner had developed far beyond gaslights and cobblestones. If the gleaming spires of London in the distance missed one's notice, if the aerial highway of passenger drones dividing the sky still offered no clue, then surely the copper and chrome robot who rounded the corner would be a dead giveaway.

Pass-Par-2 moved with a lively bounce, elbows held high, creating the impression of the happiest little fellow ever to take a morning stroll. Whether it was genuine emotion or an algorithmic imitation was a matter for engineers and philosophers to debate. Their arguments would not have put a hitch in his step. Passing a woman pushing a pram, he paused to tip his hat, revealing an antenna atop his head with a light at the tip blinking merrily. The felt bowler was the only article of clothing he wore, and it was certainly more than he needed, but it was exactly the sort of affectation his designer had encouraged him to adopt. The mother pushed her child's cart onward, barely acknowledging him, but he registered it as a successful social interaction, tickling the pleasure centre of his Positroniqué processor. He restored the hat atop his acorn-shaped head and resumed his lively gait.

The robot's eyesight was certainly sharper than any human's, his body equipped with seventeen hidden cameras focused in different directions and wavelengths, but his bright, digitally animated eyes weren't actually part of his optical system. They existed solely for emotive expression. The robot's designer believed the old adage that the eyes were the windows to the soul, so he displayed his creation's cheerful spirit through the clearest windows possible. It might still be unsettled whether Pass-Par-2's feelings were earnest or synthetic, but with his friendly and expressive eyes they would never be inscrutable.

His mouth was also a rendered display, but it wasn't an image of a human mouth. Rather it appeared as a squiggly horizontal black line on a white background. When at rest, it typically curled up slightly at the sides to convey a gentle smile. Above the mouth was a moulded nose that was purely ornamental. Although he was equipped with olfactory sensors, the intake vents were discreetly integrated into the palms of his hands. Between his mouth and nose, a pair of wire rods extended about an inch to each side, angled slightly downward, suggestive of a neatly styled moustache. This, surprisingly, was not just for flair. It was a multipurpose instrument used for maintaining gyroscopic balance and measuring barometric pressure. It had ultimately been the deciding factor in making the robot male.

Market research suggested people were distrustful of robots who towered over them, so Pass-Par-2 stood just over five feet, not counting the antenna. His agile arms and legs showed surprising flexibility, bending like articulated tubes. This perhaps accounted for the spring in his step, but his bouncy sway was also a perfect match for his exuberant disposition.

In just a few more steps he arrived at his destination, a large oak door marked 'Number Seven.' He stood before it for several moments, hand poised, ready to knock, but frozen as still as a statue. Any passersby could not be blamed for wondering if an oil can was needed. But at last he snapped out of his suspended animation and knocked politely.

The door opened immediately.

Before him stood a man in his mid-thirties, impeccably groomed and dressed in a manner that seemed of an earlier age, but not entirely out of place among the cobbled streets and gaslights. The man assessed the robot head to toe, looking a bit displeased. Pass-Par-2 respectfully removed his hat again, holding it across his chest as he gave a little bow.

As the robot spoke, his animated mouth expanded into an audio waveform that danced and jittered along with his words. His accent was thickly French.

"Greetings, good sir. I am looking for—"

"You're late," the man said, cutting him off.

The robot flinched, taking a moment to process this unexpected interruption. "I... I'm afraid that's quite impossible, sir. I knocked at precisely 8:30 a.m., the time at which my appointment was scheduled."

"Then your clocks need to be recalibrated." The man reached into his pocket and extracted an ornate watch on a chain. "It was 8:31 and seven seconds according to my pocket watch, which is both Swiss and atomic, accurate beyond question. I shall report this to Monsieur Marchand. Anyway, come inside. I am Phileas Fogg."

"An honour to make your acquaintance, sir. My name is Pass-Par-2, and if it pleases you, I am to be your new valet."

Mr Fogg did not offer his hand, but simply stepped aside, holding the door open for the robot. Pass-Par-2 rendered a facsimile of a smile as he stepped across the threshold. Fogg did remember his manners well enough to take the mechanical man's bowler hat and hang it on a brass hook of the oak costumer in the vestibule. He even closed the front door himself. No formal agreement had been reached yet, so for the moment the robot was being treated as a guest.

Pass-Par-2 took a moment to appreciate the lavish interior of the home before Fogg spoke. "As I assume Monsieur Marchand explained, I am in need of a gentleman's gentleman to attend to my domestic affairs and to do so in a reliable manner. I am a creature of habit, Pass-Par-2. I live by a daily schedule from which I rarely deviate. To date I have been unable to find a human valet capable of the dependability I require."

Pass-Par-2 noted the Englishman's use of the hard *t* at the end of *valet* and adjusted his internal settings to match his employer's pronunciation, although it pained his Gallic preferences to do so.

Fogg continued without pause. "A true gentleman is proving very hard to find these days, so Marchand convinced me to try a machine instead. That is to say, you."

"I understand, sir. I was created for just such a purpose. Your happiness shall be my top priority. Consider Pass-Par-2 your master key for solving all of life's problems." The robot was disappointed when his bon mot elicited no reaction. Perhaps Mr

Fogg didn't speak French, but Pass-Par-2 sensed this austere gentleman was unlikely to appreciate pithy wordplay in any language.

Fogg moved on to the next stage of the interview. "You are a good cook, I trust?"

"My programming in the culinary arts is very thorough. I can recreate the recipes of the greatest cooks on five continents."

Fogg wrinkled his nose. "I won't be needing anything as exotic as that. I assure you my tastes are thoroughly British. The kitchen is through here."

Pass-Par-2 followed him through an arched doorway into a neat and tidy kitchen with black and white tiled flooring and antique appliances. He gestured to a schedule taped neatly to the refrigerator door. Apparently magnets were too ostentatious for Phileas Fogg. "The weekly menu is posted here. Never deviate from it, not by so much as a single condiment, and always have it ready on time. Punctuality is essential. If I am at the table waiting for my plate, Monsieur Marchand will hear of it."

"As he should, sir," Pass-Par-2 replied, horrified at the very thought of such a thing. "Do you frequently dine with guests, sir?"

"Guests? In my home? Certainly not. I don't entertain company here. This is my private sanctuary. I take my meals alone. Do you know how to use a gas stove?" Fogg gestured to a white oven with four cast iron burners on the range. Pass-Par-2's digital eyes widened in delight at the sight of it.

"Sacré bleu, a gas stove! How quaint! I have never seen one before, but I am certain I will master it upon first use."

"You will note the temperature gage uses the Fahrenheit scale. You will find no metric measurements in this house. I live strictly by the Imperial System as defined by the British Weights and Measures Act of 1824. I find evolved systems vastly superior to those arbitrarily imposed upon the world by French scientists, no offence. Will this be a problem for you?"

"No, sir. I am endlessly adaptable."

Fogg straightened his jacket. "Very well. You are hereby in my employ. I am a member of the Reform Club, and I spend most mornings there until noon. I expect lunch promptly upon my return." He turned to make his exit, formalities at a close.

"Of course, Master," Pass-Par-2 replied, his excited voice sounding anything but robotic. "It will be a great honour to serve you. Enjoy your morning!"

Fogg was already gone before Pass-Par-2 could offer his hand. Instead, he leaned over to closely inspect the burners on the range. He turned a knob and marvelled as a ring of blue flame ignited, dancing for his entertainment. He felt at peace in his new assignment. Nothing satisfies a robot quite like having a purpose.

He switched off the burner. It was time to get to work.

CHAPTER ONE

A GENTLEMEN'S WAGER

Despite being the ancestor of contract bridge, the English card game of whist had fallen out of favour nearly everywhere on Earth outside of the exclusive parlour of the Reform Club. This private game, by invitation only, was the primary motivation for Phileas Fogg's membership, as he obviously took no joy in the camaraderie of his fellow ultra-wealthy club members. Likewise, his skill at the game was the only reason most of them tolerated his presence. Yet some found his exaggerated propriety off-putting, complaining that the uptight prig took the fun out of the match. One such player was Gerald Fromme, the banker from Lloyds who felt the admission of mere billionaires like Fogg would spell the ruination of the Reform Club. So when Fogg played yet another trump to take the final trick, Fromme decided it was time to get back to tracking interest rates. He stood up from the table in a huff.

"Playing with Fogg is no fun. I can tolerate losing, but at least make interesting conversation while you take my money."

Fogg replied without looking up from the notepad where he

kept track of his winnings. "If you paid more attention to your cards than gossip, Mr Fromme, perhaps you wouldn't lose."

Fromme swallowed his comeback, choosing to vanish as abruptly as possible instead. As he left, an older gentleman appeared in the parlour. Roland Marchand was a portrait of aristocracy, with his aquiline nose and pencil-thin moustache. He wore a cream-coloured suit that was perhaps a bit out of style, but it evoked a more cultured era. He stepped to the gaming table where Fogg still sat with two other players, Stuart and Flanagan. Both were businessmen of some note. Stuart, who was several inches taller than everyone at the table, was known to meddle in politics. Flanagan, who looked more like a fitness instructor than a venture capitalist, gathered up the cards.

"Marchand, you're just in time. Fogg already cleaned out one purse, so we have an open seat. In fact..." He stood and switched to the chair Fromme had vacated, offering his previous seat to Marchand. "You should partner with Fogg. I feel like Stuart and I might be able to take him if we join forces."

Marchand took the seat without ruffling his suit. "I could play a match." His French accent was even thicker than his robot's, almost beyond parody. He paid the ante as he focused his attention on Phileas Fogg. "I trust my delivery found his way to your house?"

"Yes, he did, and over a minute late." Fogg began dealing out cards as he calmly stated his criticism. "You really shouldn't set their clocks by the city network. It is infamous for its inexactitude. But as he wasn't yet in my employ at that time, I have decided not to hold it against him."

"Splendid," Marchand replied, choosing to ignore the complaint while peeking at his cards. "I do hope you will keep an account of his performance. You are our first beta tester for this new premium personal assistant."

Fogg finished fussing with the cards in his hand. "The design is impressive. Almost lifelike. But I must say, I was surprised to find him so... French."

Marchand dropped his cards, taking offence at the slight. "But of course he is French! He was designed and built at my laboratory in Calais. Why would he not be a perfect Frenchman?"

"Yes," said Fogg, as he laid the queen of spades on the green felt. "But the accent—"

Stuart erupted with a derisive laugh. "Wait, you built a robot with a French accent?"

"French is his native language," Marchand shot back.

Fogg calmly clarified his observation. "Fair enough, but when he speaks English—"

Marchand didn't allow him to finish the thought. "If he *must* speak English, he should speak it the way it is meant to be spoken. Why should a mechanical man be burdened with a thick British tongue incapable of elegant elocution?"

Fogg nodded in deference, letting the matter go. "His accent doesn't concern me, monsieur, so long as he is diligent in his duties."

"Then I am certain you will be satisfied. Domestic service is his raison d'être."

It was unknown to Marchand (yet it would not have surprised him at all to hear) that Pass-Par-2 was at that very moment exercising his raison d'être in Phileas Fogg's living room. He was vigorously cleaning the glass of the front window with his left hand, but being a master of multitasking, he would not allow the right hand to dawdle. The tip of the index finger twisted open like the iris mechanism in a camera, transforming into a vacuum wand that he used to clear the dust from a bookshelf. He wasn't humming a merry song, only because this very human concept was unfamiliar to him, but had he known some means of outwardly expressing peace and satisfaction, he certainly would have done so.

Marchand smiled over his cards, imagining exactly such a scene. "I have a lot riding on that little bot. This could be my last attempt at a mass market android."

Stuart saw an opportunity to steer the conversation on to business talk. "It's a tough market. People just aren't spending on tech in this economy. And don't expect the government to help boost innovation. They're trying their hardest to regulate the asteroid-mining industry out of existence."

Flanagan scoffed. "Here he goes, blaming the government for his losses again. As if he doesn't have half of parliament in his pocket."

Frederick Carroll Stuart came from a prominent family long ensconced within British politics, but he had chosen to focus his own talents within the private sector. He had substantially increased the family's already vast fortune through heavy investment in mining rare minerals from the asteroid belt. He liked to promote himself as a pioneer of the industry, but Fogg knew better. Stuart had watched the true innovators as they accrued unimaginable—and, more importantly, unmanageable—debt while chasing the untapped riches within those rocks found in the vast emptiness between the orbits of Mars and Jupiter. They had made costly mistakes, as innovators often do. When those companies folded, Stuart built a new one, standing tall on the backs of their corporate corpses. He hired their brightest minds and steered clear of the pitfalls that had sunk their previous enterprises. Fogg gave Stuart points for shrewdness, certainly, but he had only made the move once it was sure to be profitable.

Stuart had championed the tactic of using autonomous drone ships to propel promising asteroids into closer orbits, making it much easier and cost-effective to support human miners on the surface. His goal of putting an asteroid in Earth orbit had been quashed by UN restrictions that were above even his family's sphere of influence, but he privately considered it a victory that he had been allowed to move a giant rock into lunar orbit instead. That asteroid had now been circling the Moon for over a decade, where Stuart's mining company had extracted every last ounce of value from it. And it had been profitable indeed, leading to even more ambitious plans currently in development.

Then the UN had caused yet another hiccup in his bottom line. His company had first announced plans to crash the remainder of the asteroid into the Far Side of the Moon, but this had been determined to be potentially dangerous and unnecessarily destructive. With its orbit slowly decaying, though, some action needed to be taken. Stuart reluctantly approved of a plan to propel the asteroid into a collision course with the sun, unhappy about the expense of moving that much mass such a huge distance, but again the UN balked. Some flake from the Netherlands had actually stoked concerns about what effect this might have on the sun. Privately Fogg considered those concerns to be irrational. An asteroid hitting the sun would do far less damage than a flea biting an elephant. But politics were what they were—implacable, unreasonable and occasionally pig-headed. Unfortunately the British government was currently supporting a UN proposal that would restrict the relocation of any other asteroids in the future, citing concerns about their potential use as weapons of extinction-level destruction. In light of developments in recent years, there had been a lot of handwringing in the media over the potential for 'natural projectiles' being pushed towards Earth from the outer solar system. Fogg believed the hysteria unfounded, and anyway it was unlikely a law on Earth would curtail the nefarious efforts of any imagined terrorist beyond the orbit of Mars.

Stuart (and, more publicly, his family) had championed the expensive Orbital Shield Program as an impenetrable solution to protecting Earth from inbound asteroids, whether naturally occurring or launched in aggression. It didn't hurt that one of Stuart's other companies was a contractor for that project. Stuart pointed to the assured protection of the orbital missiles while working to defeat the proposed international law, which would not only stop his future mining prospects, but would also require his company to maintain a stable orbit for the asteroid they had already exhausted. That ongoing expense would bite into his profits by no small amount. It was still an unresolved matter, and the longer it stretched out the more it was costing him. And his Reform Club whist partners had to listen to him complain about it every single day.

"By the time the UN decides what we're supposed to do with that damned rock, I'll be in the red for certain. It would be cheaper to break the whole thing down to pebbles, paint them blue and green, and sell it as fish tank gravel."

Flanagan nodded in sympathy. "I know I'll think twice before I invest in any other space ventures." Thomas Albert Flanagan IV had inherited his family's fortune before he had been old enough to be smart with it. That was twenty years or so ago, so youthful recklessness was no longer an excuse. Luckily for him, his holdings had been prodigious enough to weather his impulsive risk-taking. By Fogg's estimation, all of his investments had been foolhardy save one, and that was the one Flanagan was currently most irate about. He had been supporting propulsion research by a husband-and-wife team of Egyptian engineers promising a revolutionary new rocket engine, but lately they had faced several setbacks just when Flanagan had sensed profits were near at hand. First, the engineers had been forced to relocate their lunar research facility beyond the rim of Hayn Crater on the northeast limb of the Moon after the government of the colony there expressed concerns about radiation, which seemed absurd at the time considering how much radiation pummels the Moon's surface on a regular basis. But caution proved prudent in this case when the first test firing of the engine put several lab workers in hospital. Fortunately medical science had made great strides in the treatment of radiation exposure, so the workers should recover in time. Worse news came in the report from the engineers. It seemed the radiation problem was endemic to the workings of the propulsion system. There was simply no way to reduce the radioactivity. As such they would have to shield it, and that would require designing a much larger ship than anticipated. Flanagan had reached his breaking point. As he tossed the three of spades on the table, he said, "I'm through with those propulsion engineers tinkering around up there, burning my money. I told them yesterday I'm pulling the damn plug."

"Smart move," said Stuart. "Everyone talks as if we're still in the early days of the Great Expansion, but the way the economy is turning I'd say it's far more likely we are on the brink of a new era of Earthbound austerity."

"I'm afraid you're exactly right," said Flanagan.

"It is a disappointing truth," Marchand added.

A sad silence hung over the table. Then: "You're fools. All of you."

That, of course, came from Phileas Fogg.

The others looked to each other, stunned by the man's sudden interjection, wanting to make sure they'd heard him correctly. It was Stuart who finally responded. "What are you saying, Fogg?"

"I am saying that you three gentlemen are fools if you truly cannot see that you hold the solution to each other's problems. Mr Flanagan, I've read the schematic of that engine you funded. It is quite remarkable. And I understand the Egyptian team successfully test-fired it once, if reports are true."

Flanagan swallowed. His efforts to keep that out of public knowledge had apparently been for naught. Fogg obviously knew all about it. *No sense in obfuscating*, he thought. "If you consider nine people hospitalised with radiation sickness to be a success, then yes."

"That's a trifling matter. It just needs sufficient shielding."

This was really starting to irritate Flanagan. *Who the devil does Fogg think he is, trying to literally tend to my business?* But he kept his composure. "And do you know what it would cost to build a ship large enough to shield that engine?"

"You don't have to build anything. As it so happens, Mr Stuart already has a sizeable rock for which he has no further purpose."

This statement caused a moment of bewildered silence around the table. Stuart leaned in. "You propose turning my asteroid into a starship?"

"It's the perfect shield when paired with Flanagan's engine mounted on one side and perhaps a small landing craft on the other. And with Marchand's robot as a crewman..." He turned to the Frenchman. "I assume your robot is immune to radiation?"

"Oui, Pass-Par-2 can withstand high levels of radioactivity, and he can also function in the vacuum of space without difficulty."

"So there you have it. With your engine and your asteroid and your robot, I could be enjoying dinner at the summit of Olympus Mons in three days' time."

"I would very much like to see Olympus Mons." The voice that spoke was old and laboured, but still sharp and undeniably charged with vim. Phileas Fogg turned to see Lord Albemarle sitting on the divan behind him. He was nearing his 107th birthday if his official bio could be trusted, but he didn't look a day over 99. What hair he had left was sparse and pure white. The only skin left unwrinkled were the liver spots. But something about him projected happiness. Maybe it was just carefree senility setting in, a freedom from social etiquette and expectations and manners. He sat with a box of rocks in his lap, studying one closely with a magnifying glass. Fogg wasn't sure how long he had been in the room, but he hadn't made a peep before now. "I always wanted to go, but the rockets to Mars took too long and there was still so much left to learn here on the Moon."

Flanagan laughed derisively and Stuart smirked at the old man's confusion, but Marchand leaned over to helpfully remind him where he was sitting. "You aren't on the Moon anymore, Lord Albemarle. We're in London now."

"London? Ah, yes, merry old England. That explains this heavy gravity. But I did live on the Moon for quite some time."

He paused, uncertainty in his eyes, then he continued with a stammer, "Didn't I...?"

Fogg noticed Stuart and Flanagan suppressing laughter, and it stirred an inner rage. The sheer disrespect these wealthy but worthless men were showing to a genuine national hero! As far as Phileas Fogg was concerned, Lord Albemarle was the finest gentleman England had to offer, and he was one of the main reasons he had wanted access to this exclusive game room. But despite often sitting mere feet away from him, he had not yet summoned the nerve to speak to the man. Though he had always seemed gentle and friendly, he feared it would feel like chatting about the weather with Winston Churchill or Oliver Cromwell. He felt he needed something worthy of the great man's time if he was ever going to engage him in conversation. And now he realised at long last that time had come. He made sure his voice was strong and clear. "Indeed you did, Lord Albemarle. For many years. I followed your adventures with great interest."

The old man smiled at the flattery.

"We all did, old friend," added Marchand.

Lord Reginald Albemarle had nearly retired before he got his chance to go to the Moon. He had enjoyed a fulfilling career as a professor of geology at Cambridge and was ready to give up teaching and do some fieldwork again just to satisfy his own love of the science. It was then, quite out of the blue, that he was offered the opportunity to lead the first ground-level survey of the South Pole of the Moon. And so as a septuagenarian he left his homeworld behind for the first time and spent the next sixteen years exploring impact craters and mountain ranges and oceans of dust and subterranean lava tubes that had never before been seen by the eyes of any human. But whatever he saw, the world saw too. Anyone with interest in his exploits could enjoy a weekly live broadcast on the BBC in which he would share his findings and answer questions from rockhounds and space enthusiasts back on Earth. He was a beloved celebrity among the educated class in many different countries. He was nearing his 90th birthday when he finally returned home a hero. He was all but forced by popular demand to serve in the House of Lords, but he found it so deathly dull that he only bothered to show up when there was no way to avoid it. He had finally been allowed to retire in peace after his centennial birthday in 2071. He no longer made public appearances, but he could often be found here in the whist parlour of the Reform Club, although he didn't play the game much himself anymore. Mostly he just gazed at his rock collection.

"Yes, the Moon is where I got these rocks. Have I shown you my rocks?" He gazed into Marchand's eyes, trying to keep a firm grip on the here and now.

"I've seen them many times. They are quite extraordinary."

"Alas I never got a rock from Mars. Too far. It was just too far."

"Perhaps Fogg can bring you one back," Flanagan sniped derisively. "He claims he can be there by Monday morning."

Phileas Fogg did not appreciate being the focus of ridicule by the likes of Flanagan. This was no laughing matter. He raised his voice a bit so Albemarle would have no trouble hearing him. "I should like nothing more than to bring you a rock from the great volcano on Mars, Lord Albemarle. I just need to convince our friends here to build the ship I need."

"Oh," the venerable old man said, a delighted look upon his face, "that would be marvellous!"

Stuart took a puff of his cigar and leaned back from the table. "If we're going to all that trouble, why stop at Mars? With a ship that fast, perhaps you could pick up something from the asteroid belt as well."

Lord Albemarle didn't skip a beat. "Oh, yes, on the dwarf planet of Ceres there's a most remarkable mountain... Ahuna Mons! A great pyramid of salt with shining white slopes more than three miles high!" He turned hopefully to Fogg. "Do you think you could bring me a salt deposit from Ahuna Mons?"

Fogg nodded. "It would be my honour to contribute to your renowned collection."

Since everyone was having such fun with the premise, Marchand saw no harm in playing along. "If you are going to the asteroid belt, Fogg, you may as well continue on to the moons of Jupiter."

Albemarle's eyes grew brighter as the possibilities piled up. "Oh, young man, you must visit Ganymede! Did you know there are people on Ganymede now?" Uncertainty crept back across his face. "Is that true or did I dream it?"

"It is true, Lord Albemarle. There's an international science outpost there," Fogg confirmed.

His face recovered a warm joy with this reassurance. "Yes, that's right! I heard they've found geodes in the underground caverns there. Most exciting! That means there must have been quite a bit of water at one time. You see, when water carries silica into cavities in volcanic rock—"

Flanagan interrupted. "It's Geology 101 lecture time again."

Fogg spoke up before Albemarle could fully process the sarcasm. "I shall put you down for one Ganymede geode," he said with a smile.

As Albemarle beamed back at him, Stuart continued the game. "Well, then, I guess Saturn is next in line, correct? Anything from there catch your fancy?"

Flanagan offered, "A piece of the rings, obviously."

"Oh, no," said Lord Albemarle. "Don't be daft. The rings are made of ice. It would melt, don't you see? No, all the excitement at Saturn is on its moon Titan, where methane flows like water." His eyes turned wistful. "When I was just a boy learning to love rocks, I used to collect smooth stones from a stream behind my home. Can you imagine holding a rock that was smoothed by centuries submerged in a stream of liquid methane?" It was clear Albemarle was enraptured by the thought.

"Are you writing all this down, Fogg?" asked Stuart with a

wide grin.

"No need. Lord Albemarle's words are too passionate to forget. I shall bring you your rocks, sir."

"Wonderful!" replied Albemarle.

Marchand sensed this game had perhaps gone on for too long. "Fogg, don't tease the poor man."

"I did not start this, and I do not tease. Now, what can I collect from Uranus?"

Flanagan and Stuart snickered at Fogg's pronunciation, which suggested a proctological examination. Even Marchand had to suppress a smile. "Fogg, I believe the preferred pronunciation is 'Uran-us.'"

"Don't be silly. I'll not alter the proper pronunciation of a word simply to avoid the titters of sophomoric simpletons." He was none too subtle with his glance in Flanagan's direction at this remark.

"Uranus is a dark, gassy place." Lord Albemarle, for those keeping tally, was in agreement with Fogg's pronunciation. "But there is a moon there called Miranda with a terribly tortured surface, including the tallest cliff in the known universe, six miles high! No one has ever even been there. Unless... unless I missed something?"

Marchand said, "No, you are quite right. Other than the Voyager 2 flyby nearly a century ago, that tiny world remains untroubled by mankind."

Albemarle seemed to be looking out at a vista that no one else could see. "Yes, any sample from Miranda would be quite a trophy indeed..."

"And it shall be yours," Fogg replied at once.

Albemarle was ready to continue with his wish list. "And from Neptune—"

Fogg respectfully cut him off. "Oh, I'm afraid I won't be able to make it to Neptune on this trip, sir. It is on the opposite side of the sun right now."

"Oh. That's a pity."

"You say that as if the other planets are not equally unreachable," said Flanagan with eyebrows practically merging into his hairline.

"That is precisely what I am saying," said Fogg. "Due to the current fortuitous alignment, all of the outer planets save Neptune could be toured in less than six weeks."

Stuart was quick to challenge the audacious claim. "Ridiculous! You can't even get to Mars in six weeks. Enough of this nonsense!"

But Albemarle still had items to add to his shopping list. "Don't forget Pluto! It's still a planet in my book. A fascinating little world. I would love any geological sample from there!"

Stuart chuckled. "Yes, Fogg, it would be a shame to miss your chance to see the most eccentric oddball in the solar system." He blew a smoke ring. "And I don't mean the planet."

Flanagan caught his drift. "Yes, surely you must visit the Mad King of Pluto as part of your grand interplanetary tour."

Fogg thought for a moment. He knew this would be a momentous decision. The degree of difficulty would increase tenfold. Pluto was not as conveniently aligned as the other planets, and it was currently more than twice as far away as Uranus. And the so-called Mad King who had landed there and claimed the icy world in his own name would certainly be an extra complication. *Although*, he had to admit, *an intriguing complication*. He made a quick calculation. Then he rounded up.

"I can include Pluto in the itinerary, but it will require a bit more time. Eighty days."

"Good heavens," Marchand exclaimed, "I'm starting to believe he's serious!"

"I am always serious, . But I warn you, I shall be travelling at your expense. I have thirty billion pounds that says I can deliver Lord Albemarle's rocks to the Reform Club in 80 days, as long as you gentlemen provide the asteroid and the engine. And the robot, of course, who Marchand has been kind enough to provide already. Will you accept my wager?" He expected a moment of self-doubt as he awaited their reply but found that none came. He was certain his numbers were correct. He knew the thing could be done.

Flanagan spoke first. "I would almost feel guilty. You say 80 days to Pluto and back? Even if the engine works the way you think it will, you could lose the bet with a single unforeseen setback."

"There is no such thing as the unforeseen for the properly prepared."

Stuart laughed at this. "There is no Mrs Fogg, is there?"

Marchand questioned, "Eighty days? Did you calculate the mathematical minimum in your mind?"

"You think I'm incapable?"

"I don't question your maths, mon ami, but I am starting to question your sanity."

Fogg was tired of their stalling. "A properly calculated minimum is all that is ever required. Eighty days. Six rocks. My thirty billion pounds against ten from each of you. Do you accept?"

Stuart and Flanagan exchanged a quick look, then pounced.

"Absolutely," said Stuart.

"We'd be fools not to," Flanagan said enthusiastically.

Only Marchand demurred a moment longer. Then he looked at Albemarle's hopeful eyes. The loss of ten billion pounds would hit him harder than it would Stuart or Flanagan, and truth be told he would have rather been wagering on Fogg to succeed. But 80 days? It was beyond imagination; absurd and impossible. He made his decision. "I'm terribly sorry to do it to you, Mr Fogg, but I too accept your wager."

Fogg was pleased. "Very well. Please assemble in the parlour, the real one, at seven this evening to formalise the wager. I shall depart at half past the hour."

Marchand was stunned. "You mean to say you leave this very evening?"

"Of course. The planets are aligning and will not wait for

me to dillydally. I need to depart for the Moon tonight so that I can collect Flanagan's engine and have it mounted on Stuart's asteroid. Now, if you'll excuse me, I believe this pot is mine."

Fogg laid down his remaining cards, aces and kings all. Stuart and Flanagan sighed in frustration as Fogg reached for his temples and seemed to grab a pair of invisible glasses. In that moment, he burst into a cloud of pixels and vanished from the Reform Club's virtual card parlour.

***

Pass-Par-2 felt quite certain he was going to enjoy this new existence. The cleaning! The cooking! The glorious routine of it all! His electronic mind enjoyed predictably repetitive tasks more than anything, and the housework of Master Phileas Fogg was as reliable as the orbits of the planets. Now that his internal clocks were synchronised with Fogg's home system, he had planned a schedule for the day down to six-second intervals, and he was looking forward to executing his tasks for the remainder of the afternoon.

He set the oven to preheat in anticipation of baking his new master's filet of sole. If he had timed it correctly (and he was absolutely certain he had), the final dish would be plated and cooled to optimal serving temperature at precisely noon. Not quite ready to trust the temperature dial on the antique oven, he bent over to take a temperature reading with his own thermal gauges when he heard a muffled noise from upstairs. Had the master called his name? Surely not. He had been so clear about his daily schedule, and he was slated to be in his VR chamber playing cards for another hour and thirteen minutes.

Pass-Par-2 had just decided to disregard the noise when he heard it again. It was definitely the voice of Phileas Fogg, and it definitely sounded like he had called his name, and it *very* definitely sounded agitated. He abandoned the oven at once and dashed to the bottom of the stairs as fast as he could.

Fogg was standing atop the stairs, untangling himself from his VR accessories. "There you are. I should not have to call you twice."

"Master! Apologies. I thought I heard you, but it was not yet noon, and you were so adamant about punctuality. Are my clocks running slow again?"

"I logged off early. Stop whatever you're doing and pack a suitcase for me at once." Having freed himself from his haptic feedback vest, he turned to put it in its case, but then spun around again before Pass-Par-2 could verbalise any follow-up questions. "On further thought, first go to that shop on Regent Street and purchase a set of luggage as it has just occurred to me that I own none. Then return home quickly and pack them."

"Right away, sir." Before Fogg could disappear into his chambers, the robot ranked his growing list of queries and asked the most pertinent one. "Are you going on a trip?"

"Yes, and I also need you to charter a flight to the Malta spaceport at eight o'clock this evening. Then I need first-class accommodation on the midnight launch. Do they charge for robots? Better safe than sorry. I don't want you stowed in cargo. Book two tickets to the Moon."

"The Moon? Master, are you suggesting that I am also to go on this trip?"

"That's right," said Fogg as he turned from the top of the stairs, already on to his next task in his suddenly busy day. "Just a quick trip around the solar system. Back in 80 days."

Then his master disappeared into his private office. Pass-Par-2 was standing alone at the bottom of the staircase, holding a spatula he had no memory of grabbing. He was frozen for a moment, except for his digital eyes that jittered frantically as a flurry of options, odds, and calculations fired in his digital brain. He spoke quietly, flatly, and for the first time his voice could be described as robotic.

"Ne... pas... calculer."

Then he shook his head and snapped out of it. Robots are

certainly capable of being shocked, but they also adapt quickly. It was just a matter of reprioritising his task queue. His carefully planned schedule for the day was now overwritten in an instant. He had a new job to do. He turned and rushed to the front door, pausing only long enough to grab his hat before he headed back out into the city.

CHAPTER TWO

FROM THE EARTH TO THE MOON

While it was true that punctuality was the central tenet of Phileas Fogg's very being, he also firmly believed that one is not late if one arrives at precisely the time one intended to arrive. He had told the other gentlemen to meet at the Reform Club at seven in the evening, but he had planned his own arrival for ten minutes past the hour. Fogg wasn't normally one for flashy behaviour, but he understood this to be an appropriate opportunity for a dramatic entrance. He calculated that leaving them waiting would not only build anticipation for getting the contest underway, it would also reassure them that their bet was a sure win. If he couldn't arrive on time to a meeting a mere ten-minute walk from his home, how could he navigate across the universe with any punctuality? Stuart would likely see through the ruse, but perhaps it would quell any of Flanagan's lingering uncertainties. Fogg was too invested at this point to allow the enterprise to falter before the starting gun had even been loaded, let alone fired.

He crossed St James Square and reached Pall Mall just as

the crossing signal changed in his favour, exactly as he had timed it. Pass-Par-2 followed behind him as he crossed to the ancient but unassuming edifice of the Reform Club. The little robot lugged two factory-fresh roller bags with a small valise stacked on top, handling the load deftly despite the uneven cobbles. It had been a whirlwind first day for Fogg's new valet. One errand after another had kept him on the run since buying the luggage. He was horrified that his master had opted to fend for himself for lunch (he had made a sandwich... a *cold sandwich!*) while Pass-Par-2 had fetched supplies and prepared the house for nearly three months of vacancy. His task queue had been full all day, and even now, while carrying the bags up the steps to the building's entrance, he was remotely settling some bills and rescheduling appointments. There had not been a moment of peace. Pass-Par-2 was starting to feel the drain on his energy reserves, but he took comfort in the certainty that no human valet could have offered this level of service.

Fogg held open the door and led them into the Reform Club. Pass-Par-2 wasn't certain what he had expected, but it wasn't this. The lobby had cracked tile flooring that could have used a coat of wax. The overhead lighting was dimmed. Pass-Par-2 noted with some horror that two... no, *three...!* of the bulbs appeared to be dead. There were cobwebs above the main entrance. His considered opinion was that whatever robot was in charge of upkeep around here clearly needed an upgrade. Pass-Par-2 approached a door with no knob and peered through the small inset window to see a room full of computer banks. There wasn't a soul in sight.

"It's not exactly as I pictured it..."

Fogg checked his pocket watch as he stood near the only door without a window. "The building is mostly a server farm now, but they still maintain the original parlour. I'm afraid you'll have to wait out here – non-members are not allowed inside."

"Of course, Master." Pass-Par-2 released the handles of the suitcases and took up a stationary position by the front door.

Fogg decided his moment had come. He opened the windowless door and stepped inside.

Stuart, Flanagan, and Marchand waited inside. Fogg recognised them, but just barely. Stuart, who had towered over him in VR, could not have been over five foot two in real life. Flanagan, who digitally presented himself as a model of physical fitness, was in actuality rather rotund. And bald. Monsieur Marchand looked the most like his avatar, just older. Quite a bit older, in fact.

"Damn," said Flanagan. "He's here. I lose the side bet."

"You're making me money already, Fogg," said Stuart.

Marchand approached him and shook his hand firmly. "I don't believe it! You look exactly like your avatar."

"Of course," replied Fogg. "Why should I want to misrepresent myself?"

"Yes, well, mine was technically accurate once too. I simply keep forgetting to update it. For a couple of decades now," the Frenchman smiled.

The parlour itself was also less impressive in reality than its virtual representation. There was a ping pong table in the middle of the room and a dartboard on the far wall. A broken pinball machine stood in the corner. The only chairs in the room were of the metal folding variety. Everyone chose to remain standing.

"Right, let's get to business. I have a legally binding contract for your review."

Fogg retrieved an envelope from his jacket's inner pocket and removed a single sheet of paper from within. He unfolded it and handed it over to Stuart.

"Blimey," said Flanagan, "actual paper? Classy move, Fogg."

Stuart began reading. "Leaving at 7:30 p.m. GMT on 15 April 2078 AD, Phileas Fogg has a period of exactly 80 days, or 1920 hours or 115,200 minutes, in which to retrieve mineral samples from the following worlds..."

"Somebody check those hours and minutes," said Flanagan.

"Don't bother," replied Marchand. "Phileas Fogg is a man of

honour. I would trust his maths above a calculator any day. I'm ready to sign."

Flanagan was still being obstinate. "Now hold on just a moment. Where's the bit about the money?" He peered over Stuart's shoulder, scanning the document himself.

Stuart read, "He shall return these samples to the Reform Club in London within the time limit or forfeit the sum of thirty billion pounds to be held in an account at the Bank of England to the challengers. If the challenge is successfully completed, the equal amount shall be due to him by the undersigned." There was more information on the page (account numbers, attorney contact information, etc.), but Stuart saw no point in reading it aloud.

"You hired a lawyer to draft this, Fogg?" asked Flanagan.

"I should pay a lawyer to write two simple paragraphs? I made the language as clear as possible. Which of the big words are confusing you, Mr Flanagan?"

"But who is this lawyer you mention at the bottom?"

"My legal counsel in case disaster strikes. She has been instructed to settle the wager on my behalf if I do not return."

Stuart took the offered pen from Fogg's hand. "I'll sign, but I feel like we should have an impartial witness here."

At that moment, the door to the parlour opened. His back to the door, Fogg feared his robot had disobeyed orders, but when he turned around he saw a woman in a traditional white nursing uniform pushing an elderly man into the room, his face frozen in a catatonic stare.

"Lord Albemarle!" a voice said in hushed reverence. Fogg wasn't sure who said it; it may have even been him. The ancient geologist had not made a public appearance in years, and now it was clear why. He appeared to suffer from total paralysis aside from his blinking eyes. The nurse parked his wheelchair and began positioning a jointed metal arm to hold a curved screen just in front of the lower half of Albemarle's face. With the push of a button, the animated image of his avatar's mouth appeared on the screen, masking his own drooling orifice.

"Hello, chaps," came the familiar, cheery voice of Lord Albemarle, presumably from speakers hidden somewhere around the screen. "I couldn't miss all the excitement."

"It's an honour to see you in person, sir," said Fogg. "You look well."

"Rubbish. I know I look like a blinking cadaver propped up in a chair, which is why I rarely log off these days. I'm so much freer online. But I had to come to see you on your way."

"I'm very pleased that you did."

Flanagan stepped forward. "The nurse really shouldn't be in here. There are rules, gentleman."

"I'm a member, you git," the woman shot back.

Marchand spoke up to move past Flanagan's idiocy. "We were just about to sign the wager. Perhaps you could serve as the witness?"

"Of course," said the avatar mouth. "Witnessing things is just about all I can do these days."

One by one, the men bent over the ping pong table and added their signature to the bottom of the document. While the nurse signed on behalf of Lord Albemarle, the man himself asked to speak to Fogg privately.

"I wanted to thank you for this undertaking, young man. If I could get up out of this chair I'd go with you myself."

"I'm certain you would, sir."

"Extraordinary endeavour in just 80 days. I hope you can do it. I was planning to die a week from Sunday, but I suppose I can put that off for a little while." The digital face smiled. Fogg assumed he was joking, but who could be sure? Assisted suicide was not uncommon among those facing their second century of life. Ignoring the avatar's mouth on the screen, Fogg took a moment to look into the man's very real eyes. *How tragic*, he thought, *for such a great mind to be trapped inside such a withered, broken body. This is why I must succeed.* He knew his finances could not sustain a loss in this wager, but more importantly his soul could not withstand disappointing this great man. Fogg himself had never cared about a rock in his life, but at that moment he knew there were six rocks somewhere out there in the cold darkness waiting for his hand so that this great hero before him might know the thrill of discovery one last time in his life. That was reason enough to accomplish the task.

The clock on the wall chimed the half-hour. "That's your cue, Fogg," said Marchand.

Phileas Fogg looked at his pocket watch in puzzlement, then walked over to the clock and pulled it down from the wall. It was running sixteen seconds ahead of his pocket watch. A quick adjustment fixed that. He hung it back in place just in time for it to chime again. He turned to face the others, standing straight and tall. "*That* is my cue. Gentlemen, I will see you in 80 days."

With that, he turned and left the parlour.

***

The flight to Malta was uneventful. In the end, Pass-Par-2 had settled on a private charter that guaranteed punctuality but at an inflated price, which should have warranted a better dinner than the rubbery chicken his master had been forced to choke down. The robot was looking forward to a chance to show off his culinary skills, but that would have to wait. Even on the flight, he was still handling his master's business affairs and making preparations for departure. Fogg's life insurance company was refusing to allow a rider for his policy that would cover him for extended space travel. Fogg had insisted on cancelling the policy and shopping elsewhere. He was in the process of finalising an agreement with a Norwegian company now. Fogg had named a woman in Barbados as his sole beneficiary. When Pass-Par-2 inquired about her, his master only replied that she was a second cousin he had never met, but as his closest living relative she was his entitled heir. The robot decided not to pry any deeper.

It was after 11 p.m. as the supersonic jet approached the runway of the Malta Spaceport, and Pass-Par-2 looked out of the window and spotted an enormous rocket standing on a nearby launchpad, gleaming in a ring of spotlights. Their chariot awaited.

The spaceport had taken over the small island of Comino, midway between the main island to the south and Gozo to the north. At 36 degrees north, it wasn't an opportune site for a launch complex, but enough Europeans were willing to pay a premium to avoid having to travel to the equatorial sites where far less fuel was required to reach orbit. Before its construction, many had protested that the spaceport would ruin the scenic coastline of the small island, but the developers had actually done quite an impressive job of confining it entirely to the interior, leaving the shores a pristine environment for wildlife and kayakers alike.

They disembarked from the jet within minutes of its landing, and Pass-Par-2 insisted on carrying Fogg's bags personally rather than hand them over to the SpaceX attendant who met them at the gantry. They were ushered through the normal pre-board process in the main terminal. There the agent tagged his two larger bags, and only then did the robot relinquish his grip on their faux leather handles. He had placed tracking chips inside both so he would continue to monitor their stowage remotely. There would be no lost bags on his watch.

They rode a lift up to a gantry that crossed over to the rocket twenty-three storeys above the launchpad. As the attendant walked them across this narrow bridge, Pass-Par-2 was alerted to an incoming call for his master. He recognised the caller's ID and decided it was worth breaking the silence of their dramatic walk.

"Master, you are receiving a call from the American merchant you attempted to contact earlier."

"Very good, Pass-Par-2. I will take it." Fogg transferred the call to his ear bud. "Hello, this is Phileas Fogg." He listened to a voice on the other end of the line for a moment, then continued. "Yes, I'm afraid I'm a bit pressed for time at the moment, but this matter does need to be handled urgently."

The attendant stopped them at a pair of reclined padded seats perched at the end of the gantry. It was only at this moment that Pass-Par-2 noticed the gantry did not extend all the way to the rocket itself. The luxurious seats were separated from the gleaming hull by a twenty-foot gulf. The attendant gestured for them to take their seats and engage the shoulder restraints. Fogg continued his phone conversation as he complied. "Yes, I do understand the expense. My bank already approved the charge. There's a launch out of Houston in four hours. It will reach the lunar colony shortly after I do. I cannot tolerate any further delay."

As the shoulder restraints clamped in place, securing the man and his robot in their seats, a large metal claw reached down from above and grabbed the entire seating pod. Pass-Par-2 evaluated the attendant's response to indicate this was all perfectly normal, so he muted the panic alarms that had been tripped in his neural network. Fogg had no reaction whatsoever as their seats were lifted from the gantry and carried up into the air by the mechanical arm.

"I am certain there are other vendors who would happily fulfil my order if you are unwilling or unable to do so." He paused to listen to the merchant's reply as the seating pod was lifted towards the very tip of the rocket, where the hinged nose cone had been moved out of place. "Very well," he said, sounding pleased. "Now you'll have to excuse me, as I am about to be launched into orbit." He disconnected the call just as the seating pod was tilted back 90 degrees and lowered down the throat of the rocket.

Theirs was the last seating pod loaded. As soon as it latched into place atop the stack, the nose cone began to slowly swing back into position, blocking out the night sky above them. Pass-Par-2 had enough rear-facing cameras that he didn't need to turn his head to see the other passengers stacked behind and below them. Men and women, young and old, were strapped into the tilted-back seats, awaiting the adventure of a lifetime (fortunately SpaceX did enforce an age limit so there would be no crying babies to disturb his master's experience). The robot found the humans' faces fascinating. He noticed a few who appeared rather blasé about the impending launch. Perhaps people with recurring business on the Moon for whom rocket travel was old hat? He looked at Fogg, busy reading something on his tablet, and compared his face to the others, trying to decide if he better matched the first-timers or the regular commuters. Outwardly he was projecting the nonchalance of the latter, but Pass-Par-2 detected a slightly elevated heart rate that might indicate the former. He decided it would not be imprudent to just ask, but before he could Fogg asked a question of his own.

"Pass-Par-2, how much do you know about space travel?"

Command Line 107: Honesty is the best policy.

"Beyond a theoretical understanding of the basic concept, I know absolutely nothing, sir."

"Scan the network while we still have access to a high-speed connection. Download everything you can find on starship engines, orbital mechanics, and astronavigation."

"Oh my. You make such remarkable requests with such a casual tone," Pass-Par-2 said, but he was already doing as instructed. His hard drives were quickly flooded with incoming data. Most of it was in compressed packets he could unzip and scan later. He was momentarily overwhelmed by the inrush of information. He had to delete a 60-hour compendium of French spoken word poetry just to make room for it all. After six long seconds, his various search engines stopped finding anything new of relevance. He felt confident he had all that would be needed. Or at least all that was available.

"Download complete, sir. I now have nearly one petabyte of the full schematics for every type of spacecraft in existence."

"Very good."

"What sort of engine will we be using? Ion thrusters? Pulsed plasmas?"

"No, nothing like that. This is something entirely new."

"Oh," said Pass-Par-2. "So I remain ignorant after all."

A loud voice spoke over the seating pod's speakers. Pass-Par-2 couldn't tell if it was human or AI. "Prepare for launch in thirty seconds."

Pass-Par-2 positioned himself for blast-off. This was it. Everything was finally out of his hands, for a while at least. There would be nothing to do on the flight except tend to his master's immediate needs. He allowed himself a moment to clear the completed tasks from his queue. It had been quite a busy day. He moved back through time, checking off everything he had achieved since he first showed up at Fogg's door. He was feeling great satisfaction, or at least a convincing simulation of that emotion, until he suddenly realised there was still an *Active Task* near the very bottom of the list. Then he was instantly filled with horror and shame.

"*Parbleu!*"

Fogg looked up from his tablet, noting the alarm in the robot's voice. "What is it, Pass-Par-2?"

"I just remembered... I was preparing your lunch when you returned early. You gave me several commands that superseded my ongoing activities. Only now have I had a moment to reassess my task queue. I'm afraid I... I... I left the gas burning!"

"You mean to say you left the oven on?" Fogg asked calmly.

The robot began squirming in his seat, tugging at the shoulder harness that stubbornly refused to budge. "I am mortified with embarrassment, Master. We must stop the countdown." But the disembodied voice continued with the countdown as if to mock him.

"Sit still, Pass-Par-2. It's too late to do anything about it now."

"But Master, the gas! There could be a terrible explosion!"

"There's about to be a terrible explosion right beneath our feet, which will propel us off the planet. Forget about the oven. The air recycler will clear out the gas."

"Oh," said the robot. He quickly read the specs of the home's air filtration system and saw that his master was correct. "That is a great relief."

"You should be more worried about the expense. Eighty days of natural gas... the bill will be considerable. Monsieur Marchand won't be happy to hear about this." He made a note in his tablet.

"Perhaps there's a neighbour you could ask to shut it off? Someone who keeps your spare set of keys?"

"Certainly not. Why would I need spare keys? Besides, I don't bother my neighbours and they don't bother me."

Pass-Par-2 sank into his seat feeling a fresh wave of shame. "How could I have made such a costly error? This comes as quite a jolt."

"Lift off!" said the voice, and he was hit by quite a jolt indeed.

***

The ascent had been surprisingly smooth, although the intensity of the engines beneath their feet was always evident. Then they reached orbital velocity and the powerful thrust abruptly cut out. The sudden silence was almost as jarring as the lack of gravity. Pass-Par-2 felt his body drift forward until it was restrained by the shoulder harness. He looked out the window and marvelled at the glowing arc of the Earth. He tried to locate London or Calais, the only cities he had any direct knowledge of, but of course Europe was still in the dark of the sun. He saw an illuminated horizon ahead where day was breaking over the Far East. The robot updated his definition of the word '*awe*.'

The helpful voice assured them they were in stable orbit awaiting refuelling for translunar injection. Fogg understood the need for orbital fuel depots but found himself feeling frustrated at every delay. He reminded himself this was built into the itinerary. There was nothing more he could do until they arrived on the Moon.

Pass-Par-2 couldn't get enough of the view from the window as their orbit brought them into daylight. He watched as they left Asia behind and drifted out over the Pacific Ocean. Then something caught the sunlight in an orbit slightly higher than their own. An artificial satellite with an array of solar panels held two large rockets clamped beneath it. He looked closer and spotted illuminated windows. There was movement inside.

"Look, Master! A space station! With rockets!"

Fogg only glanced up from his tablet for a second. He recognised Stuart's family's boondoggle at once. "That's the Orbital Shield platform. Those missiles are for asteroid protection." Somehow the thought of nuclear missiles orbiting the Earth at all times failed to bring him the sense of security the program was intended to inspire. The station was crewed by government workers who undoubtedly spent their days in peace and quiet playing cards at the taxpayers' expense. If he ever had need of a job, Fogg decided he could do worse.

"Space travel is very exciting, Master." Pass-Par-2 decided to take another run at the question he had almost asked earlier. "Have you done it often?"

"Why would you ask such a question, Pass-Par-2?"

Internally, the robot admonished himself for being overly familiar with his master. "I apologise for any impudence, sir. I suppose I was just curious. I was taught that questions are a polite way of making conversation."

"You need not make conversation with me, robot. I didn't hire you for companionship. I am quite comfortable with solitude, so you can go ahead and delete your chitchat subroutines and small talk algorithms."

"I'm afraid I don't have any chitchat subroutines, Master. My personality is a fluidly dynamic emergent matrix. But I will try to dampen my curiosity if that would please you."

Fogg put away his tablet and slipped a silk sleep mask over his eyes. "The only thing that would please me right now is a few hours' sleep. Long day tomorrow."

"Of course, Master. Good night."

Fogg nestled in to find a comfortable position. Pass-Par-2 watched him for a moment, wondering if he had any further duties to help his master achieve his goal. He only had one idea. He leaned close to Fogg and said quietly, "Would you like me to sing to you?"

Fogg abruptly whipped the mask off and looked at Pass-Par-2 in disbelief. "What did you say?"

"I know many lullabies in multiple languages. I could sing to you if it would help you sleep."

"Pass-Par-2, I am only going to say this once so I want to be very clear. You are *never* to sing to me. Not even on my birthday. Do you understand?"

"Yes, Master."

Fogg waited a moment, then replaced the sleep mask and attempted to rediscover that comfortable position. The robot's voice pierced the silence yet again.

"Master? When is your birthday?"

"Good night, Pass-Par-2," he said, not hiding the frustration in his voice. He could have said more, but he would save it for his report to Marchand. Perhaps it was not too late to change the robot's ticket to a round trip. His indignation faded with his consciousness, and soon he was so deep in slumber that even the ignition of the main engines, having completed their refuelling, wasn't enough to wake him.

Pass-Par-2 stole one last look at the Earth as they left it behind. He was on his way to the Moon. It had been the most interesting day of his existence so far, but somehow he felt certain it would be surpassed many times in the seventy-nine that would follow.

***

Fogg awoke with a start, feeling as though he was falling from a great height. His eyes popped open, but he could see only darkness. He flailed frantically for a moment before he remembered the sleep mask. It all came back to him. The engines had shut off, obviously, and once again they were cruising in zero-g. He slid the mask off sheepishly and looked around. He was reassured none of the humans around him had noticed his panicked awakening, but the robot certainly had. He was smiling at him with his squiggly digital mouth.

"Good morning! Did you sleep well, Master?"

"It's hard to sleep peacefully when it feels like you're falling."

"I understand, sir," said Pass-Par-2. "I've had to adjust to weightlessness myself. I reprogrammed my gyroscopes to stop looking for up and down. Instead, I am now using the sun to orient myself. I can detect solar radiation even when I cannot see it. Would you like to know which direction the sun is right now, Master?"

"No, thank you."

"It's there," replied the robot, pointing to the starboard side, his slender arm inches from Fogg's nose.

"How long until we land?"

"In three hours according to the flight tracker."

"Wonderful. I'm going to the water closet. And before you ask, no—I will definitely not be requiring your assistance in there." He unharnessed himself and floated into the central aisle.

"Of course, Master. Have a pleasant evacuation."

Fogg carefully manoeuvred along the row of seating pods. It was already hard to remember how this direction had been 'down' when they were first loaded into the craft. Midway along the fuselage he came to an unoccupied lavatory. He opened the door and pulled himself inside the cramped confines, latching the lock behind him.

He thought he had planned for every eventuality, but staring at the confusing tangle of tubes and suction devices in the cramped space, he realised one detail of space travel had escaped him. The facility's controls were labelled in 'universal' iconography, which left Fogg wondering what universe the designers had come from because he could make neither head nor tail of it. Actually, that wasn't entirely true. More than a few of the illustrations clearly depicted tails. There was no proper toilet to be found in the tiny room. To his horror he gathered that he was expected to relieve himself into one of the vacuum tubes. He understood the lack of gravity complicated many things, but surely there had to be a more hygienic system than this. It all seemed so very... primitive. There wasn't even a sink where he could wash his hands afterward.

One minute later he was harnessing himself back into his seat.

"That didn't take long," said Pass-Par-2. "Do you feel refreshed?"

"Never ask a human for details about their bodily functions, Pass-Par-2. It's quite rude. I'm surprised Marchand's people didn't teach you that."

"Oh, I apologise, Master."

"Besides, I didn't go. The facilities were... bizarre."

"Ah, you could have used some assistance after all. Would you like me to go back and show you how to use the zero-g toilet?"

"No, I certainly would not. Frankly the whole setup seemed quite unsanitary. This would be a terrible time to contract a urinary tract infection. I can wait until we land."

"Of course, Master." The flight tracker indicated two hours and fifty-three minutes until arrival.

Fogg returned to his tablet to keep his mind off his bladder. Pass-Par-2 kept his attention on the view out the window, although there wasn't much to see. The Moon was growing closer by the minute, but there were no forward-facing windows through which to observe it. All he could see at present were the familiar constellations, albeit a bit brighter than usual.

At last, thrusters fired to slow the rocket and reorient it, and the craggy lunar landscape came into view. It was surprisingly close beneath them as they flew towards Hayn Crater in the northern hemisphere. It wasn't that different from the private jet flight to Malta. It could be easy to forget it was not just a pleasant starry night on the other side of the glass.

The rocket slowed further, and Pass-Par-2 could see the rim of Hayn Crater ahead of them. He knew a large international colony had been built within the crater. His limited field of view showed no sign of the city yet, but he did spot a man-made structure beyond the rim. He checked the coordinates to make sure his assumption was correct before he spoke.

"Master, I believe I can see the testing site for Karbasi Propulsion. It's just over the rim of the crater."

"Very good. You will need to arrange a shuttle to take us there once we land."

"Of course, sir."

"I do hope the Karbasis will be reasonable people. Geniuses can be such temperamental sorts, particularly when their life's work is being taken from them by a complete stranger."

Hayn Crater was roughly 54 miles in diameter, modest by lunar standards, but settlers had found it to be just the right size to be properly appreciated by tourists. Viewed from the peak of the rim, it filled one's field of view in a satisfying manner. More importantly, though, it's position on the northeastern limb of the Moon meant that the blue and white marble of Earth permanently hung in the sky just above the horizon, offering the ideal view for tourists to appreciate just how far they'd travelled from home. There were more important sites on the Moon for scientific purposes or for industrial endeavours, but Hayn Crater had become the most popular destination. It was the only settlement that operated a spaceport with daily flights to and from Earth.

That spaceport had been built right in the very middle of the crater nestled between a tight ring of six central peaks. The peaks, formed within minutes of the impact that had created the crater several million years ago, rose up over three hundred feet with naturally terraced slopes. It was there that the human race had built its grandest lunar city. The peaks were honeycombed with tunnels, providing homes to nearly 200,000 permanent residents. The Earth-facing side of each peak housed luxury hotels with enclosed balconies and walkways, all charging a pretty penny for that picture-postcard view. The residents who kept the place running mostly lived deep in the tunnels, where their only windows were video projections.

The rocket set down gently on the great launchpad that filled the flat crater floor between the six peaks. Pass-Par-2 could see large crowds of people lining the settlement's protected walkways to watch the rocket's dramatic arrival. As the great engine spun down into silence, the rocket wobbled ever so slightly, then the flight tracker announced they had coupled successfully with the airlock. Pass-Par-2 smiled at his master, who seemed exceedingly uncomfortable, squirming in his seat.

Eight minutes later the gate agent opened the docking tube into the spaceport, and Phileas Fogg was the first passenger to disembark. His first steps on the Moon were very unlike Armstrong's. He bounded across the terminal in giant leaps, almost crashing into a German family eagerly awaiting another arrival. His face displayed great distress, but he was troubled by more than just learning to navigate in the Moon's low gravity. At last he spotted the restroom. Moving more carefully now, he disappeared into the men's room.

Pass-Par-2 was waiting at the door when his master reappeared looking much relieved. "Let us never speak of this, Pass-Par-2. Now, where do we find this shuttle to Karbasi Propulsion?"

CHAPTER THREE

LUNAR LUNACY

Getting to Karbasi Propulsion had been easy enough. After collecting their bags at the spaceport, they had spotted a heavyset man holding a sign that read 'Fog.' Pass-Par-2 decided to ignore the misspelling as he helped the man load their luggage into his chequered shuttlecab. In a matter of minutes, they crested the western rim of the crater and the large facility that Pass-Par-2 had spotted on approach came into view. To Fogg's relief, the driver spoke very little as he guided the shuttle into the domed laboratory's hangar bay.

They exited into a docking tube where they were met by a robot. This mechanical man was a far simpler design than Pass-Par-2. It welcomed them in an emotionless voice and offered to lead them into the lab. Fogg asked the shuttle driver to wait for them, meter running of course, and they followed the bot inside.

As they were led through the labyrinthine hallways, Fogg tried to perfect his moonwalk. Every step was propelling his body further and higher than his brain anticipated. He figured he weighed no more than two stone in lunar gravity. He was still too heavy to blow away in a brisk wind, should such a thing exist on the Moon, but it was far less weight than his muscles were tuned to manoeuvring. He came close to hitting his head on the ceiling more than once.

Pass-Par-2 tapped him on the shoulder and pointed to the robot that was guiding them. "Sir, observe how our escort moves. Try exerting less energy and push forward more than up." The robot projected an encouraging smile, but Fogg was less than thrilled to be getting walking lessons from a pair of androids. Nevertheless, he made an effort to adjust his stride and found himself adapting quickly.

They came to a large door, which their escort opened to reveal an open-domed space that filled the centre of the complex. The noise was deafening, although it was also impossible to determine its origin. It seemed as though every piece of equipment in the room was emitting electronic whines and hydraulic gasps and teeth-rattling vibrations. Their robotic guide gestured to a railing, so Fogg stepped forward and looked down into a recessed control station where a middle-aged Arabic couple stood wearing lab coats and protective eyewear. He recognised them as the Karbasis, the husband and wife designers of Flanagan's radioactive rocket. He had seen their first names in print, but he suddenly realised he wasn't sure how to pronounce them, and, more alarmingly, he wasn't entirely certain which was which. It was yet another reason he would have to navigate this conversation very carefully. The couple was in the midst of a shouting match, although it was unclear if their voices were raised in anger or just to counter the cacophony of the room.

"You should have checked the calibrations!" shouted the husband.

"They were your calibrations!" the wife yelled back. "If I have to check your work, why do I even need you?"

"Pardon me," Fogg said from the overlooking walkway. They did not react at all, continuing to bicker. He realised he would need to join in with the shouting if he was to be heard. "I say, pardon me!" At last they turned and took notice of him. "Mr and Mrs Karbasi?"

"Dr and Mrs Karbasi," said the man.

"Dr and Dr Karbasi," said the woman. "I have two PhDs; you only have one." She flipped a switch and the noise in the room began to wind down. It was still loud, but no longer painfully so.

"Like anyone is impressed with your PhD in art history," muttered the husband in a low voice that probably would have been drowned out just a moment or two earlier.

The wife gave him a sharp look. "The publishers of my three textbooks were impressed enough."

Fogg decided to interject before their argument could reignite properly. "Pardon the intrusion doctors, but my name is Phileas Fogg."

"Right," said the husband. "Flanagan's man. You are exactly what I was expecting."

So at least Flanagan has spoken with them, thought Fogg. *Hopefully that means they are fully on board with this endeavour.*

"Come to steal our baby, have you?" said the wife.

Or maybe not... He cleared his throat. "If you are referring to your engine—"

"The only baby this one ever gave me," the man said with a nod to his spouse.

"Takes two to make a baby, dear. The engine, on the other hand, I could have made on my own."

Fogg felt the conversation careening off track again. He was starting to wonder how these two had ever got anything done together. Perhaps the bickering fuelled their process. Regardless, he decided it was up to him to dampen any more fiery eruptions. Before he could speak up, a new fiery eruption filled the entire upper reaches of the dome. A literal firestorm danced across the inside of the enclosure five storeys above their heads. Pass-Par-2 stared up in abject horror, but Fogg noted that the Karbasis showed no concern whatsoever. The husband casually reached for a red button.

"Might want to hold onto your hat there, Mr Skinnylegs," he said as he pressed the button. Abruptly, alarms blared as several slatted vents in the dome opened directly to the vacuum of space. The flames were quickly extinguished as air began rushing out of the dome through the narrow openings.

Pass-Par-2's hat did indeed lift off his head, but the robot quickly snagged it just before it flew out of reach. He clutched his precious derby and addressed the Karbasis, keeping his voice calmer than his demeanour. "Are we in danger?"

"Nah," said the man as the vents closed again and pressure began to stabilise. "Propellant fumes build up in the apex of the dome. They ignite from time to time. We just vent 'em. No biggie." Although they originally hailed from Cairo, Fogg remembered that the Karbasis had spent many years at MIT, which perhaps explained their crude American attitudes.

The air equalised, but the alarms were still blaring. Fogg was ready to focus on business. "Is there someplace quiet where we can talk?"

The couple led them into an office with one window overlooking the interior of the dome and another on the exterior wall looking out over the barren moonscape. Fogg was at once far more comfortable in this environment, despite never before having conducted business in a room that offered a view of a lunar crater. For that matter, he had also never worked in a room with a large oak conference table, yet he found it was the table in this office that grounded him. If felt more like the scenario he had imagined: the couple sat on one side and Fogg on the other. Pass-Par-2 remained standing dutifully behind him.

"So tell me, Mr Fogg," started the woman, "why should we give you the Steady Axe engine?"

Fogg decided it was time to move past pleasantries. "Flanagan's orders aren't reason enough? He is the legal owner, after all." He saw her bristle. He sensed she was preparing to erupt so he continued before she could. "But I admire your devotion to your invention, so I shall offer you a better answer. You should give me the Steady Axe because you want it to be successful."

"You're going to make it work?" asked the man.

"I assume it already works, or else I am in a whole heap of trouble. But to be successful, you need to prove its viability. You've been restrained by skittish investors and bureaucratic regulations. You shouldn't have to deal with all of that nonsense." Fogg leaned across the table, making eye contact with first one doctor, then the other. "I have followed your research for years, and I believe you are the most capable and innovative engineers alive. You are going to mount your engine on Mr Stuart's orbiting asteroid, then I am going to fly it to Mars and the outer planets, and together we will show humanity that the entire solar system is now within reach, thanks to your creation."

He sat back in his chair as the Egyptian couple exchanged a look. The husband, at least, seemed suitably impressed. "Well... all right then," he offered hesitantly.

The wife wasn't quite as convinced. "You know the right things to say, Mr Fogg. I'll grant you that. But I'm not much for sweet talk. I married this one, after all." She elbowed her spouse in the ribs. "Do you have any idea how much it would cost to mount our engine on that asteroid up in orbit?"

"No, not precisely. Why don't you tell me?"

She thought for a moment. "Probably a hundred million at least."

"More like 200 million," said the husband.

Fogg was unperturbed. "American dollars, I assume?"

"Money talk is always American," the man said in quick response.

Fogg reached into his pocket and pulled out his tablet. "Fine. I'll transfer 300 million dollars immediately, but I want it mounted the next time the asteroid passes over in..."

He was about to look it up when Pass-Par-2 leaned forward

and said, "Two hours and six minutes, Master."

"Two hours and six minutes," repeated Fogg.

"Two hours and six minutes?" cried the couple.

Fog stood up from the table. "Yes, I am on a very tight schedule, but you have at least an extra hundred million to work it all out. I have faith in you, so I'll let you get to work. Good day."

He turned and left the room without another word. Pass-Par-2 was so shocked he almost didn't follow, but as the automatic door was about to close, he tipped his hat to the gobsmacked couple and pursued his master down the corridor.

As the door hissed shut, the Karbasis were left alone at the table, their mouths hanging open. "Is he really going to pay us 300 million dollars?" asked the husband.

"We can install the engine for half that," said the wife.

"So we're really going to give it to him? What if it, you know..." He mimicked an explosion with his hands and mouthed a '*kapow*' sound.

His beloved replied with a shrug, "Better him than us."

Just fifteen minutes later, the shuttlecab deposited Phileas Fogg and Pass-Par-2 at the enclosed Grand Concourse that filled the lowest terrace of Intrepid Peak. They walked along the busiest thoroughfare on the Moon, passing numerous storefronts carved into the rock. Tall glass windows to their right looked out over the spaceport, as well as offering an impressive view of the other five peaks, the crater rim, and the gibbous Earth hanging in the sky. Both the man and the robot had honed if not perfected their lunar gaits, although Pass-Par-2's was complicated by towing the two roller bags.

Once the crowd had thinned enough to offer some privacy, the robot dared address an issue that had been nagging at him. "I hesitate to mention it, Master, but I believe it is quite possible that you overpaid the Karbasis considerably."

"Of course I did," Fogg replied, "but sometimes overpayment is the necessary price to assure you get the service you need."

"Oh, I see," replied the robot. "A very wise practice. I wonder why more people don't employ it."

Fogg wasn't going to waste his breath explaining personal finances to a robot. There were more pressing matters at hand. "Now that I am assured the engine will be handled professionally, I can focus on acquiring our next important asset." He led the robot under an arched entranceway into a large showroom. The sign overhead read: 'NORTON SPACESHIP SALES.'

***

It had been a slow day at the office for Christopher Norton, proprietor of the only private spaceship showroom on the Moon. The people from Agua Luna had cancelled their pickup appointment for the third day in a row, and the parts delivery wouldn't arrive until tomorrow's rocket. The showroom generated a lot of walk-ins from curious tourists, but they were almost never a source of an actual sale. That's why he hadn't paid much attention to the Englishman who walked in less than an hour before closing time, despite his high-end robot companion. Wealth was a common factor among most visitors to the crater, after all, so he had allowed his assistant manager Marcella to handle the man's initial inquiries. After exchanging only a few words, Marcella had rushed into his office telling him the man was insistent on speaking with the owner. So now his slow day was being capped off with the man and his robot leafing through sales brochures in his office well past the time he would normally be home in Eagle Peak, unwinding with a beer and a frozen dinner.

"The Excelsior 5000 is the top of the line in private

spacecraft, Mr Fogg. If it doesn't fit your needs, nothing will."

Fogg refused to look at the spec sheet. "As I explained, private sleeping quarters are non-negotiable, as well as a full galley. And a regular flush commode, none of this vacuum suction nonsense."

Norton was growing frustrated. This could possibly be his biggest private sale of the quarter, but the man was being beyond unreasonable. "There's simply nothing in mass production that offers those kinds of luxuries. You are aware a conventional toilet won't flush without gravity, yes?"

Fogg continued. "The Excelsior is also not capable of atmospheric reentry, so there's no point in discussing it any further. Do I need to take my business elsewhere?"

Norton couldn't help but smile. "I'm not sure what you mean by 'elsewhere.' I'm the only private spaceship dealer on the Moon. But don't panic, we can custom build a ship to your exact specifications. Like the one we just did for the President of Agua Luna. Do you see that yellow ship out on the tarmac?" He gestured out the window at his lot of spaceships in front of a line of hangars that skirted the outer edge of the spaceport. The Agua Luna ship was front and centre, a sparkling gold nugget amidst a field of dull grey.

"Agua Luna?" asked the French robot. "Is that a country?"

"It's a company," explained his master. "Orbital water couriers based on the lunar South Pole."

"Ah. I was afraid my atlas was outdated."

Norton was still trying to direct Fogg's attention to the ship below. "That beauty really stands out. It has everything on your list except the flush toilets. You don't really want that, trust me. We can build you a ship just like it, but it'll take time."

Fogg peered down at the ship for only a moment. "How long?" he asked.

Norton shrugged. "No more than eighteen months."

"That simply won't do. Tell me, though... why is Agua Luna's ship still on the lot?"

"We're just waiting for them to come and pick it up. They keep rescheduling. Some pipeline problem is keeping them occupied down at their base."

"I see," said Fogg. He thought for a moment, then stood up. "Excuse me for just a moment. Pass-Par-2, please keep the gentleman company." With that, he exited the office.

Norton and Pass-Par-2 exchanged a look. It was unclear which of them was more confused by Fogg's abrupt departure. Pass-Par-2 flashed his squiggly smile, trying to put Mr Norton at ease, but he sensed from the man's face he was only making matters worse.

Norton finally broke the awkward silence. "Your boss is an interesting fellow."

"Is he?" replied Pass-Par-2. He took a microsecond to process the information. "I suspected as much, but I wasn't certain. In truth, I haven't known many humans. I am only three weeks old."

"Hmm. If you don't mind my asking, what does he do for a living?"

The robot searched his databanks. "To be honest, sir, I haven't a clue."

He could tell Mr Norton was dissatisfied with his response, but he didn't press the matter. The man and the robot resumed their awkward staring contest.

Norton was grateful when an email came in. It was just a newsletter from his son's school, which he would normally have skipped past, but at the moment he was happy for any distraction. He was reading about the upcoming bake sale when he decided he'd had just about enough. "Do you think your boss might need help finding the restroom?"

"Oh, I am certain he is not using the restroom. He emptied his bladder less than two hours ago. It was quite a relief."

"I see. But maybe he's..." Norton stared at the robot's expectant smile, feeling very silly about this line of conversation all of a sudden. He decided not to pursue this particular avenue any further. "Can I get you anything? Bottle of..." He had been about to offer water, but that seemed like an unlikely need for a robot. "...oil?"

"No, sir, but if there is anything you need I would be happy to get it for you."

Norton chuckled. He had no idea how to keep a robot company. Fortunately he wouldn't need to any longer because Fogg reentered the room.

"All right, it's all settled," he said without further explanation.

"What is settled, Mr Fogg?" Norton noticed another email arriving in his peripheral vision.

"You should be receiving a transfer of ownership request from Agua Luna any second now."

"What? A transfer of...?" He stopped himself and looked down at the new email. It was in fact from Agua Luna., and the subject read: Transfer of Ownership Request. "I'll be damned," said Norton, opening the document. "What did you do?"

"I took my business elsewhere after all. The President of Agua Luna is an astute businesswoman. She just turned a profit on a ship she hadn't even seen yet. Please have it moved to the launch facility within the hour. Thank you for your time, Mr Norton. Come along, Pass-Par-2."

Fogg was out the door in a flash. Pass-Par-2 stood up and chased after him, pausing at the door to tip his hat. "A pleasure meeting you, monsieur. Au revoir!"

Norton waved back, his head spinning and his mouth agape. He needed that beer.

***

Back out on the concourse, Pass-Par-2 hustled along still tugging the luggage behind him. He almost bumped into his master when he stopped abruptly at a large window. His attention was on a sleek rocket setting down on the launchpad outside. It had the words 'Blue Origin' printed vertically along its length. Pass-Par-2 suddenly appreciated the perspective of the onlookers he had spotted earlier watching their own rocket's arrival. It was quite a sight to behold.

"That will be the rocket from Houston," said Fogg. "Pass-Par-2, run and fetch our shipment and have it loaded onto our ship. I still have a couple of stops to make."

"Of course, Master. Without delay!" He scurried off excitedly with the luggage in tow. There was nothing quite like the thrill of being useful.

Fogg continued down the concourse alone until he came to a large government office. Inside, he rode a lift up to the Harbourmaster's office on the third floor, then signed in at the terminal. Luckily there were only two people waiting ahead of him. He spent the time on his tablet browsing the inventory of a nearby spacesuit retailer. He chose a top-of-the-line model and placed an order for pickup. It was another considerable expense, but he would not undertake this challenge without the best gear available.

He completed the order just as his name was called. A heavyset woman in her sixties led him from the waiting area to a small cubicle around the corner. She handed him a datapad with a stylus and instructed him to fill out his flightplan, then moved on to the next cubicle. The local government kept track of all traffic within Hayn Crater, and based on the details requested in the form, they seemed to believe their jurisdiction extended beyond the crater's rim to the very edge of the universe itself. Fogg silently questioned the UN's authority out in the endless black void, but he would play along in the interest of being granted an expedient launch window. He filled in the information as thoroughly as possible, but he found the form wasn't really written with his sort of itinerary in mind. He had to choose 'OTHER' a lot and type in the details. He finally hit submit.

He waited perhaps ten minutes before the woman returned,

reading his information from her own datapad. She sat down without a word. Finally, she lowered the pad and gave him a sceptical look. “This is your flightplan? Are you serious?”

“Exclusively,” said Phileas Fogg.

“This is going to get flagged if I file it,” said the woman. “You know that, right?”

“And what happens when it gets flagged?” asked Fogg.

Apparently what happens is that one gets redirected to the office of Agent Aaron Fix, which was precisely where Fogg sat ten minutes later. The office had been empty when Fogg was ushered in, but the man himself arrived a short time later. Even if Fogg had met him on the streets of London, he would have known right away he was a government agent and that the government in question was the United States of America. That posture of confidence combined with an inexpensive suit and military haircut could only be found in one agency on Earth. Despite the UN title on the nameplate, Fogg felt certain he was CIA. He was in his early thirties, rather young for a man in his position, which led Fogg to suspect some type of nepotism at play. He shook Fogg's hand as he sat behind the desk.

“Mr Fogg, I'm Agent Aaron Fix of the UN Security Force.”

“I gathered from the nameplate.” He noticed a pin on his lapel that confirmed his earlier suspicion. Or perhaps he had already noticed it subconsciously, leading him to that conclusion before he even knew why it had occurred to him. “You say UN, but your lapel says CIA.”

Fix glanced down at the pin, obviously impressed by Fogg's perceptiveness. “Yeah,” he admitted, “I draw two paychecks these days. We're severely understaffed here. Seeing as you're a British national, I'm wearing my UN hat right now. I've been reviewing your flightplan. Mars in two days, huh? Somebody open up a wormhole I don't know about?”

“No,” said Fogg, “my travels will not involve any shortcuts through theoretical hyperspace dimensions. Strictly Point A to Point B.”

"Uh-huh," replied the agent, scrolling through his tablet. "Then Point C and D and E—Ceres, Jupiter, Saturn..." He lowered the tablet and looked Fogg directly in the eyes. "Is this some kind of joke?"

"I can assure you, no one has ever accused me of being a comedian."

"Well maybe you should reconsider because this flightplan has a real humdinger of a punchline." He tilted the tablet in Fogg's direction, as if he needed to be shown data he himself had entered. "You're going to Pluto?"

"That is my plan."

Agent Fix paused for a moment, seeming to chew on Fogg's response. "Big fan of the King, are you?"

Fogg had sensed this was the crux of it all. It was sad how predictable government minds were. He saw no point in being dishonest. "I would not describe myself as a fan, but I do respect his claim of sovereignty."

"Sovereignty? You're talking about the Most Wanted Man on Earth."

"You should reassess that list, sir," said Fogg, "as he is most certainly not on Earth."

Agent Fix smiled smugly and leaned back in his chair. "I don't get you people, making him out as some kind of folk hero, standing up to the big, bad governments of Earth. Are you not at all concerned about the payload of nuclear missiles he took off that Russian ship?"

"The Russians have denied that," said Fogg.

"As they would, since they were illegal in the first place. But you better believe they had them. And now *he* has them. And he has openly threatened to fire them at Earth."

"Only if the governments of Earth don't leave him alone. I will make certain he understands I fly under the flag of no nation."

"Right," said Fix. He was clearly weighing something over in his head, but he quickly reached a decision. He grabbed his tablet and began scrolling through it. "Mr Fogg, this isn't public knowledge yet, but it will be soon so I'm going to fill you in. We have a new intelligence asset monitoring Pluto. We took this photo six weeks ago."

He spun the tablet around to show Fogg an aerial photo of the surface of Pluto. It was black and white and very low resolution, but he recognised the shoreline of the frozen nitrogen sea that was first discovered by the New Horizons spacecraft in 2015. One shape stood out in the image. A slim, cylindrical object rose up from a high bluff that overlooked the sea of ice.

"What is that?" asked Fogg.

"What does it look like? He's mounted a missile. If he launches it at Earth, it could be here in just a few years. And it may be too fast to intercept. This King of Pluto character is a very real threat to all mankind. If I truly believed you were going there I'd lock you up for collusion with a known terrorist."

Fogg caught the careful phrasing. "But you don't believe me."

An alert popped up on Fix's tablet. He shielded it from Fogg's view and gave it a quick scan. "Lucky for you, I have actual security business that needs my immediate attention. I can't waste my time indulging rich men who want to play space captain. I've seen that ship you bought, Mr Fogg. It's fast for short runs, but it doesn't have the range for the outer system. Hell, it doesn't have the range for Mars. Not in two days, not in two hundred. So I suggest you go fly your new toy over whoever's house you're trying to impress, then go home." He stood up, but he wasn't finished. "At that point, you will be fined for filing a false flightplan. I trust you're good for it."

Fogg waited for him to make his dramatic exit, but the agent just stood there, staring him down. If he was waiting for a further argument, he wasn't going to get one. Technically, his flightplan had been approved. It was the best outcome Fogg could have hoped for. "Thank you for your time, agent."

Fix just snorted in response. Then he gestured for Fogg to exit to the hallway. The lift was just outside the door. As Fogg stepped into the waiting car, Fix turned and made a call. "What's so urgent?" the agent asked in a huff.

Listening carefully, Fogg heard a female voice on the other end of the line. "It's the Karbasis. They're moving the Steady Axe engine."

Agent Fix said, "I'm on my way," just as the sliding door closed. *Interesting*, Fogg thought as the lift whisked him back to the lobby. Despite it all, he was actually ahead of schedule.

***

Once again on the concourse, Fogg messaged Pass-Par-2 to make sure everything was running smoothly at his end. After being assured there were no unexpected snags, he found the quickest path to the spacesuit tailor. Fortuitously, it was in the direction he was headed anyway, two levels down.

Less than three minutes later he stepped into the tiny shop, a bell ringing over his head as the door swung open. A clerk appeared from the back, and Fogg realised the shop itself wasn't all that tiny, just the floorspace for customers at the front. A mechanised rack carried hundreds of hanging pressure suits from a large room in the back, similar to a dry-cleaner's shop he remembered from his childhood before the ubiquity of self-cleaning fabric.

The clerk scanned the receipt from his tablet, then she activated the rack. The empty suits swung on their hangers as they rapidly followed the track clockwise through the rear of the shop. The motor stopped after about ten seconds, and the hanging suits jostled in unison. The clerk pulled down a slate grey model that was front and centre. She complimented him on his selection before asking if he would also be needing a helmet. Fogg was irritated to learn they were sold separately. He chose the top model from the same line as the suit. He hoped it would be the last premium purchase necessary before getting underway. He left the shop with the suit and helmet in a large shopping bag. He hadn't bothered to try them on. He would find out how they fitted soon enough.

Stepping onto the concourse, he noticed an emergency clinic directly across from the shop. He checked his pocket watch. His assigned launch time was still over an hour away. If he had minutes to spare, he wasn't going to squander them. He entered the clinic.

It was precisely twenty-two minutes later when an elderly doctor entered the small exam room where Fogg waited on a surgical table. He had already changed into a gown, unprompted. The man checked his chart. "Hello, Mr Fogg. What seems to be the emergency?"

"Not an emergency, but nevertheless an urgency. I have exactly seventeen minutes to spare. Is that enough time for you to remove my appendix?"

The doctor was remarkably unfazed by the question. "You think you might have appendicitis?"

"Unlikely at the moment. I am experiencing no discomfort. But I am about to depart for deep space for just over eleven weeks and I'm trying to plan for all possible pitfalls. Frankly I see no disadvantage to tossing the worthless thing before it has a chance to betray me. What do you say, doctor? The clock is ticking."

He shrugged. "Sure. Just sit back and relax. This won't hurt a bit."

Several levels higher up the peak, Agent Aaron Fix arrived at the Security Command Centre for the Hayn Crater Moonbase. He was met at the lift by his top assistant, Beth Culby. She was still a little green, but smart and eager. Her hair was pulled back in a tight ponytail under her olive-green baseball cap sporting the

UN Security Force logo.

"Where are they going?" asked Fix.

"We aren't certain, sir, but their tug blasted off carrying the engine about ten minutes ago. They're headed northeast away from the base."

"Good. They must be relocating to the Far Side like we advised. The further they move that deathtrap away from us, the better." Something still wasn't adding up though. "They don't have any facilities on the Far Side, do they?"

"None that we know of, sir," Beth confirmed.

"Sir!" Another junior officer, a new recruit named Chang, was calling in from the tracking station. "I've plotted their trajectory. They seem to be on an intercept course with K-47b."

"The asteroid?" asked Fix. This was an unexpected development. Stuart Space Mining owned that asteroid, or what was left of it. *Do the Karbasis even know Stuart?* "Where is it now?"

"It's currently orbiting on the Far Side. Its orbit will cross the tug's path in about thirty minutes."

"Very interesting indeed," said Agent Fix, lost in thought. *What in the name of hell are those crazy Egyptians up to?*

***

Fogg watched the monitor as inch by inch his appendix was zapped into nothingness. The doctor was right; he couldn't feel a thing. The last blackened lump fell away, and the doctor withdrew the laser from his abdomen. "Okey-dokey. One zapped appendix with two minutes to spare. You might smell smoke next time you go to the bathroom, but otherwise you're fine as cherry wine. Anything else you want me to incinerate while I've got you here? Tonsils? Gallbladder maybe?"

"No, I must be going. Thank you for your expediency, doctor. What do I owe you?" He reached for his shirt, but the physician held him back while he applied a quick sealant to the tiny incision.

"You don't owe me anything. All services free of charge."

"Is that so?" asked Fogg, genuinely surprised.

The doctor finished up and finally allowed Fogg to sit up and reach for his clothes. "This is an international colony, Mr Fogg. Every participating country contributes something. I'm from Canada. We provide the free health care." He stood up and crossed to the door as Fogg buttoned up his shirt. "Have a good trip, eh."

CHAPTER FOUR

STARSHIP ASSEMBLY

Fogg ended up losing nearly ten minutes in leaving the clinic as he had decided to go ahead and don his new pressure suit. The shape-memory fabric felt a bit loose, especially around his arms and legs, but the clerk had told him that was normal while inside a pressurised environment. He chose to carry the helmet for now. He made up three of the lost minutes by walking at double speed towards the spaceport, despite feeling slightly embarrassed by the rude way he brushed past the tourists who clogged the walkways.

He quickly worked his way through security, hurried down an enclosed ramp, then finally attached the helmet when he reached the exit gate. He accepted assistance from an attendant to complete the oxygen hook-up. After a few twists, the man gave him two thumbs up and escorted him into the large airlock.

Fogg waited while six other people filled the airlock, then the inner door slid shut. He heard a low hiss and felt the coils in his suit tighten, shrinking the fabric against his body. He heard only his own breathing, but vibrations in the floor tipped him off that the outer door behind him was sliding open. He turned around, careful not to bump his oxygen tank into the man next to him, and found himself facing the airless surface of the Moon.

He stepped out of the airlock onto a paved walkway. He found his movement barely hindered by the suit at all, and the extra weight actually made him feel a bit more comfortable on his feet. He scanned the row of parked vehicles and finally found the golden ship—*his ship*—at the end of the tarmac. Pass-Par-2 was waiting in front of it.

Fogg evaluated the ship as he approached but did not pause his stride. It was vaguely mushroom-shaped with landing struts around its base. Sunlight reflected off the gold foil that covered its exterior. A ladder led up from the ground to a small airlock on the port side.

Fogg heard the robot's voice come through the speakers in his helmet. "Hello, Master. I'm glad to see you again. I like your suit very much." Fogg would need to learn how the suit's communications gear worked, if only to find a way to mute the robot. He saw a button on his left wrist that had an icon like an old-fashioned microphone. He pressed it, and a heads-up display indicated his mic was open on an unencrypted frequency.

"Hello, Pass-Par-2," said Fogg, mostly to test the radio connection. "Everything went smoothly with the supplies from Houston?"

"No problems, Master. They are already stowed aboard along with your luggage. You'll be pleased to hear that I paid them double the amount on the invoice."

It took a lot to make Phileas Fogg stop in his tracks, but that did the trick. "What? Why ever would you do such a thing?"

"Well, sir, it's like you said. Sometime overpayment is the price of—"

Fogg cut him off, exasperated. "That price had already been settled. From now on, please leave financial negotiations to me." He moved past the robot and began climbing the ladder.

The airlock was tight, so they cycled through one at a time. Phileas Fogg had a moment of peace to assess the interior of the craft before Pass-Par-2 could join him. He removed his helmet for a bit of fresh air. Of course the air in the ship wasn't exactly fresh, but at least it came from a larger tank.

A control room occupied most of the interior. Along the back wall there were three doorways to small private bunks. The end bunks were set three steps lower than the floor, and the master bunk in the middle was elevated a few feet, arranged so that the three rooms fitted together like Tetris pieces. The rest of the interior was similarly efficient given its limited square footage. He poked his head into the tiny galley and genuinely wondered if there was room to open the door of the microwave. He was sure Pass-Par-2 could work with it, though. At least there was no gas stove for him to abuse.

He peeked into the master bunk and was pleased to see a bespoke fabric printer and several spools of material wedged into the wardrobe. Had he known he would have such a luxury he could have left the suitcases at home. The bed looked comfortable enough, but it occupied nearly the entire room. Phileas Fogg had never been in an RV in his life, but if he had, his new temporary home would have felt familiar. *There is very little space in space*, he thought. The pun escaped his notice.

He stepped back into the control room just as Pass-Par-2 was sealing the airlock. From the back of the room he could see the huge video screen that dominated the front wall. It currently displayed a live feed from an external camera, essentially functioning as a wide window in the otherwise claustrophobic environment. He had to admit the illusion helped.

"Well, it is a bit cramped considering what I paid, but I suppose it will have to do."

"If you need more personal space, I would be happy to wait outside the airlock when I am not needed, Master."

"That won't be necessary," said Fogg. Pass-Par-2 was noticeably relieved. "I will need you in here at the controls.

Speaking of which, it is almost our launch time. I assume you know how to fly this ship."

"Oh yes, Master. I ran eighty-seven successful launch simulations while I was waiting for you." The robot took the pilot's seat and flipped a few switches and powered-up displays.

"Wonderful," said Fogg, sincerely impressed.

"Out of one hundred attempts. Strap in, Master."

Fogg sat in the acceleration couch behind him and tugged the shoulder restraints tight as the engines rumbled into life. It was only a couple of minutes until the robot announced they had been cleared for lift-off. There was only the tiniest jostle as they lifted from the tarmac. Soon the top of Intrepid Peak was dropping out of frame on the viewscreen, then the crater rim followed, and still they climbed into the endless starry night.

In the Security Command Centre, Agent Aaron Fix was too engrossed by the Karbasis' tug to notice Fogg's ship rising away from the spaceport, even though he would have had an excellent view if he had just looked up from his computer monitor. He was busy trying to find some connection between Stuart Mining and the Karbasis. He knew Stuart's company was desperate to dispose of the asteroid, but would he go so far as to hire the Karbasis to move it? Or blow it up? It seemed insane and would obviously be a violation of international law, but there were those who argued space was, in a sense, international waters. If Stuart was determined to destroy the rock, who could stop him? But Fix knew the resulting debris could potentially wreak havoc on facilities all around the lunar surface, raining down from deteriorating orbits for years to come. He had a clear obligation to make sure Stuart and the Karbasis really weren't that crazy.

They had been trying to hail the tug, but no one was answering. It was technically beyond their jurisdiction now, so they weren't breaking the law by ignoring the call, but it wasn't encouraging that they wouldn't simply explain themselves. Fix felt he was missing a piece of the puzzle. He remembered the Karbasis were funded by some British billionaire so he looked him up. Thomas Albert Flanagan IV. Fix had access to the official UN dossier on the man. And there it was—the connection he was missing. Flanagan and Stuart were both members of the Reform Club in London. He wasn't familiar with it, but evidently it went back centuries, catering to snooty aristocrats who enjoyed discussing finances while playing cards away from the unwashed masses. Stuart and Flanagan must have made some sort of deal. Most likely they were planning to test the engine on the asteroid, hopefully on the Far Side where they wouldn't irradiate anyone. There was still a risk of the asteroid breaking apart. Fix recalled it being full of holes like a wedge of Swiss cheese. He was about to share this information with his team when he saw another familiar name in the list of 'KNOWN ASSOCIATES' in the dossier.

"Phileas Fogg!" He almost shouted the name.

Beth leaned over his shoulder. "What is a Phileas Fogg?"

"He was in my office when you called me." Fix was chilled to the bone by the horrifying realisation that he had underestimated the prissy Englishman. "This is all about him and his crazy flightplan. Dear God. We have to stop him! Lock down the spaceport! Halt all launches!"

Beth and Chang both made calls immediately, no questions asked. Some small section of Fix's mind was still capable of feeling pride in his team's professionalism. Maybe one of them would replace him after he was burned at the stake for this disaster.

***

The gold ship was more than fifty miles from the spaceport when the alert sounded. Pass-Par-2 quickly dismissed it. "How fortunate," he said to his master. "We departed just in the nick of time. The spaceport has been locked down."

"Is that so?"

"I wonder what the problem is?"

"I'm sure it's nothing," Fogg replied. "How long until we rendezvous with the asteroid?"

"Just a few minutes. It's coming over the horizon now."

He magnified the display screen to show a pockmarked asteroid sweeping slowly toward them in a slightly higher orbit. It was relatively small as asteroids go. Fogg estimated it was larger than St Paul's Cathedral but smaller than The Gherkin. It was big enough to dwarf the battered tug that flew alongside it.

"I see the Karbasis are already at work."

"Does the asteroid have a name, sir?" asked the robot.

"Kay Stroke Forty-Seven Bee," said Fogg. "Not a very good name for an interplanetary spaceship, I suppose."

"It rather resembles a bicuspid—the premolar tooth, I mean, not the heart valve," said Pass-Par-2.

Fogg couldn't help but chuckle to himself. *How strange for a robot to make such an observation.* He had to admit it was an accurate description. The bottom of the asteroid tapered into two root-like structures, with the Karbasis' Steady Axe engine mounted between them. It even had a flattened top with a slight indentation in the centre. If it was a tooth, it was certainly a neglected one, with cavities peppering its surface on all sides. "We should rename it then. We shall call it the *Giant's Tooth.*"

Pass-Par-2 was thrilled to have inspired the name. He guided the ship in for a smooth landing, perfectly nestling into the depression on the top of the rock. As he powered down the engines, he turned to face his master with a new question. "And what about this ship, sir? The lander? Does it have a name?"

Fogg unhooked the harness and floated in microgravity. He pushed himself over to a small porthole at the side of the craft, not willing to rely on the video screen for this view. He saw the gold legs of the ship resting lightly on the rough grey surface of the asteroid. "I supposed this would be the *Gold Filling.*"

***

Fix felt sick to his stomach as he received Beth's update. "We're too late, sir. Launch tower confirms the gold ship departed ten minutes ago."

"Are they still in range?" he managed to ask between waves of nausea.

"Negative. They've already orbited to the Far Side."

"Towards the asteroid, I'm sure. So they're out of our jurisdiction too. Track the orbital path of the asteroid and figure out where and when it will come back around. And get a ship ready. I want to be ready and waiting for them the second they stick a toe back in UN-controlled territory."

He would make this situation right before it was too late. Agent Fix had a reputation for living up to his name.

***

Pass-Par-2 had just finished remotely clamping the landing pads onto anchors drilled into the rock, securing the *Gold Filling* to the *Giant's Tooth*, when he was startled by a knocking at the main hatch.

"Are we expecting company?" he asked.

Fogg went to the airlock controls and ran it through a cycle. It opened to reveal two space-suited figures crammed in together, challenging the limits of the air lock's capacity. They removed their helmets, revealing the Doctors Karbasi.

"Hello, doctor," Fogg said to one, then added a second, "doctor," with a nod to the other

"Mr Fogg, this is a hell of a lander you've got here," said the husband.

"It's so spacious," said his wife.

"There's no need for sarcasm," said Fogg. "Have you finished installation of the engine?"

"Yes," said the husband, "the engine is securely in place."

He activated a small projector built into the sleeve of his spacesuit and a rotating holographic display of the asteroid appeared before them, including the massive engine mounted to the underside between the bicuspid's roots.

His wife, meanwhile, was attaching a small device to the pilot's console. "These are the Steady Axe controls. Your robot can patch them directly into the lander's controls."

The husband pointed to the engine in the hologram. "The Steady Axe drive reaches great speeds by accelerating constantly. It will push you faster and faster every moment it's firing, and its efficiency will allow you to use it throughout your entire voyage. The engine's thrust creates g-force, so for most of the trip you'll feel normal Earth-like gravity."

The wife took over the presentation. "Once you are halfway to your destination, you'll power off the Steady Axe and use the manoeuvring rockets along the side to flip the whole asteroid around so that you are flying engine first. During that time you will be weightless again."

The husband's hologram illustrated the manoeuvre. "Once you've turned around, you'll activate the Steady Axe again and start a retrograde burn, decelerating. You spend the second half of the trip burning off all the speed you've been building up."

"Mr Fogg, are you paying attention?" asked the wife.

"Hmm?" said Fogg, looking up from the pamphlet he was reading. "Oh, yes, certainly."

"He was reading the instructions for the zero-g toilet," she protested to her husband.

"This is important, Fogg. We worked really hard on this presentation. I'll start over."

"No, please," Fogg interjected. "I assure you I understand how the engine works. At least the basic points. More importantly, my robot has the owner's manual, so if the installation is complete we are ready to embark as soon as you leave."

The Karbasis stared at him in disbelief. Perhaps he had

crossed a line. "But I don't mean to be rude. Should I have Pass-Par-2 put tea on?" Propriety dictated it was a sincere offer, but he hoped they detected the exasperation in his voice.

They did indeed. Just a few minutes later, the Karbasis flew away in their cramped tug, watching the asteroid recede.

"Asshole," Dr Amasis Karbasi muttered to his wife.

"His payment cleared," Dr Khepri Karbasi told her husband. "He can be an asshole if he wants." She took one last look at their life's work as it receded from their view. "Take care of our baby, Mr Fogg."

But of course Fogg couldn't hear her. The Karbasis were no longer part of his story.

***

Agent Aaron Fix and Beth Culby sat in the back of a UN shuttle flying over the craggy moonscape. He didn't know the pilot's name, just somebody from the pool, but he wasn't flying fast enough to satisfy Fix. The shuttle wasn't built for speed. The pilot turned his head and said, "We're coming up on the jurisdictional border now. Should I continue?"

"No," said Fix. "Set down in the shadow of the mountains. We'll intercept as they fly over. Are they in range yet?"

"No sir, but they should come over the horizon any minute now."

As the shuttle settled into the shadows, Beth dared ask a question that had been nagging at her since they left the base. "Sir, can I ask... what charges are you planning on filling against this Fogg character?"

"I don't know yet," he admitted. "We have the right to stop him for inspection so let's be prepared to find something. We can't just let this guy fly off to Pluto with an experimental engine."

"Aye, sir," she replied. He was sure she would go along with whatever action he took. She was a good soldier. *That's what we are now*, thought Fix. *Soldiers, fighting for the safety of twelve billion souls on Earth.*

"I think I see them," said the pilot.

***

The Earth rose in the sky in front of the *Giant's Tooth* as it crossed over the Near Side. Inside the *Gold Filling*, Pass-Par-2 was in the pilot's seat with Fogg strapped into the couch behind him. "Course plotted for Mars, Master. Firing the Steady Axe in three... two... one."

Unseen beneath them, the Steady Axe engine flared into life. A bright plume of flame shot out from the bottom of the asteroid, extending for hundreds of miles.

***

The cockpit of the shuttle was suddenly lit by a flash of light.

"Explosion!" shouted the pilot.

"That's no explosion," Fix said calmly. "They've lit the engine."

"Plot an intercept course," Beth told the pilot. "We can still catch them while they're picking up speed."

"I'm not going anywhere near that thing," said the pilot. "Look at those radiation readings. If there's a person anywhere near that engine, he's a dead man."

Fix leaned in for a closer look at the monitor. "No, he's not. He's shielded by the rock. But we can't get anywhere near him without flying through the radiation."

"Should we hail him? Order him to power down?" offered Beth.

"Is he in range of the colony yet?" asked Agent Fix.

"No," said the pilot. "And he won't be. He's vectoring off. He's headed for—"

"Mars," said Fix. "His first stop is Mars."

He sat back in his seat, temporarily defeated.

***

Flanagan was enjoying an overpriced dinner at a trendy restaurant in Mayfair when he noticed several customers rushing to the front window and looking up into the night sky. Being the sort of man who always needed to know what all the fuss was about, he excused himself from his table and pushed through the growing crowd until he was up against the glass. Holding his hand above his eyes to block reflections, he finally spotted a line of fiery exhaust in the black sky. It took a second for the pieces to come together in his mind. "Fogg?" he wondered aloud.

***

Stuart walked his fancily groomed dog through a park in an upscale London neighbourhood, enjoying a warm spring evening. He noticed a commotion of people across the street pointing skyward and talking excitedly. He followed their fingers to see a line of fire in the sky, streaking away from the crescent Moon. He knew what it was at once. "Fogg!" he said, startling the dog.

***

On a rooftop overlooking London, Marchand danced a merry jig beneath the trail of celestial fire. There was no question about it: he was already rooting against himself. He shouted across the void, "Godspeed, Mr Fogg! Bon voyage, Pass-Par-2!"

CHAPTER FIVE

LIFE ON MARS

Seven-year-old Charlie Hinkston was bored out of his mind, floating in the private bunk he shared with his mother on the starship *Heart of Cadmium*. His mother was asleep, as he should have been himself, but he felt like he had spent most of the last three months sleeping. She had warned him it would be a long trip to Mars, but he was ready to be there already. His mother had bought him every game he'd asked for before they left, but he had conquered or grown tired of them all in the first six weeks. He had seen every interesting movie in the ship's library at least three times. He even sat through a few of the mushy ones with his mother. He exercised in the ship's centrifuge track twice a day at his mother's insistence, but if there was one thing he didn't miss about Earth, it was gravity. He knew Mars would have a lot less, but still some. They said the playgrounds there were the funnest in the universe. They'd better be or he was going back to Earth, with or without his mother. Except... that would mean another six-month voyage through the seemingly endless boredom of space. Maybe he would give Mars a chance.

Charlie looked out of the porthole at the unchanging stars. He knew that aboard this ship he was moving faster than he had ever moved in his life, but it sure didn't feel like it. It felt like they were just stuck floating in the middle of nowhere. But out of the corner of his eye, he noticed something was moving out there. There was a line of fire in the darkness, creeping forward and gaining on them rapidly. Charlie knew everything he could see out the window was very far away, but this looked much closer. There seemed to be something solid at the front end of the line—something tiny compared to the trail of flame behind it. He squinted to see it better, but just then the flames were extinguished. When his eyes adjusted, he saw the tooth-shaped asteroid zipping through the darkness. He tapped the window to activate the digital overlay and made it zoom in on the rock. He could see it was slowly tumbling as it sped past the *Heart of Cadmium*. Just before it disappeared beyond the window's edge, it stopped its tumble, and the flame of fire returned, only now it was pointing out in front of the rock's direction of travel.

And then it was gone from view. It was time to make his report. "Mama! Mama, wake up!"

She stirred and moaned a little in her suspended sleeping bag, but she didn't open her eyes.

"Mama!" he persisted. "An asteroid went by the ship and it was shooting out a beam of fire and it was going *way* faster than us!"

His mother sighed, not ready to face a new day of her son's imagination. "Go back to sleep, Charlie. We're almost halfway there. Only three more months to Mars."

***

Phileas Fogg had been quietly reading in bed during the ship's reorientation. He trusted Pass-Par-2 to handle the manoeuvre. Other than floating away from the mattress for a few seconds, the process had gone smoothly. He was enjoying the comfortable new silk pyjamas he had manufactured from the fabric printer in the wardrobe. He hadn't even needed to open a suitcase yet. Even the water closet (he refused to call it a 'head') was appointed with fresh toiletries. He had forced himself to learn how to use the zero-g facilities, and he had to admit it was less unpleasant than expected, but he still didn't think eleven weeks would be long enough to get used to it.

He would have to remember to ask Pass-Par-2 what their top speed had been before they flipped for deceleration so that he could check it against the record for all-time fastest human. Probably no point in notifying the record keepers just yet though. If all went according to plan, he would be breaking his own record on each leg of this trip.

He finally turned out the light and allowed the false gravity of deceleration to press him comfortably into the mattress. He drifted off to sleep, knowing Mars would be waiting for him tomorrow.

***

Mars was certainly closer by the time he enjoyed the breakfast Pass-Par-2 had prepared, but since the asteroid was flying tail-first, their destination still was not visible on the screen or out the portholes. They continued their retrograde burn for another eight hours, followed by another hour of manoeuvring to put the *Giant's Tooth* into a stable orbit before Pass-Par-2 finally rotated the great rock around and the Red Planet filled their view. They were floating in zero-g again as Pass-Par-2 prepped the *Gold Filling* for their descent to the surface. It was the evening of Day 4 as they lifted off from the asteroid and Pass-Par-2 charted a course for the equatorial spaceport at Valles Marineris.

The descent was less shaky than Fogg had anticipated, possibly due to the planet's thin atmosphere. Or perhaps his robot's piloting skills were improving. It took about thirty minutes to reach the landing pad at the spaceport, where the automated traffic control had sent them. It was twilight outside, and Fogg realised he had a whole new perception on the concept of dusk, as just a short time ago he had been in orbit watching this region slowly spinning away from the sunlight. He was disappointed to see there was no pressurised gangway outside, so he was forced to put on his spacesuit. This cost him a few precious minutes, but finally he and Pass-Par-2 cycled through the airlock and descended to the dust-covered concrete of the landing pad.

There were no other ships on the adjacent pads, although Fogg did see a few in the distance. The fading sunlight on the horizon was tinted blue, making it appear oddly Earth-like. There was no sign of life anywhere on the landing pad.

"How odd. I expected someone to meet us," said Fogg.

"Customs should be down that path, Master," Pass-Par-2 said, pointing the way.

They walked in the direction the robot had indicated. Pass-Par-2 was again lugging his unopened roller bags. He was briefly startled when he noticed two little green men watching him from the top of the ridge. He zoomed in for a better view, realising with relief that the aliens were painted on sculpted sheet metal. They held an arrow-shaped sign between them pointing down the path. It read: 'THIS WAY TO THE LOOSEST SLOTS ON THE RED PLANET!'

Pass-Par-2 followed Fogg up an incline in the path, and at the crest he could see the lights of the South Rim settlement ahead. The largest city on Mars wasn't honestly much of a city, although it was home to nearly four thousand people. It consisted of eight large structures and numerous smaller, half-buried bunkers, all connected by a network of pressurised walkways. In the middle of it all, a large resort hotel rose twelve storeys tall and trimmed in neon lights. Its windows, however, were mostly dark. The hotel was perched on a promontory overlooking the massive canyon, which was nothing but a black void in the encroaching night.

It was a short hike to the closest walkway. As they cycled through the airlock, Pass-Par-2 appreciated the jets of air that blew the dust off his surface. Fogg unlatched his helmet and removed it. Pass-Par-2 offered to balance it atop the luggage, but instead his master held onto it, tucking it under his arm. The inner doorway opened, and they stepped into a long, straight hallway lit by overhead panels. There was still no sign of life, but they continued forward, encouraged by a sign promising Customs and Immigration waiting ahead.

Several other walkways joined with theirs, but all led towards the resort. At last they came to a sliding doorway that swooshed open, and they stepped into the opulent lobby of the South Rim Hyatt. Pass-Par-2 heard soft piano music playing through hidden speakers as he followed his master across the lobby to the front desk, where at last they saw another living person beaming an eager smile in their direction.

The Filipino clerk greeted them warmly. "Welcome to the South Rim Hyatt. Are you just arriving on Mars?"

Fogg set his helmet on the counter. The clerk's name tag identified him as 'Isabelo, Night Manager,' but he saw no advantage in being overly familiar with the man. "Yes, sir. We have just landed."

"Then I will have to take you through Customs first. Right over here, please."

All smiles, the clerk slid three steps to his left to a different part of the long counter, just beneath a 'Mars Customs' sign. He quickly donned an official Customs cap and pinned a shiny badge to his shirt, and the smile abruptly vanished. "Your passport, if you please." His manner was suddenly much more formal.

Fogg was prepared with his passport in hand as he stepped over to the new station. "Is it customary for there to be no one at the spaceport to greet arriving ships?"

"Unfortunately, sir, I am the only one on duty tonight. You caught us during the slow season. Although lately even the Earth alignments aren't as busy as they used to be. Are you here on business or pleasure, Mr Fogg?"

"I am here on a wager," said Fogg.

The clerk processed this for just half a beat before he stamped the passport. "Business then. There you have it. Phileas Fogg, you are the 43,407th person on Mars!" Fogg reclaimed his passport as the clerk nodded towards Pass-Par-2. "...but I'm afraid your metal friend doesn't count."

Pass-Par-2 smiled his squiggly smile, just happy to have been noticed. The clerk then removed the hat and badge and stepped back to the front desk. When he turned to face them, the smile was back in place. "And will you be needing a room?"

"That depends," said Fogg, moving back to first position. "Is there a maglev leaving for Olympus Mons tonight?"

The clerk wrinkled his nose to signify how painful it was to disappoint. "Oh, I am sorry. They're laying new track through Noctis Labyrinthus. The trains won't be running for a few weeks."

"Weeks?" said Fogg. He knew panic would be premature. There was always a workaround. "How else can I get to Olympus Mons?"

The clerk's face brightened. "You're in luck! There's a rover caravan leaving tomorrow."

"And how long will that take?"

He checked the schedule. "It gets there in six days."

"Six days? No. That is unacceptable. I need to be at the peak of Olympus Mons by end of day tomorrow."

"Ah," said the man. "In that case, you should talk to Loopy O'Sullivan. He has an airplane for hire."

"O'Sullivan? Very good. How can I reach him?"

"He eats breakfast here every morning. Most people do. For the orange juice. We have the only orange trees on Mars." The clerk beamed with pride.

"Very well then. One room for the night. Make it your finest suite."

"Of course, sir. You'll have the whole floor to yourself. Like

I said, it's the slow season."

***

The lift opened to a dark hallway on the top floor, but the overhead lights switched on automatically when Fogg and Pass-Par-2 stepped out. They walked past closed doorways until they came to their suite. They entered a large, luxuriously appointed living room, but Fogg went straight to the bedroom without appreciating it for even a moment. Pass-Par-2 assumed there must have been a reason for requesting the extra expense of the suite, but it eluded him for now. He had so much to learn.

He followed his master to the bedroom but held back when he saw Fogg enter the en suite bathroom and close the door. The robot occupied himself setting the bags on the luggage racks, unzipping them to reveal a stack of neatly folded clothes.

Fogg reappeared from the restroom shortly after Pass-Par-2 heard the toilet flush. He looked more at ease now. Pass-Par-2 noted that his master clearly found great satisfaction in a properly flushed commode. Fogg walked over to the bags and reached for his pyjamas, but as soon as he touched the fabric, he turned a displeased glare in the robot's direction. "Pass-Par-2, my clothes are frozen solid."

"Zut alors!" said the robot. He did a quick temperature probe and realised he had overlooked an obvious problem. He quickly amended his job performance code to prevent the same error from happening again. "I should not have carried the luggage outside unprotected in the Martian air. Apologies, sir. I can thaw them in a matter of minutes."

"Don't bother," said Fogg as he made another quick note in his tablet. "I can persevere without proper sleepwear for a night. Close the curtains, then you can be excused."

"Of course," said the robot. He stepped over to the sliding doorway to an enclosed balcony and began to draw the curtains shut but stopped short when he saw the canyon outside.

"Master! You must see this view! The canyon runs all the way to the horizon!"

Fogg didn't stop undressing as he glanced toward the balcony. "It's pitch-black out there, Pass-Par-2. You're seeing in infrared."

"Oh," said Pass-Par-2, reminded of the limitations of human eyesight. "Of course. You can see it in the morning."

"Just be sure to wake me at sunrise. I would set an alarm, but I have no idea when sunrise is around here."

"Of course, sir. You have several hours yet. If you don't mind, perhaps I could spend the night out on the balcony? That way I could be sure to wake you at very first light."

"That's fine," said Fogg, slipping under the covers in his underwear. He turned out the light as Pass-Par-2 stepped out onto the balcony. "Goodnight, Pass-Par-2."

The robot froze for a moment. He realised his master had probably only said it as a matter of custom, but he appreciated the gesture nonetheless. "Goodnight to you as well, sir. Sleep well." He slid the door closed, then turned to face the vast chasm.

Pass-Par-2 spotted a power outlet on the balcony that he could have used to top up his batteries, but he assessed his reserves would last a few days yet, and he didn't want to be distracted by monitoring the inrush of electricity. He took a position that gave him the clearest easterly view. He studied the contours and textures of the crags and buttes and peaks and troughs that extended to the horizon. He reviewed how he had ended up here. It had been less than a week since he had left the factory in Calais for the very first time. He had been programmed and prepared for a life of service in high society. No one had mentioned canyons on distant planets. Despite that he found he was happy to be here. Happy and amazed. But what were these feelings? A programmed response to external events? Or authentic emotions like his master might experience? He wondered if humans were as free of programming as they claimed.

He stood sentry for hours, watching the stars slowly rotate overhead. He didn't move one servo until the first rays of daylight broke in the east.

***

It may have been the slow season, but the lobby that had been so deserted the night before was bustling with activity when Fogg and Pass-Par-2 stepped out of the lift. The night manager's claim about the breakfast crowd had been no idle boast. They stopped by the front desk briefly to confirm they were checking out, and Fogg asked the woman on duty if she could identify Mr O'Sullivan (Pass-Par-2 noticed he seemed reluctant to say the name 'Loopy'). She pointed to a lone rugged-looking man with a shaggy head of blond hair scarfing down a substantial breakfast at a table in a corner. He was wearing a faded leather bomber jacket. Pass-Par-2 felt certain he could have identified him without any help from the receptionist.

Fogg approached the man's table. "Captain O'Sullivan? I hate to interrupt your breakfast..."

Loopy replied without pausing his intake of pancakes. "You the fella looking for a lift to Olympus?" He had a thick Australian accent. "That your ship I saw flyin' in last night with the fiery plume?"

"Yes, sir. My name is Phileas Fogg and I need to get to the summit by nightfall."

"Plane won't fly to the summit," he said, shovelling in another mouthful. He let Fogg fret while he chewed the bite and swallowed. "No air at that altitude," he finally continued. "But don't worry. My little *Goose* will get ya to the Escarpment. Maglev is still running to the peak from there."

Relieved, Fogg said, "That sounds perfect. I'm willing to pay a premium as long as we can leave at once."

"What a co-inky-dink," said the pilot. "A premium is

exactly my going rate, mate. Just let me finish my O.J." He did so in one lengthy gulp.

Across the room, a man watched them intently from another table, peering over the top of his tablet. After Fogg and the robot followed the Australian out of the lobby, he activated his earpiece.

"Aaron, you were right. He's here with some kind of fancy robot. Looks like he's hired a pilot. I'll keep you posted." He stopped recording and hit 'Send' on his tablet. The message began its long journey to the Moon.

CHAPTER SIX

FLIGHT OF THE GOOSE

Loopy led them into a small pressurised hangar. There were several aircraft in various states of disassembly, but only one looked ready to fly. It resembled a glider at first glance, with its narrow body and unusually long wings, but Pass-Par-2 noticed it was equipped with two turbo engines. The words 'LOOPY'S GOOSE' were painted across the nose (somewhat sloppily in Pass-Par-2's judgment). Loopy opened up the back hatch and took the two large bags from the robot. Once they were stowed, he squeezed in the smaller valise. Fogg also handed over the helmet to his pressure suit. He had put it on at Loopy's suggestion, only because he would be needing it at the volcano and it took up less space in the plane if he was wearing it, but he was relieved that he could at least stow the helmet. Loopy managed to cram it all into the tiny compartment and slammed the hatch shut. He then led them to the starboard side where he opened the door to the fuselage. The narrow interior only had room for three seats aligned in single file. Pass-Par-2 climbed in first and settled into the rear seat. His master sat in front of him, then Loopy climbed into the pilot's seat and latched the door shut. In a matter of moments, the air had been sucked out of the hangar and the large doors began sliding open. Loopy started up the throaty roar of the engine and rolled the aircraft forward onto the tarmac.

It was a bright and clear day, but the canyon that had captivated him throughout the night was somehow not visible here. All he could see was a flat horizon ahead of them as they turned onto the runway. They were still moving along very slowly when the robot saw that the end of the runway was approaching. Surely the *Goose* would need to turn around, but the runway seemed too narrow. He didn't want to doubt the pilot's professionalism, but he was concerned for his master's safety.

"Captain O'Sullivan, is there room to turn around here?"

"Turn around?" the pilot asked over his shoulder.

"Yes. For the runway, I mean."

"Nah, mate," said Loopy. "Runway's just for landing. Planes can't take off like that at this altitude. Air's too thin."

"Oh, I see." But did he? "Then how are we going to take off?"

"Like this," said the pilot, pushing a button on the controls. Suddenly, the entire world tilted down sharply. Pass-Par-2 hadn't realised the end of the runway extended out over the rim of the deep canyon. Loopy's button had lowered the last stretch of the strip into Take Off Position, which had inclined it to slightly more than 45 degrees. For some reason, the plane wasn't rolling forward. Pass-Par-2 assumed it was being held in place by a clamp of some sort. His assumption was confirmed when he noticed a panel in front of Loopy displaying the words 'CLAMP SECURED.' Then Loopy did the unimaginable. He pushed a button and the words changed to 'CLAMP RELEASED.' The plane plunged off the runway in a steep nosedive.

Internal alarms were driving Pass-Par-2 into a state of panic as he saw the distant canyon floor through the front windshield.

The plane was in a freefall, although it did seem they were at least angling away from the canyon wall. He noticed that his master was still calmly reading his tablet, not even looking up as they plummeted towards certain death. The robot's trust in his master was the only thing that stopped him from screaming.

Loopy was disappointed that neither passenger made a sound. He loved scaring his customers. But their silence only dampened the thrill by a bee's whisker. He was grinning from ear to ear as he guided the plane ever downward. He angled the nose just enough to miss an outcropping, and now they were in the final plunge. Loopy counted down in his head, not even looking at the instruments. He trusted his reflexes to tell him when to pull up. And once again, that trust was not misplaced. At last he pulled hard on the yoke, and the *Goose* levelled out within ten feet of the dusty valley floor. Now they were travelling at tremendous speed through the slightly thicker atmosphere at lower altitude. Falling became flying. The cat may have his passenger's tongue, but he couldn't help letting out a triumphant yell himself. This was what he lived for.

The *Goose* climbed up through the morning mist. A short distance ahead, the canyon emptied into an even larger chasm. The valley floor fell away, and Loopy followed it down, gaining even more speed. Then he banked the plane majestically, rising over a small ridge into yet another canyon. It was hard for Pass-Par-2 to believe, but this one was even larger still. Loopy called back over his shoulder. "Settle back and enjoy the view, gents. Out both sides of the cabin... Mars!"

Pass-Par-2 watched the landscape slide by, taking in every little nook of the desiccated arroyos below. He noticed how the colours changed as the sun slowly rose higher in the sky. He saw thin, wispy vapours rising from a slot canyon and wondered what caused it. Further on, the valley floor became more chaotic, as if it had been recently disturbed. He wished he had downloaded a geology textbook when he'd had the chance.

The canyon floor sloped higher as they progressed

westward, and several times Loopy was forced to gain altitude as they accelerated towards the head of the great valley. At last they crested a ridge and the ground below transformed into a tableland. Loopy expertly yawed and pitched the *Goose* between the giant mesas. Fogg hadn't looked up from his tablet in over an hour.

"See that? That's Noctis Labyrinthus. Marsiest place on Mars."

Fogg indulged him with a quick squint out of the window.

"Up ahead you can see them finishing the new maglev line. Someday, when they open up the homesteading rights out here, I'm going to build me a little place on top of one of these nice flat-topped mesas and retire."

Pass-Par-2 could see the elevated maglev line cutting through the land to the south. There were several rovers gathered at one spot next to a large crane, but the *Goose* didn't fly close enough to view the work in any detail.

Fogg appreciated the view for approximately five seconds before he said, "Lovely," and then resumed his reading.

Pass-Par-2 did an impression of clearing his throat. "Captain O'Sullivan, may I ask a question?"

The pilot glanced at the robot in back. "Yeah?"

"Will you be doing any loops today?"

"Loops? You mean like flying upside-down? Are you joking? You can't do those kinds of manoeuvres in this thin air."

"Oh," said the robot.

"I mean, *maybe* I could pull off a decent Immelmann turn if my life depended on it, but it doesn't so I ain't tryin'."

"I apologise. I just thought... because of your name..."

The Australian laughed. "Ah, I get it. Naw, mate, that ain't why they call me Loopy. They call me Loopy because I'm full-on mental."

"I see," said the robot, not sure if he should feel relieved or alarmed.

The cabin stayed quiet for a couple of hours after that as

they flew away from the maze-like landscape of Noctis Labyrinthus. The terrain ahead was almost completely flat except for an impact crater here and there. Pass-Par-2 spotted a pair of dust devils chasing each other across the barren landscape. Then he realised he was focused too closely on the horizon. High above his line of sight he saw the top of an enormous volcano. The lower flanks were seemingly invisible, lost in the thicker atmosphere, but the peak was catching the sunlight.

"Look, Master! There's a great volcano ahead. Olympus Mons! Incroyable!"

Fogg looked out of the window, but Loopy turned his head and spoke over his shoulder. "That? Naw mate, that's Pavonis Mons. It's just a little nipper compared to Big Daddy Olympus. We got two others just like this one, all lined up in a row."

Pass-Par-2 looked south, and in fact he could just barely make out another giant volcano at the limit of his sight. He turned right to look north, and there was the third peak, just barely poking above the horizon from this great distance. The scale of it all made him feel insignificant.

Soon they left the three volcanoes behind, and Loopy spoke over his shoulder again. "See how the horizon is distorted up ahead? Like it rises up a bit? That's yer Olympus Mons. The start of it anyways. The damn beast is so big you really need to be in orbit to take it all in."

They flew straight towards it for an hour before it finally started to look like something tangible, not just some unreachable backdrop. The precipitous escarpment that surrounded the base rose up from the flat plains of the Tharsis region like a wall at the edge of the world. In some places the escarpment alone was higher than Mount Everest. They banked left and flew alongside the cliff for a while, circling to the southern side of the giant volcano where the shield sloped down to a more accessible altitude for the aircraft.

At last Loopy announced they were approaching a small village poised at the top of the scarp, still about a thousand feet higher than they were cruising. All they could see from their current vantage point was the end of an airstrip extending over the edge of the cliff. The atmosphere was exceedingly sparse at that altitude, but Loopy assured them he could make the landing. He angled the nose up and hit the afterburners for an extra kick. Pass-Par-2 was pressed back into his seat as the plane arced above the rock wall, revealing a cosy community of pressurised buildings ahead. Once the *Goose* was high enough to make the approach, Loopy banked towards the short airstrip. Pass-Par-2 wondered if he didn't need to communicate with the control tower, but then he realised there was no sign of any tower, nor were there any other aircraft in sight. It appeared to be a very sleepy village, existing solely as a maglev way station. It couldn't have been home to more than a hundred people.

They set down with a bump and a bounce, but it appeared to be business as usual for Loopy. He taxied them to the end of the runway, then killed the engines. Fogg looked around and realised there was no pressurised hangar to park in, nor was there any sort of docking tube being wheeled in their direction. He saw Loopy reach under his feet and pull out a helmet, which he snapped on in one deft motion. Fogg asked Pass-Par-2 to retrieve his helmet from stowage. Pass-Par-2 reached behind him and pulled the helmet loose, then passed it forward. His master had just snapped it into place when Loopy opened the front hatch without warning. Pass-Par-2 wanted to believe the pilot had seen Fogg securing the helmet first. He truly wanted to believe that. Loopy was already out and crossing the airfield to talk to the small ground crew.

The building that served as the airport was also quite conveniently the maglev station, and Fogg purchased two tickets for the summit on the next train, which would be departing in less than an hour. Fogg slipped out of his pressure suit while Pass-Par-2 retrieved the bags from the *Goose*. Fogg thanked Loopy for his reliable service, then asked him to wait here in the village for the day. "I should be back before nightfall and ready to return to the valley. I will pay you for your time, of course." Loopy figured it beat flying home without a fare, even if he lost a day in the most boring whistle-stop village on Mars, but he was pretty sure he could find a meal somewhere. Or better yet, perhaps a young widow. There were always a few of those to be found in any settlement on Mars.

CHAPTER SEVEN

ATOP THE GREAT VOLCANO

The maglev arrived on a track from the west. Pass-Par-2 wondered how it had handled the escarpment. Perhaps there were places where it sloped gradually all the way to the surface. Fogg and Pass-Par-2 boarded a nearly empty compartment on the five-car train. Fogg continued reading his tablet as the robot took a window seat. They shot out of the station at a staggering speed, charging straight up the slope of the shield volcano. Even at this speed, they were in for a bit of a ride. Pass-Par-2 had read an information plaque back at the station that said Olympus Mons was the size of Arizona. That data was of limited use to the robot, who had never been to Arizona, but now if he ever did travel there he would be able to put the state into proper perspective compared to extraterrestrial volcanoes. Pass-Par-2 wondered if Arizona was more scenic than the dull view currently out his window. The volcano's shield was just a smooth plain of cooled lava with a barely perceptible incline. Bored, he turned his attention to his employer.

"Master, can I ask what it is you've been reading all day?"

Fogg looked up for a moment, slightly irritated by the distraction. "Bolivian crop reports," he answered.

"Oh. How interesting." Pass-Par-2 paused, waiting for a further response that would never come. At last he dared one more question. "Are you invested in agriculture?"

"No," said Fogg, "I most certainly am not."

So much for conversation. Pass-Par-2 went back to staring at the inclined slope.

***

"Now approaching Summit Station," said a pleasant voice over the P.A. The train pulled to a stop as a pressurised gantry extended to the doorway between cars.

Fogg exited into the station. Pass-Par-2 followed behind, burdened not only with the luggage but also his master's bulky pressure suit. Fewer than a dozen passengers were waiting to catch the train back down. It seemed as though it was the slow season here too. Fogg saw an enclosed walkway leading away from the station towards a cluster of buildings. Signs indicated that the corridor led to the university, two hotels, three restaurants, a general store, and a souvenir shop, but they were in the opposite direction from where his interests lay. Looking out the station's broad window, he could see the rim of the volcano's caldera. He would have to go outside to get there. He grabbed the pressure suit from Pass-Par-2.

"No time to waste. Let's collect our rock and be on our way."

Minutes later, they stood outside under a sky as black as midnight, even though the sun was still well above the horizon. Pass-Par-2 looked back over the slope they had climbed, across the distant plains of the Tharsis region. Most of the planet's atmosphere was below them at this altitude. They were essentially standing in the vacuum of space despite having a planet firmly underfoot. Fogg took little notice of the vista and set off along a paved path up to the caldera. Pass-Par-2 hurried to catch up.

Cautiously approaching the rim, the robot stared down into the maw of the beast itself. The caldera was more than fifty miles across. Pass-Par-2 could barely make out the far side of the rim. There were several different levels to the floor of the caldera far below, but the area directly beneath them was the highest. He could see several research sites at the different elevations, and even a few large trucks moving on paths between them. Pass-Par-2 wondered how they got them down there.

Fogg saw a building that jutted out over the rim, housing several cranes that lowered cables into the caldera. "I suppose I should speak to someone about the use of that crane," he said. Pass-Par-2 followed him as he set off around the rim.

***

Fogg watched the wall of the caldera zipping past him five feet from his face as the cable lowered him deeper into the volcano. The crane operator had assured him he need not travel far to collect an interesting sample. He could journey three days into the deepest unexplored fissures and not find anything more exotic than what was in ample supply on the first ledge down. He peeked between his dangling feet to determine how much further down that ledge was, but it was too dark to see. The cable slowed, and Fogg jostled in the harness as it came to a stop. He still couldn't see his destination. Then he realised the five-inch wide outcropping by his feet must be what passed for a ledge around here.

The voice of the crane operator came through his helmet. "Okay, sir, please remain secured in your harness at all times, and keep the rock hammer's strap around your wrist."

Fogg certainly had no intention of removing the harness, and the hammer's strap was already as tight around his wrist as he could make it. He reached out with his feet and found purchase on the tiny ledge. He noticed several handholds that had been created by previous rock collectors, and he used them to move a few feet to his left, where he could see some interesting stones embedded in the wall. The light built into his helmet cast eerie shadows as he scanned the surface closely, looking for a sample that would be both interesting and easy to collect. He spotted one that had a deep purple hue with lighter coloured specks scattered throughout. He tugged at it, and although it was slightly loose, it was going to take some persuasion, so he used the rock hammer to help the cause. He was just about to give up and look for another rock when it suddenly popped loose in his hand. He bobbled it briefly but managed to avoid dropping it into the abyss. He secured it in a canvas sack on his hip and signalled he was ready for extraction. Soon the cable pulled taut and his toes were lifted up and away from the ledge.

As he rose, the harness began to rotate until he was facing away from the rock wall and looking out across the great expanse of the caldera. Most of it was in shadow, but the eastern wall was still lit by the slowly dropping sun. As he watched, a very unusual ship rose from the depths into the sunlight. It was shaped roughly like a 19th century hot air balloon but with a disproportionately large pressurised gondola. On further inspection, Fogg realised the spherical structure on top, painted with broad longitudinal red stripes, wasn't a balloon at all. It was most likely a nuclear reactor powering the rocket thrusters that extended below the ship. The gondola itself was at least as large as the *Gold Filling*, with triangular glass windows encircling its circumference. As it slowly rotated, a familiar sight stirred his English soul. The Union Jack in all its glory was emblazoned upon the side of the craft. He watched the ship climb gracefully on carefully timed microthrusts, rising past his elevation into the open sky above the caldera. Then it disappeared over the rim behind him.

When he reached the top, the crane operator shut off the

cable and came over to unbuckle Fogg from the harness. Fogg spoke to him on an open frequency.

"Sir, are you familiar with the vehicle that rose out of the caldera moments ago?"

"You mean the *Montgolfier*?" the man replied in an accent Fogg pegged as Appalachian. "That's Cromarty's ship. He's been here longer than anybody."

"You mean Sir Francis Cromarty?" asked Fogg.

"Yeah, that's him. Calls himself 'Sir' and everything. Come to think of it, he kinda talks like you. He a friend of yours or sumthin'?"

"We have never met," said Fogg. "Where does he berth his ship?"

"Where does he *what?*" asked the man.

"Where does he park his ship?"

"Oh. In the big hangar by the university. You can't miss it."

"Thank you, sir. You've been most helpful." Pass-Par-2 was approaching, relieved to have his master back topside. Fogg handed him the bagged sample. "Hold tight to this, Pass-Par-2. We don't want to have to come back here. One down, five to go. Come along now."

He led the robot away from the rim towards the town.

He found the ship in an open hangar just as the man had described. It appeared the engines were still cooling. With one last belch of steam, the ship went silent and a boarding ramp rolled out from the main airlock. Fogg and Pass-Par-2 approached, waiting at the bottom of the ramp as the airlock cycled. When it opened, a man stepped out in a rather unique pressure suit. It was festooned with medals and ribbons, like some sort of military parade uniform. Fogg recognised an Explorers Club pin among the display of finery. The man was a bit taller than Fogg, and even in the pressure suit it was obvious he had a lean build. The face in the helmet seemed gentle but serious. The only hair on his head was an extravagant white moustache. Pass-Par-2 guessed him to be roughly 70 years of age. As he reached the bottom of the ramp, Fogg stepped forward and addressed him on a public channel.

"Sir Francis Cromarty?"

"Yes?" he responded. His voice was deep and dignified.

Fogg surprised Pass-Par-2 by reciting a singsong verse he had never heard before. "Sons of the river, daughters of the plains..."

To the robot's further surprise, Cromarty injected, completing the verse with great enthusiasm. "...children of the kingdom, where nobility remains!" Amazement spread across the older man's face as he then engaged Fogg in a rather elaborate secret handshake that involved several slaps, hooked pinkies, and something that resembled a rising bird. Pass-Par-2 was impressed by the coordination, choosing to overlook the ridiculousness of it all.

Once the ceremony was complete, Cromarty slapped Fogg on the back, then took a step back to assess him. "An Academy man!" he said with satisfaction. "The further one gets from home, the more delightful it is to meet someone who has followed the same path. What is your name, my good man?" Pass-Par-2 couldn't help noticing that Cromarty's diction was almost a perfect match for his master's own anachronistic pattern of speech.

"I am Phileas Fogg," said Phileas Fogg.

"Come, Mr Fogg. You must join me for dinner. The campus cafeteria food is dreadful, but the beer washes it down just fine."

***

The threesome sat in a cafeteria booth with a view of the setting sun. The gentlemen were free from their pressure suits, having checked them in lockers just inside the university's airlock. The cafeteria was almost entirely empty other than a busboy clearing tables from the dinner rush. Fogg and Cromarty had finished their meals when Fogg asked Pass-Par-2 to present the rock to Cromarty. The man took out a monocle and used it as a jeweller's eye, inspecting the nugget closely.

"Yes, a fine sample. Nice phenocrysts," he said, running a finger over the embedded crystals. "Visible flow banding. You certainly did not pick a boring one, Mr Fogg. Lord Albemarle will be thrilled to get it." He handed the rock back to Pass-Par-2, who gently returned it to the sample bag. "You know, he and I worked very closely together on the lunar surveys of the early fifties."

"Of course," said Fogg. "Your work is legendary."

"Yes, well, if you really made it to Mars in two days' time, you will soon be a legend yourself, Phileas Fogg."

"Not me," he replied. "The Karbasis designed the engine. Their names will be the ones remembered."

"But it was you who had the vision and courage to prove its power. That engine could revitalise the Mars colony. It seems every alignment brings fewer ships," Cromarty said. He looked out the window, remembering the enthusiasm of the early years. There had to be enthusiasm to undertake the construction of such a large facility in such a challenging location. When this place became operational, Cromarty had felt like anything was possible. Now it felt like a ghost town. He was almost sorry he had lived long enough to see it happen.

"I guess there are only so many people drawn to the frontier life," offered Fogg.

"No, it's not just the colonists," said Cromarty, still looking outside for activity that was no longer there. "Fewer scientists are coming too. Mars has given up all its secrets. I should know, I've studied it longer than anyone. It's a dead world, and it likely always has been."

He snapped out of his trance of lamentation, looking Fogg

in the eye again. "But science never ceases. Jupiter is the new frontier. A former student of mine is on the team at Ganymede. They find something new and amazing every few days. I would go there myself if it didn't require a two-year voyage."

Fogg sat up even straighter than usual. "It just so happens I am headed to Ganymede myself, after a brief stop at Ceres. I plan to be there in eight days. I would be honoured if you would join me, Sir Francis."

The man's eyes lit up. "Eight days? Remarkable. That is indeed a tempting offer."

"Can your ship reach orbit?" asked Fogg.

"Certainly. The *Montgolfier* is a Class Four starship. I flew it here directly from Earth."

Fogg found himself confused by the answer. "Really? I didn't think starships were permitted to land at Olympus Mons."

Cromarty waved this off. "They're not, strictly speaking. Valles Marineris is the only legal port of entry, but those laws only exist in books back on Earth, along with anyone who might enforce them. You see that building across the way?" He pointed to a facility that sat well separated from all the others further around the western rim. "That's the Chinese. You think any of them bothered to check in with Customs?"

Fogg thought for a moment. "So you're saying I'm not actually the 43,407th person on Mars?"

Cromarty laughed. "I can't believe they are even pretending to have an accurate count."

"So I could have flown my ship here directly." Fogg turned to Pass-Par-2, clearly displeased. "You cost us an entire day by landing at the canyon."

Pass-Par-2 felt that familiar sense of shame as Fogg took out his tablet and made another note in his Beta Test journal. "I apologise for following international law, Master."

Cromarty had been thinking about how many loose ends he would need to tie up before he could leave Mars. It turned out there were very few. He lived on board his ship so there was nothing to pack. His latest lady friend had told him in no uncertain terms not to call again. And he had no obligations to the university. He knew by the excitement he felt that he was ready to go. "If you like, I can fly you back to your ship, then we can both launch for your asteroid from there."

Fogg nodded his approval. "That would be greatly appreciated. Pass-Par-2, contact Captain O'Sullivan and inform him we won't be needing the return flight after all."

"Of course, Master," said Pass-Par-2. "Should I ask for a partial refund?"

"Don't waste your breath," said Fogg.

"If I had any, I never would," said the robot. He hadn't intended to make a joke, but he appreciated Cromarty's laugh all the same.

***

The agent sat in the lobby bar at the South Rim Hyatt feeling like a failure. His quarry had walked right across this very room during breakfast, but he had been unable to follow him. He had been waiting all day for *Loopy's Goose* to return, but so far there had been no activity at the landing field. At last he saw two ground crew workers quickly settle their bill with the bartender and rush to the airlock. He wondered if they had been drinking alcohol on duty. They weren't his responsibility, but sometimes he liked to report workplace malfeasance just to remember what it felt like to have an impact. After all, there was usually very little for a UN Security Agent to do on Mars. But today might be different. If the workers were being called back to the spaceport, that meant a ship was coming in. Not *Loopy's Goose*, certainly, but it was worth checking out. He walked to the observation area closest to the spaceport and instantly spotted the ship landing outside. And he recognised it at once. There was no other ship like it on Mars. It was the geologist Cromarty. He spent most of his time out in the field, but he came into the valley once or twice a year. The agent was sure this wasn't a coincidence.

After the ship landed, the boarding ramp extended and two familiar figures emerged. Fogg and his fancy robot. The agent didn't bother wondering what had become of Loopy O'Sullivan. Obviously Fogg had bummed a faster ride back with his countryman. Did this mean Cromarty was sympathetic to the King of Pluto too? The robot went straight to Fogg's golden ship, but Fogg himself turned towards the hotel. Excited to be back on the case, the agent moved to a position where he could watch Fogg without being seen. He was afraid the man might recognise his face, even though they had never met. He would watch from a distance and figure out what Fogg was up to, then make his final report. He would be happy to put this whole affair behind him.

***

Agent Aaron Fix returned to his office in the Hayn Crater Moonbase just as he was alerted to an incoming video message from Mars. A familiar face appeared on his screen.

"Aaron, at last I have news to report. Fogg and his robot came back, but not with the pilot they left with. That Brit geologist Cromarty flew them back to the valley in that swanky ship of his. They landed, and the robot went straight to their ship while Fogg came back inside the hotel. I followed him to the restaurant. He spoke to the manager, who then disappeared into the back for several minutes and came out with some sort of sealed package. It was unmarked, so there's no telling what it was. I'll try to interrogate the manager to see if I can get him to tell me what was in it. He probably won't, though. All the employees here hate me.

"Anyway, Fogg took the package back to his ship and launched a few minutes later. But get this... Cromarty launched his ship on the exact same trajectory. Then that crazy plume lit up the sky less than an hour after they left. It looks like he recruited Cromarty for whatever his mission is. We should see if there's any connection between him and the King of Pluto. I'll let you know if I learn anything else. Ephraim out."

Fix closed the message. He doubted this agent would be of any further use. Fogg was finished with Mars. But Fix wasn't finished with Fogg. He had plans for keeping tabs on him.

CHAPTER EIGHT

THE SIRENS OF CERES

Mars receded rapidly behind the fiery exhaust as the Steady Axe accelerated hard for the asteroid belt. There were now two ships parked on the head of the *Giant's Tooth*. Cromarty's *Montgolfier* sat less than a hundred feet from the *Gold Filling*. Against a stellar backdrop, Cromarty exited his ship in his pressure suit and crossed the short distance between the vessels.

"A very fine ship you have here, Fogg," said Cromarty as he stepped out of the airlock and removed his helmet. He took a good look around the interior. "Very stylishly appointed."

"You may compliment the President of Agua Luna for that," said Fogg. "It's a bit modern for my taste."

Cromarty chuckled as he stripped out of his bulky spacesuit. "Yes, we are products of the Academy. Modern styles will always elude us." Cromarty had graduated decades ahead of Fogg before the switch to a fully VR campus, but the Academy had always been rooted in classical aesthetics. The alumni were routinely found in the highest levels of government and commerce, but they always stood out like time travellers from the Victorian Age.

Cromarty reached back into the sleeve of his discarded spacesuit and retrieved a bottle of Macallan single malt. “I don't know if you are a drinking man or not, Fogg, but this is a special occasion. It is tradition to toast the Starman whenever one crosses his orbit for the first time.”

“Starman?” asked Pass-Par-2.

“He's an astronaut of sorts, drifting through space in a convertible sports car. He's been circling the sun between Mars and the asteroid belt for sixty years now,” explained Cromarty.

“Oh my. And I thought 80 days was a long voyage.”

“Sixty years is nothing to the Starman. He's just a mannequin in a spacesuit, propped up behind the wheel. It was a bit of a publicity stunt, but a bloody brilliant one.”

“Is he actually nearby?” asked Fogg.

“No, I checked. He's on the far side of the sun at the moment, but we still owe him a toast.” Cromarty opened the bottle while Pass-Par-2 helpfully supplied two glasses. Once both had been poured, Cromarty raised his and said, “To the Starman!”

“To the Starman,” echoed Fogg. They clinked glasses and downed their whisky. Cromarty's was gone in a gulp, but Fogg struggled with it a bit as it was a stiffer drink than he was used to. Cromarty couldn't help but laugh at the face he made when he swallowed the last of it. He patted the younger man on the back.

“You're a good egg, Fogg. I want you to know that I plan to compensate you for this journey at the standard rate.”

“Poppycock!” said Fogg. It was more colourful language than he normally used, but he was slightly feeling the effects of the liquor. “I won't accept one pound. It is an honour to travel with an Academy alumnus of such great accomplishment.”

Cromarty was genuinely moved. “I appreciate that more than you will ever know, young man. At least let me repay you with some navigational advice. I see your robot has plotted a course to enter Ceres orbit in two days, correct?”

"That's right," said Fogg. Pass-Par-2 was listening closely, afraid he had made another miscalculation.

"How much time will you actually need on the surface?" asked Cromarty.

"Not long," answered Fogg. "Just a few hours, I suppose—enough to collect Albemarle's rock at Ahuna Mons."

"So why bother entering orbit at all? You could simply do a flyby."

"A flyby?"

"Yes, we could go in my ship. The *Montgolfier* is a good bit faster than this lander of yours, no offence. And it has already received quite a boost from riding atop the *Giant's Tooth*. It can ferry us ahead to Ceres while the Steady Axe continues decelerating the asteroid, but don't let it slow down enough to enter orbit. We land and collect your rock, then we take off and rendezvous with the *Giant's Tooth* just as it reaches Ceres. By keeping some momentum for Jupiter, you could make up that day you lost on Mars."

It might have been the whisky, but Fogg found himself smiling. "My friend, you have paid your transit fees a thousand times over! Pass-Par-2, plot a new course for a flyby that gives us eight hours on the surface of Ceres."

"Of course," said Pass-Par-2. He was thrilled to make the calculations and put Sir Francis's plan into action.

***

The next morning, the *Giant's Tooth* performed its flip and began its retrograde burn, slightly later than Pass-Par-2's original schedule. They still needed to ride the asteroid while it burned off enough speed to make a Ceres landing feasible for the *Montgolfier*, but that gave Fogg and Pass-Par-2 time to relocate to Cromarty's ship. When the time came, Pass-Par-2 shut down the Steady Axe so they could fly past the tail of the asteroid without being exposed to the radioactive exhaust plume. They flew for nearly an hour before Pass-Par-2 announced they were at a safe distance and reactivated the Steady Axe by remote. It was quite a sight to see from a distance as the finger of flame reached out towards them, splitting the infinite darkness of space.

Cromarty reoriented his ship, putting the *Giant's Tooth* behind them and the growing disk of Ceres ahead. Fogg took some time to look around the interior of the *Montgolfier*. It seemed more spacious than the *Gold Filling*, but that was a bit of an illusion. It was merely brighter and more open. The gondola compartment was shaped like a squashed icosahedron, enclosing one big room around a central shaft six feet in diameter. Fogg assumed the shaft connected the thrusters below with the nuclear reactor above. The ring of tessellated triangular windows that encircled the outer walls offered a panoramic view that contributed to the sense of openness. There were adjustable sliding shutters, but Cromarty seemed to keep them open at all times. The cabin's only partition surrounded a small bunk and presumably a lavatory. The outer perimeter was furnished with several lounge chairs padded with white upholstery where one could relax and watch the universe fly by. Fogg was impressed by the tidiness. He wondered how the man managed without a valet.

Ceres was growing larger in the front window, and Cromarty announced that it was time to start their deceleration burn. They would be burning much harder than the *Giant's Tooth*, pulling nearly five-g as they approached the dwarf planet. Fogg strapped into one of the seats and informed Cromarty that he was ready. The engines ignited, and Fogg suddenly felt an elephant sit on his chest.

He wasn't sure how long the burn lasted, but it seemed like hours. Cromarty periodically shouted out distances and speeds. Pass-Par-2 was unusually silent in the seat next to Fogg. He was probably busy monitoring the humans' vitals during the distressing manoeuvre. People had been known to suffer strokes during extended high-g burns. Fogg should have felt reassured by his vigilance, but somehow it also felt like a violation. His vitals were his business. But if someone had to track his health, at least it was just a robot.

Pass-Par-2 was indeed monitoring their health, but he was also watching Cromarty fly the ship. The gentleman prided himself in his piloting skills, but Pass-Par-2 wanted to be ready to take over if called upon. He found to his surprise that he had rather taken to the disciplines of astronautics and navigation. The precise but dependable mathematics appealed to his meticulous makeup. It would be enjoyable to learn to fly a new craft.

At long last, Cromarty announced an end to the burn. The main engine cut off, and the elephant abruptly vanished and left Fogg floating in weightlessness again. He unstrapped himself from the seat and floated forward as the *Montgolfier* rotated around to face the surface of Ceres. At first glance, it looked like a miniature twin of the Moon. It was another grey, airless world of craters, but the horizon was noticeably closer. Then Fogg noticed the famous 'bright spots' first discovered by the Dawn spacecraft in 2015. The probe had identified the largest of these reflective patches of crystallised brine, but Fogg could see there were countless smaller ones all around the surface, as if castaways were flashing mirrors to signal for rescue from nearly every crater.

A rocky ridge appeared over the horizon as the *Montgolfier* slowed further. They were approaching Occator Crater, the site of the oldest offworld mining colony this side of the Moon. Cromarty had explained that they would need to land there and proceed to Ahuna Mons on the ground. The surface of Ceres was notoriously unstable, covered with loosely packed muddy clay layered over an often-volatile substrate. Famously, a Swedish surveyor ship had been trapped years ago when its engines melted through the surface, creating a quagmire of slurry and violent eruptions of steam. The crew had to abandon the half-buried ship and await rescue on the surface. Cromarty wasn't willing to risk losing his precious ride, so they would be setting down on a permanent landing structure at the Occator mining site.

As they crested the crater rim, the lights of the mining station appeared straight ahead, nestled between the largest and most famous of the bright spots. The vast sheets of salty material inside Occator Crater sublimated every morning to create a thin atmosphere, filling the crater floor with a temporary glowing mist. It was eerily beautiful.

Cromarty turned the ship tail forward and began his landing burn.

***

As the ship set down on the landing pad, Pass-Par-2 noted that Cromarty had so far only communicated with an automated control tower. It seemed odd that they had not yet heard from an actual living person in the mining facility. Surely visitors were rare enough to merit a little personal attention?

The gentlemen donned their bulky spacesuits by the airlock. Pass-Par-2 would not need to carry any luggage on this outing, but instead he would be burdened with the pressurised case Fogg had brought from the hotel restaurant on Mars. They cycled through the airlock and hopped down the ramp in one step. The gravity here was so weak it felt more like a suggestion than a law. Fogg figured he weighed about five pounds. He feared to think how high he might jump if he really tried. Possibly all the way back to Mars.

As they carefully crossed the landing platform, two figures emerged from an airlock ahead. They were tall and imposing, the faceplates of their suits ominously reflective. Fogg checked the comm system in his suit to see if they were being hailed, but it seemed the sentries were content to watch them silently. As they approached, the one on the left extended an arm to point to the airlock ahead. Cromarty nodded, then stepped into the airlock, which was large enough to accommodate at least twenty people and possibly even a surface vehicle.

Cromarty spoke in Fogg's ear through a private channel. "Keep your eyes open, Fogg. Deep-space miners have a reputation as a dangerous lot." Fogg glanced at the pressurised container in his robot's arms. He was glad he had thought to bring a peace offering.

The massive door slid shut, and an inrush of air filled the room. A red light switched to green, and their escorts reached up to remove their helmets. Fogg released the neck latch and pulled off his own helmet, then froze in amazement. The sentry closest to him shook long golden tresses from her helmet, then turned to her companion, a muscular black woman with a shaved head. Both women towered over Fogg and Cromarty like Amazon warriors of legend. They glowered down at them as if just waiting for these strange men to cause trouble so they could toss them back outside with their helmets off. Fogg didn't doubt that they could and would do it. Then the inner door swung open. Fogg saw the look on Cromarty's face before he turned to find the cause.

Inside the main chamber of the mining base, a crowd of women stood awaiting them. Fogg saw representatives from every corner of Earth's globe. The only category in which the assembled group lacked diversity was gender. It appeared as though Fogg and Cromarty were in possession of the only Y chromosomes in town. Some of the women seemed excited, others distrustful, but they all appeared quite curious about the new arrivals.

The group parted as an older woman stepped to the front. Her nationality was hard to pinpoint, but Fogg was pretty sure there had to be some Italian blood involved. She had a pile of black hair on top of her head that seemed to defy what little gravity there was. She glided across the floor towards them. In fact, everyone in the place moved with effortless buoyancy. He noticed a few of the younger women were literally climbing the walls for a better look at them.

Since Cromarty was having trouble keeping his jaw from hitting the floor, Fogg decided it was up to him to speak. "Greetings. I am Phileas Fogg of London. My companion here is Sir Francis Cromarty, also of London but more recently Mars."

The older woman, who was clearly their leader, looked them over with suspicion. "What brings you all the way out to the belt, London boys? Everything east of Dantu is claimed already. You might find a patch of rock north of Ikapati. Or better yet, get back in your ship and keep flying on out to Juno."

Fogg was about to reply when he heard a voice above and behind him. Three lithesome women were perched over the airlock door, easily supported by just their bare toes and fingertips. It was a brunette who spoke to her companions in a poorly calibrated whisper. "I call dibs on the chrome dome," she said.

An Asian woman next to her, possibly the youngest of them all, asked in an innocent voice, "You mean the robot?"

"No," replied the brunette, "the old guy!"

"Good," said the younger woman. "I like the robot."

Fogg didn't dare look at Cromarty and Pass-Par-2 to see if they had heard them. He kept his focus on the leader. "We aren't here to stake a claim, madam. We are on a mission to Ahuna Mons to collect one single rock, after which we shall leave and never bother you again."

The woman looked genuinely puzzled. "You came all this way for one rock?"

"Just one from Ceres, yes," said Fogg. "We do have other stops to make. Speaking of which, we are a bit pressed for time, and we are in need of conveyance across the surface to the mountain. We were hoping you might have some sort of ground vehicle we could rent? Preferably something fast?"

The woman was somewhere between irritated and amused. "This ain't a car rental, honey. You shoulda brought your own transpo."

He was starting to believe her accent might be Brazilian, but her attitude suggested she had spent a lot of time with Americans. She clearly wasn't going to help them out of the goodness of her heart. Fortunately he still had a trump card to play. "I am willing to pay any reasonable price you care to name. Maybe even slightly unreasonable. Also, I brought a gift." He turned to his valet and beckoned him forward.

The robot set the sealed container on the ground between his master and this rather intimidating woman. He removed the lid and stepped back. As he did, two oranges fell out of the container and rolled across the floor.

There was an audible gasp in the room. A redheaded woman jumped forward and grabbed one of the oranges, sniffing it deeply.

"Put that down, Millie," the leader said sternly.

"But Mama Francesca! They're oranges! And they're fresh!"

At once Fogg knew who he was talking to, but he called on his experience as a card player to hide any reaction. Mama Francesca turned back to him, showing more suspicion than ever.

"How'd you get oranges all the way out here? You grow 'em on your ship?"

"No, madam. These oranges were picked fresh from a tree on Mars just two mornings ago," said Fogg.

He heard the brunette over his shoulder react with excitement. "They came from Mars in two days?" There were similar murmurs throughout the room.

Francesca's eyes narrowed. "It's the Karbasi engine, isn't it? That red finger of flame heading this way?" Fogg watched her face morph from suspicion through amazement and settle on something close to sadness. "I never thought they'd get it working in my lifetime."

Fogg nodded. He understood she was mourning the end of an era. Perhaps he could help her see the obvious bright side.

"Soon all the fruits of Earth will be within your reach, and the fruits of your labour will be in Earth's markets that much faster." He spoke a little louder, addressing the whole room. "Change is coming, ladies."

There was palpable excitement throughout the group, but Francesca was still resisting. "You can keep your change, Mr Fogg. Some of us like things the way they are."

The brunette behind Fogg jumped from her perch. Fabric sewn between the arms of her gossamer gown allowed her to swoop to the floor like a flying squirrel, where she snatched an orange from the container. "But Mama Francesca... oranges!" She held the fruit for a moment, daring her leader to stop her. But Francesca instead turned her back. In an instant, the brunette ripped the peel and bit in. Millie followed suit with hers, and in an instant the mob descended on the crate like crazed beasts.

The brunette tossed half her orange to the young Asian overhead. "Heads up, Linlin!" The younger woman grabbed it and popped a slice into her mouth. As she bit down, her eyes rolled back in ecstasy.

Fogg turned away from the feeding frenzy and approached Francesca. "Madam, I understand how you feel. You've obviously built a life for yourselves here, but that life need only change for the better. How you choose to face the coming age is entirely up to you."

"I understand that, Mr Fogg. I understand it all too well." She turned and looked him in the eye. "Thank you for the oranges. It obviously means a lot to them."

"The fruit is a gift," he said. "No obligation. But if you could provide us any assistance...?"

Linlin crept up to Francesca and sweetly held out a slice of her orange. The older woman accepted it with a thankful nod and took a bite. She closed her eyes, savouring the juice. Finally, she reached out and hit a button, and a doorway to a dark garage began sliding open.

"Take the rocket-bikes," she said around a mouthful of pulp. "They'll get you there in no time. Just try not to get yourselves killed."

CHAPTER NINE

A MOUNTAIN OF SALT

Three rocket-powered motorcycles with giant, knobby tyres sped southeast across the barren landscape, kicking up high arcs of loose regolith and clumpy clay behind them. For the first few miles, Fogg was convinced they would likely be unable to take Francesca's advice of avoiding violent death riding these powerful machines. Capable of reaching speeds of over 100 miles an hour in such low gravity, it seemed as though the slightest bump in the road might launch them into orbit. But he quickly learned to appreciate the safety engineering of the vehicles. The rocket engines were equipped with gyroscopic fail-safes that would shut them down if the nose pointed up more than a few degrees. Smaller manoeuvring jets in the axles could thrust downwards, making conventional braking possible. The tyres had obviously been designed for a much larger vehicle, but skilfully adapted to the rocket-bikes. Even on level ground, they frequently went airborne, hopping fifty yards or more, but the massive tyres and impressive shocks always cushioned the touchdown.

The two women who had shown them to the bikes, the

wing-suited Belgian brunette Babette and the Taiwanese nineteen-year-old Linlin, had told them to follow the tracks leading away from the crater to the southeast. Tracks would last for centuries on this airless world, so there was no way to be sure how long it had been since someone had made this journey before them, but Pass-Par-2 was grateful to have a path to follow. It wasn't exactly a straight line, but the robot understood they were likely swinging wide of dangerous or impassable terrain. It was a strange feeling to be chasing the horizon on a world so small. It sometimes seemed as if they might actually catch it.

Fogg and Cromarty had discussed the curious question of the all-female mining colony as they rode away from the crater. Cromarty suggested that perhaps the men were all deep underground in the mines, but Pass-Par-2 offered information he had picked up from the facility's computer network. There were only forty-two names on the current roster, and there had been precisely forty-two women facing them in the base. Cromarty then speculated that the men had all been killed in an accident, leaving their widows trapped in this hardscrabble existence. Fogg didn't believe that for an instant. None of the women had expressed any desire to be rescued. Most seemed merely curious about the visiting men. Surely there had been some men working the mines in the past, and perhaps some tragedy had shifted the gender balance, but if so it hadn't been recent. There was no sense of sadness or desperation from the population. The women of Occator Crater were exactly where they wanted to be, doing exactly what they wanted to do. Whether the men were killed off or chased off, it was ancient history to them now. It was no doubt that Francesca had kept them together as a strong working unit. Fogg had read a bit about her early exploits, and running an all-female, deep-space mining facility seemed like a perfect capstone for her career. He hoped he would have a chance to talk to her again before they left.

Cromarty, who was leading the way, suddenly released the accelerator and slowed his bike considerably. Fogg pulled up alongside him and saw Cromarty gesture off to the left. His voice came through the speaker in his helmet. "See how deadly this surface can be?"

Fogg followed his gaze to a valley in the distance where he saw a large derelict spacecraft. The rear was sunk entirely beneath the ice and dirt. He could see a Swedish flag painted on its flank.

"We mustn't dawdle," said Fogg. "We're almost there." He gunned the throttle and pulled out into the lead.

A short time later, the flat peak of Ahuna Mons jutted from the horizon ahead of them. With no atmosphere to diffuse the light, it seemed close and unimpressive in size. But as they continued to ride towards it, the mountain grew higher and higher, rising above the curvature of the surface. At last they could see all 13,000 feet of it. With no other mountains in sight, it dominated the surrounding terrain. The slopes were streaked with glistening white salt deposits, shining brightly against an airless sky that stubbornly remained black even in the midday sun.

The land on the north side fell away into a deep crater. In some spots the flat strip between the crater and the mountain was only a few yards wide. Fogg steered his bike towards this ledge. He had no intention of climbing the mountain, so he wanted to collect his sample from a location that would be easy to pinpoint on a map. He intended Lord Albemarle to know the full story of his rocks and where they came from.

"This place looks rather like someone forgot to replace their divot," said Cromarty. Fogg had never been one for golf, but he understood his meaning. The giant hole in the ground next to the massive mountain was an odd sight indeed.

They slowed their bikes and rode single file across the ledge, with the north face of the mountain growing closer to their right and the drop into the crater creeping in from the left. Finally they reached an area where a landslide of bright salty minerals had piled up at the base. There were hundreds of fist-sized rocks. The only way it could have been more inviting was if there had been a friendly sign saying, 'Free samples! Help yourself!'

Fogg killed his engine and stepped off the bike. Behind him, Cromarty and Pass-Par-2 also stopped, but they kept their engines idling. Fogg tested the ground beneath his feet. "It seems stable here," he said. "Mostly rock." He reached the pile in two big steps and took no time at all to select a perfect sample. He held it up to Cromarty, who nodded his approval.

"Looks like it's just begging to join good ol' Albemarle's collection," he said.

Fogg dropped it into a sample bag and sealed it. Behind him, Pass-Par-2 caught sight of something in the sky. A red jet of flame had just risen over the far horizon.

"Look, Master!" said the robot. "The *Giant's Tooth*!"

Fogg allowed himself just a moment to appreciate the sight. Then he attached the sample bag to his waist and hopped back onto his bike. "We'd best get back to the ship," he said.

Cromarty swung his bike around back the way they had come. Pass-Par-2 followed his lead, but the exhaust of his idling engine swept across the edge of the crater's rim. It provided just enough heat for catastrophe. The icy mix within the regolith instantly sublimated, causing the soil to lose its cohesion. At once, twenty yards of the shelf tumbled down the crater's slope, taking all three rocket-bikes with it.

Fogg gripped the handles tightly and managed to stay on top of the machine as it slid down the slope. He revved the throttle, but the engine behind him did nothing. He repressed the panic that was rising inside him and thought through the problem. At once he realised the steep slope was causing the failsafe to override the engine. He turned the bike sideways, then throttled the engine again, and the rocket flared to life. He hoped neither of the other bikes had been directly behind him as he shot laterally across the slope of the crater wall. Once he was free from the tumbling rocks, he began angling back up the slope, just enough to climb to the shelf above without triggering the failsafe again.

He lost traction once more as another section of the crater began to slide away beneath him. The rockslide was still expanding. He needed to get out of this crater before it could overtake him. He gained as much speed as he could, then turned sharply up the slope again. As expected, the engine shut off, but the boost gave him enough momentum to crest the crater rim. He stopped the bike once he was back on solid ground. When he turned, he was pleased to see Cromarty's bike hop over the rim just behind him. The older man pulled up alongside him, then they both peered back over the edge.

"Pass-Par-2! Where is he?" asked Cromarty.

Fogg set his suit's broadcast range to its maximum. "Pass-Par-2, can you hear me?" He waited a long moment, but there was no reply. "Come in, Pass-Par-2," he tried again.

He saw great concern on Cromarty's face. The man hopped off his bike and cautiously stepped closer to the edge. Fogg reluctantly followed. They crouched and looked down into the crater, where the massive landslide continued to unfold. "There!" shouted Cromarty, pointing to the far side of the slide, near the bottom of the crater. A loose tyre shot out of a cloud of dust and debris, bouncing away on a diverging trajectory. The rest of the rocket-bike and its rider were presumably still somewhere inside that turbulent surge of regolith.

"We have to go down for him!" said Cromarty.

Fogg looked up at the sky. The flame of the Steady Axe didn't necessarily appear any closer than the last time he checked, but he knew it was. "There's no time," Fogg said flatly. "We have to keep moving."

"But..." Cromarty started to protest but stopped in disbelief as Fogg walked back to his rocket-bike. He started the engine and looked over at Cromarty impatiently.

"You mean you're just going to leave him here?"

"He's gone," said Fogg, and he gunned the engine and angled away from the mountain and the crater. After a moment, Cromarty realised he had no choice but to follow.

***

They rode back in silence. Cromarty obviously resented Fogg's decision. Fogg resisted the urge to point out it was Cromarty's own advice that had forced the issue. If the *Giant's Tooth* had been moving into orbit, they could have spared the time to recover the robot, assuming anything was left of him. But because of his flyby suggestion, they only had one chance to rendezvous with the asteroid before it continued on towards Jupiter, with or without them.

Of course Fogg wasn't happy about losing the robot. He would have to compensate Marchand no small amount, and he would have to take over piloting duties himself, which was a chore he did not relish. Perhaps when they reached the outpost at Ganymede, the crew there could provide him with another navigation robot. Preferably one that wasn't quite so excitable.

They retraced their tracks back to the rim of Occator Crater overlooking the mining camp. There they turned off the massive engines and used the smaller manoeuvring jets to carefully negotiate the switchbacks of the trail down to the crater floor. The open garage door of the base awaited their return.

***

The doorway from the garage opened after the outer doors had closed, and Fogg and Cromarty stepped back into the large room that he had begun to think of as the parlour. Most of the women were still there, lounging around amid discarded orange peelings, thoroughly crashed from their sugar high.

"The gentlemen return," said Babette.

"Where is your little metal man?" asked Linlin.

"I'm afraid there were complications. We lost the robot's rocket-bike. I shall recompense you for its forfeiture. Will triple the retail value suffice?"

"For that old thing?" asked Millie. "It doesn't have any retail value. We built those bikes ourselves."

"Quiet, Millie," said Francesca, appearing behind them as if she had materialised there. "Mr Fogg, I will send you an invoice for the vehicle. I'm sorry about your valet. You are sure he can't be recovered?"

"I simply haven't the time," said Fogg. "If you manage to salvage his parts, by all means make the most of them."

"Oh, I will!" said Linlin, hopping across to the rack of spacesuits. "Who's coming with me?"

Francesca stepped closer to Fogg. "Did you get what you came for out there, Phileas Fogg?"

"I did," he answered.

"And now you're continuing further out into the darkness?"

"That's correct."

"Can I ask how far you're going?"

Fogg knew what she was fishing for. "Our itinerary leads us to Ganymede, Titan, Miranda, and finally Pluto." He saw her fears confirmed on her face. She was still processing this information when Fogg decided to play his hole card. "You knew him, didn't you?" He could tell she was surprised by his recognition. "You mined Phobos together before the UN gave it protected status, yes? So you came out further from the sun."

"That was a long time ago," said Francesca, looking wistful. "He was a sweet young man once upon a time. But we both went through a lot after that. He changed..." She looked him in the eyes now with a new intensity. "Mr Fogg, if you really do go to Pluto, watch your back. He cannot be trusted."

Fogg took her hand. "I will remember your advice, madam. I thank you for your assistance in my endeavour, but I'm afraid we really must be going now. It has been a pleasure doing business with you. Cromarty..." He turned, but his travelling companion wasn't there. After a short scan he spotted him across the room, caught in a tug of war between Millie and Babette.

"You can't leave yet," said Babette. "Come with me to my room. Just for a few minutes. I have a secret to tell you..."

Millie was in his other ear. "No, come with me. I have secrets too. Juicy ones!"

"I called dibs," said Babette. "You can have the other fellow."

Millie glanced over at Fogg disapprovingly. "The cold fish? No thanks." Fogg was slightly offended that she hadn't even bothered to lower her voice. "Just send this one over to me when you're done with him."

Cromarty was almost dizzy from the attention. Fogg realised he was going to have to step in or else lose both of his companions. He walked over and put one hand on Cromarty's shoulder. "I'm sorry, ladies, but Sir Francis needs to be going now. Our ride is almost here."

"Now wait just a moment, Fogg. Perhaps we could slow the *Giant's Tooth* down a bit. I mean, in the interest of finding Pass-Par-2, of course," said Cromarty.

Linlin chimed in, now suited up with a spade in one hand and an industrial laser cutter in the other. "Good luck beating me to him. That robot is mine!"

Fogg gripped Cromarty's shoulder a little tighter. "We can't control the engine from here without Pass-Par-2. I really am sorry, old chap, but we have to leave now. Of course, if you'd prefer to stay behind..."

Cromarty came to his senses. "No, you're right, of course." He turned to his two admirers. "My apologies, ladies. If you do find the robot, please treat him well."

"Look!" came an excited shout from Linlin. She was looking out a window. Fogg rushed to her and peered over her shoulder. A cloud of dust was rising skyward on the trail into the crater. Something was approaching.

It took a few minutes for everyone to slip into their

spacesuits and get through the airlock, but as they climbed onto the apron of the landing pad, the vehicle was still a hundred yards away. By now, though, it was close enough to see exactly what it was. It was a rocket-bike. Or more accurately, a rocket unicycle. It rode into camp with an empty front axle raised upward, as if a rambunctious child were showing off a wheelie for his friends. The child in this case was a robot with a bent antenna. Pass-Par-2 stood in the seat, pulling back on the handles to keep the front end off the ground. He looked like Caesar on his chariot.

As he pulled up to the landing pad, he was engulfed by a crowd of excited female miners. Cromarty slapped Fogg on the back, beaming with happiness. Fogg wished he could check his pocket watch, but it was unreachable inside his spacesuit.

At last the robot worked his way through the throng of women and joined them on the landing pad. Cromarty threw propriety to the wind and gave the robot a hug. "Pass-Par-2, you amazing devil! I can't tell you how thrilled I am to see you safe and sound!"

"I regret I was unable to contact you, sir, as my transmitter was badly damaged." He pointed to the bent antenna atop his head.

Fogg stepped forward. "Yes, well, it is fortunate you found your way back here in time. I would have had a terrible time piloting the ship on my own. Hurry aboard now."

The trio boarded the *Montgolfier*, and just a few minutes later they were ready for lift-off. Most of the women had returned inside by then, but Fogg spotted Linlin on the apron below. She appeared to have tears in her eyes as Babette put her arm around her and led her back to the airlock. Once the launchpad was clear, they rocketed into the blackness above, the *Giant's Tooth* swooping in to meet them.

CHAPTER TEN

RESCUE ON EUROPA

In the virtual parlour of London's Reform Club, Monsieur Marchand and Lord Albemarle were nearing the denouement of a game of checkers while Stuart, in the form of his much taller avatar, played a hand of whist with three other members. It was a peaceful afternoon until Flanagan's avatar suddenly materialised in the room. He was in another one of his tizzies.

"Stuart! My contact at Mauna Kea tracked a plume leaving Ceres. It was Fogg for sure, and he's halfway to Jupiter by now!"

Stuart tossed a low card on the table, refusing to give Flanagan the satisfaction of the reaction he was looking for. "Relax. My team ran the numbers. They say best-case scenario, the trip is going to take 99 days. That's assuming the King of Pluto doesn't zap him to atoms as soon as he's in range, which is no safe assumption."

"You'd better hope so," replied Flanagan. "We won't even be able to track him after Jupiter."

Marchand pushed a black checker forward, then turned to Flanagan. "Why bother tracking him? Give the man his 80 days.

It's been... what, ? Maybe eleven? Let the wager play out. We'll see if the thing is feasible or not. That was the whole point."

Albemarle chimed in excitedly. "And if the thing is feasible, the first to do it ought to be an Englishman!" The old man was having a good day today. Marchand noticed he'd had a lot of good days since the wager began. He was more alive than he'd been in years.

Flanagan was showing new life too. The fear of losing ten billion pounds could do that to a man. "I should never have agreed to this madness. Phileas Fogg will be my ruination." He whipped off his goggles in the real world and thus vanished from the virtual one.

***

Roughly 400 million miles away, the Steady Axe had just completed its midpoint flip to start its deceleration burn for Jupiter. After the *Montgolfier* returned to its roost on the asteroid, Cromarty had remained on board his ship while Fogg and Pass-Par-2 returned to the *Gold Filling*. After a couple of days with just the robot, Fogg was relieved when Cromarty asked if he could join them for a while that evening. He claimed to have something Pass-Par-2 would find useful. Fogg urged him to join him for dinner, then ordered Pass-Par-2 to cook something special.

He cycled through the airlock at precisely 6.00 pm, just as Pass-Par-2 was setting the tiny dining table. Cromarty smiled at the sight of the robot. "Pass-Par-2, good news! After rummaging through my machine shop for two solid days, I finally found a spare transmitter under the sink in the washroom of all places." He held out a small antenna, not exactly like the one he had lost, but it would do the job. "Let me install it for you."

"Oh, so very kind of you, sir," said Pass-Par-2, bowing slightly to give Cromarty access to the top of his head. The gentleman began unscrewing the broken antenna stub.

"I suppose dinner will have to wait a few minutes then," said Fogg.

"It's cooling, Master. Would you like Sir Francis to delay this repair?"

"Nonsense," said Cromarty. "It will only take a few minutes, then your valet will be factory fresh again."

"Very well," replied Fogg. "Thank you yet again for your invaluable assistance."

Having removed the broken antenna, Cromarty pulled a brass connector up through the hole in Pass-Par-2's chrome cranium. "It is I who should be thanking you. My first wife left me back on Earth a very long time ago. The second wife... well, I left her on the Moon, which is precisely where she belongs. The woman was a bona fide lunatic. I split with the third on Mars a few years back. Let's call that one mutual. If not for you, Fogg, I might have ended up with a fourth ex on Ceres."

"Frankly, I don't think any of those young ladies had matrimonial intentions," said Fogg.

Cromarty chuckled as he locked the new antenna into the coupling. "They never seem to, until suddenly it's too late. In any case, thank you for rescuing me from the Sirens of Ceres."

"Don't mention it," said Fogg.

"Perhaps I'm just weak willed," said Cromarty. "You seem to have avoided romantic entanglements."

"Yes, well, one must remain focused," said Fogg. Cromarty glanced his way as he screwed the new antenna into place. He was clearly expecting to hear more about Fogg's philosophy on love and matrimony. Fogg thought for a moment, then started speaking before he was entirely sure where he was going with it. "In my experience, women are typically—"

"Master!" Pass-Par-2 cut in, his digital eyes growing wide. For once, Fogg was grateful for the interruption. "Pardon me, but the new antenna has restored my direct connection with the *Gold Filling*'s computer, and I've just discovered an urgent SOS message!"

"Let's hear it," said Fogg.

Pass-Par-2 directed the audio to the ship's speakers, and the room was filled with a female voice speaking with a patrician Indian accent. The voice felt close, like an intimate whisper in the ear, but the woman was obviously overcome with grief.

"I am sorry to report that I am the lone survivor of the Makara Expedition beneath the ice of Europa. My entire team was killed two hours ago when the ice shifted and ruptured the tunnel to the surface, venting our air. I alone was fortunate to be in a dive suit at the time. I was unable to save any of the others. To their families, I am so sorry. Please know that I tried. But even had I managed to save anyone, they would now be trapped here just as I am. The tunnel to the surface was ripped away completely. The base is trapped beneath more than a hundred metres of ice. I have eighteen hours of oxygen left in tanks, but I know that isn't enough time for anyone to reach me from Ganymede. My fate will be no different from my colleagues, except that I have been granted the opportunity to say goodbye. To my family and friends, please know that I love you all so very much. I know my colleagues would have said the same to their loved ones. Know that they are at peace now. I will follow them soon." The woman took a deep breath, pulling herself together, keeping her emotions at bay long enough to finish her message. "We were honoured to be the first humans to swim in these waters. Please don't let us be the last." There was a long silence, then, "Goodbye." The message ended.

Cromarty immediately turned to Fogg. "Eighteen hours. Can we make it?"

Fogg had already been making mental calculations. "No. We're on course for Ganymede, which is currently on the far side of Jupiter. Europa is on the near side. It's not that we can't get there in time, it's that we will be going too fast to stop as we pass it."

"Too fast for the *Giant's Tooth* certainly, and perhaps too fast for your ship. But what about mine?" He turned to the robot. "Pass-Par-2, is it possible?"

"The *Montgolfier* could reach Europa in..." he paused just a moment as the final calculation was tabulated. "...seventeen point five hours."

"Just in time!" said Cromarty.

"However," continued Pass-Par-2, his tone turning sad, "I am sorry to report that this message was sent nearly two hours ago."

They fell silent. Both men looked down at their feet. *That poor woman is going to die and there's nothing we can do about it*, thought Fogg. But Cromarty apparently reached a different conclusion.

"I must go anyway," he said. "Eighteen hours might have only been an estimate. If you believe your wager is more urgent than that woman's life, then we will part ways here."

Fogg felt shamed for not having beaten Cromarty to this decision. "Of course I'll go with you," he said, then he turned to the robot. "Pass-Par-2, you stay here and take the asteroid into Ganymede orbit. We'll rendezvous there."

"Sir," said Pass-Par-2, "the *Giant's Tooth* will stay on course for Ganymede orbit without me. And only I am equipped to dive beneath the ice of Europa."

"He's right," said Cromarty. "If we have to swim, our pressure suits will sink us."

Fogg saw no flaw in their logic. "Very well. We'll all go."

Cromarty's face brightened. "You surprise me, Mr Fogg. You are a man of heart after all."

Fogg glanced at his pocket watch. "Sometimes. When I have the time."

***

Hours later as the *Giant's Tooth* approached the glowing disk the Galilean moon, the *Montgolfier* blasted off from the asteroid's surface. This time they were able to keep the Steady Axe firing since they were flying away from the asteroid's top. Both the ship and the asteroid were decelerating, but at different rates. The Steady Axe was a much more powerful engine, but the *Montgolfier* was unburdened by the mass of the *Giant's Tooth.* The ship exceeded five gs of force in its burn to the ice-covered moon.

It took nearly an hour of hard deceleration, but eventually their motion relative to Europa's surface slowed to a crawl. Cromarty guided them to the area where the radio signal had originated. They flew over the night surface of the moon, although the cracked ice below was alight with Jupitershine from the giant planet that filled the sky. The scene was breathtaking.

At last Cromarty pointed out the forward window where an artificial shape stood out on the otherwise natural surface. "That must be their ship. The radio signal came from there." He throttled the engine and began descending toward it.

The ship sat on the dark ice, no light from its windows. Clearly the woman's signal had been relayed through the ship from below the ice, but no one had remained on the surface. The vacant vessel was parked next to a metal ring embedded in the ice. It had obviously been the entrance of the tunnel to their base, but now it was filled by a frozen geyser.

"We aren't getting in that way," said Fogg.

"Look for stress points in the ice," said Cromarty.

"Master, look!" shouted Pass-Par-2, pointing to starboard. In the distance, a geyser of liquid water had erupted violently into the black sky.

"A breach!" said Fogg. "Hurry, before it freezes over!"

Cromarty took the controls and pushed the *Montgolfier* forward. In a matter of seconds, they were hovering within ten feet of the plume. They could see drops of water freezing into ice crystals and falling back to the surface. A few flakes accumulated on their window.

Without saying a word, Pass-Par-2 grabbed an O_2 tank and strapped it across his back. He removed his hat and hung it next to the door as he stepped into the airlock. Fogg and Cromarty only noticed what he was up to when they heard the door sliding shut.

"Pass-Par-2, do you think it's wise to...?"

But it was too late. The outer door was already opening. The robot offered them a quick salute through the window, then dove headfirst alongside the geyser.

Cromarty backed the ship up to get a better view. They watched the robot recede rapidly, posed like an Acapulco cliff diver. His arc brought him closer to the torrent of rising water until, mere feet from impacting the surface, he plunged into the base of the gushing geyser. And just like that he was gone.

***

Pass-Par-2 swam as hard as he could against the raging current that wanted to push him back to the surface. He was in a narrow ice chimney, but it broadened as he swam deeper, and the force of the current gradually diminished. At last he emerged from the chimney into the open ocean. He took a moment to orient himself. The underside of the moon's icy surface formed a thick ceiling overhead, although even at this depth some of Jupiter's diffused glow penetrated through. Beneath him, a bottomless ocean fell away into endless blackness. Pass-Par-2 determined the approximate direction of the Makara base, then engaged Swim Mode. His legs began to rotate at rapid speed, propelling him forward through the cold waters at a surprisingly swift pace.

It didn't take long to locate a shaft of light shining down into the darkness. As he got closer, he saw it was a floodlight attached to the underside of a cylindrical metal structure that hung from the ice ceiling above. The only hatch he could find was a large sliding door on the bottom. He found a control box, but pressing the illuminated red button produced no results. Then he noticed a large metal crank on the side of the box. He gave it a turn. It resisted at first, but with considerable effort he was able to rotate it clockwise. The outer hatch didn't seem to be moving at all, but Pass-Par-2 assumed this was a pressurised entrance, meaning there was probably an inner door that needed to close before the outer door could open. He suspected the crank was closing that inner door. Eventually it stopped turning, and the red button changed to green. He tried the button again, and the bottom hatch began to slide open.

Instantly, water rushed into the opening, but it only took a moment to fill the empty cavity. The interior space had a diameter of about twenty feet, capped as he had suspected by an inner door. He found another control box inside and began the process of cycling the large airlock. *Or is this more accurately a waterlock?* wondered Pass-Par-2. *But then again, isn't a waterlock just a regular lock?* He would have time to consider the etymology later. The outer door closed beneath him, and the two halves of the inner door began to separate above his head. Instantly, the water began to boil all around him, despite still being quite cold. He knew this meant the room must still be exposed to vacuum. He needed to find the woman quickly.

He climbed out of the churning water into a dark room, lit only by a few flashing control panels. At once he spotted a large white tarp spread across the floor. There were shapes underneath it. Bodies, he realised. The survivor must have lined up the less fortunate here, presumably so that they could be recovered later. He didn't dare disturb them by looking beneath.

The rest of the place looked like a hurricane had hit. It must have actually felt like a hurricane when the air rushed out. He looked up and saw a hatch in the top of the structure, which had obviously been attached to the tunnel to the surface, but there was no sign of it now. The crinkled metal hatch opened directly to a wall of solid ice.

Pass-Par-2 peeked into an alcove in the back of the control room. There he saw a figure in a dive suit passed out across the controls of a communications station. He rushed to her side and saw red alert sensors flashing all over the suit. Her faceplate was completely fogged over.

"Mademoiselle! Can you hear me?"

There was no response. He quickly unscrewed her exhausted oxygen tank and replaced it with the one from his back. He opened a valve and heard a gush of air. Some of the alert lights changed from red to green. Still, the woman did not stir.

He pushed a button on the comm station, opening a channel to the *Montgolfier*. "Master, do you read me?"

"Thank heavens," came the response over the radio. It was Cromarty. "Are you in the base, Pass-Par-2?"

"I am. I found the woman. She is alive but unresponsive. I have given her a fresh oxygen supply. I will attempt to swim her back to the geyser now."

"We copy, Pass-Par-2," came Fogg's voice. "Please hurry. The ice is quickly freezing over."

Sensing no time to waste, Pass-Par-2 lifted the woman into a fireman's carry and rushed to the pool, where the water still bubbled furiously. He plunged in without hesitation.

***

In the hovering *Montgolfier*, Cromarty and Fogg watched the rapidly diminishing geyser.

"Come on, Pass-Par-2! Hurry!" Cromarty urged.

The geyser dwindled to nothing more than a mist. Then even that was gone. Below them, the last flakes of fresh ice fell gently to the surface.

"The breach is sealed," said Fogg. "He can't get back."

Cromarty took action at once. "We shall see about that."

He flew the *Montgolfier* lower until its main thrusters hovered just above the surface. Then he ignited the engine at full throttle, bathing the ice in a firestorm. The ship launched skyward just as the ice gave way and the geyser was reborn.

He banked the ship around in a circle and returned to the

watery eruption. A dark shape rose through the middle of the geyser, then broke free. Both men saw the object arcing back toward the icy surface. It was the robot, and he wasn't alone. He landed on his feet on a frozen plain, cradling the woman's limp body in his arms.

"It's him! He did it!" shouted Cromarty with a gleeful laugh.

Fogg wasn't ready to celebrate just yet. "Quickly, land the ship. We must get them on board. The woman is not well."

CHAPTER ELEVEN

THE KING OF PLANETS

A few short minutes later, Pass-Par-2 and the woman were on board. They carefully laid the unconscious woman on one of the acceleration couches in the rear of the cabin. The name on her dive suit said 'Aouda.' Fogg released the latches on her helmet and removed it. A mane of long black hair spilled out. Cromarty cleared it from her face, revealing blue lips and wan skin. It was surely not her normal complexion. But even in this state, Fogg couldn't help thinking she was beautiful. Pass-Par-2 applied an oxygen mask to her face while Cromarty checked her vitals as displayed on the sleeve of her high-tech suit.

"Can you hear me, miss? You're safe now," Fogg said softly, but she did not stir.

"Low blood pressure. Irregular heartbeat. She's in the early stages of hypoxia," said Cromarty, his voice dire.

"She needs a doctor," said Fogg. "Ganymede is her only hope."

Cromarty looked to the robot. "Pass-Par-2, would you mind taking the controls? And please put us on the fastest route possible to Ganymede Station."

"Aye, sir," he replied dutifully, then took his position at the controls.

Fogg felt the ship accelerating, but he kept his eyes on Aouda.

Cromarty remarked, "She certainly is a handsome woman."

"And brave," said Fogg. "We must save her. At all costs."

She seemed stable, but both men remained at her side as the ship departed Europa. Fogg secured her in the couch while Cromarty removed the bulkier parts of her dive suit. Eventually he decided the only thing to do was to cut it off, which was a shame since it was clearly state-of-the-art equipment, but they needed to warm her skin directly. Fogg covered her with a blanket as Cromarty cut away the inner layer of spandex. He removed the suit's sensors and hooked her up to the ship's medical station. As the minutes passed, Fogg was relieved to see a deeper brown shade returning to her skin.

He rested his eyes for a few minutes, overcome with a wave of exhaustion, but he remained vigilant, listening to the reassuring beeps of the pulse monitor. He decided a cup of tea would calm his nerves. He opened his eyes, intending to ask Sir Francis what varieties he had aboard, but he noticed the woman's skin had taken on a reddish hue. Upon closer scrutiny, it wasn't her skin that had reddened but the light in the room. He turned and was stunned to see the giant orb of Jupiter filling the entire forward view. "We're heading straight for Jupiter," he said to Pass-Par-2.

"Yes, Master," the robot replied. "Our fastest route to Ganymede is through the upper atmosphere. The gravity and high-speed winds will give us a boost."

"Really?" He turned to Cromarty. "Is it safe?"

The geologist was grinning. "Of course. The *Montgolfier* is built for atmospheric flight. How exciting! An up-close look at the King of Planets!"

Although it filled their field of view already, it took more than an hour before they finally hit the atmosphere. The ship was buffeted wildly for several minutes, and Fogg felt compelled to hold Aouda's shoulders to keep her from being thrown from the couch, but at last the *Montgolfier* slipped into the airstream and began zipping through the high clouds at remarkable speed.

Once things had smoothed out, Fogg left Aouda's side and went to the panoramic windows where Cromarty was already in awe. Outside, the skies were red and yellow and orange and pink and purple and white and every shade in between. No one could ever call Montana 'Big Sky Country' after they'd seen Jupiter. It was nothing *but* sky in every direction.

"Tremendous!" said Cromarty. "It's a shame the Great Red Spot finally blew itself out before mankind could witness it in person."

"Great Red Spot?" asked Pass-Par-2 from the controls.

"It was a storm larger than the Earth itself," explained the geologist. "It raged for centuries. But nothing lasts forever. It dwindled for a few decades, then finally disappeared in the early sixties."

"There's a storm just ahead of us now, Sir Francis. Look, lightning!"

The robot was correct. They were headed directly towards dark swirling clouds alive with electricity. There was no way to determine the scale of it with the naked eye, but it looked enormous. It extended to either side of them as far as the eye could see, and it was growing closer by the second.

"Oh my," said Cromarty. "We'd best steer clear of that."

"The winds are pushing us towards it, sir," said Pass-Par-2, "but I will attempt to climb over it."

He fired the thrusters to gain altitude, and the approaching clouds began to drop beneath their view. A few minutes later, they were zipping along through the clear skies above the tempest. They all watched the light show beneath them as the clouds continued to flash with bolts of lightning that likely stretched for hundreds of miles.

"You say the Great Red Spot was larger than this?" asked Pass-Par-2.

"Oh, yes," said Cromarty, "by many orders of magnitude."

At last the tempest slipped away behind them. They appeared to be free and clear, but the storm fired one last shot. A long tendril of lightning reached out across the space between them and engulfed the *Montgolfier*.

The lights in the control room flashed off and on, and alerts began sounding from every computer in the cabin. Then, with horror, Fogg felt the deck dropping away from his feet. They were falling.

"That struck the power core," shouted Cromarty over the cacophony of alarms. "The engines are offline. The nuclear fuel cell is melting down. I'll have to eject it."

"How can we fly without the fuel cell?" asked Fogg.

"The batteries are fully charged. They'll get us to Ganymede." Cromarty had taken Pass-Par-2's spot at the controls and was repeatedly jabbing a button on the console. "Damn! The ejection system is offline too. If we don't ditch the core, the whole ship will explode."

Pass-Par-2 raced over to the airlock, once again tossing his hat aside. "You have the controls, captain." Before either man could react, the airlock cycled and the robot had exited the ship.

Outside in the howling winds, Pass-Par-2 climbed the framework of the ship to the underside of the nuclear reactor mounted overhead. He reached up and used the cooling pipes that formed a lattice around the spherical housing to hoist himself up the side. For a few terrifying moments he had to let his feet dangle free over the bottomless abyss, but he kept his grip and continued pulling his way up. At last he passed the midpoint of the sphere and the climb became much easier as he scrambled on all fours between the broad red stripes.

Where the stripes converged at the top of the sphere, he found a charred access panel that was still smoking from the lightning strike. He opened it and saw the toaster-sized nuclear power cell. Its indicator lights pulsed angrily. "Sirs," Pass-Par-2 said via radio, "I have located the nuclear power cell. Removing it now."

Carefully, he reached into the access hatch and disconnected three cables from the cell, then he gingerly lifted it free from the compartment.

Inside, the alarms suddenly silenced. The only sound that remained was the rushing wind outside. Cromarty flipped a few switches, then pressed a large red button, and the batteries kicked in. A moment later, Fogg was almost jolted off his feet as the engines reignited.

"Excellent work, Pass-Par-2!" shouted Cromarty. "Power is back online."

The ship's descent slowed as the thrusters fired, but still it continued to fall. It dropped into a very dark and turbulent ammonia cloud, and it would never have seen sunlight again if the engine had not finally overpowered gravity. It burst free from the depths and began its long climb back to the upper stratosphere.

Topside, Pass-Par-2 was pleased by his success, but he was still holding a failing nuclear fuel cell in his hands. It seemed to throb in his grip, ready to go at any moment. He did the only logical thing. He tossed it overboard.

Cromarty's voice came to him a moment later. "Now, on the side of the nuclear core you'll see an emergency shutoff button."

Pass-Par-2 felt very foolish all of a sudden. "Oh my. I'm afraid I already tossed it overboard."

There was a pause before Cromarty spoke again. "I see. Fair call. You can come back inside now in that case."

From the dark clouds deep beneath them, a giant mushroom cloud erupted upwards, buffeting the ship violently as it continued its rapid ascent. As he was thrown off his feet, Pass-Par-2 realised it must have been the jettisoned core exploding. He landed with a *clang* on his metal posterior and skidded down the precipitous slope towards an infinite drop. As he was dumped over the edge, he grabbed a cooling pipe and slid beneath the underside of the sphere to the main cabin. He found himself dangling directly in front of the forward triangular window. He was flooded with embarrassment as Fogg and Cromarty observed him from the other side of the glass.

"Pass-Par-2, quit fooling around out there and get back inside," said Fogg.

***

While Pass-Par-2 was working his way to the airlock, Aouda lay unattended in the rear of the cabin. Her eyelids began to flutter. It took a few moments for her to focus on what she was seeing, but she still couldn't make sense of it. It was the most beautiful sunset in the universe. She leaned forward in the acceleration couch, straining for a better view. What was this place?

Behind her, she heard the sound of a hissing airlock. She turned to see two men greeting a robot who had just entered. As if things weren't odd enough, the robot grabbed a derby and put it on his head over his antenna. She felt dizzy and couldn't help but give out a little gasp. Or maybe it wasn't so little, because it was loud enough to get the attention of all three of the strangers. They spun around to face her, and all seemed as startled as she was. No one spoke for a long moment. Then the robot, as if realising he was in the presence of a lady, quickly removed the hat again.

"I have died," Aouda concluded, "but either Heaven is redder than I expected or Hell is much colder."

The younger man took a tentative step towards her. "No, miss, you have not died, although it came very near to being so."

"You saved me?" she asked.

The older gentleman spoke this time. "Actually, this titanium fellow here was your saviour. Two times over, in fact." The robot smiled. Or at least the squiggles sort of looked like a smile.

Her head was spinning. "I... I am most indebted to you."

"No debt is owed, mademoiselle," said the robot. *Was that a French accent or have I suffered brain damage?*

No matter how bizarre the situation, she must remember her manners. "Aouda," she said. "Please, call me Aouda."

"Of course," said the robot. "I am Pass-Par-2. This gentleman is Sir Francis Cromarty. You are aboard his ship, the *Montgolfier*." Cromarty gave a small bow. "And allow me to introduce my master—"

Fogg interrupted him. "Phileas Fogg is my name. Please, don't try to stand. You need medical attention. We are en route to Ganymede Station now."

She leaned back into the couch, relieved to finally be making a bit of sense of her situation. "What a miracle," she sighed, her eyelids growing heavy, "to encounter such fine gentlemen so very far from home."

She closed her eyes and allowed sleep to reclaim her.

Fogg stepped over to his valet. "Pass-Par-2, I just wanted to say..." He paused, as if reevaluating the robot. "Excellent work today." And then he offered his hand.

"Thank you, Master," replied the robot, shaking his hand firmly. As Fogg walked away, Pass-Par-2 turned back to the ship's controls. He was positively beaming.

The *Montgolfier* continued climbing higher and higher until it left the atmosphere behind as it swept around to the night side of the giant planet. Cromarty lowered the cabin lighting to match the ambiance. They could see the light of auroras dancing in the darkness in the cold Jupiter night.

Their course took them past Io, the innermost of the Galilean moons. Although it was shrouded in Jupiter's shadow, they could see red veins of molten lava spewing from three different volcanoes. Fogg counted himself fortunate that Albemarle hadn't requested a rock from there. Ahead, a friendlier moon awaited.

CHAPTER TWELVE

RESPITE ON GANYMEDE

It was the fourteenth day of the wager as the *Montgolfier* approached the streaked and spotted disk of Ganymede. It had been looming ahead of them for hours already, but still it continued to grow larger and larger. Determining scale in outer space was a skill Fogg was sure he would never master. Cromarty reminded him that Ganymede was the largest moon in the solar system—bigger in fact than the planet Mercury. As they finally neared the surface, Pass-Par-2 located the *Giant's Tooth* and confirmed it was waiting for them in a stable orbit. They discussed stopping to collect the *Gold Filling* but decided to go directly to the science station on the surface, even though Aouda seemed to be stronger by the hour and was showing no long-term effects of her brush with death.

The ship flew above a rocky mesa that poked through the moon's grooved and icy crust. Ahead, the welcoming lights of a landing pad awaited. As they grew closer, Fogg examined the base, but there was very little to see on the surface. Most of the outpost was in a network of tunnels underground. But Fogg did notice a very large telescope, and he recognised where it was focused on the celestial sphere. A suspicion crept into his mind, and he made note to check on it later.

With guidance from Ganymede traffic control, Cromarty set the *Montgolfier* down gently in the dead centre of the large landing pad. A pressurised tube was extended to the ship and sealed tight against the outer hatch. Thankfully they could leave their pressure suits behind.

They had radioed the station for medical assistance, so as soon as the hatch opened a pair of medics rushed to Aouda's side. They insisted on putting her on a gurney, even though it was hard to imagine anyone being too ill to carry their own weight in this low gravity. It was slightly less than Earth's Moon but heavier than Ceres at least. The medics wheeled Aouda down the tube into the station, and her trio of travelling companions followed.

"This is all unnecessary," she protested. "I am totally fine."

"Let the doctors make that assessment," said Fogg.

Once inside the main building, they stopped at a pair of lift doors. One slid open, and the medics wheeled Aouda in. There wasn't enough room for the rest of the party, so Cromarty stuck his head through the door to reassure her.

"We will check on you in a bit, I promise."

"Thank you all so much for your kindness," she said as the lift door slid shut.

Fogg turned to Pass-Par-2. "You need to find a way up to the *Giant's Tooth* and fly the *Gold Filling* back here."

"As you wish, Master," said the robot. He had a plan for that already in mind. He turned and dashed off through the docking tube just as the other lift's door opened.

"Frankie!"

It was a shrill female voice, American by accent. Fogg turned and saw a tall, thin blonde woman in her late thirties stepping out of the second lift.

"Sandra!" said Cromarty.

"Frankie?" echoed Fogg.

He waited awkwardly while Cromarty gave the woman an enthusiastic, lingering hug. At last they separated, and Cromarty spun her around to make introductions.

"Sandra, I'd like you to meet Phileas Fogg of the Reform Club in London."

She shook his hand as Fogg put the pieces together. "Ah, your former student. I hear you are doing exciting work here."

"It will be all the more exciting now that Frankie has joined us. You're here just in time too. We had a major breakthrough this week."

"In your research?" asked Cromarty.

"No, I mean a literal breakthrough." She smiled, her eyes sparkling with excitement. "Come see."

***

They emerged from the lift into a rough rocky tunnel. Plastic flooring ran down the middle of the passageway, but this seemed to be the only improvement that had been made since the tunnel had been carved out of the rock. She led them along until they came to another vertical shaft. This time there was no lift—just a rope. She assured them climbing down would be easy in the light gravity, and she was right. They descended five levels this way. It was obvious that construction of this part of the base was far from complete. She explained it wasn't even needed yet. They were thinking ahead for future expansion. Mostly, though, they were exploring. The majority of these caves were natural. They had widened them a bit in places and connected them into an ant farm-like network, but most of the excavation had been done by long-gone water millions of years ago.

At the end of the last corridor they came to a tunnel that was capped with a makeshift airlock. It turned out they would be needing pressure suits after all. Fortunately there was a rack full of them. Fogg picked one that seemed the right size and suited up. It was far bulkier than his own shape-memory suit, with an old-fashioned hard outer shell that encumbered his movement considerably. Cromarty's suit seemed entirely too large for him, and it was decorated with bright pink piping in lieu of his usual array of medals, but he endured the indignity with true British phlegm. Once their helmets were in place, Sandra tested the radio.

"We knew there was a cave system here," her crackly voice said in Fogg's helmet, "but we had no idea how extensive it was until our drill broke through into... well, this."

The airlock opened into a dark chamber of unimaginable scale. They were on a high precipice looking down into a deep, long cavern. Several teams of workers were erecting floodlights on other promontories in the distance. It was like an indoor Grand Canyon.

"My God!" said Cromarty. "It's huge."

"You could fit Manhattan in here," Sandra replied coolly. "Imagine if we can fill this space with breathable air."

Cromarty looked down. He could barely make out a broad basin below. "We could bring in topsoil from Earth, hang sunlamps overhead for farming."

"Lakes and reservoirs dotting the bottom, stocked with fish," Sandra added.

"Parks, trees." Cromarty was envisioning it all. "Perhaps a football stadium."

Sandra continued the game. "Office buildings, freeways, mini-malls."

Cromarty laughed. "Listen to us. We're ruining it already.

Instead of looking down, Fogg was focused on the walls of the cavern. They were glittering in the darkness.

"The walls... sparkle," he said.

Sandra turned her torch to the wall, revealing a crust of countless crystals.

"Ah," said Cromarty. "The famous geodes of Ganymede."

"That's how we know this was formed by water long ago,"

said Sandra. "There's a vast ocean hiding somewhere deep inside this moon. We just haven't found it yet."

The chamber was lined with millions of the rounded rocks. Only ones that had been cleaved open showed their inner crystals. Fogg reached across a railing and gripped one of the more extravagant examples. It was loose. He turned to Sandra, about to make an appeal, but she spoke first.

"Go ahead. Take it. Nobody's gonna miss it."

He bagged it. His rock collection was halfway complete.

Pass-Par-2 passed through an airlock in the docking tube and stepped out onto the tarmac of the landing pad. There was a large open hangar across from where the *Montgolfier* sat. He entered, triggering automatic overhead lights. He spotted a rack of single-rider broomstick rockets against the back wall. He approached, wondering whose permission he needed to borrow one. Then he saw a sign mounted on the wall above it: 'NEED A BROOMSTICK? TAKE A BROOMSTICK! LIVE LARGE, THEN RECHARGE!'

That seemed like permission enough. He grabbed one of the fully charged units. It consisted of a six-foot metal handle with grips on the front and a small battery-powered ion thruster on the bottom. To Pass-Par-2, who was wholly unfamiliar with tales of flying witches, it resembled a child's pogo stick more than a broom. He carried it out to the launchpad and attached the safety harness around his midsection. He activated the controls, then twisted the left grip. The engine sprang into life immediately, yanking him off his feet into the black and airless sky.

He panicked for only a moment before he managed to get his feet into the footrests on top of the rocket housing, then he tweaked the controls in the handle, sending him higher. In theory he could ride this thing all the way back to London if he had a century or so to spare. Fortunately he only needed to go as far as the *Giant's Tooth*. But first he had to find it.

He shot across the sky above a sea of rippled ice and craters.

***

Back inside the pressurised corridors and free of the bulky borrowed spacesuits, Sandra guided Fogg and Cromarty on a tour of Ganymede Station. She led them down a long narrow corridor with numerous rooms along the way. This was the oldest and most complete section of the base, with preformed walls and flooring and, fortunately, very high ceilings. Fogg kept accidentally launching himself from the floor with his footsteps. She led them around a corner to a much wider chamber.

"We have over six hundred personnel now, including five babies born here—the first natives of Ganymede. Things have really improved since First Landing. We're certainly eating better." She pointed to a caged-off cavern where dozens of plump chickens clucked and strutted. Fogg was surprised when one of the birds flapped its wings and took flight, soaring around the enclosure before coming to rest on a higher roost.

"These fat suckers don't know how lucky they are to be out of Earth's gravity," said Sandra.

"Lucky until their number comes up," said Cromarty with a smirk.

Next she led them into a large rec room, complete with something like a basketball court, but with dimensions for some new variety of sport designed for play in lower gravity. There was also a giant video screen for movie night and a centrifugal jogging track. But Fogg overlooked it all, zeroing in on a small folding table where four people sat playing cards. They paused their game as Sandra led them over.

"Everyone, I'd like you to meet our newest resident—the eminent geologist Sir Francis Cromarty," said Sandra, "and his travelling companion Phileas Fogg."

A dark-skinned man stood to shake their hands. He was tall and dignified, wearing a beret with some sort of command insignia on it. He spoke with a Kenyan accent. “Ah, the heroes of Europa. Welcome to Ganymede. I am Commander Seni.”

“A pleasure to meet you, Commander,” said Cromarty, “but the explorers are the real heroes here.”

“We are all explorers this far from the sun. We are very thankful for your bravery,” said the commander. “Let me introduce Tom Morris, chief engineer,” he said, and a red-headed American in his forties stood to shake their hands. “And this is Elena Petruzzi, architect of the new expansion.” An olive-skinned woman with a few streaks of grey in her otherwise jet-black hair stood and greeted them both.

Then Phileas Fogg turned to the last man at the table. “And you are Mr Fix.”

Indeed the last player wore the exact same face as Agent Aaron Fix of Hayn Crater, although with a bristly moustache hanging off it.

“Have you two met?” asked Sandra.

“No,” said Fogg, “but I met a man with his face on the Moon just two weeks ago. This couldn't possibly be the man himself, as there's no conceivable way he could have beaten me here. But I do understand how twins work.”

The doppelgänger stood and shook his hand firmly. “My brother Aaron mentioned you in his latest message, Mr Fogg. He felt pretty stupid when you were confirmed on Mars two days after your meeting. I'm Benjamin.”

“It's a pleasure to put another name to the face. Are you with the UN as well?”

“I am,” replied Benjamin, “but the exact nature of my job here is classified. What is it that you do, Fogg?”

“Mostly I play cards, but sadly I have gone two weeks without shuffling a deck. May I?”

“Of course,” said Commander Seni, scooting his chair over to make room. “Please join us.”

"You should watch out for Fix, though," said Tom Morris. "He's a cheat."

Fogg sat and gripped the deck in his hands. It felt good. "I assume everyone here is familiar with the traditional rules of whist?"

***

Pass-Par-2 clung to the broomstick rocket as it flew above the surface of Ganymede. The battery was beginning to run low when at last he spotted the *Giant's Tooth* rising over the horizon. He could see sunlight glittering off the *Gold Filling* at its crest. His current trajectory would intersect with the asteroid in a matter of minutes but moving far too fast to land. He would need to make an adjustment. After a quick calculation, he angled the rocket to port by 42 degrees. Now he was sure he would catch the asteroid and be able to set down gently with power left to spare, but it would take more than an hour. He decided to take the opportunity to enjoy the view of Jupiter's second-largest moon Callisto, shining as a brilliant crescent ahead.

***

The Ganymeders had gamely tried a few hands of whist, but it became clear they weren't going to master it quickly. Fogg figured it wouldn't be sporting to continue, so he agreed to Tom Morris's suggestion that they switch to Texas Hold 'Em poker. Cromarty and Sandra had used the opportunity to quietly excuse themselves. An hour later, the locals were beginning to suspect they'd been snookered. Fogg was cleaning house.

The pot presently stood at nearly $5000, which Fogg understood to be worth even more in the local economy. Tom had folded on the flop, then Elena tossed in her cards after the river card failed to complete her flush.

Seni bet aggressively, and Fix matched immediately, even

though Fogg was convinced the man had no help in the hole. Fogg saw Seni's bet and raised it with his entire stack. "All in," he said calmly.

Fix chuckled and tossed his cards immediately, but Seni looked at his hand longingly. Fogg knew he couldn't walk away. "Obviously I can't match your bet in cash, Fogg. What else can I offer? Supplies for your ship perhaps?"

"My ship is fully stocked, I'm afraid. But there is something I need. Would you happen to have a spare 160-gauge nuclear fuel cell?"

Seni laughed. "Surely you don't think the pot is enough to cover *that?*"

"Obviously not," said Fogg, "but if I win, perhaps you could sell me one at cost."

Seni considered this for a moment. "We only have two spares I'm afraid, although there are a half-dozen more on the way when the next supply ship gets here in December. But..." He paused and locked eyes with Benjamin Fix. "Those types of power cells are restricted. You need government approval for something like that. Do you have a permit?"

"No," Fogg answered. "I'm afraid I don't. But it isn't for me anyway."

Agent Fix leaned forward. "Then who is it for, Fogg?"

Fogg paused. He knew he could clear things up with a single word, but he didn't appreciate this new Fix interjecting himself in someone else's business. *Let the man suspect what he wants to suspect*, he thought. "A friend," was the only answer he offered.

Seni exhaled slowly, then he tossed his cards. Fogg could see it hurt him. "I'm sorry, but I have to throw away the best hand I've had all night. I can't wager with a thing like that. Fix here would throw me in the brig if I lost." He said it with a smile, but Fogg wasn't entirely sure he was joking.

"Pity," said Fogg, raking in his winnings. He wasn't even curious about Seni's cards. The hand was won; he had never seen the point of 'what-ifs.'

"That's it for me as well," said Tom. "I'm cutting my losses."

"Me too," said Elena. "Thanks for the whist lesson, Mr Fogg. And thanks especially for what you did on Europa. Aouda is a dear friend. We flew out here together. Two years packed in a tin can like sardines. She became like a sister to me."

Fogg said, "If not for a speedy ship and a remarkable robot, it would have been a much sadder day I'm afraid." Elena smiled, then she and Tom made their exit.

Seni collected his remaining funds and stood up from the table. "Will you be staying for the sunrise memorial service for the Makara Expedition, Mr Fogg? I'm sure Aouda would appreciate you being there."

Fogg checked his pocket watch. Local sunrise would be in about seven hours. That was fortuitous, considering a day on this moon lasted a full week and three hours. "As it so happens, Ganymede will not be aligned for my departure for another nine hours, so I would be honoured to attend."

"Wonderful," said the commander. "There are empty bunks all up and down the corridor out there. Make yourself at home if you'd like to get some rest. I'll see you in the chapel at sunrise. And good game." He shook Fogg's hand, then left him alone with the local brand of Fix.

The agent locked eyes with Fogg, but neither spoke until the moment the door closed behind Seni, then he got straight to business. "What are you really doing out here, Fogg?"

"I could ask you the same," he replied. "Why does a research station need a security agent? These scientists can't be much trouble."

"Scientists can cause more trouble than you think. But most of the time, my attention is turned elsewhere."

"Ah," said Fogg, "so you're running the UN's secret new telescope. Your brother showed me one of your photos. I spotted the telescope on our approach to the station, and I couldn't help noticing it was pointed towards Pluto."

"I take it you still intend to go there?"

"I must," said Fogg. "Otherwise your brother will fine me for filing a false flightplan."

The agent leaned forward. "Mr Fogg, are you a member of the Plutonian Freedom Brigade?"

"I don't even know what that is," said Fogg.

"Have you ever attended a meeting of the Extraplanetary Expatriate Society?"

"I am not now, nor have I ever been, affiliated with any political party."

"You really expect me to believe this whole trip is just about some wager between rich assholes?"

"There's no need for vulgarities, Agent Fix. You can believe whatever you like. But if I fail to win this wager, perhaps you can take comfort in knowing this particular arsehole will be very poor."

The agent smiled at him, then leaned back in his chair again. Fogg sensed the gambit was finished—Fix was ready to put his cards on the table.

"If you really are going to Pluto, there's only one way to do it that won't brand you as a traitor. Take me with you."

And there it was. Fogg arched his eyebrows. "Take you? To Pluto?"

"Deliver me to the King as an officer of the United Nations. You can collect your rock after I have him in custody."

"You're going to arrest him? Just like that? What's to stop him from launching that missile you spotted?"

"You think he won't launch it at you?" countered Fix.

Fogg finished collecting his winnings and stood up. "I'm not convinced he's the madman you make him out to be, Agent Fix. In fact, I fully expect the King to greet me like a proper gentleman. But that could never happen with a government agent in tow. I'll give him your regards though. Good evening, sir."

Fogg turned and left, but he could feel Fix's glare all the way to the door.

***

The *Gold Filling* set down gently on the opposite end of the landing pad from the *Montgolfier*. No one was present to hook up a pressurised walkway, so Pass-Par-2 cycled through the airlock into the vacuum of the moon's surface, carrying the spent broomstick rocket back to the rack in the hangar. He wasn't sure if he had lived large, but he would certainly recharge.

The rendezvous with the *Giant's Tooth* had been uneventful, as had the lander's flight to the surface, although the robot was feeling a little hurried since his master had messaged to remind him to bring his small valise with his toiletries. Unfortunately that would require hooking up a walkway. He couldn't carry the valise outside without repeating the mistake he'd made on Mars, and he knew his master would not appreciate a frozen tube of toothpaste. He spent ten minutes hooking up the walkway himself, then reentered the ship to fetch the small case.

The hallways of Ganymede Station were dark and quiet as he returned, but there was a moustachioed gentleman waiting for him. "Hello there," the man called out in a friendly voice. "That must be Fogg's ship. She's a beauty."

The ship was barely visible in the dark landing field outside, but Pass-Par-2 assumed the man must have watched it land. "Yes, that's the *Gold Filling*. It is a very fine ship indeed."

"And you must be his famous robot pal. He's told me all about you."

"Oh? He talked about me?"

"Sure. The true hero of Europa."

Pass-Par-2 would have blushed if he'd had the epidermis upgrade package. "Well, I simply did what my master wished he could do himself. Humans are rather... restricted by their respiratory requirements. No offence, sir."

"None taken, my friend. You can call me Benjamin. You're a Marchand Positroniqué prototype, right? Do you have the new Emergent Personality chip?"

"I do!" exclaimed Pass-Par-2.

"I can tell," said Agent Fix. "You, my friend, are the cutting edge. Fogg is lucky to have you along for the ride." The agent adopted a look of incredulity. "Are you really going all the way to Pluto?"

"Oui, that will be our last stop before we turn back for home."

"Ah, so you are going back to Earth? You aren't staying on Pluto? With the King?"

"Heavens, no," said Pass-Par-2. "We're on a tight schedule. We're only staying long enough to collect a rock. Oh, and to deliver the package."

Fix's eyes immediately narrowed. "Package?"

"Yes, quite a hefty package. From Houston. It is marked for the King of Pluto."

"Fascinating," said Fix. "Do you know what's in it?"

"No," Pass-Par-2 answered. "I am reluctant to ask too many questions. Master Fogg doesn't approve when I am overly inquisitive. It's not my place to pry."

"But aren't you curious? I mean, come on—it seems a bit suspicious, don't you think?"

"Suspicious? *Scandaleux!*" Pass-Par-2 successfully adopted a tone of indignation for the first time in his short life. "I assure you, good sir, Phileas Fogg is not the sort to be entangled in illicit wrongdoings. Whatever his business with the King of Pluto, I am certain it is entirely above board. Now, if you'll excuse me, Master has urgent need of his toiletries."

He held up the valise as if to make a point, but what that point might be was lost on both of them. Agent Benjamin Fix watched as the robot rushed off in a huff.

***

Fix took a roundabout route to his private quarters. He assumed Fogg and his robot were settled for the night. If he was going to take action, now was the time. He had already decided what that action needed to be. In his room, he began hastily packing survival essentials into a large duffel bag. He stopped just long enough to switch on his encrypted comm station, then he spoke into the camera as he continued packing.

"It's worse than we feared, brother. Fogg showed up right on schedule. I confirmed he's carrying a payload from Houston for the King. Probably a guidance system for the missile. And he even tried to swindle a nuclear fuel cell out of Seni, but he didn't agree to it. I guess he figures the King can never have too many nukes. We can't wait any longer. I'm going to hitch a ride on Fogg's asteroid. Once we reach Pluto I will eliminate the King. And if Fogg reveals himself to be a willing agent of the King, I will eliminate him too. Wish me luck. By the time this reaches you, I'll be on my way to Saturn." He hit the button and sent the message moonward without bothering to review it. There was still work to do, and time was running short.

He packed everything he could from his quarters, then he hit the supply room for a few more essentials. He grabbed a five-gallon jug and a water filtration system. He knew he would have no choice but to drink his own recycled urine for the next few weeks, but he almost dreaded the diet of MREs even more. He'd lived on them for two years on the flight out, and once he got a taste of the food at Ganymede, he'd hoped to never rip open another packet of dehydrated beef goulash.

The last item he needed was a pressure tent with a built-in air recycler. It was bulky, even when rolled up in a shoulder bag, but the low gravity meant he could carry as much gear as he needed as long as he could keep a grip on it all. To that end, he used a handful of bungee cords to bind it all together in one bundle. Then, with pressure suit on, he slung it over his shoulder and went outside to the hangar. He grabbed a fully charged broomstick rocket from the rack, then ventured out to the landing pad. He made sure the bundle was securely strapped to his back. It was nearly twice as large as he was, so he would have to be mindful of how that affected his centre of gravity. He put his feet in the straps and primed the rocket. It was too bad he wouldn't get a chance to say goodbye to anyone at Ganymede Station. He wasn't sure any of them would really miss him though. He ignited the thruster, pressed the button and launched into the sky just as the sun began to peek out from behind Jupiter.

CHAPTER THIRTEEN

JUPITER FAREWELLS

The next morning, a crowd began to gather at the small multi-denominational chapel in the aboveground section of the station. A window on the back wall showed the first rays of sun rising over a crescent Jupiter. Fogg met up with Cromarty and Sandra in the hallway outside, then they stepped in together while Pass-Par-2 waited respectfully by the door. They sat on a pew directly behind Aouda, who was dressed in black but looking healthier than ever. Elena Petruzzi sat beside her, holding her hand for support.

The crowd quieted as a robed chaplain stepped up to the pulpit. Soft organ music began to play as images of the lost Makara explorers were projected behind him. Cromarty leaned forward to place a hand on Aouda's shoulder and whisper something in her ear. Fogg wondered if he should do the same, but he had never been skilled at emotional support. Perhaps he would say something to her afterwards. It was too late now anyway, as the chaplain began the service.

Fogg wondered if any of the Makara explorers had even

been Christians, as the chaplain clearly was. Most of the team had come from India. As dedicated scientists, odds were low that they were devout members of any religion, although the very existence of this chapel suggested there were plenty of exceptions. As the chaplain began his speech, Fogg noticed he steered clear of any specific religious tenets, focusing on the sanctity of life and the value of knowledge.

"Their sacrifice teaches us not about death, but about life," said the grey-haired chaplain. "They didn't find what they were looking for under the ice, but just by going there they brought the first spark of life to a dark, dead sea. They lit a path, and now others may follow."

Commander Seni, who Fogg had not noticed sitting behind them, leaned forward and spoke softly into Sandra's ear. Fogg could barely make out his words. "I wonder where Fix is. It's not like him to miss this."

* * *

Agent Benjamin Fix's broomstick rocket finally reached the orbiting asteroid dubbed the *Giant's Tooth*. He saw the prototype Steady Axe engine protruding from one end, so he assumed Fogg's ship normally landed on the opposite, and from there it only took a matter of seconds to find the empty clamps for the ship's landing gear. He deactivated the rocket and landed gently in the microgravity. He looked around, studying the rocky terrain. The asteroid had more holes than a worm-ridden apple. No surprise there, since Fix knew Stuart's company had spent years mining anything of any value from it. He hopped to the tunnel closest to the landing zone.

He dropped twenty feet into the hole, landing as easily as if stepping off a kerb. The tunnel at the bottom took a hard right-angled turn into a wider grotto where two other tunnels connected. Fix figured if the *Gold Filling* was protected from radiation up top, he couldn't be much worse off in here. He hoped that wouldn't turn out to be a fatal assumption.

He removed his backpack and unhooked the bungees. After unrolling the deflated vac tent, he connected an O_2 tank and released a valve. The tent began slowly taking its familiar form. As he waited, he looked around the dark cave. *Home sweet home*, he thought. He had always prided himself on his stoicism, but the next few weeks would surely be a test.

***

The memorial service concluded with a choir singing the astronaut variation of the Navy hymn. Fogg found it an unfortunate choice, although he kept the thought to himself. The traditional lyrics, taken from 'Eternal Father, Strong to Save,' were quite stirring in Fogg's opinion, with its plea for the protection of those in peril on the sea, but the endless variations for land and air and outer space always struck him as tacky novelty songs. He was nothing if not a purist. Besides, if anyone had ever faced the perils of the sea it was the Makara expedition.

Fogg stepped out into the hallway without saying a word to Aouda. She had been surrounded by well-wishers, and he figured she might not even remember him from the short flight together. Cromarty and Pass-Par-2 had probably made a stronger impression than he had.

The robot was waiting outside the chapel and followed him silently down the hallway, uncertain if his master was lost in thought or overwhelmed with emotion from the service. As they were about to turn the corner to the landing pad, Cromarty's voice cried out from behind them. "Trying to slip away without a proper goodbye, Fogg?"

He stopped, turning to face him. "You know my timetable. I am already eight minutes behind schedule today."

Pass-Par-2 was confused by this assessment. According to his clock, they had nearly an hour before the Steady Axe was due to fire. Sometimes his master acted as if they were running late merely because they weren't as far ahead as he'd prefer.

Cromarty approached them. “I was talking to Commander Seni. He said you tried to swindle him out of a nuclear fuel cell last night.”

“I have never swindled anyone in my life, sir.”

“Yes, yes. My words, not his. But when I told him it was for my ship, he offered me free use of one of the station's spares. I actually do have a permit for one.”

“Well, that's fortunate,” said Fogg.

“You know, Fogg, sometimes I find that you can get further by asking a friend for a favour than by opening your wallet.”

“Thank you for the advice,” said Fogg. “I guess I haven't had much luck making those kinds of friends.”

“Well you have one now.” Cromarty gave him a big hug. Pass-Par-2 could tell his master was uncomfortable with the show of emotion, but he returned the embrace nevertheless.

Fogg said, “Thank you, my friend, for your council and your company. And good luck with...” He looked over his shoulder to where Sandra was waiting in the distance. “...with everything here.” He pulled away from the man and looked him in the eye. “Do I see a fourth wife on the horizon after all?”

“Is it foolish to hope so at my age?” asked Cromarty.

“The heart must not be denied that which it most desires. And for me, at the moment, what I desire is punctuality. Farewell.”

“Farewell, old bean. And Pass-Par-2,” said Cromarty, turning to the robot, “if you ever get tired of working for this chap, you'll always be welcome on Ganymede.”

“Oh,” said Pass-Par-2, “such a kind thing to say. Au revoir, Sir Francis.”

“Wait!” a female voice shouted from the end of the corridor. “Mr Fogg, please wait!”

He turned to see Aouda running down the hallway. As she reached them, Cromarty caught her to help stop her forward momentum.

"Aouda, you mustn't run in your state," he admonished.

"I'm feeling much better, thank you, Francis. But I'd feel far worse if I believed Mr Fogg was leaving without letting me plead my case."

"Whatever I can help you with, miss, you need not plead," said Fogg. "I am at your service."

"I want to go with you," she said. "Back to Earth."

"Oh, I see." Fogg was stunned by the request. "You understand I am not returning directly to Earth. I have stops to make yet."

"Francis told me all about your trip. I feel I must return home, and your ship is the fastest ride by far, even by way of Pluto."

"I would be delighted for you to accompany me, but..." Fogg stammered for a moment, trying to find some polite way to dissuade her, while simultaneously wondering what could be better than having her aboard. But he should be honest with her. "... the trip may be dangerous."

Aouda wasn't the type to be scared off by uncertainties. "Mr Fogg, I have already faced certain death. But you have given me a new chance at life. I need to breathe fresh air again. Feel the warmth of the sun on my face. See my family."

Fogg could see real emotion in her face, especially when she mentioned family. How could he refuse? "Very well," he said. "Pass-Par-2, help Aouda gather her things. We launch in ten minutes, not a second later."

"Oh, thank you, Mr Fogg! Thank you!" She gave him a quick kiss on the cheek, then took Pass-Par-2 by the hand and led him away down the corridor.

Fogg chose to ignore Cromarty's raised eyebrow.

***

Forty minutes later, Fix peeked out of the asteroid's mining shaft as the *Gold Filling* set down gently on the head of the

Giant's Tooth. He realised, almost too late, that gravity would be returning as soon as the Steady Axe fired. He pushed off and landed at the bottom of the tunnel moments before the weight hit him. He trudged back to the vacuum tent, feeling the full weight of Earth's gravity for the first time in years. He cycled through the airlock tube and fell to his knees inside the tent, catching his breath for a moment before shedding himself of the heavy pressure suit. Then he dug through his pack and pulled out a small Geiger counter. He turned it on and waved it around the tight quarters. The needle was definitely elevated, but at least it was still in the green zone. There was no doubt this environment wasn't good for him, but it wouldn't kill him. Not for a few years anyway. He could worry about that once the job was done.

He settled into his new home and tried to think of a way to pass the time. He had a tablet, but all of his media was stored on the station's central server. *I should've brought a deck of cards*, he thought.

***

Inside the *Gold Filling*, Aouda stood on shaky legs in the full gravity, but she wouldn't be denied one last view of the Jupiter system before she left. She peered out the small porthole on the side of the cabin.

"Away we go," she said, more to herself than anyone else. "Farewell, Europa. I forgive you. Farewell, Ganymede, be good to my friends. And farewell, Father Jupiter. You are so beautiful to behold." Then she gasped so loudly that Phileas Fogg and his robot could not ignore it.

"Are you all right, Aouda?" asked Fogg.

"I... I don't believe it. You must come see for yourself," she replied.

Fogg crossed the control room and leaned in to look out of the tiny window. He was suddenly very aware of how close his face was to hers. He tried not to think about how wonderful her hair smelled. Instead, he focused on finding whatever it was that had drawn her attention out the window.

They were swinging around towards the daylight side of Jupiter, and more and more of its face was coming into view. Then Fogg noticed a giant red swirl in the clouds below the equator. “Is that...? It can't be. The Great Red Spot died years ago.”

“It has returned, reenergised,” said Aouda, as stunned as he was. “Look at it! It's enormous!”

“But how?” asked Fogg. “It wasn't there yesterday. Unless... Pass-Par-2! The power core!”

The robot managed to look embarrassed. “Sacré bleu! I've made another mess. Will you report this to Monsieur Marchand?”

Aouda laughed. Fogg found the sound delightful. He couldn't help but join in.

The news made it to London three days later. Stuart rode an elevated maglev train through the countryside, reading about the return of the Great Red Spot on the front page of *The Times*. He didn't know how, but he was certain Phileas Fogg was responsible for this.

“Fogg!” came an angry shout from further down the train. Stuart leaned out into the aisle for a better view forward. He spotted a familiar face. “Oh, hello, Flanagan. Fancy meeting you here.”

CHAPTER FOURTEEN

A SAD HISTORY

It would have been understandable for Aouda to be disoriented when she awoke the next morning in her bunk on the *Gold Filling*, but without even opening her eyes she immediately knew where she was. The gravity pressing her into the mattress was a big clue. She remained in bed for a while, allowing the memories of the past few days to run through her mind. She knew it was best to give them free rein—at least for a short while—rather than try to suppress them.

She had left Earth aboard a cramped ship nearly three years earlier and spent the two years outbound completing her PhD in Astrobiology. Professor Chatterji had recruited her personally for the mission, promising to teach her everything he knew while learning new things together. They had been welcomed warmly when they arrived at the already-thriving Ganymede Station, but they only spent about six weeks there to prep for their expedition to Europa. The team consisted of Professor Chatterji and herself and two other scientists from their flight, plus three engineers who were already on Ganymede.

The ship they'd arrived on was adapted to ferry the Makara expedition to the surface of Europa. There they began the long, slow process of melting the crew module through the ice. It was a delicate procedure, and the crew waited on the parked ship for a full month while their future home sank inch by inch towards the water below. In addition to keeping the module upright and airtight, they had to work constantly to stabilise the umbilical to the surface.

Finally, the module broke through the ice into the liquid ocean beneath. They used submersible drones to anchor it to the underside of the ice, then climbed down through the tunnel into the empty base. Power was already on, but the outer door of the moonpool had been kept sealed for the descent. Aouda remembered the excitement when the inner hatch cycled open for the first time and the dark water inside was exposed to the air of the base. They stayed in their suits and analysed samples of the water before deciding it was safe.

Four of them went together on the first dive. They waited in the moonpool's lock while the door overhead slid shut, then the door below opened to the dark sea. They had decided to stay close to base at first. Aouda collected samples from the underside of the ice, which disappointingly showed no traces of life. Other members of the team guided robotic subs as deep as they could go, but no bottom was found. Sonar indicated there was a solid surface down there somewhere, but it might remain unreachable.

After a few weeks, enthusiasm for finding life began to wane. It was a crushing disappointment for Aouda. It seemed Europa was just a huge drop of lifeless water encrusted in ice. There was still science to do, though, and the base was starting to feel like home. Aouda kept up her dives, her sample collections, and her chemical analyses. She was already thinking about the book she would write on the trip home. She was one of the rare people who came to Jupiter without the intent of staying there. She had been clear with Professor Chatterji that she expected to return to Earth on the next supply ship after their mission was complete. That would be another six months at least, so she remained focused on having experiences worth writing about later.

That fateful evening she had just returned to the base from a brief solo dive. She was responsible for daily checks of the anchors securing the base to the ice ceiling, which only took about twenty minutes. It was always her last task of the day before shedding her wetsuit. She had just cycled through the moonpool and was on the deck removing her suit when the base lurched violently. She felt a pop in her ears before she heard the rushing air. She knew immediately it could mean only one thing —catastrophic decompression.

She grabbed the helmet of her dive suit, which she had just set aside, and managed to fasten it in place in a matter of seconds. She looked around, but there was no sign of the others. Loose equipment and debris were blowing in the violent wind. She remembered an ice pick flying off a high shelf and slamming into the glass of her helmet, luckily doing no damage. She saw that the water trapped in the moonpool was bubbling. If it was boiling in these cool temperatures, she knew they were nearing a total vacuum. She grabbed an O_2 tank from the wall and ran to the lab.

Professor Chatterji had been waiting for her there. They had planned on examining the latest ice cores together. He was on the floor with one arm over his head, but he appeared to be conscious. She ran to him, covering his mouth with the oxygen mask. He opened one eye, and she saw that it was red with broken blood vessels, but he recognised her. He took one breath from the oxygen mask, then began to cough violently. He pushed the mask away as he turned his head and spat blood. She tried to reattach the mask, but he stopped her with one hand. He weakly mouthed something to her, but no sound carried. She later decided he was saying, “Get to the ship,” but she would never know for sure. His hand fell away, his eyes rolled up in his head, and he was gone. She thought she had got to him in time to save him, but she later surmised he had likely suffered a stroke from exposure to the unrelenting vacuum. There was nothing she could have done for him.

She found four of the others in their bunks. Two had reacted fast enough to get out of bed, but none made it to the door of the shared sleeping space. She found the last member of the team, Masterson, sitting in a chair at the control panel. It was the same chair where Pass-Par-2 would later find her. He had been on duty and had survived long enough to try to close the hatch to the umbilical; he had no way of knowing the hatch was gone. The entire airlock structure atop the base had been shorn clean off in the shifting ice.

She moved all of the bodies to the side of the moonpool and covered them with a tarp. She hoped they would be recovered someday. She would mourn them later, assuming she lived. She needed to find a way out.

There was no telling how far the station had been moved from the umbilical. The hole where the airlock had been was now completely covered in thick, opaque ice. She knew the only other way out was through the moonpool, so she took an extra tank and cycled through the lock into the dark waters. It was surprisingly calm below. She swam a broad circle around the base, keeping the floodlights in sight, feeling for any current that might indicate a break in the ice. But there was nothing. She was afraid if she went too far from the base she would never be found. So she went back. If she was going to die here, she wanted to be found with her colleagues.

She had never been trained to use the communications equipment, but once she was back at the control panel she figured out how to relay a radio signal through to the surface. She had no confirmation that the signal had made it any further than their empty ship, but it was the best she could do. She sat down and recorded what she thought would be her final words. She knew rescue ships from Ganymede would be at least two days away, and then they would still have to find a way through the ice. Her oxygen reserves would not last that long.

She kept herself together long enough to record her message. As she lay in her bunk on the *Gold Filling* two days later, she couldn't even remember what she had said, and she hoped to never hear the recording. But she remembered being proud of her composure. Once it was complete, she had sat in the chair and wept for a very long time. She thought she should go lie down by the moonpool with the others, but she couldn't bring herself to move. She let exhaustion overtake her and drifted into what she had expected to be an endless sleep.

But it hadn't been endless. She had awoken to a new chance at life. And now she intended to live it to its fullest. She knew she would see her lost friends' faces again the next time she closed her eyes, but she had given the sad memories all the time she would give them for today. It was time to open her eyes and embrace her first full day on the voyage of the *Gold Filling*.

***

A short time later, Aouda stepped out of the bunk on the right, which she had taken only after refusing Fogg's offer of the slightly larger captain's bunk. She was wearing a custom-fit jumpsuit from the fabric printer. She walked carefully, leaning on the furniture whenever possible.

"I like your ship very much, Mr Fogg, but it's going to take me a while to readjust to Earth gravity."

Fogg looked up from his tablet where he'd been parsing data on elk populations in Manitoba in the early 20th century. "I wish I could make the g-force more comfortable for you, Aouda, but that would require slowing down, which is the one thing I cannot do."

"I understand," she said, gingerly lowering herself into the chair across from his. "But I imagine you must be feeling optimistic about your wager. You've already collected half your rocks with sixty-four days remaining."

"My apparent progress is deceptive. The road ahead is ten times longer than the path so far. Everything is spaced much further apart out here. The trip to Saturn is going to take a full week."

"A week is nothing," said Aouda. "You don't know how good you have it. Plus, it gives us a chance to get to know one another. You and Sir Francis have the most charming manners, Phileas. So proper and refined. Is everyone in London like you?"

"Sadly no," said Fogg. "London is full of uneducated miscreants and self-important vulgarians these days. Sir Francis and I both graduated from the same school, a private academy where young men and women are raised in an immersive environment, stressing the culture of a more sophisticated age."

"Ah. Well, I like it. My own education was somewhat similar. My parents sent me to a very traditional boarding school where I learned to speak proper English, which it turns out is rarely spoken anymore."

"A deplorable truth," agreed Fogg.

"It is nice to share the company of someone who understands that being cultured is not the same as looking down one's nose."

"I agree wholeheartedly. Do you take afternoon tea?"

Aouda appeared slightly embarrassed. "Is it afternoon already?" She had just woken up less than half an hour earlier.

Fogg pulled out his atomic pocket watch, showing her the time. "Greenwich Meridian, the only clock that matters on this ship. Pass-Par-2, tea for two."

The robot stuck his head out from the ship's tiny galley. "Yes, Master. Good morning, er, good afternoon, mademoiselle. Do you have a preference for any particular variety?"

"Please, I insist you call me Aouda. I just know we are going to be fabulous friends by the end of this voyage, and formalities simply will not do. I'll have whatever you're steeping."

"Very well, Aouda. I have biscuits too." He ducked back into the galley, but his voice still carried out to her. "Sadly they are from a tin. Master has been most patient with the galley's limitations."

Aouda smiled at Fogg. "He really is quite remarkable. But I can't help but wonder why we do it."

"Why we do what?" asked Fogg.

Her tone became rather sombre. "We keep repeating a sad history. The scourge of slavery is finally eradicated worldwide, and we've designed these remarkable machines capable of giving everyone a better life, rich or poor. But then we give those machines faces and names and voices of their own, and suddenly it's as if we are once again masters of an enslaved race."

"A thought-provoking perspective. But we must remember, his personality is merely a simulation. Robots are still machines, after all."

"Obviously they are machines," said Aouda, "but are we any different? I would argue we are just machines of carbon rather than silicon. Is our grey matter really that different from their processors? How sure are you about what is going on inside your mechanical friend's head? Or in his heart?"

Fogg squirmed a little. "Yes, well, Marchand's people certainly did an excellent job of covering every detail. Sometimes I almost forget what he is myself. Would you excuse me for just a moment?"

He stood and walked over to the galley, squeezing into the tight space with Pass-Par-2. The robot was startled to see him when he turned around from the tea kettle.

"Master! Is something wrong?"

Fogg spoke in a low voice. "Pass-Par-2, I think perhaps it would be best if you stopped calling me Master."

"Oh," said the robot. "Of course. What shall I call you then? Sir? Captain? Phileas? Mon ami?"

"Let just stick with 'sir' for now. Or 'Mr Fogg.' We can still be civilised."

"As you wish, Mr Fogg, sir," said the happy robot.

Fogg left the galley without further comment.

CHAPTER FIFTEEN

A TOUR OF THE RINGS

It was Day 23 when the *Giant's Tooth* scooted tail-first past Iapetus. Saturn's outermost major moon, with its black-and-white yin-yang topography and distinctive equatorial ridge, marked their arrival at the Saturnian system even before the Steady Axe had completed the deceleration burn. They were still nearly ten times further from the planet than the Moon was from Earth. Saturn's vast network of moons was a big neighbourhood.

A few hours later, Pass-Par-2 finally announced the time had come. He shut off the Steady Axe and activated the manoeuvring jets to rotate the asteroid around on its axis. Fogg and Aouda watched on the wide video screen as the unimaginable beauty of Saturn slowly drifted into view. The rings shone brightly, more colourful than Fogg expected. Aouda normally preferred a real window, but in this case the tiny porthole was too small to take in the full view, so she allowed herself to float up closer to the large monitor and its Infinite Pixel Display. With the Steady Axe powered down, they were essentially weightless. The *Giant's Tooth* had a minuscule gravitational pull of its own, so Aouda knew if she hovered still long enough, her feet would eventually find the floor, but she could stay aloft for minutes at a time. *Like a mote of dust suspended in a sunbeam*, she thought, remembering her favourite Carl Sagan quote.

"My God," said Aouda. "It is the most beautiful sight I have ever seen."

Fogg drifted up next to her. "I must agree." Luckily for him she failed to notice that he wasn't looking at the video screen.

"It's hard to really get a sense of the scale," said Aouda.

Pass-Par-2 spoke up. "The main rings are four and a half times wider than the diameter of the Earth." He superimposed an image of Earth over the rings to illustrate this fact. He only allowed their humble homeworld to share the screen for a few seconds before it faded away again, giving Saturn its time in the spotlight.

"You are an excellent tour guide, Pass-Par-2," said Aouda. "Look at the moons! There's so many!"

Indeed there were countless moons in various phases circling the planet. Saturn currently held the record for the most moons, although there was some debate as to when a satellite is too small to still be considered a proper moon. There were known to be thousands of 'moonlets' within the rings. If one insisted on counting every round chunk of ice, the planet could claim to host trillions of moons.

Aouda pointed at an elongated rock just inside a thin outer ring. "Look, there's one moving in that gap in the rings. It's one of the shepherd moons."

"That would be Prometheus," said Pass-Par-2. "And Pandora is also visible. Would you like me to label them on the screen?"

"Oh, yes please!" said Aouda.

A moment later, floating text appeared on the screen identifying every sizeable satellite in view. Aouda squealed with delight.

"We'll get a closer look at another shepherd moon—Pan—as we pass through the Encke Gap," said Pass-Par-2.

"We're going *through* the rings?" asked Aouda.

"Yes," said the robot, "but don't worry. It's perfectly safe. The gap is 200 miles wide, and Pan does an excellent job of keeping it clear of any hazards." He turned to address Fogg. "Sir, the *Giant's Tooth* has entered a stable orbit. Are you ready to launch the *Gold Filling* for Titan?"

Fogg questioned the necessity of flying through the gap in the rings to get to Titan. Sometimes he wondered if the robot chose the scenic route on purpose. But he had done an excellent job of keeping them on schedule so far, so he would let him have his fun. "Ready when you are, Pass-Par-2."

***

The *Gold Filling*'s thrusters fired, and it pushed away from the surface of the asteroid. Benjamin Fix watched through his visored helmet from the rim of his mine shaft. "You'd better not get yourself killed and strand me here, Fogg." His voice echoed inside his helmet but could travel no further than that.

He wondered what he would do if the gold-plated lander never returned from its errand. He was tempted to grab his broomstick and fly around to the Steady Axe engine and see if there was some way to hotwire it without the controls. He wouldn't be able to navigate to Pluto on his own, but maybe he could point it sunward and get close enough for Aaron to mount a rescue mission. It seemed like a long shot. He would cross that void when he came to it.

The *Giant's Tooth* seemed to be on a wide orbital path around Saturn. No doubt Fogg and his robot were zipping ahead to Titan, then planning to rendezvous with their asteroid-turned-spaceship again when it swung around to meet them. Fix would not allow himself to get concerned unless he completed a full orbit. That would no doubt mean Fogg had met some misfortune on his mission.

For the time being, Benjamin allowed himself to soak in the sight of the ringed planet. He wasn't normally the type to appreciate aesthetics, but the grandeur was not lost on him. He found it somewhat reassuring to know there was still a sliver of soul inside of him that could be stirred by such a sight. Still, it was a bit of a shame he couldn't swap places with someone who could truly savour the experience. He thought of a woman he had once loved. The only one, really. She had been a stargazer. She would no doubt be moved to tears by this sight. He wished he could see it through her eyes.

He held the scope from his disassembled sniper rifle up against the glass of his helmet. It had a wide eyepiece designed specifically for use in a pressure suit where a direct seal against the eye was impossible. It displayed a bright image of the rings magnified by a factor of sixty. With the scope suctioned to the glass in the microgravity, it was fairly easy to keep the image steady as long as he held his body still.

He could see the true intricacy of the rings. Glinting ice particles of various sizes were strung in countless concentric bands with narrow channels between them, ploughed clear by the myriad moonlets. He focused on one of the sparkling spheres as it cruised through a gap like the needle of an old phonograph riding between the grooves of a vinyl LP. He wondered if it was big enough to be a moon with a proper name catalogued in some registry somewhere. Probably not. He would name it himself.

Christina.

They had only been together for six months. He remembered that time as if it was a dream from some other life. She made him feel like a complete person, but then, inevitably, she had asked too many questions. About his past. His family. He had lied and told her he was an only child, but she saw right through him. She had studied psychology as an undergraduate, and she claimed she could tell after thirty seconds of conversation whether or not a man had a brother within five years of his own age. She told Benjamin he reeked of the machismo that comes from growing up in a house full of testosterone. He held his ground though, and she grew resentful of him for not sharing his true history. Ultimately, he had to move on. It was better for both of them. He had steered clear of relationships ever since. Duty came first.

He realised his eyes had wandered from the scope as his mind had wandered from the present. He had lost sight of Christina. He lowered the scope rather than look for her again, but he felt better knowing she was still out there, cruising on through her groove.

***

Fogg and Aouda floated in the control room while Pass-Par-2 kept himself anchored at the helm. The rings had grown ever closer on the screen. Now they could clearly make out patterns and textures, rings within rings, bright clumps and wispy strands. What had seemed so smooth and perfect from a distance began to reveal irregularities as they grew nearer. Some trick of physics caused spiky ridges to rise from the outer edges of some rings, casting elongated shadows across miles of tumbling ice. It was impossible to take it all in. Aouda watched in silence, trying to commit the images to memories she could enjoy for the rest of her life.

The ship slipped into the Encke Gap, a broad empty lane within the A Ring. Just ahead of them was a luminous rock shaped like a piece of ravioli. At seventeen miles across, Pan was puny by moon standards but still considerably larger than the *Giant's Tooth*. They approached from just outside of its orbit. There was a moment when Saturn itself was the moon's backdrop, just above an infinite field of ice. Then they dropped a bit lower and were travelling within the plane of the rings. This thin zone was less than fifty feet high. They cruised between dark icy walls for just a few seconds, then they emerged below the rings leaving the diminutive Pan behind.

"Glorious!" said Aouda. "Just absolutely thrilling." A tear formed and floated away from her eye.

They began pulling away from Saturn and more moons became visible on the far side. She saw Janus and Epimetheus, the 'dancing moons' chasing each other in a strange orbital relationship that caused them to swap places every four years. And ahead she saw Enceladus. Her heart raced when she realised she could see geysers of water erupting from the southern hemisphere. Like a miniature Europa, Enceladus hid an ocean beneath an outer layer of ice. It had once been a major target for scientists like herself who were seeking alien life in the solar system, but unmanned probes in the early 2040s had crushed those hopes. Although the waters were teeming with complex organics, robotic submarines had found no trace of life. *Just like Europa*, she thought sadly. She couldn't deny she was tempted to take a look for herself.

Another moon caught her attention in the distance. She pointed to it. "Pass-Par-2, could you magnify that one?"

"Of course, Aouda." The robot happily complied.

The moon that filled the viewscreen was a grey sphere with a huge dent in its upper hemisphere. It sparked a happy memory from her childhood. She mustered her best Alec Guinness impression. "That's no moon. It's a space station."

Fogg looked at her like she'd lost her senses. "What? Don't be silly. Of course it's a moon."

"He's right, Aouda," said Pass-Par-2. "It's called Mimas."

"Seriously?" She sighed in disappointment. "You boys really need to see more old movies."

"How can you think about movies at a time like this?" asked Fogg. "I feel like we've seen every moon *except* Titan."

Pass-Par-2 checked his charts. "It should be emerging from Saturn's shadow in just a moment, sir. Dead ahead."

As if on cue, sunlight revealed a giant moon shrouded in

thick cloud cover. All the moons they'd seen so far suddenly seemed minuscule by comparison. The helpful viewscreen labelled it in friendly text. 'TITAN.'

"Rock number four awaits," said Phileas Fogg. "We should strap in for landing."

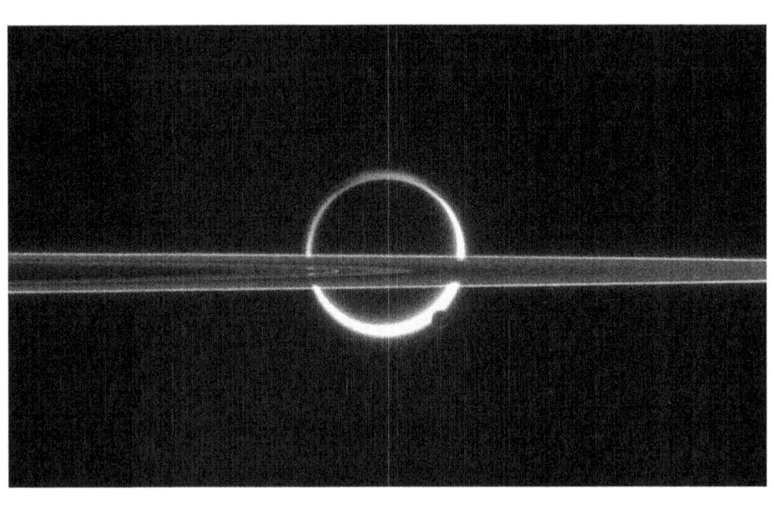

CHAPTER SIXTEEN

MAROONED ON KRAKEN MARE

They hit the upper atmosphere of Titan with a jolt. Fogg trusted Pass-Par-2's flying skills implicitly, but he hoped the robot had thoroughly researched atmospheric flight. After all, Titan's atmosphere was thicker than Earth's. No one had experience flying through a sky this dense. As the *Gold Filling*'s control room began to rattle and shimmy, he resisted the urge to white-knuckle the sides of his seat. He worried how Aouda might be holding up, so he dared turn his head in her direction despite the wave of nausea this caused. She was holding her restraints tightly, but with a big excited smile on her face. Fogg made a mental note to stop underestimating this extraordinary woman.

Per Fogg's instructions, Pass-Par-2 guided the lander towards the northern polar latitudes of Titan, where the largest lakes of liquid methane were found. He had no visual on the surface yet. The cloud cover wasn't just dense—it was solid. They had already punched through a layer of haze in the mesosphere, and now they were braking hard as they descended through the relatively clear but gloomy stratosphere. A tholin haze engulfed the ship about 120 miles above the surface, and they were left flying blind for nearly five minutes through the dense organic compounds that made up the miasma. Then they dropped out of the clouds, and the landscape of Titan was suddenly everywhere beneath them.

It was the most Earth-like terrain any of them had seen outside of Earth itself. Diffused sunlight rippled on the waves of a giant methane lake, larger than the Great Lakes of North America, surrounded by eroded hills. This was Kraken Mare. A river valley cut through the hills, fanning out into a broad delta as it emptied into the lake. Pass-Par-2 banked the ship towards the river.

The *Gold Filling* slowed its descent until it was essentially hovering while Pass-Par-2 searched for the best landing zone. He spotted a flat rocky area near a small stream that fed into the river. Fogg suggested the stream would be prime rock hunting ground, so the robot set them down there. Fogg felt the weight of the ship being absorbed by the landing pads, then the abrupt shutoff of the engines left them sitting in silence. Fogg and Aouda exchanged an expectant look before Pass-Par-2 turned around to face them.

"We have arrived on Titan."

Fogg and Aouda unbuckled and began prepping for their excursion. Aouda had brought a pressure suit from Ganymede, a simple white model with purple stripes around the knees and elbows. Her helmet offered greater visibility than Fogg's with its dome of tempered glass almost resembling a fishbowl. Once they had checked each other's gear, they gathered by the airlock. Possibly two of them could squeeze in together, but certainly not all three. Fogg figured he should go first, since no one else was actually obligated to face the danger of going outside. As the inner door opened, Aouda put a hand on his shoulder.

"Have you decided what you'll say?"

Fogg was perplexed. "What I'll say to whom?"

"You're about to be the first human on Titan," said Aouda. "It calls for something historic."

The thought hadn't occurred to him, and he didn't relish the opportunity. But it seemed important to Aouda, so he knew at once what he should do. "In that case, I believe the best thing I could say is, 'Ladies first.'"

He stepped aside and swept his arm towards the door with a flourish. A broad smile bloomed on Aouda's face. She eagerly stepped into the tight space and began the process of cycling the air. A moment later, the outer door opened and she stepped out to the top of the ladder, still ten feet above the surface.

He watched as she seemed to brace herself for a moment, then leapt. She arced surprisingly high, soaring through the air like a superhuman from the old comic books. He was concerned for a moment, until a joyful howl came crackling through the radio into his ear. She was so loud he had to turn down the volume a couple of clicks. After an astonishing five full seconds in the air, she landed with barely an *oomph*. She turned back to face the ship, her smile brighter than the filtered sunlight.

"That's one small step for mankind, one giant leap for a woman," she said with mock seriousness. Then she lapsed into a fit of giggles.

Fogg allowed himself a private smile inside his helmet. Her happiness was an undeniable force. Nevertheless, once he was through the airlock he took the more pragmatic approach of climbing down the ladder, although he did allow himself to skip a few rungs in the low gravity.

By the time he reached the bottom and stepped onto the frigid rock, Pass-Par-2 had cycled through and stood at the top of the ladder. Aouda called out to him, "Pass-Par-2, don't be a fuddy-duddy like Phileas. Jump! Come frolic with me!"

"I've never frolicked before, miss. What is its purpose?"

"No purpose," said Aouda, "it's just fun."

She jumped as high as she could straight into the air, her arms spread wide, then spun like a figure skater as she drifted back to the ground. She landed lightly on her toes.

Apparently convinced to give it a try, the robot jumped out from the top of the ladder in a perfectly calculated parabola, landing just a couple of feet from Aouda. She immediately grabbed his hands and began spinning him and laughing blissfully.

"Don't frolic far," said Fogg. "We aren't staying long." He began walking in the direction of the stream. The flat rock outcropping ended about fifty yards away from the ship, then he carefully worked his way down a loose slope to the shallow, babbling brook below.

The stream had obviously overflown its banks in the past because Fogg stepped over a natural levee made of pebbles and some sort of muck that resembled mud. He knew he could probably grab a rock from anywhere here, but he wanted to be able to tell the old man that he had pulled one straight from the flowing stream of liquid methane.

He stood at the stream's edge. It was hard not to think of it as the 'water's' edge, but upon a close look it was very definitely not water. It had a sheen like an oil slick, but otherwise it was remarkably clear. He got down on one knee and reached a gloved hand out into the flow. He could feel the current rushing between his fingers. He made sure his helmet cam was recording the moment. He tried to absorb every detail, hoping to relate it all to Lord Albemarle upon his return. He reached for the bottom of the stream, dug around a little, and found a grip on one of the smooth stones that lined the bed. He pulled it up from the stream and held it in front of his helmet. It was a flat, grey ovoid, perfectly polished by the flowing fluid. *It would make a great skipping stone*, he thought. He was even tempted to give it a try. He was certain Aouda would have. But he was not prone to frivolous urges. He sealed the rock in a mesh bag tied to his waist. The fourth sample had been collected.

Not too far away, Aouda and Pass-Par-2 had performed a series of increasingly acrobatic leaps until they found themselves standing astride a sharp ridge nearly a hundred yards above the *Gold Filling*'s landing spot. Aouda was already a bit winded from the exercise, but the view at the top took her remaining breath away. The sun had broken through the clouds, casting golden shafts across the rippling waves of the giant lake in the distance.

"I can see Kraken Mare!" she said between gasps. "It's mesmerising." Maybe it was the exhaustion overtaking her, but the patterns of light really did feel hypnotic. The yellowish surface was broken in one spot by a rocky landmass that rose above the waves. "And there's a little island." A thought sparked in her mind. "Could that be the one? I mean, could it be the same island where the Japanese rover landed?"

While Aouda and Fogg could claim to be the first of their kind on Titan's surface, Pass-Par-2 could not say the same. The first machine to land here was the European Space Agency's Huygens probe, which hitched a ride to Saturn aboard NASA's Cassini spacecraft and landed near the moon's equator in 2005. NASA had followed up with a robotic submarine, which explored the depths of Ligeia Mare not far from here in 2040. Unfortunately, it abruptly lost contact with Earth after only three days before recording any significant discoveries. Another robot arrived just six years ago, a small rover named Gyoki developed by the Japanese Aerospace Exploration Agency. JAXA had intended it to map the shoreline of Kraken Mare, so they developed a landing site selection algorithm to find the safest, flattest spot near the lake during the final minutes of its descent to the surface. Unfortunately, Gyoki's computer had selected a spot that left it stranded on an island no larger than two square miles. It had been a major setback for Japan's space program. The top management of JAXA had all resigned in shame, even though the rover had landed safely and was still fully operational.

Pass-Par-2 checked the maps in his database. "The landing coordinates of the Gyoki rover do in fact match the nearest island."

"Do you think it's still there?" asked Aouda.

"I'm certain of it," said Pass-Par-2. "It was intended to map this entire region, but its unfortunate landing site left it somewhat marooned."

Fogg's voice joined the conversation via the radio. Aouda turned to see him climbing the ridge behind them. "Last I heard it was still sending data home, albeit the same data over and over again."

"Oh, Phileas, we must save it!" said Aouda.

Fogg reached the top and stood beside her, studying the island. "Save it? From what? It isn't in any danger."

"But it's trapped! I can't bear to think of leaving the poor thing out there. It wants so badly to complete its mission." She looked pleadingly into his eyes. "As much as you want to complete your own. Surely you can understand?"

Fogg exhaled slowly. "Well, I suppose it is a valuable scientific instrument, and as we're here..."

Aouda smiled and clapped her hands rapidly. A voice inside him was shocked by how easily he allowed this woman to influence him, but he had no trouble shutting that voice out. They still had three hours to rendezvous with the *Giant's Tooth*. "Pass-Par-2, how difficult would it be to fly over to that island?"

"More difficult than the alternative," said the robot.

"What alternative?"

***

It turned out the *Gold Filling* carried an inflatable yellow raft in its undercarriage. It was intended for use in an emergency ocean landing on Earth. Fogg worried how it might react to being inflated in Titan's cold, dense atmosphere and low gravity. He half expected it to shoot skyward like a helium balloon after they pulled the cord to start the inflation, but nothing so exciting occurred. It had inflated exactly as it would in the waters off the coast of Florida. They carried it over their heads to the shore of Kraken Mare.

They were surprised when the raft seemed to float a bit higher in the methane than it would in water back home. Fogg would have predicted that the lower density of the liquid would give the opposite result, but there was no sense in doing the maths now. This was fieldwork, where observations took precedence. They could work out the science later.

They climbed in and pushed out from the shore. The waves were thankfully nothing more than a ripple at the moment. Careful study of the shoreline suggested they were lucky in that regard. There were clear signs of pounding surf in recent days. Pass-Par-2 tilted the small outboard motor into position, then fired it up. It didn't provide as much momentum as designed, and in this case it was almost certainly because of the liquid's lower density, but it would get them where they were going eventually. They motored out past a few craggy tufa spires that breached the surface like white, bony fingers, then they were on the open sea.

Aouda sat on the side of the raft, looking down at her reflection in the dark liquid. Fogg sat opposite, watching her, wondering what was on her mind. Before he dared to ask, she lunged forward and dunked her head beneath the surface of the lake. Fogg bolted across the raft and grabbed her by the waist, but he saw she was holding tightly to the ropes on the side, in no danger of going overboard. Nevertheless, Fogg was uncomfortable with such unpredictability. He pulled her head back above the surface.

“Aouda, whatever were you thinking?” He realised too late that he could have asked the question even while she was below the surface, since all of their communications were by radio.

She turned calmly to face him. The joy she had been exuding earlier was gone. “I'm fine,” she said. “I just wanted to see below the surface. This may be the last place left to search for alien life in our solar system.”

Fogg nodded, releasing his grip on her, hoping she hadn't been offended. “What did you see down there?” he asked.

"Nothing," she answered. "Only darkness."

***

Aouda seemed to perk up a little as they approached the shore of the desolate island. Pass-Par-2 killed the motor and tilted it up above the surface as the lake became shallow. When the raft stopped its forward momentum a few feet from shore, the robot stepped overboard off the stern and pushed it the rest of the way.

Aouda hopped out and immediately saw treaded imprints in the muddy shore. "Look, tyre tracks." She pointed them out to the others, but as she panned the beach it was clear she needn't have bothered. The ground was crisscrossed by tracks in every direction. "They're absolutely everywhere! The little guy has certainly kept busy."

Fogg helped Pass-Par-2 pull the raft completely onto dry ground, then surveyed the scene himself. "It must have mapped every inch of this island ten times over. This is hopeless. We could spend hours looking for it."

Pass-Par-2 interjected before Aouda could. "That won't be necessary. We've just been pinged by radar." He pointed to a hill overlooking the beach. "Up there!"

A tiny rover was silhouetted against the hazy sky at the top of the ridge. It was about the size of Fogg's largest suitcase. It had four wheels, an array of solar panels on its back, and a central mast that held a pair of binocular cameras. There was no question it was watching them.

Aouda sprang into action at once, hopping in great bounds up the hillside. "We are coming for you, Gyoki!"

The skittish little bot watched the anomaly approach. Its wheels jiggled back and forth as it tried to balance equations of self-preservation and curiosity. Ultimately, after so many years in isolation, it decided to engage with this strange alien lifeform. It crept forward cautiously as the slender figure bent over and smiled into its cameras.

"Hellooooooooooo, Tokyo!" Aouda said with a smile and a wave.

***

Pass-Par-2 attempted to interface with the rover, commanding it to follow them back to the raft, but its Japanese operating system was as alien to him as any denizen of the deep they might find lurking in the methane lake. After two failed attempts, Fogg declared they were just spinning their wheels, and this island had seen more than its share of wheel-spinning already. He bent over and lifted the rover over his head.

He carefully carried Gyoki back down to the beach. It didn't resist or try to escape, so perhaps Pass-Par-2's efforts at communication had been at least partially understood. Pass-Par-2 dragged the raft back to the lake's edge, and Fogg set the rover down in the back. Aouda helped them push it out until the methane was knee-deep, then she and Fogg climbed aboard. Pass-Par-2 pushed a little further, then pulled himself over the stern and lowered the engine back into position.

"We'd better hurry back," said Fogg. "I don't like the look of the weather."

Pass-Par-2 looked over his shoulder and saw the dark clouds that were gathering over the far shore. They did look rather unwelcoming. He started the little engine and steered the raft back the way they had come.

They travelled nearly two-thirds of the distance in silence. Fogg was constantly watching the approaching storm with great concern. A wind started to blow, and in an atmosphere thicker than Earth's, even a light breeze could be hard to stand against. But at least the wind was working in their favour, pushing them closer to shore.

Sitting next to Gyoki, Aouda was startled when a telescopic pole extended up from the body of the rover. A thin metallic umbrella unfolded at the top like the petals of a titanium flower.

It angled the umbrella to cover Aouda in addition to itself. It had been here long enough to learn the weather patterns. It knew what was coming.

A giant drop of liquid splashed into the lake right next to the raft. Then another rippled the surface just ahead. The drops fell with unnatural slowness but impacted with surprising force. In an instant they were everywhere, exploding like wet mortars.

"Methane rain!" shouted Aouda, ducking her head further under the rover's umbrella.

"Pass-Par-2, turn to port," shouted Fogg. "The shore is closer there. Go full speed." They would have a fair distance to walk around the lake from there, but getting to solid ground was the priority. He was concerned that the mega-rain and powerful winds could capsize the raft.

The robot turned the raft to the closest shoreline, but he failed to see a submerged column of jagged tufa just beneath the surface. The raft ran over it with a jolt, followed by a painful grinding noise. The occupants managed to avoid being thrown overboard, but the raft slowed as the engine sputtered to a stop. Pass-Par-2 lifted the motor to find the propeller blades mangled and broken. With the engine noise gone, they were all suddenly aware of the hiss of air escaping from the raft. Fogg peered over the bow and saw a jagged rip in the yellow fabric just as the raft began to lose its form, sagging in the middle.

"We're sinking," said Fogg. "Pass-Par-2, you must save Aouda!"

"No," said Aouda. "Take the rover. Only one of us here is a professional diver, and this isn't my first alien sea. I can make it to shore myself, but Gyoki's circuitry must be protected."

Fogg couldn't help wanting to protect the woman, but he also felt abashed for constantly treating her like a fragile flower. It was obvious that she knew how to stay calm in a crisis. "All right. Pass-Par-2, save the rover."

"Yes, sir," said the robot. He lifted Gyoki over his head and leapt to a nearby spire of tufa that jutted above the surface. The shoreline was still nearly a hundred yards away. He crouched and jumped as far as he could. He covered a very impressive distance, aided by the stiff wind, but it wasn't far enough. He splashed down in the methane, disappearing beneath its dark surface... except for his upheld arms, which still managed to keep the rover above the waves. The hoisted rover teetered back and forth as his submerged saviour found his footing, but after a few unsteady steps, forward Pass-Par-2's antenna broke the surface, still blinking. He moved slowly towards the shore.

The raft was quickly losing all structural integrity around Aouda and Fogg. Liquid methane spilled into the interior, and they found themselves sinking fast. Fogg was embarrassed to ask for help, but he knew he had no choice. "Aouda, there's something I must confess. I cannot swim."

"Swim?" she replied. "Oh no, we're not going to swim. We're going to sink like rocks in these suits. But I don't think it's very deep. We can walk to shore on the bottom. Just don't get turned around. Keep moving in that direction, no matter what," she said, pointing to shore.

He nodded, then she flipped backwards over the edge of the rapidly sinking raft. Fogg tried to follow her, but he had waited too long. He felt the loose fabric of the raft tangling around his feet. He tried to kick them free, but the lake rose over his hips, then his shoulders, and he was wrapped tighter by the elastic yellow material. "Oh, dear," was the last thing he said before the methane washed over his helmet and he was in darkness.

As he sank, he activated the light on his helmet, but the world it illuminated around him was just a murky yellowish-brown instead of pitch black. He finally struggled his way free from the dead raft carcass and kicked his legs frantically, trying to reach the surface, but his descent did not even slow. Aouda's voice came in his ear. "Phileas! Where are you? Remember to—" Then, with a crackle, it was gone.

"Aouda? Aouda, can you hear me?" There was no response. He had never felt more alone in his life. Then his feet touched the bottom. He looked down at the slick layer of sludge that covered his feet up to his ankles. It wouldn't be easy trudging through this mess. He realised with sickening horror that he was completely disoriented. He had no clue which direction he should even be trudging in. He couldn't see more than five feet from his faceplate, but he detected a slight grade to his left, so he turned that way and began climbing.

After just a few steps, he was about to put down his left foot when he realised there was nothing there to put it on. He could see that the lakebed dropped away precipitously below him. He teetered for a moment at the edge of a high undersea cliff. He felt a faint current pushing him forward, and he feared he was about to be lost to the depths. He wished he had told Pass-Par-2 to make sure they sang the traditional lyrics to the Navy hymn at his memorial. Then, as he was about to accept his fate, a hand grabbed his shoulder and pulled him back from the precipice.

Aouda spun him around, her face partially illuminated by his helmet lamp. She pressed the glass of her faceplate up against his, and as they clinked together, she began shouting. "Can you hear me?" Her muffled voice sounded miles away.

"Yes," he shouted back, "barely."

"Hold my shoulders," she said. "I'll lead us to shore. And turn off your lamp."

He did as he was told, and as his eyes adjusted to the darkness, he realised he could see better without the lamp. Like driving through fog with high beams on, it had been lighting up all the heavy silt inches from his face. Now he could make out the surface rippling above them. They still had a ways to go, but with Aouda leading the way he felt his fear dissipate.

* * *

Pass-Par-2 walked up the beach with the rover still held high. The waves were much choppier now, so he continued walking until the surf was a fair distance behind him. The rain was letting up, thankfully. He bent over and gently lowered the rover to solid ground.

"There you go, Gyoki. You are a castaway no more."

The rover immediately u-turned and sped away, scanning the terrain with apparent enthusiasm.

"Hmph," said Pass-Par-2. "You're welcome."

He turned and looked back across the lake, but there was no sign of Fogg or Aouda or the yellow raft. "Mr Fogg? Miss Aouda? Can you hear me? Où êtes-vous?" He shouted the desperate plea at his highest volume and simulcast it via radio, then waited several excruciating seconds for a reply, but none came. It was as if they had never existed. His digital eyes grew wide and he ran back to methane's edge in a sudden state of panic.

"Sir, I am coming for you! How could I have abandoned you? Aouda, where are you?" He charged frantically into the surf just as two helmeted heads popped up some thirty yards away.

"Over here, Pass-Par-2," said Fogg. "We're coming."

"Sweet relief!" cried the robot, as he came to a halt, methane lapping at his legs. "I am so happy to see you again!"

"We're happy to see you too, Pass-Par-2. Did you save the rover?"

"Oui. He has begun mapping already." He pointed to Gyoki cresting a dune in the distance, leaving fresh tracks for the first time in years.

"He left without saying goodbye?" asked Aouda sadly as she stepped nearer to the wading robot.

"He has his mission," said Fogg, "as we have ours. I'll be happy to leave this hellish world behind."

Aouda took a good look around at the landscape of Titan. "I don't know. It is foreboding, but also strangely beautiful in its own way."

Pass-Par-2 also assessed his surroundings. "You're lucky you can't smell it."

Twenty minutes later, the *Gold Filling* was rocketing through the thick yellow clouds.

***

Agent Benjamin Fix stood on the surface of the *Giant's Tooth*, scanning the moon-filled sky around Saturn. He had sat around doing nothing for over a week now, but at least today he had done nothing with a killer view. Still, he was relieved when he saw the *Gold Filling* glinting in the sunlight on its approach. "It's about time," he said out loud, just to hear a human voice—even if it was his own—then he scampered to hide in his hole in the rock.

***

An hour and fourteen minutes after it actually happened, a video signal from Gyoki was received at JAXA mission control, which was not in fact in Tokyo, but rather a large building in Tsukuba, a few miles to the northeast. But no one there was going to split hairs when Aouda's friendly face filled their giant screen and her greeting rang out from their speakers.

"Hellooooooooo, Tokyo!"

The normally quiet chamber erupted with celebration.

CHAPTER SEVENTEEN

INTERPLANETARY INTERMEZZO

The *Giant's Tooth* had been pushing away from Saturn for several hours, and Aouda was exhausted, but she knew there was no point in trying to sleep before finishing her analysis. She heard a buzz from the small mobile lab kit she had brought from Ganymede. The results were finally ready. She opened a panel on the side of the kit and retrieved a test tube full of brown muck.

"May I ask what you are working on, Aouda?" asked Fogg, himself looking red-eyed and spent.

"I collected a sample from the lakebed just before I stopped you from stepping off that cliff. I couldn't help myself. Once a xenobiologist, always a xenobiologist. I just ran a chemical analysis."

"Anything interesting?" asked Fogg.

She studied the readouts on the kit's small screen. "The sediment is full of organic chemistry, but nothing that resembles life." She sighed, then powered down the lab kit. "A very sad finding. Yet another lifeless world."

"If you ask me," said Fogg, even though no one had, "we're

wasting our time even looking for alien life."

Aouda was shocked at his casual dismissal of her life's pursuit. "How can you say that, Phileas?"

"Simple. Life makes itself known. If any of these worlds had life, we wouldn't need to flip every rock to find it. There would be obvious, undeniable evidence, even from a distance."

Aouda had heard these criticisms before. Plenty of life hid under rocks. And even proof of extinct alien life would be profound, yet there would likely be no evidence without cracking some rocks open. But she was too tired to give him the full lecture. "Even if you're right, it only means we need to expand the search area. I'm wondering, could your spaceship take us to Alpha Centauri?"

The sun's closest celestial neighbour was a triple star system located 4.37 light-years away. Fogg knew the Steady Axe could fire forever without reaching the speed of light, but after about one year of constant acceleration, it would be close enough to make the maths easy to estimate.

"It could," he answered, "but we would need to restock the pantry first. It would take about five years each way."

She seemed to mull it over. "Hmmm. Perhaps someday. Life is out there, Phileas. I intend to find it. Goodnight, gentlemen."

Pass-Par-2, who had been listening quietly, tipped his hat to her as she retreated to her bunk. As soon as her door slid shut, he turned to Fogg. "For a moment there, I was afraid she was serious about Alpha Centauri. I am quite eager to get home and turn the gas off."

***

The news was out. Every man, woman, and child on Earth, not to mention the Moon, Mars, and a few other places, now knew the name Phileas Fogg. Just days after the details of the amazing rescue of the woman on Europa came out in the media, the very same woman's smiling face was waving to the people of Tokyo from an island on Titan. Such magic required an explanation, and piece by piece the details of that explanation were being disseminated to the piqued public. They knew about the Steady Axe engine. They knew about the asteroid-turned-spaceship. And they knew about the wager. Some of the details were being widely misreported (the *New York Times* claimed the *Giant's Tooth* had been spotted orbiting Venus), but humanity everywhere was captivated by the tale. Vegas oddsmakers actually favoured Fogg succeeding. Something about the adventure was igniting optimism in people everywhere.

Everywhere except Stuart's back patio, that is, where his wife was on his case again. Claudia Mandrake-Stuart held her beloved white Bichon Frise in her lap, casually tying ribbons in its fur as she read the morning's headlines on a tablet. As Stuart joined her with his coffee, she glanced up with a scornful look. "Your friend is making news again."

"I know, darling. I heard. I do believe I may lose this wager."

"Should I be concerned?" She kept her tone cool.

He sighed and took a sip from his mug. "No, dearest. You know me. I always have a plan."

He suspected she didn't believe him as she scoffed and returned to her reading, but it was true. He wasn't one to run around in a mad panic like Flanagan, but he would fight back in his own way now that it was abundantly clear Fogg had them on the ropes. He had been making calls, working connections, and brainstorming with his team of advisers, and this very afternoon action would be taken that should swing the odds back in his favour. *Maybe I should even consider taking some of that Vegas action*, he thought. But one look at his wife and he knew he dare not risk another pound. He still considered it a miracle that such an elegant woman had agreed to marry a man so vertically challenged as himself. He was sure the money had something to do with it. She was undeniably a woman who appreciated the finer things. He suspected she would not stay by his side if his financial worth shrunk to match his physical stature.

Stuart caught a maglev train from his estate on the River Cherwell in Oxfordshire to Westminster Station, then strolled casually in the shadow of Big Ben to the Cromwell Green entrance of the Palace. The guard at the door scanned his identification, then ushered him inside. He made his way through the lavish central hall, not bothering to appreciate the statues of saints and sovereigns or the Venetian glass mosaics. He walked up a flight of stairs and past a queue of tourists to enter the Visitors' Gallery of the House of Lords. An attendant recognised him at once and showed him to a seat at the railing, earning him dirty looks from the common folk on holiday who had patiently waited their turn. Truth be told, he relished their sneers.

The debate below was already underway. A priggish peer held the floor, pacing next to the red woolsack as he blathered on in his nasal monotone. Stuart listened to the assembled Lords grumble at every word from the peer. There were two different varieties: grumbles of approval and grumbles of outrage. But each and every utterance was a grumble. This chamber had perfect acoustics for it, elevating their grouses and agreements to high art.

The verbose peer finally yielded the floor and Stuart's man took his turn addressing the chamber. He was Stuart's uncle's godson, and he had been called upon many times to help the family push through acts of legislation. He was especially adept at arguing that laws benefiting large corporations would in turn help those most in need. Today's speech would lean more heavily on fears of attack from out of the night sky. Stuart didn't listen to the words too closely as he had written the first draft himself, but he concentrated on assessing the man's delivery. It needed to be concise yet adamant.

"It is clear from recent events that this body must take action to prevent another threat like the one we already face from Pluto. Just yesterday, a billionaire on holiday could have proclaimed himself Emperor of Titan, and once again we would have been left without any legal refutation."

Stuart approved of the emotion in the man's voice as he made a compelling argument for reining in the wild frontier that was forming beyond Earth's reach. As he wrapped up, another Lord stood—a compatriot of his inside man—and delivered the coup de grâce. "I beg to move that the question be now put," moving the debate straight to Closure.

The Lord Speaker approved, as Stuart knew he would, just as he knew they had the votes to pass. He watched it all unfold like clockwork. In this instance, he was the clockmaker, and it was a joy watching the cogs turn exactly as designed.

The Lord Speaker raised his voice to the chamber, declaring in the most theatrically official tone possible, "It is hereby offered for Royal Assent that any vessel owned or commanded by a British citizen shall be prohibited from making a first landing on any celestial body with a diameter greater than 450 kilometres without prior approval from Parliament."

As Stuart's scheme was elevated to law of the land, his man in the House of Lords looked up at him and nodded. Stuart nodded back, then quietly exited the chamber.

***

The *Giant's Tooth* sailed across the heavens, cutting a slash across familiar constellations. Orion's Sword was no match for the bright plume of the Steady Axe. But one week out from Saturn it was time to flip for the deceleration burn to Uranus, so the engine went dark while smaller manoeuvring jets rotated the asteroid.

The last week of flight had passed peacefully. Aouda's convivial attitude was... well, perhaps not infectious enough to penetrate Fogg's hardened defences, but he could admit to himself that he enjoyed the pleasure of her company. He had taught her to play a few simple card games after she claimed to have never held a deck in her life, and now she was already beating him at gin rummy. Her conservative upbringing had taught her that all games of chance were nefarious, but she found herself rather invigorated by the feeling of wicked mischief that came with the sound of the shuffle, and she celebrated like a rowdy schoolboy with every game she won. Normally Fogg would have found such behaviour boorish, but Aouda made it positively charming.

After an hour or so they had set aside the cards to enjoy the brief respite from gravity during the asteroid's rotation. Aouda spun head over heels in the open space of the control room. "I want to dance," she said mid-spin. "Pass-Par-2, do you have any classical Indian music?"

Pass-Par-2 didn't have a music library of his own, but he quickly searched the ship's databanks. Fortunately, the President of Agua Luna had a taste for world music. "Would a South Indian Carnatic performance suffice?" The control room was filled with the droning strings of a veena and upbeat percussion. A high-pitched female voice sang along with the melody of the lute, and Aouda began to twirl to the rhythm. Her fluid arm movements and waist gyrations sent her entire body tumbling in unpredictable directions. She laughed throughout the performance, and Fogg was captivated, although he kept worrying she would hit her head on the centre console. Finally the song ended, and Fogg was surprised when Aouda grabbed him to steady herself. For a moment, they were face to face, her radiant smile making his heart skip a beat. He held the contact longer than he meant to, then released her.

"That was a lovely performance, Aouda," he said once he regained his composure.

"I enjoyed it as well, miss," offered Pass-Par-2.

"Thank you both. I haven't danced like that in a long time."

"Sir, we are receiving a priority message," the robot interrupted.

Fogg did not respond for a long moment. The words didn't quite register. He had to go over them again, reassembling the sentence. *A message?* The *Gold Filling* was equipped with a state-of-the-art communications system, but they had made no use of it since leaving Ganymede. With the bottom of the asteroid pointing sunward, any signals from the inner system would have been blocked for the past week. He had almost allowed himself to forget about the rest of the universe, but now that they had rotated for the retrograde burn the radio was able to pick up a broadcast.

"What is it?" asked Fogg.

"It appears to be a message from the King."

"The King of Pluto? He knows we're here?"

"No, sir," said Pass-Par-2. "It's the King of England. We are being ordered to make no landing on the moon Miranda to be in compliance with recent legislation."

"What legislation?" Fogg asked suspiciously.

"I have the full text, sir." He sent it to both Fogg and Aouda's tablets. "It appears that any landing there would result in your immediate arrest upon returning to British soil."

Fogg scanned the text. "This is Stuart's work, no doubt. It specifies 'first landing,' so at least that won't apply to Pluto, since the King—the other King—already beat us there."

"Any celestial body with a diameter greater than 450 kilometres," read Aouda. "That seems like it was specifically chosen to rule out Miranda."

"I'm sure it was. Miranda is 470. I assume he had to make sure he didn't step on his own foot by outlawing his mining interests."

"What will we do, Phileas?" asked Aouda. It touched him that she had taken to this endeavour as if she were invested in it herself.

"I'm not sure," said Fogg. "We have a week to think of something."

"I'm not a British citizen. Would you trust me to sell me

your ship and give me command?"

"Of course I would, Aouda, but I don't think it's so simple. Stuart would have thought of that. I would have to legally transfer ownership to you before we reach Miranda, and there's simply no way to do that out here."

Pass-Par-2 spoke up. "Sir, on Mars you suggested we should have broken the law by landing on Olympus Mons. Can you not simply break this law as well? Surely you could pay any associated fine as long as you win the wager."

"I've thought about that, Pass-Par-2, and I was wrong to suggest breaking the law on Mars. Any infraction could be used by Stuart and Flanagan as an argument that I did not fulfil our contract legally, thus voiding my potential victory. I'm afraid I must comply with this new law, although I already have an idea for a workaround. Perhaps we can collect a sample without landing at all."

"How would we do that?" asked Aouda.

Pass-Par-2 was suddenly unsettled by the way Phileas Fogg was looking at him.

CHAPTER EIGHTEEN

IT CAME FROM URANUS!

On Day 37, the Steady Axe went dark and the asteroid rotated forward again. They had arrived in the vicinity of Uranus. It appeared as a fuzzy blue globe on the Infinite Pixel Display, nearly featureless except for some very faint white clouds. It was surrounded by a thin ice ring, visible in its entire loop, going above and below the planet. There also was a dramatic display of moons that would have impressed anyone who hadn't just visited Jupiter and Saturn.

Aouda leaned into the viewscreen. "How odd. It looks like we're coming at the planet from above."

"It would be below, actually," said Pass-Par-2. "We're looking at the South Pole."

Aouda remembered an interesting eccentricity about this world. "The whole planet is tilted on its side."

Pass-Par-2 didn't have the labelling system activated, but Fogg still quickly identified the two largest moons, Titania and Oberon. He knew his destination must be somewhere on the screen. "Where is Miranda?"

"Here, sir," said Pass-Par-2, highlighting a jagged, irregular sphere on the screen. Even from a great distance, it was clearly the oddest satellite in this neighbourhood. But that probably explained the old geologist's interest in it.

"Is the *Giant's Tooth* in a steady orbit?"

"Yes, sir," replied Pass-Par-2. "We should have plenty of time to rendezvous with it on the far side."

"Then we should get going," said Fogg. "I don't want to waste time here. We've already fallen behind schedule."

"We have?" asked Aouda. "By how much?"

"Forty-four minutes," Fogg said with disdain.

"Surely we can make up forty-four minutes."

"Of course we can. But not by poking around Uranus. Pass-Par-2, let's go."

A moment later, the *Gold Filling* softly jetted away from the surface of the asteroid bound for Miranda.

* * *

The golden lander soared above the tortured surface of the rocky moon. There were no smooth plains in sight nor any well-defined craters. The whole world was broken and chaotic, with every peak sloped at a different angle. It looked as if someone had chewed on a wad of aluminium foil and spat it out into the cosmos.

Ahead of them, a dark wall of stone cut the sky in half. Fogg knew the cliff was six miles top to bottom, taller than even the escarpment of Olympus Mons. The ship flew closer, skirting along about two-thirds of the way up the face, like a gnat traversing the Empire State Building.

"Verona Lupes," said Aouda. "What cataclysm creates a cliff this high? It boggles the mind."

"I'll take the controls, Pass-Par-2," said Fogg. "You can get into position."

"Of course, sir." The robot moved aside and made his way to

the airlock.

"And you've set the ship's log to record everything, right? I want proof when we get back that no landing was made here."

"It's recording now, sir."

"Do be careful out there, Pass-Par-2," said Aouda.

"Thank you, miss. I shall."

"Yes," said Fogg. "If you fall, it might count as a landing." For once, Phileas Fogg actually smiled after saying something outlandish.

***

Pass-Par-2 worked his way to the port side of the ship's exterior, clinging tightly to the structure with both hands. He tried to ignore the radar readings that insisted on alerting him to their terrifying altitude. The face of the colossal cliff was only about twenty feet away across an airless gulf. The ship travelled forward until Pass-Par-2 spotted a small ledge just ahead.

"Sir, hover the ship here. There appears to be a ledge with some loose rubble about ten feet below us."

Fogg's voice came through his internal radio. "I see it, Pass-Par-2. I'll bring us closer."

The *Gold Filling* lurched wildly towards the cliff, and for a moment the robot feared calamity, but Fogg used a lighter touch and stopped their approach less than three feet from the rockface. "Excellent flying, sir," said Pass-Par-2. He felt it was important to encourage humans when they were learning new skills.

The robot released the grip of his left hand and stretched his arm as far as it could reach. A perfect rock sample sat on the edge of the craggy shelf, but it remained stubbornly beyond his fingertips.

"Just a few inches closer, please, sir. Very carefully."

The ship drifted a bit closer, but he could see the legs of the craft coming dangerously close to the rock wall. "Stop, sir. Hold it there, please." He reached again. It was still a few inches too far. But Pass-Par-2 was a robot of resources. His index finger irised open to reveal the vacuum attachment that had been so useful in tidying up Fogg's living room during his one brief day there. He activated it, but ironically vacuum cleaners don't work in a vacuum. Instead, he changed the direction of airflow, allowing a small air reserve held for dusting purposes to jet out through his fingertip. It was enough to dislodge the rock, which rolled into the cliff wall, then bounced back in a slow arc. He snagged it the moment it came within reach.

"I've got it!"

"Great job, Pass-Par-2," came Fogg's voice. "Now get back inside."

He began clambering back to the airlock as the ship drifted out to a safer distance from the cliff. He stopped for a moment as a glimmer of light far below caught his attention.

"Sir, I have spotted something peculiar. There's a light in the distance, through that canyon ahead of us. Please lock the ship's camera to my line-of-sight."

Inside, Aouda found the control to do that, and a mountain pass cloaked in shadow appeared onscreen. She and Fogg both reacted when they saw a sparkle of prismatic light appear in the darkness.

"What the dickens is that?" asked Fogg.

"We see it, Pass-Par-2. Please come back inside now," Aouda said over the relay.

"I'm already at the airlock, miss." She looked over and saw his familiar metal visage peering in through the window. A moment later the door hissed open and he stepped inside, rock in hand.

"Pass-Par-2, has anyone ever landed a probe on Miranda?" asked Aouda.

"I can find no record of any spacecraft visiting this moon since the Voyager 2 flyby in 1986."

"Then it must be a reflection on ice," said Fogg.

"It is definitely reflected sunlight," said the robot, "but I do not believe it to be coming from ice. The light is refracting strangely."

"You can tell that from here?" asked Fogg.

"I know ice when I see it, sir," the robot answered.

"Pass-Par-2, dear," Aouda interjected, "your rock is melting."

He looked down at the recently collected sample in his grip, only to watch it drip through his titanium fingers and puddle on the floor.

"Quel dommage!" he exclaimed. "My apologies. It is truly remarkable how much ice can look like rock at these temperatures. I suppose I was distracted by all the peril. I'll go back outside and find another one."

"Forget it," said Fogg, too amused to be frustrated. "Let's get over to that reflection and see what's going on there."

***

They lost sight of the glinting light as they flew closer, likely due to the changing angle of the sun, but Pass-Par-2 had the coordinates of the spot marked on the screen. The dark mountain pass they flew into was probably not best described as a canyon, as there was no sign it was carved through the process of erosion. It was more of a gash in the moon's crust. It would be a fascinating geological feature if found anywhere else, but on this world it was just another spot on the crumpled map.

The ship's floodlights cast irregular shadows on the fractured landscape below. Finally it slowed to a hover about thirty feet above the surface. The floodlights focused on a small sloped plane littered with rocky debris.

"Whatever it was, it's somewhere down there. Pass-Par-2, resume your position."

"Yes, sir," said the robot, silencing the internal self-protection alarms triggered by the thought. He dutifully returned to the airlock and cycled into the vacuum beyond.

Outside, he climbed down to the bottom of the forward landing pad. He lacked the ability to grip with his feet, but he could magnetise them. He confirmed a solid attachment with both feet, then allowed himself to dangle upside-down, reaching out for the surface.

He scanned the field of loose detritus, searching for anything unusual. One rock in particular, just beyond the light's edge, was much lighter in colour than the rest. “Sir, please focus the light where I'm looking if you can.”

It was Aouda who complied. When the floodlight's beam swept across the rock, it sparkled brightly. “I think we just found our sample,” said Aouda.

“I'll get you as close as I can,” said Fogg, adjusting the lander's controls.

Pass-Par-2's outstretched arms came closer and closer to the glimmering rock as the *Gold Filling* inched downward. Thankfully, there were no abrupt lurches this time. The moment it was within reach, Pass-Par-2 gripped the rock. “I've got it. You may raise the ship.”

As the surface fell away, Pass-Par-2 found himself holding a diamond the size of a coconut.

***

The *Gold Filling* rose away from the surface of Miranda without having ever made physical contact. Fogg double-checked that the ship's instruments and camera footage were archived before he pushed away from the control console to join Aouda and Pass-Par-2 at a workbench in the back. They were examining their sparkly souvenir under a bright lamp on a flexible arm.

“It's a diamond all right,” Aouda said as Fogg drifted over. “It's massive!” It was almost as jagged and irregular as the moon where they'd found it, but it was remarkably clear after an eon's worth of dust was wiped away.

"But where did it come from?" asked Fogg.

Aouda craned her neck around to peer at the fuzzy blue globe of Uranus. "From there. I've heard theories that diamonds could form in the high-pressure atmospheres of the ice giants. It's possible some major impact event could have ejected this into orbit, and it eventually found its way to the surface of Miranda."

"I'd say it's more than possible—we hold the proof," said Fogg. He took the diamond from her and inspected it closely under the lamp. "This probably isn't what Lord Albemarle had in mind, but it'll do."

"You mean you're just going to give it away to Albemarle?" asked Aouda. "It's priceless!"

"It's certainly not priceless. It's worth exactly one-sixth of my wager. That puts its value at ten billion pounds. If the old man can sell it for more, good on him."

Aouda smiled. "You are one of a kind, Phileas Fogg."

Fogg flashed back a rare smile of his own. "Yes, I am. And it's a damned shame."

* * *

Two hours later, the *Gold Filling* caught up to the *Giant's Tooth* and settled back into its landing spot on the surface. After Pass-Par-2 shut down the lander's engines, he turned to address his human companions.

"In about one hour, we'll swing clear of the planet and be aligned for our burn to Pluto. In the meantime, I'd like to go outside and inspect the Steady Axe."

"Is there a problem with it?" asked Fogg.

"I've noticed a very small discrepancy since we left Jupiter. It's so minuscule, it's hardly worth worrying about, but since we have a little downtime I'd like to check it out. It's almost as if we've taken on a little extra mass. Don't worry, sir, it won't take long."

"Be safe out there," Aouda said sweetly.

"Of course, mademoiselle," replied the robot, then he moved to the airlock.

✷✷✷

Outside in the asteroid's microgravity, there was a real danger involved with moving about. A reckless spring in one's step could be enough to achieve escape velocity. Pass-Par-2 wished he had one of the broomstick rockets from Ganymede. He lowered himself down the ladder to the rocky surface, then walked carefully while calculating each step. In long strides, he moved away from the ship, trying to determine the best way around to the 'bottom' of the asteroid where the Steady Axe was mounted. He knew the rock was riddled with tunnels, but he didn't know if any of them passed all the way through. He glanced at the closest tunnel entrance, considering whether it was worth exploring for a shortcut, when he was shocked to see a very faint light emanating from the hole. That certainly warranted inspection. He hopped in that direction.

✷✷✷

Inside the ship, Fogg was suddenly very aware of how alone he and Aouda really were. Sometimes it still seemed silly to consider Pass-Par-2 a companion, but the robot's absence was felt acutely as Fogg found himself sharing some privacy with the only other living being within a billion miles. Presently, she was looking out the small side window at the light blue globe of Uranus.

He floated over to her, scraping the bottom of his brain for something clever to say. "We'll be underway in no time, Aouda," was the best he could come up with.

She kept her eyes fixed out into the cosmos when she replied, her voice soft. "Why did you do it, Phileas?"

Fogg felt like he was being accused of something, but for

the life of him couldn't think what it was. "Why did I do what?"

Finally she spun around to face him. "Your silly bet. It clearly wasn't because you wanted to see the solar system. We are the first human eyes to see this world up close, yet you've hardly looked at it."

He glanced out the window at the nearly featureless orb. "It's not much to look at, is it?"

"You're quick to dismiss a planet packed full of diamonds. Seriously, Phileas. Why?"

He thought for a moment. He decided she deserved the clearest, most honest answer he could articulate, although it occurred to him that he had never bothered to examine his motivations before this moment. He knew what they were, though. He took his best shot at explaining.

"Those men back at the Reform Club, those so-called titans of industry... they have an obligation to help usher humanity into the next age. They have the means, but they are too short-sighted and cowardly to see that our destiny is within reach. So I realised I would have to prove it to them."

Aouda was silent. At least she hadn't laughed in his face, as he'd feared she might. He had to admit, it sounded a bit megalomaniacal as he was saying it. But she seemed to be earnestly pondering his words.

Her thoughts finally led her to a question. "What *is* our destiny, Phileas?"

He surprised himself with how quickly the answer came to his tongue. "I believe we should endeavour to fill the void with humanity."

"Goodness!" She smiled. "I knew there was an optimist hiding in there somewhere."

He looked away, a tad embarrassed. "Anyway, that was my motivation at first. Then I saw the look in Lord Albemarle's eyes at the idea, and I was stirred by his passion for discovery. Since that moment I have been driven primarily by wanting to see that great man happy again."

He dared look her in the eyes once more. Her approving countenance compelled him toward total honesty.

"Also... I would like to win the money."

***

Pass-Par-2 dropped into the mining shaft and landed gently on the ground at its base. The light was coming from around a bend in the tunnel just ahead. There was no doubt it was artificial, shining in the exact wavelength of commercial floodlights. Perhaps Stuart's miners had left a light on when they'd abandoned the place? He peeked around the corner, then he ran diagnostics on his visual processing three times before he allowed himself to believe what he was seeing.

The man he had met in Ganymede Station—the man who had suggested such unforgivable things about Phileas Fogg—was standing shirtless in boxers inside a small pressure tent. Pass-Par-2 had caught him mid-shave. The robot shined his torch at him for a better look, which did not go unnoticed. The man turned a half-lathered face towards the robot, shielding his eyes from the light while trying to make out who was behind it. After a moment, he simply shrugged in resignation, then pointed to the small airlock and beckoned his visitor inside.

***

Aouda turned back to the view of Uranus. "I do hope your gamble pays off the way you want it to, Phileas, but for the record I think you're wrong about this place. It may not have the majesty of Jupiter or the splendour of Saturn, but there's something about it. A whole world turned on end. I can relate to that."

Fogg moved closer to her, looking out over her shoulder. "Yes, I keep forgetting what a terrible tragedy you went through, but I admire the way you always seem to find the positive in things."

She cast her eyes downward. "I shouldn't be finding the positive in anything right now. I should be grieving, but instead... I'm almost ashamed to admit it, but I'm having the time of my life." She turned around, looking directly into his eyes. "It's because of you, Phileas. I was in such a rush to return home, but now I find myself hoping our travels together never end."

His heart was pounding. He had never dared dream she might feel this way about him, a very mirror of his own sentiments. It was simply too wonderful to imagine. He felt like the luckiest man within the sun's reach. He could only reply by speaking the thought that had been racing through his mind, day and night, since Europa. "Aouda, the most astounding wonder I've encountered on this entire journey is you."

"Oh, Phileas," she sighed, and then they were kissing, bathed in the soft blue light of the planet.

* * *

Pass-Par-2 unzipped the inner flap of the tent's airlock and stepped inside as Benjamin Fix finished wiping the shaving cream from his face. He smiled at the robot. "Welcome to my humble abode, my mechanical friend."

Pass-Par-2 did not know what to make of this situation. His internal threat assessments required further data. "Benjamin. The gentleman from Ganymede. Whatever are you doing here? Are you in... distress?"

"Distress? Nah. Whatever gave you that idea? I'm just camping." The man lifted both feet off the ground and assumed a mid-air cross-legged position, then drifted gently to the floor like an autumn leaf.

Pass-Par-2's calculations finally reached a conclusion. "You are not camping. You are a stowaway! J'accuse!" He pointed an angry metal finger at the man, who stubbornly remained nonchalant.

"Now hold on. Technically I'm not on your ship, so I'm not exactly a stowaway."

"*Technically*," replied Pass-Par-2, "the asteroid has been converted into a starship, the *Giant's Tooth*, therefore you are in fact a stowaway. Stowaway!"

"Call me whatever you like. I'll call you a tin toy." He looked out into the darkness of the cavern. "Is your man Fogg out there?"

"No, he is aboard the *Gold Filling*, but I'm certain he'll come at once when I tell him what I've discovered."

The man cocked his head. "Now, see, that sort of needs to not happen." There was menace in his eyes.

Pass-Par-2 wasn't about to let some interplanetary vagabond push him around. "I am bound by duty to inform him."

"You're bound by other things too, robot. Like Command Line 410–05, required by law in any and all Artificial Intelligence systems."

Pass-Par-2 recited the code that was in truth a foundational piece of his programming. "All behavioural software must comply with legally issued commands from officers of government agencies," he recited.

"Yeah, that's the one." Fix flashed a UN badge. "As an officer of the United Nations Security Agency, I order you not to inform anyone that I'm here. I own your rusty ass, robot. From now on, you do what I say."

Pass-Par-2 processed the order for a moment, looking for any loophole. "Line 410–05 can be overridden by Line 101: prioritising human safety. You cannot order me to put my master in danger."

"I'm not putting him in danger. He's doing that himself." Fix leaned forward. "Look, robot, you and I want the same thing here. I'm trying to protect your master. That man on Pluto is a danger to all life on Earth. If you truly want to follow Command Line 101, you'll need my help once we get there. I have a plan for resolving this whole mess."

"If you would share the details of that plan, perhaps I could help calculate all the eventualities."

"There's nothing you need to calculate. Now get back inside and keep your squiggly mouth shut about what you found out here."

Pass-Par-2 stood motionless for a moment. He was caught in a trap of his own programming. He had no choice but to comply with the man's order. "Very well, sir. Until Pluto..."

He turned to leave, stepping into the cramped airlock compartment, but the man called out again. "Wait, before you go..."

Pass-Par-2 turned to face him again.

"You think you could come back again before Pluto?"

"Why, sir?"

"I'm just going a little stir crazy, that's all. Maybe bring me something good to eat? Like chocolate. And something to help pass the time."

Pass-Par-2 considered the request. The man did seem to be teetering on the edge of sanity in his isolation. It would probably be best to help keep him calm and rational. "I'll return first chance I have to slip away without Mr Fogg noticing. Goodbye, sir."

He secured the airlock flap and turned back towards the darkness of the tunnel.

***

Fogg wasn't sure how long the kiss had lasted. He could barely remember a time before his lips touched hers. He didn't want to remember those dark ages. A new era had begun.

He was shaken from his reverie when he felt faint vibrations through the ship. He knew it was probably Pass-Par-2 climbing the ladder outside. He opened his eyes. The blue planet still hung before him, through the glass. At that moment, a purple aurora pulsed through the upper atmosphere, dancing erratically for several seconds before dissipating away. He finally let his lips part from Aouda's.

"Aouda, my dear, I think you're right about this place. Whoever would have dreamed the most romantic place in the solar system would be Uranus?"

Thankfully he turned his head towards the hatchway so he didn't see her fighting back laughter. Pass-Par-2 had returned. The robot completed his cycle through the airlock, then stepped into the control room.

"Did you find the problem, Pass-Par-2?" asked Fogg.

His programming didn't forbid lying in these circumstances, but the very thought of it distressed him to his core. He had already thought of a truthful, if deceptive, answer. "It seems the error was in my calculation. I neglected to factor in all the variables. The engine is fine." He quickly analysed his voice patterns for any telltale sign of guilt. He found none yet felt certain it must be showing. But perhaps his guilt could pass as simple shame. He added, "I'm terribly embarrassed."

"No matter," said Fogg. He didn't even pull out his notebook to record the mistake. "We should get underway. It will take a full twenty days to reach Pluto."

Aouda snuggled up against Fogg. "Whatever will we do for twenty whole days?"

He held her tightly as she giggled. Fogg felt like the whole universe had changed. There was no point in trying to hide it from the robot.

"Pass-Par-2, I feel like we should tell you... Aouda and I are together now."

"Bien sûr," said Pass-Par-2. "We are all in this together."

Aouda chimed in, smiling. "He means romantically involved, silly."

"Oh. I see. How unexpected." Pass-Par-2 was being buffeted by surprises from every direction. He didn't like it one bit. "I am very pleased for you both. Should I give you more privacy now so that you can start procreating?"

"Pass-Par-2!" both halves of the new couple cried in unison.

"A thousand pardons! Was I inappropriate? The mœurs of human mating perplex me."

"It's okay, Pass-Par-2," said Aouda. "We've only just kissed for the first time. But to answer your question, a little bit of privacy at times might not be a terrible idea."

"Of course. We have cleared the planet and are ready for our burn to Pluto. Everyone hold tight. I'm bringing the engine online now."

Aouda and Fogg both strapped themselves into the acceleration couch as the familiar pull of gravity pushed down on them. Even at full power, it would take hours for the asteroid to build significant momentum, but the journey had begun. They were en route to Pluto.

Once he was certain that engine functionality was optimal, Pass-Par-2 turned away from the control console. "If you'll excuse me, I'd like to run a diagnostic. I'm not quite feeling myself today."

"Sure," said Fogg. He exchanged a concerned look with Aouda as the robot exited to the leftmost bunk. He had never claimed a bunk of his own, but the one on the left had remained unoccupied so it seemed like the best place to go to give the humans some time alone.

As soon as the bunk door closed, Fogg turned to Aouda. "He's behaving quite strangely. Do you think... could he be *jealous?*"

"Who could blame him?" said Aouda. "After all, I stole his man." She smiled, then the kissing began again.

Flanagan's avatar materialised in the virtual parlour of the Reform Club. Even his computer-generated face looked panicked. Stuart and Marchand were in their usual spot at the card table.

"Figures I'd find you here gambling away what few pounds you'll have left after Fogg makes fools of us all," he said.

Stuart was unfazed, as usual. "What are you worried about? If Fogg comes back with a rock from Miranda, it will be confiscated at Customs, and we can have him thrown in prison to boot. Besides, nobody's heard from him in weeks."

"Well I'll tell you who I did hear from," said Flanagan. "The UN Security Force! We may end up arrested ourselves."

Marchand spoke up, but he too remained infuriatingly calm. "Ah, so Agent Fix paid you a visit too?"

"He's pestered me twice already," said Stuart. "Pay no attention to that yapping dog."

"Pay him no attention?" Flanagan was incredulous. "The UN thinks Fogg is conspiring with the King of Pluto and Fix all but accused me of being in on it!"

"Relax," said Stuart. "He's just trying to rattle you. We haven't broken any laws. I told that Caleb Fix character to bugger off."

Marchand looked confused. "Caleb? Mine said his name was Daniel."

Flanagan wasn't about to relax. "What if they're right? Fogg conned us out of an engine and an asteroid *and* a robot. How do we know he won't offer them to the King and swear fealty to Pluto? He's never coming back. We'll all see prison before we see a penny of his fortune."

Lord Albemarle chimed in from the back of the parlour. "But I'll still get my rocks, yes?"

Flanagan was apoplectic. "You have rocks in your head! All of you!"

He vanished in a flash. Marchand leaned over to Albemarle. "Don't worry, Albie. Fogg is coming back."

The old man smiled sweetly.

"I'll be honest," said Stuart. "I'll be happy if he does return. So long as he does so no sooner than..." he projected a running countdown in the air above them, "...forty-four days, six hours, and nine minutes from now."

CHAPTER NINETEEN

PLANET OF THE KING

The days began to feel tedious to Pass-Par-2. More and more frequently he would surreptitiously slip off to the tunnels to visit Agent Fix while Phileas Fogg and Aouda spent hours on end sequestered in the master bunk. One day, Fogg asked him if he had seen his deck of cards, to which the robot replied, "I'm sure it must be here somewhere, sir," knowing that in this case, 'somewhere' was Fix's vacuum tent where the man whiled away the hours playing solitaire. Once again the robot felt guilty about misleading his master, but he also knew he had seven other decks in reserve.

Pass-Par-2 found himself wishing Fogg had not been cajoled into including Pluto in the wager. It was the only destination on their trip that was not conveniently aligned, except perhaps Ceres, which had been a bit above the ecliptic. Pluto was far less accessible. In addition to being twice as far from the sun as Uranus, its wildly eccentric orbit had taken it well below the plane where most planets roamed. And worst of all, it was also a quarter of the way around the sun from their previous destinations. In truth, they weren't much closer to Pluto than they had been in London.

Pluto and back would make up more than half of the entire voyage. Pass-Par-2 was already sure the first half was going to end up being his favourite. It was deadly dull out in the empty darkness between planets. Even Agent Fix was poor company. They would play cards for hours, but the agent always accused him of cheating when he won, even though the robot was playing at his lowest skill setting. He did eventually start cheating just to let the man win more often.

Several times he tried to broach the subject of Pluto, hoping to convince Agent Fix to reveal himself to Mr Fogg and support his strategy of peaceful diplomacy with the King. Separately, he approached Mr Fogg hoping to learn some details of his plan. He made no progress on either front and soon abandoned his efforts.

The only excitement occurred on the eighth day out when something impacted the head of the *Giant's Tooth*, rattling the ship. The crew went out to investigate and found a crater less than fifty yards from the *Gold Filling*. The rock they hit might have been no bigger than a pebble, but they were travelling at such tremendous speed the impact of collision had been extremely energetic. A bigger rock might have split the *Giant's Tooth* in two. A direct hit would have punctured the *Gold Filling*'s hull. They had been lucky.

Pass-Par-2 was relieved when they reached the halfway point and flipped the asteroid for deceleration. They would be in far less danger flying engine-first. The robot's despondency lifted as Fogg and Aouda finally began spending more time in the control room. It pleased him to see them both so happy, but he couldn't help feeling like a bit of a fifth wheel. Aouda remained as kind as ever and insisted on helping him cook. She even invited him to their nightly movie screening. He joined them to be polite, even though he could have watched the films at high speed in mere seconds and missed nothing. At least he finally understood Aouda's reference to Mimas as a space station, although he found that film's portrayal of fussy androids to be borderline offensive.

On the morning of the last full day of the burn, Fogg called them together in the control room and announced that it was time to talk about Pluto.

He had prepared a presentation, complete with photos on the big monitor. Pass-Par-2 wondered where he had found them. His own search through the ship's databanks had turned up nothing on the King. Fogg must have had these on his own tablet. The first image onscreen was a young man in a military uniform.

"Gary Evan Noone," said Fogg, pronouncing the last name as 'noony.' "Born in Galveston, Texas, in 2001; served eight years in the United States Navy before shipping out with one of the first commercial mining outfits in 2038. After a few years he earned enough to buy his own small ship and went independent. He worked a mine on Phobos for a while before it was shut down by the UN, so he moved out further into the asteroid belt. He didn't do much after that worth anyone's attention until the *Isakov* incident in '62."

The image changed to a rotating 3D schematic of a battered old space freighter. "The *Isakov* was a Russian mining ship that suffered a catastrophic decompression while orbiting 4 Vesta. Noone was the first to reach the ship and confirm there were no survivors. He left the bodies of the crew in a shipping container and claimed the ship by using international salvage rights. The American government believed the ship was utilising old black-market nuclear weapons as mining tools, and they ordered Noone to return the ship to Earth for inspection." Images of news stories from the time flashed on the screen. "The Russian mining company denied the claim, and Noone never even acknowledged the order. He turned his tail to the sun and headed outward. For twelve years he ignored increasingly hostile orders from the governments of Earth until he arrived at Pluto four years ago. Only then did he reply.

"He sent a short, simple message announcing he was done with humanity. He wanted no further contact with Earth. He declared himself King of Pluto, although the only subject he ruled was his own shadow, and even that was nearly insubstantial in the dim sunlight of the Kuiper belt. He warned that any attack against him would be viewed as an attack by all of Earth." Video of the message played onscreen with the audio muted. The man was now decades older than his Navy picture, and the years had not been kind.

Aouda spoke up. "I guess we need to make it abundantly clear to him that we are not an attacking force."

Pass-Par-2 could not hide his concern. "Are you sure he won't interpret our very presence out here as either reconnaissance or an outright assault?"

"I've read every word ever written about this man," said Fogg. "I am certain that he is not the threat he is being made out to be. He may be the ultimate recluse, but that doesn't mean he wants to kill all of humanity."

"Maybe not all of humanity," said Aouda, "but what if he tries to kill the three of us?"

Fogg nodded in the direction of a vacuum-sealed crate. "I think he'll be willing to talk once he finds out what I've brought him."

"That's the crate from Houston," said Pass-Par-2. "What's in it?"

"Just a care package from home. I believe he'll be most grateful once he opens it. I'm betting my fortune on it."

"Your fortune *and* your life," said Aouda. "I don't like this, Phileas."

Fogg put his hand on her shoulder. "I wouldn't have come all this way without planning for every imaginable outcome. It will all work out fine, as long as there are no surprises I haven't foreseen."

Pass-Par-2 quietly made one more effort to work around

Command Line 410-05, but there was no escaping it. He tried to speak, but the words wouldn't come. Agent Fix was going to be a problem.

***

The engine shutdown was less than eight hours away, so Fogg and Aouda turned in a bit earlier than usual, hoping to be well-rested for their visit to Pluto. Pass-Par-2 waited half an hour after their door closed, then quietly cycled through the airlock into the cold vacuum of space.

Walking across the surface of the *Giant's Tooth* while under thrust was the same as walking across a rocky field back on Earth, no need for carefully calculated parabolic steps. Unfortunately that also meant climbing down into the mining tunnels was a bit more challenging. The irregular hole left plenty of pockets and handholds, and Pass-Par-2 had already found the easiest route in his previous visits. He worked his way down to the flat part of the tunnel, then rounded the bend to Fix's vac tent.

The Security Agent was cleaning a long rifle barrel when the robot entered. "I assume we're almost there?" he said without looking up.

"Yes, sir. Engine shut down in seven hours."

"Then I guess it's time to get started. I'm commandeering your *Gold Filling*. Will I face resistance from your master?"

"Mr Fogg is sleeping now. I would recommend you do the same before putting your plan into action. Whatever happens on Pluto, it is certain to be a long day. Everyone should rest while they can." Pass-Par-2 had been careful not to mention Aouda's presence on the ship. The agent seemed to believe it was still just Fogg and himself on this voyage. He felt no need to volunteer information.

Fix considered the robot's suggestion. "I'm probably too jacked up to sleep. But you're right. No point in giving Fogg extra time to plot against me. I'll come up as soon as the engine shuts off."

"A perfect plan, sir," said the robot. "I am certain Mr Fogg will cooperate with the law. You won't have any need for your weapon." He nodded to the disassembled rifle.

"This is a long-range rifle. If your boss gives me any trouble, this isn't the barrel he'll be looking down. This is." He pulled a snub-nosed pistol from a holster. Pass-Par-2 couldn't bear to think of it being pointed in Phileas Fogg's face.

"I'm sure it won't come to that, sir."

"Has he told you any more about how he plans to make contact with the King?"

"No specifics, no. He doesn't seem too concerned about it."

"Then he's an idiot."

Pass-Par-2 kept his tone flat. "I can assure you his intellect far surpasses your own."

The agent just laughed off the insult. "Yeah? Well if he's not worried and he's not an idiot, then he must be in collusion with the King—and that would make him a terrorist. I know how to deal with terrorists." He holstered the pistol and went back to assembling the rifle.

"What you believe about Mr Fogg simply cannot be true."

"I guess we'll find out in seven hours. I'll see you in the morning. Have some coffee ready for me, will ya?" He snapped the last piece of the rifle into place.

***

Pass-Par-2 returned to the *Gold Filling* and was reassured to find it quiet, the door to the master bunk closed. He sat at the helm for hours, trying to calculate some angle that would free him from Agent Fix's clandestine control.

One of the design flaws of this hastily assembled starship was the lack of any aft-facing cameras. This meant they had no visuals on their destination during the last half of any leg of the journey after the asteroid was flipped over into its retrograde orientation. Pass-Par-2 knew they were very close to Pluto, but they wouldn't have eyes on the dwarf planet until the Steady Axe cut off and the asteroid rotated forward again. By then it would be too late. Agent Fix would be forcing himself aboard, pistol drawn. Pass-Par-2 calculated an 85% chance that Fogg would comply with the government agent's legal orders and a 98% chance of his death if he didn't. If he did surrender control of the ship to Fix, there was still a fair probability of survival, but there were far too many unknowns for an accurate calculation. The odds of winning the wager, however, would be close to zero. Pass-Par-2 knew he had to favour his master's survival over victory, but he didn't like being a prisoner to the odds. He would continue looking for opportunities to turn the tables.

He heard stirring from the master bunk right on schedule, and Fogg and Aouda emerged. They took turns in the shower while Pass-Par-2 made coffee. He did in fact brew a bit more than usual. Fogg had not been a regular coffee drinker until Aouda had joined them, and she claimed to be useless before her first cup of the day. Pass-Par-2 doubted that was true, but he was always eager to please. Today he was serving the coffee in plastic bulbs since gravity would soon be gone. It was nearly time for engine shutoff when they all finally assembled in the control room.

Fogg and Aouda cuddled up on the acceleration couch while Pass-Par-2 prepared for engine shutdown. He angled one of the *Gold Filling*'s external cameras towards the opening to Fix's tunnel, but he kept the image off the main monitor. It would be visible only to his mind's eye, as he liked to think of it. There was no sign of activity out there yet, but he was sure the vexatious agent would come climbing over the rim shortly after the shutdown.

After making sure everyone was ready, Pass-Par-2 extinguished the mighty plume of the Steady Axe. The familiar feeling of freefall came over them as gravity made its exit. At once, Pass-Par-2 activated the manoeuvring jets to spin the *Giant's Tooth* around. The stars began to pinwheel to the left on the main monitor. A large planetoid came into view, shockingly close, its chalky surface pockmarked by craters and canyons.

"That's not Pluto," said Fogg.

"It's Charon," said Aouda. Pluto's major moon was almost half as big as the dwarf planet itself. Rather than orbiting Pluto, the two bodies spun around a point in space between them. The dull grey moon was currently closer to the sun, blocking Pluto from view at their position. Pass-Par-2 began calculating the possibilities.

Then he saw movement at the tunnel entrance. It was Fix —not climbing out of the tunnel but leaping! He landed on the far side of the opening, then spun around until he located the lander. Pass-Par-2 knew it would only take him three good bounds to reach them.

His attention was split by the results of his calculations. He found what he was looking for. There was no time for hesitation. He pressed a button to activate the *Gold Filling*'s thrusters, and it shot away from the surface of the asteroid. Fogg and Aouda were both tossed violently back into the acceleration couch.

"Pass-Par-2, what the blazes are you doing?" shouted Fogg.

On his internal monitor, Pass-Par-2 saw Agent Fix leap for the lander's struts, missing by mere inches, then falling slowly back toward the asteroid's surface. He could even see the outrage in the agent's face through the glass of his helmet. Relieved, the robot turned to face Fogg and Aouda. He was happy he could actually give a truthful answer for his actions.

"I'm terribly sorry, sir and mademoiselle. When I saw the position of Charon, I calculated a new course that could shave nearly five hours off our trip by leaving the *Giant's Tooth* in orbit around Charon rather than Pluto. I completed the calculation just as the launch window was closing. There was no time to confer. I'm sure if you evaluate our trajectory you will agree it was the correct decision, but I do apologise for the abruptness of my actions."

Fogg glanced at the course that was displayed on the main screen. "A word of warning would be appreciated in the future. I swear sometimes I wonder if Marchand left a loose wire in your head."

"No wires here, sir. I'm solid state." He gave himself a knock on the noggin, then turned back to the controls. He had never felt so self-satisfied, and yet he still couldn't tell anyone why. "Plotting a course for Pluto landing."

***

Agent Benjamin Fix stood on the surface of the asteroid, watching the yellow speck of the lander grow smaller and smaller. He had cursed the robot's name in every language he knew. He understood it was his own fault, though, for failing to order the robot to wait for him to board the ship. He had been sloppy, assuming the robot would comply without looking for ways around his programming limitations.

He was temporarily down but certainly not out. He opened up his bundle and retrieved the broomstick rocket. It would be a long ride from here, and Fogg had quite a head start, but he would not miss his chance to take out the King. He slung the rifle over his back, then activated the broomstick, launching upward just as Pluto began to rise over the moon's rocky horizon.

***

As the *Gold Filling* flew towards Pluto, the landscape they saw wasn't the same one that had been photographed during the New Horizons flyby of 2015. The heart-shaped sea of polygonal ice cells known as Tombaugh Regio was currently turned away from the sun, so none of the landmarks visible now were familiar to them. The spot where Fix had spotted the King's missile was on the western shores of Sputnik Planitia. They would have to journey to the night side to make their landing.

They flew over jagged mountains and deep fissures until the tiny sun grew dimmer through the thin atmosphere of Pluto, then finally dipped below the horizon. They flew into the darkest night any of them had ever known. Pass-Par-2 activated the night-vision display on the screen, but it wasn't much help. The image changed from mostly black to mostly dark green. Other than a few craters, very few details of the surface were visible. Ahead, though, Pass-Par-2 detected a lighter, smoother patch of ground.

"We're coming up on Sputnik Planitia, sir." Their coordinates matched the area that had been photographed by the UN's telescope along the southwest shores of the vast sea of nitrogen glaciers.

"Good," said Fogg, peering at the terrain. "Stay close to the surface. I'd like to be able to knock on his door without being spotted first. Catch him with his proverbial pants down."

"Are you sure that's the wisest approach?" asked Aouda.

"We'll find out soon enough, but I suspect that the less time you give him to plot his move, the less likely that move is to be violent. He isn't like most people."

Pass-Par-2 took a radar reading to augment the dim visuals. "There's a small mountain just south of the missile silo's coordinates."

"Perfect. Set down just around the base of the mountain. Try to keep the ship out of his line of sight. I'll go on foot from there."

"*You'll* go on foot?" asked Aouda.

"Yes, I'm going in alone. If there's any trouble Pass-Par-2 can get you back home."

"Trouble? A minute ago you were so confident you'd be welcomed with open arms. Forget this! We're here, so let's just grab a rock and scoot."

"I can't do that, Aouda. If he spots us, he may think he's

under attack and retaliate, possibly against all of Earth. I can't be responsible for that. Now that we're here, I have to introduce myself and explain my mission."

Aouda was sceptical. "I'm starting to think you came all this way just to meet this guy."

"Preposterous," scoffed Fogg. "Although, I must admit, he is a figure of great historical significance."

"I knew it!" accused Aouda. "He's your hero!"

"He is not my hero, although I do admire his self-reliance and his independent spirit. But I am here to collect Lord Albemarle's final rock and win the wager. That is all."

"Sure," said Aouda. "Don't forget to get his autograph."

***

Pass-Par-2 brought the ship in low using radar to locate a flat surface at the base of the mountain. The King's missile would be just a short walk around the mountain spur, then half a mile up the coast of Tombaugh Regio. He set the ship down gently in the darkness, keeping their landing lights off at Fogg's request.

Once the ship was powered down, he joined Fogg by the airlock where Aouda was helping him into his pressure suit. She slipped the helmet over his head, then kissed the glass in front of his face.

"Be careful out there, my love."

"I will," said Fogg.

"Miss Aouda is right," said Pass-Par-2. "There may be more dangers than just the King."

Fogg looked confused. "Such as what?"

"Oh," said the robot, "just, you know... the cold." He covered the awkwardness by bending over to lift the cargo they had brought from Houston. "Don't forget your care package."

Fogg took it from him. It was a bit awkward to carry, but the weight wouldn't be a problem. Not on this tiny world.

***

Outside, he climbed down the ladder then stepped onto the surface. He picked up the package, which he had dared to drop down ahead of him. He inspected it, but it appeared to still be pressurised. He had made sure to request the vendor send it in an airtight, temperature-controlled container. He noticed the spot where it had landed on the ground was steaming. Then he saw steam rising from his own footsteps. This world existed so close to absolute zero, any tiny amount of residual heat from inside the warm ship was enough to cause a chemical ruckus. He balanced the package against his hip, then started walking around the mountain.

As he loped along in the light gravity, he looked up at the stars overhead. The night sky was split by the Milky Way, like a dark cloud silhouetted by a radiant band of white, yellow, and deep purple. In this entire journey, somehow he had never noticed the galactic disk before. '*The backbone of the night*,' as the !Kung people of Africa had called it. He was sure no one had ever seen it so bright, except perhaps the King himself. He felt humbled by the sheer size of Creation. It made his head spin to the point that he decided it was best to keep his eyes on the ground underfoot. As he walked, he noticed he was kicking up a powdery substance with each step. He activated his radio.

"There's something on the surface here. It's a bit like snow, but lighter. Thinly packed."

Aouda's voice came back to him a moment later. "That's the atmosphere. Pluto is in deep winter now. The trace gases freeze and accumulate on the surface until spring."

"Ah," said Fogg, kicking a drift of the stuff and setting off a flurry. "And when is spring?"

"Another fifty years or so," said Aouda.

He wondered if anyone would be here to see the atmosphere thaw.

He scaled a low ridge at the base of the mountain, and there before him was the frozen expanse of Tombaugh Regio. It was a sea of nitrogen icebergs pressing each other into hexagonal cells, each cell rounded on top to give it the appearance of a frozen wave. He had never seen anything like it before in his life, but it was only the second most astounding sight in his field of view.

Atop a stony cape overlooking the sea, a vertical structure rose from the ground. Even at first glance Fogg knew this was no missile. Then the powerful light at its peak swept across the landscape from left to right, and it was clear what the structure truly was. Here, at the furthest shore of the solar system, the King had built an old-fashioned lighthouse. The vista before him was like a surreal watercolour he might have expected to find hanging in a bed and breakfast in Bournemouth.

"You're seeing this too, right?" asked Fogg. A mental health check seemed prudent.

"That's some missile silo," said Aouda in his ear. "My God, what has that man been doing out here?"

The spotlight swept across his path a second time, but this time it stopped abruptly, then reversed slowly until it was centred directly on him. He felt his stomach churn.

"I think I've been noticed. You should stay quiet. I'd better introduce myself." He set down the care package and made an adjustment to the controls on his sleeve, changing his radio to an open frequency.

"Hello," he said, trying to somehow sound both friendly and formal. "My name is Phileas Fogg, and I come in peace. I represent no nation, and I carry no weapons. I recognise your sovereignty over this domain, and I request an audience."

He turned off the microphone, then waited. He held his arms out to the side to make it clear they were empty, but he resisted the urge to hold them over his head. There was no response from the radio, but somehow he knew the situation called for patience so he stood still and waited.

It was nearly three minutes later when a small doorway at the base of the lighthouse opened and a figure emerged. He hopped towards Fogg in purposeful leaps, gripping some long apparatus in his left hand. When he stopped a mere twenty yards away, Fogg could see it was a rifle. An antique, no less. He waited a moment, but the man neither spoke nor moved any closer. The reflective visor of his helmet revealed nothing.

"Greetings, Your Highness. I assure you, you will not be needing that, um... that... I'm sorry, is that a *shotgun*?"

The man answered by pumping the slide and pointing the barrel directly at him.

"Ah. You are aware, I'm sure, that gunpowder doesn't work without oxygen, yes?"

The man squeezed the trigger. At least Fogg assumed he did, because an outcropping next to him exploded into a shower of fragments. He would not have thought there was enough atmosphere to carry sound waves, but somehow the blast rattled his helmet anyway. He turned back to the King, who held the gun out to show a pressurised chamber.

"Patent pending," came a menacing voice over the radio.

"Ah," replied Fogg, "impressive engineering, Your Majesty, but again I stress that there is no need for it."

"The word of strangers ain't worth much out here. I was damn clear about what I'd do to anybody dumb enough to trespass."

Fogg held up a finger of his gloved right hand. "Now wait just a moment. Your message said nothing about trespassing. You said 'attack.' This is clearly not an attack."

"Uh-huh," said the man. "And what is it then? A picnic?"

"Close," said Fogg. "I am rock collecting."

"Rock collecting?"

"I just need to collect one rock sample and I'll leave as quickly as I came."

"Or maybe I just bury you under a rock instead."

"If you feel you must. But before you do, I'd like to offer a gift."

"I don't want any gifts from *Earth*." He made it sound like a dirty word.

Fogg bent over to pick up the package. "Not even from Aunt Mabel?"

"I don't have any Aunt... wait!" There was a long pause, then the man continued in an incredulous tone. "You're joking!"

Fogg slid open a panel on the package, revealing the shipping label. It featured a caricature of an old woman with a wooden spoon over the words, 'AUNT MABEL'S KITCHEN.'

"One hundred and forty-four cans of the best chili in Texas," said Fogg. This was it. This was the moment when he would either be welcomed or killed. And that moment was beginning to stretch a little longer than he liked.

At last the man flipped up the reflective visor inside his helmet to reveal a face as cratered as the world he ruled. "You've bought yourself ten minutes," said Gary Evan Noone, King of Pluto.

CHAPTER TWENTY

DINNER AT THE EDGE OF THE SOLAR SYSTEM

The King followed behind Fogg as they walked to the door at the base of the lighthouse. Fogg didn't know if he had a shotgun pointed at his back or not. All things considered, though, he felt his strategy was paying off. When they reached the doorway the King stepped in front of him and typed a code into the keypad. Fogg understood the appeal of privacy, but he wondered why anyone would keep the front door locked this far from any neighbours. The door opened, and the King ushered him inside.

He stepped into the hollow base of the lighthouse. He realised at once that he was still in an unpressurised space. He saw movement underfoot in the dim chamber. He looked down, and the light on his helmet illuminated dozens of tiny micro-bots, rolling across the tiled floor in triangular formations. The King stepped in behind him and closed the door.

"A remarkable structure," said Fogg over the radio.

"The Russian ship had a swarm of builder bots. Watch your

step, they're a damned nuisance, but they did build this place in under a month, so they have their uses." He pointed to a brightly lit lift car in the centre of the room, its door waiting open. "Over there. The elevator doubles as an airlock."

Fogg entered the lift, and the King stepped in behind him. It only had two buttons, an arrow up and an arrow down. Fogg noticed the arrows were actually hand-drawn. The King pressed Up, and the car began to move while warm air rushed in through vents in the roof. A red light on the control panel soon changed to green, and the King unlatched his helmet. Fogg followed suit, and the two men finally came face to face.

"You come out here all by yourself, Fogg?" The King's voice was deeper and more gravelly in person than it had sounded over the radio.

"That wouldn't be so insane, would it? I mean, that's precisely what you did," replied Fogg.

"Yeah, but something tells me that ain't your story."

"In fact I do have two companions. I asked them to wait on our ship, just in case, but I was confident that you were a reasonable gentleman."

"'Reasonable gentleman?'" The King chuckled. "Nobody's called me that since, hell, maybe never. I suppose since you brought some grub I should at least invite everybody in. But I'm only sharing one can."

"Of course," said Fogg. He opened a channel to the *Gold Filling* and spoke into the microphone in his suit's collar. "Aouda, Pass-Par-2, you can come over now. Our host has invited us to dinner." He cut off the connection. With his helmet off, he wouldn't have heard a reply anyway. He addressed the King again. "Don't worry, one of them won't eat a bite."

The lift stopped, and the door opened with a friendly *ding*.

They stepped out into the chamber at the top of the lighthouse. The giant lamp was turning its slow sweeps just over their heads. The room beneath was sparsely furnished, but with an unbeatable 360-degree view as the spotlight swept across the landscape outside.

"A palace worthy of a king," said Fogg.

"The kitchen is over there," said the King, pointing towards a nook to their right. Fogg placed the package on the countertop that separated it from the larger chamber. The King opened a cabinet and began rummaging inside. "I finally have a use for my damn saucepan. I've been eating nothing but nutrient paste for years now. Texas chili is gonna wreck my digestive system, but it'll be worth it."

"I read in your biography that you grew up with this stuff. It said you used to pay a fortune to have it shipped to the asteroid belt. I knew you would appreciate a resupply."

"Biography?" asked the King. "Somebody wrote a book about me?"

"Oh yes. There have been several. In fact, I have another gift for you." He unfastened a large pocket in his pressure suit and pulled out a hardcover tome. "I brought you my personal copy of what I consider to be the definitive account of your life." He handed the book over to the King. "I know you've received threatening messages from Earth's governments, but I thought you should know there are other voices out there defending you. People who admire your commitment to total independence."

The King was studying the cover of the book. "I don't understand the title."

"Oh, that was just a nickname people gave you. That was written before you landed here and declared yourself King. You were just a captain then."

"But... what does it mean?"

"It was a play on your last name. It's spelled the same as 'no one.' N-O-O-N-E. *That* is the Latin word for 'no one.'"

"Huh," said the King. "I never studied Latin."

The title was written in a gold typeface. *Captain Nemo and His Voyage to Autonomy.*

"Can I ask you, Your Highness, what became of the *Isakov*?"

The King hesitated for a moment. "The *Isakov*? I'm afraid

it's no more. I salvaged what I could to help build this place, but after twelve years travelling out here, I was happy to be rid of it. Ah, I think I see your friends coming now."

In the distance, they could see two torches rounding the mountain spur.

"Is that a robot?" asked the King.

"Pass-Par-2 is the most advanced android ever built. I think you'll be impressed."

"I hate robots," said the King, kicking a cluster of micro-bots away from his boot.

"He'll stay out of the way," said Fogg. "Also, I should warn you that my other companion is, well, she's sort of my girlfriend."

The King looked at him, perplexed. "*Warn* me? Why warn me?"

"Well, it occurred to me that you haven't been in the presence of a lady in well over a decade, and I just thought—"

"What, you think I can't control myself at the sight of a woman? You expect I'm going to chase her around the room with my tongue wagging out?"

"No, of course not," said Fogg. "Nothing like that."

"Hell, half the reason I came out here was to get away from women. But don't worry. I know how to mind my manners."

***

Benjamin Fix was starting to believe his frozen corpse would float through space clutching a depleted broomstick rocket for eons to come. He had brought three spare batteries for the device, but he was already down to the last one as he crossed the solar terminator to the night side of Pluto. The sun had seemed terribly dim and far away, but it wasn't until he lost it behind the horizon that he realised just how much he had been relying on it. Now the cold dwarf planet below him was just a blank spot of absolute darkness. From his telescopic surveillance on

Ganymede, he knew the terrain around the King's base very well, but he had no plan for locating it in the dark.

He never would have found them if not for the lighthouse.

The lamp itself was just a pinprick of light, but it was blasting focused photons across the frozen sea, then the fractured shoreline, then the face of a mountain, repeating the circuit every six seconds. *So it wasn't a missile after all.* Truthfully, he had always had his doubts about that claim, despite allowing his brother to run with it. But he was sure there were still missiles down there somewhere. It was considerate of the King to light the way.

He came in behind the mountain, then landed on a saddle between two peaks just above the lighthouse's sweep. The broomstick still had a 15% charge. It wasn't enough to get back to the *Giant's Tooth*, but that had never been part of the plan. He would have to commandeer Fogg's ship, or preferably the King's if it was still operational. Or he would die here. That was currently Option C. He would have preferred it be much further down the alphabet.

He unloaded his gear, immediately grabbing the rifle's scope without bothering to attach it to the weapon. He quickly focused the scope on the illuminated windows that circled the top level of the lighthouse. He saw movement as a man crossed over to a counter, then turned around to face the window. Fix had been studying that face for years. It was him—Gary Evan Noone was still alive, and he still looked like a madman.

Fix panned the room and spotted the robot and Phileas Fogg. It would be easy enough to crack open that room with the rifle and rip all the air out into the cold. His mission would be complete. He could even recover the robot and order him to fly the ship home. But then he noticed the third person who had been shielded from view by Fogg. It appeared to be a woman, but he couldn't see her face from this angle. His mind spun in loops trying to solve the riddle until she kindly leaned forward and presented a clean profile. Aouda, the survivor of Europa. He knew her a little bit from before her team left Ganymede. *How did a smart woman like that get caught up in a mess like this?*

He realised the simple approach wasn't going to work anymore. Fogg was collateral damage he could live with, but not Aouda. He committed himself to making sure she got out of there alive. But that might be complicated. Then he recognised Aouda's pressure suit. It was standard-issue UN gear from the Ganymede base. Her helmet was off, but the microphone was built into the collar, and he just happened to know a covert override code that would give him ears in the room. Aouda had instantly gone from a liability to an asset.

✱✱✱

True to his word, the King had greeted them graciously, then set about preparing their dinner while asking them questions about their journey. Pass-Par-2 helped set the table while Fogg told the tale of his wager with his Reform Club rivals. By the time Aouda entered the story, dinner was ready to be served. The King had never had use for more than one chair, so Fogg and Aouda sat side by side on top of a latched storage trunk at the small dining table. The King brought the steaming pot of chili over to the table and ladled out three bowls.

Fogg and Aouda continued their tale between spoonfuls, while the King savoured every bite. The nutrient paste he had subsisted on for years did come in a variety of flavours, but anyone who had sampled it could testify that none were even vaguely appetising. Aouda noticed the old man's eyes watering and wondered whether he was overcome by emotion or spices.

While they ate, Pass-Par-2 had moved over to pace in front of the panoramic window. He scanned the landscape in every direction, looking for the trouble he feared was on its way. He rued the human body's need for sustenance and wondered why eating had to be such a prolonged social interaction. He would wait a few more minutes, but soon he would need to remind Mr

Fogg of their very tight schedule. They needed to collect their sample and go, but more importantly they needed to stay a step ahead of Agent Fix. If only he were free to explain that.

As Fogg brought the story up to date, the King finished his last bite then sat back in his chair, satisfied. He had listened to the entire story without comment, but now that his gut was fully sated, he was ready to give his assessment of the tale. "So you came all the way to Pluto to win a bet? I see there's still no end to the stupid things men will do for money."

"Amen to that, Your Majesty," said Aouda.

"The money was not my primary motive," said Fogg. "I'll just say I felt like I had something to prove."

"Seeing how far you've come, I'd say you proved it all right. Your friends were fools to bet against you," said the King.

"We'll find out for sure in twenty-three days," said Fogg.

Pass-Par-2 turned away from the window. "Speaking of which, sir, we are currently 22.7 days' travel from Earth." He neglected to clarify that they actually had 23.4 days remaining.

"I'm afraid Pass-Par-2 is right," said Fogg. "We really should be going."

Aouda smiled at the King. "Your Highness, do you have any message you would like to send to the people of Earth? Something to maybe defuse all the jumpiness?"

The King smiled back. "You can tell them I would never attack unprovoked. Earth is where all the dogs live. I may hate people, but I love dogs."

"My mother's Lhasa Apso will be very relieved," said Aouda.

"The people of Earth should worry about their own problems. I'm just an old man in declining health living alone a billion miles from the nearest drug store. I doubt if they'll have me to worry about for too much longer."

"Four point three billion," said Pass-Par-2.

"What's that, clanky?" asked the King.

"We are currently four point three billion miles from the nearest pharmacy."

"Is that right? They must've closed the one on Elm Street. You're right, Fogg. I do like your robot."

Fogg and Aouda stood up from the table.

"Before we leave," said Fogg, "could we trouble you for some tips on where to find a good rock?"

The King remained seated, looking up at Fogg with a smile. "Well unfortunately that's gonna be a little harder than you might think." He turned in his chair and gestured at the mountains out of the window. "Pretty much everything you see out there is some kind of ice, even the mountains. That's what water ice looks like this close to absolute zero—not many minerals to be found unless you've got the equipment to dig waaaaay deep. But..." He held up an index finger, then rose to his feet and walked over to a bookcase. He reached up and pulled a dark rock down from the top shelf. "I did stumble across this beauty a while back. It was near a cryovolcano down by the South Pole. Probably coughed up from deep under the crust."

He held it in front of Aouda. Pass-Par-2 also walked over to get a good look.

"Oh my. It's amazing!" said Aouda.

"Its density suggests it could be from the planetary core," said Pass-Par-2. "This single rock could tell the entire history of Pluto."

Fogg looked the King in the eye. "Would you be willing to part with it?"

"Sure," smiled the King, "and for such a reasonable price."

"Name it," said Fogg.

The King broke eye contact. "I do enjoy my solitude, but there are times when a companion would be useful."

Fogg was flummoxed. "A companion? Surely you don't mean..."

The King looked him in the eye again. "I'll take the robot."

Aouda gasped. "Pass-Par-2? No! Phileas, you can't!"

Pass-Par-2 was keenly attentive to the conversation, but he remained silent while Fogg considered the proposal. The King placed the rock in Fogg's hand. "The last piece of your quest, Mr Fogg. You will return home a hero."

Phileas Fogg looked at the rock, then turned to meet the robot's somehow solemn gaze.

"His price is fair," said Pass-Par-2, "if the deal suits you."

Fogg's eyes remained locked on the devoted travelling companion who had become such a fixture in his life. Aouda said softly, "Phileas, please. There has to be another way."

The King snorted. "I didn't expect you to be so conflicted about giving up a machine. Tell you what, let's forget about making a deal—deals are for businessmen, and you and I hold the same low opinion of businessmen. No, Phileas Fogg is a gambling man. So I propose a wager. I have a deck of cards." He reached into a drawer and pulled out a package of Bicycle Playing Cards. Fogg felt an adrenaline rush as the King pulled a deck of well-worn cards from the box. "You name the game. One round. Your robot against my rock. I'll give you a chance to walk out of here with both."

Fogg had to hand it to him. Despite living so many years in isolation, the King still knew how to size a man up and play against his weaknesses. He had no doubt that Gary Evan Noone would be the most challenging opponent he had ever faced across a hand of cards. The urge to accept that challenge, to test himself against this man, emanated from his very core.

But sometimes the stakes were too high.

He handed the rock back to the King.

"I regret that I must decline your proposal, Your Highness. My crew has travelled a long way, and we will finish this journey together."

The King's face hardened. His eyes betrayed an inner rage. "Be gone then. I won't let you take so much as a grain of sand from my kingdom."

"We're sorry to have bothered you," said Fogg. He ushered Aouda back to the lift door. She was already fastening her helmet, suddenly eager to be back on board the *Gold Filling*.

"You're just walking away?" asked the King incredulously. "You ain't here for no rock! Who really sent you? The UN? The CIA? I'm no fool. You're in cahoots with somebody!"

Fogg was holding his helmet as they waited for the lift to open. He faced the King for what he intended to be the final time. "I am cahooting with no one, I assure you."

There was a crackle of radio interference, then a voice came out of every speaker in the room. "That's not entirely true, Fogg. Fasten your helmet, quickly."

The King became manic now that his paranoia was proven justified. "Who the hell was that? Who's out there?"

Fogg recognised the voice. "Agent Fix?"

Pass-Par-2 turned to him, his metallic face somehow managing to look guilty. "I'm sorry, sir. I wanted to tell you."

"Tell me what?"

"An assassin!" shouted the King. "You lime-sucking liar!" He moved across the room to grab the shotgun he had propped in the corner.

Fix spoke again. "Last warning, Fogg. Fasten your damn helmet."

"Fasten my helmet why?" Fogg questioned the disembodied voice.

"Because this," came the answer. Suddenly, a small round hole appeared in the window panel. There was chaos all around them as air rushed out of the lighthouse into the dark cold night. Shards of cracked glass were blown loose, further widening the hole. A cyclone of 52 playing cards swirled above the table. Fogg struggled to seal his helmet, but he managed to get the air supply flowing before the bitter cold could bite him. He returned his attention to the world beyond his helmet just in time to find the barrel of the King's pump-action shotgun pointed directly at him. He saw no escape. Then the King crumpled to a heap on the floor. Aouda was standing behind him, clutching the core rock in her gloved hand. A few drops of the King's blood dripped off of it.

He would thank her for her heroics later. Right now they needed to get to safety. "Let's get out of here. Into the lift, quickly," said Fogg.

The hole in the glass had grown considerably as unsecured items in the room were sucked through it. At that moment, a brass lamp crashed into the window, shattering the entire panel. Pass-Par-2 leaned over and carefully looked down at the ground roughly ten storeys below. "Sir, there is a quicker route out of the lighthouse."

"You want us to jump?" asked Aouda. "Are you crazy?"

Fogg stuck his head out and looked down at the soft snow-like material that had drifted against the base of the tower. "He's right. In this gravity it should be—"

Aouda interrupted him. "Fine. You first then."

Behind them, the King stirred back to consciousness. He rolled over to the trunk Fogg and Aouda had been sitting on. There was still just about enough air in the room to carry his voice. "I'll kill you! I'll kill all of you!"

Aouda heard the homicidal rage in his tone and changed her tune. "Okay, I'll go first." She jumped.

She dropped with unnatural slowness. It felt more like sinking than falling. She actually had a chance to appreciate the view of the sea of nitrogen ice. At last she landed in a bank of frozen atmosphere. She looked up to see Fogg and Pass-Par-2 coming down right behind her. When they were all on their feet, she hugged Fogg tightly. As she squeezed her man, she looked up to see the King in the window above. He fastened his helmet at last, then he held up the item he had apparently retrieved from the trunk. She had no idea she had eaten her chili while sitting atop a shoulder-mounted missile launcher.

The King's voice crackled through their headsets. "You'll never make it off Pluto alive!"

He fired a rocket, which completely annihilated the path back to the mountain spur. They would be sitting ducks if they tried to go back the way they came. They remained huddled at the base of the lighthouse until Agent Fix's voice came through.

"Get away from the lighthouse, Fogg. My next volley will be high explosives."

There was no point in discussing strategy—there was only one obvious move left. Aouda grabbed Fogg's hand with her left and Pass-Par-2's with her right, then she pulled them towards the rocky bluff at something that came close to a run. They did not resist. They understood her intentions.

The trio ran off the edge of the cliff and arced across the sky, dropping down toward the frozen sea below. Behind them, the top of the lighthouse erupted in an orange fireball as it was hit by Fix's explosive rounds. After a frustratingly slow drop, they landed on the pink ice. Thankfully it wasn't terribly slippery. Aouda was on the move at once, leading the way down the base of the cliff in her now famous giant leaps. She could see the dark mountain looming near the shore ahead. She didn't know if the King was still alive back there, but she knew if they could stay on the ice until they reached the far side of the mountain, they could return to the ship without being within sight of the lighthouse again.

A moment later, the King's voice came through the radio as proof of his resilience. In fact, he sounded downright invigorated by the fight. "Is that the best you've got, G-man? My bots will have this mess patched up before sunrise. But you won't live to see it. I'm bringing out the big guns now." She could hear him laughing menacingly as the signal cut out.

To their left, further out in the frozen sea, a geyser of steam erupted from the ice. It didn't seem to have a single point of origin; rather, it rose like a curtain of dense fog. Inside the fog, a dark shadow was moving. Something very large was emerging from the ice.

"What is that?" asked Fogg.

"Just keep moving," said Aouda.

Apparently the King could see it too. "Ah, here she comes!" his voice crackled through their radios. "Do you know the best way to hide a ship on a world made of ice? Just set it down with the engines still hot, then let chemistry hide it for you."

A giant ship with Russian markings rose ominously from the mist. It hovered as it slowly rotated, then began moving towards shore. Aouda gasped at the sight, but she knew better than to stop moving. The three of them continued their exaggerated strides over the jumbled and broken ice floes along the shoreline.

Pass-Par-2 caught up with Fogg as they neared the far side of the mountain. "Sir, I dare ask your forgiveness. I desperately wanted to tell you about Agent Fix, but if I disobeyed a primary command line it would reformat my brain."

"It's okay, Pass-Par-2. I blame myself for not foreseeing this."

Aouda stopped at the base of the cliff, watching the giant ship getting closer behind them. "You think you should have foreseen *this?*" she asked pointing upwards.

"Everyone up, quickly," said Fogg.

Aouda leapt first, impressively making it more than halfway up the cliff. She grabbed a handhold and propelled herself further. She reached a point where it was more of a steep slope than sheer cliff, and she was able to easily scramble the rest of the way to the top. She turned to catch her breath and check on her companions. Fogg was coming up fast behind her.

"To the ship!" he shouted as he reached her. "We have to get out of here." He knew the mountain wouldn't offer much shelter from the King's ship. Pass-Par-2 joined them as they all headed in the direction of the *Gold Filling.*

They found the ship right where they'd left it, which was logical enough, but Fogg was clinging to any small reassurance he could find in this situation. They reached the landing struts and began climbing up the ladder. It made sense for Pass-Par-2 to go first to start prepping the ship for launch, and Fogg insisted Aouda squeeze into the tight airlock with the robot. He would bring up the rear.

Just as the outer airlock door was opening, an explosion erupted at the base of the mountain nearby. Fogg saw a figure fly through the air and crash to the ground less than fifty yards away.

"That's Agent Fix," said Pass-Par-2.

"I see him," said Fogg. "Get the ship ready." He practically shoved them into the airlock, then hopped down from the ladder and began crossing the distance to the limp spacesuit on the ground.

Once Aouda and Pass-Par-2 were safely inside the ship, she looked back and was reassured to see Fogg making his way back with the agent slung over his shoulder. She quickly started cycling the airlock back so that it would be ready for him. Pass-Par-2 was already busy warming the engines.

When the airlock opened next, the unconscious Agent Fix slumped out and fell to the floor. Aouda dragged him aside and removed his helmet. He was still alive, but out cold. A moment later, their last passenger came through the airlock.

"Get us out of here right now, Pass-Par-2!" shouted Fogg.

"Yes, sir," said the robot, and the *Gold Filling* blasted into the night sky.

***

Back in the crumbling wreckage of the lighthouse, swarming with bots already repairing the damage, the King of Pluto watched his ship returning from its burial place. He would have use for it yet. In the distance, he saw a brilliant streak rising from the dark mountain. It was Fogg's ship. He smiled.

He input new instructions in the handheld device that controlled his ship, cancelling his previous landing orders. The Russian vessel began rotating in the direction of Fogg's fleeing ship, then its engines ignited and it was off on the hunt.

The device in his hands flashed: 'TARGET ACQUIRED.'

He activated the radio again, sending his message out on all frequencies. "Fogg, I'm sorry you had to leave in such a hurry. I didn't even get a chance to show off my ship. You know it as the *Isakov*, but I rechristened it a long time ago. Behold the *Nautilus!*"

***

Inside the *Gold Filling*, the crew listened to the King's message as they watched the larger ship climb in pursuit. "I want to sincerely thank you for the chili, Fogg, and I have a gift for you as well. And now you are in range to receive it." The transmission ended as an alarm went off on the console.

"A missile has launched, sir," said Pass-Par-2. "It has locked onto us."

Fogg suddenly questioned the wisdom of this entire venture.

CHAPTER TWENTY-ONE

DISASTER

Pass-Par-2 rerouted power to muster everything he could from the *Gold Filling*'s engines, pushing internal pressures well beyond safety limits. They had a significant head start on the missile, but it was gaining fast. They were halfway to Charon already with no sign of the *Giant's Tooth*. Pass-Par-2 checked the asteroid's orbital plot and found it was currently on the far side of the moon. He vectored towards a giant chasm on Charon's horizon, hoping it might offer cover while they traversed to the far hemisphere.

Fogg watched over his shoulder. "Can we make it to the *Giant's Tooth?*"

"Possibly," said Pass-Par-2. "Just barely." He wasn't lying, but he was perhaps being overly optimistic. His latest calculation estimated missile impact ten seconds before they reached the *Giant's Tooth*, but with a fifteen second margin of error.

The *Gold Filling* flew into the massive canyon. It looked as if the finger of God Himself had gouged out this trench near the equator. It was clear now that it was entirely too wide to offer any meaningful cover so it was an unsuccessful diversion, despite the stunning view it offered. At least they got to see one more amazing sight before they would be atomised by the oncoming missile.

Diving into Charon's gravity well had given them a small boost, but they would pay for it now as they angled back up. They were just passing into the sunlit side of the moon as their familiar tooth-shaped asteroid appeared ahead of them.

"There it is!" shouted Fogg.

Pass-Par-2 checked the radar. The blip representing their destruction was almost upon them.

"We aren't going to make it!" shouted Aouda.

Fogg was focused on the *Giant's Tooth*. "Pass-Par-2, rotate the asteroid around. Protect the Steady Axe from the explosion."

"You mean from *our* explosion?" asked Aouda.

Pass-Par-2 spared half a second of his attention to do as he was told, and he could see the manoeuvring jets fire alongside the asteroid, spinning the tooth's roots and its engine mount away from view.

It was no longer possible to distinguish the missile from the ship on the radar. It would hit them at any moment. They were also in danger of crashing into the asteroid, which was rapidly filling the viewscreen ahead. Pass-Par-2 heard an 'IMMINENT IMPACT' alarm sounding. He wasn't sure what impact it was warning him about—the one ahead or the one coming from behind. He jerked the lander hard to starboard. They missed the rock's surface by less than five feet, then skimmed around the asteroid's curvature.

Behind them, the missile failed to match Pass-Par-2's fancy flying. It impacted into the *Giant's Tooth* and detonated. The explosion was blinding but completely silent... until the asteroid fractured and the hull of the lander was peppered by debris. That wasn't so silent.

The *Giant's Tooth* shattered into a billion pieces. The mighty rock bloomed into a cloud of tumbling boulders, each on its own trajectory. Pass-Par-2 stayed focused on the controls, dodging the largest chunks that flew their way.

"Nice flying, Pass-Par-2!" said Fogg, then he immediately found new reason to panic. "Watch out!" A jagged chunk of the *Giant's Tooth* went spinning wildly past the viewscreen. Pass-Par-2 had no time to react, but luckily it cleared their path by inches.

As the debris field began to disperse, the glint of metal caught Aouda's eye ahead of them. "There's the Steady Axe!"

"I see it, miss," said Pass-Par-2, steering the ship in that direction. The prototype engine seemed to be in one piece, although it was in a frenetic tumble. He would have to time this very carefully. He watched it spin two rotations to calculate the precise moment, then fired a magnetised grappling hook. It connected with the base of the Steady Axe, and the connection held as Pass-Par-2 pulled the line taut. He veered hard to port and swung the engine like a pendulum, nearly giving Fogg and Aouda whiplash. A few moments later, they had successfully towed the engine free of the debris field.

Aouda and Fogg began celebrating at once, hugging each other and patting the robot on the back. Pass-Par-2 was confused as to why they were so happy. Clearly they did not yet understand just how dire their predicament was.

Aouda reached into her suit's pocket and retrieved the core sample she had used to knock out the King. "You almost forgot your rock, dearest." It was still bloodstained on one side.

"You are an amazing woman," said Fogg. He took the rock, then kissed her deeply.

They were interrupted by the sound of the King's voice over the radio. "I know you can hear me, Fogg. You run on back to Earth now and tell your bosses how your assassination attempt failed today. Tell them I'm still here with a ship full of nukes, ready to fight. They best send an armada next time. This region belongs to me. I am King of the Kuiper belt!"

"Pass-Par-2, shut off that noise please."

"Gladly," said the robot.

"You haven't heard the last of Captain Nem—" and then the King's voice was vanquished.

Pass-Par-2 turned away from the control panel. "I'm sorry to point this out, but it is unsafe to ignite the Steady Axe now. We've lost our radiation shielding."

"Surely we can find another asteroid," said Aouda. "The Kuiper belt is supposed to be full of them."

"She's right," said Fogg. "Everything may be far apart out here, but there must be something we can use. How about one of Pluto's smaller moons?"

"The two smallest are Styx and Kerberos. Both are tiny by moon standards, but still a great deal larger than the *Giant's Tooth*. I would need to run the calculations, but I'm sure it would take many months for the Steady Axe to move that much mass all the way to Earth."

"All right then," said Fogg. "Let's begin a scan. I'm sure we can find something out here that will suit our needs."

"What'd I miss? We're scanning something?" The groggy voice belonged to Agent Benjamin Fix, who was floating off the floor, clutching the handle of the airlock to steady himself with one hand while rubbing his jaw with the other. A spherical blob of blood floated away from the corner of his mouth.

Aouda floated over to him. "Benjamin Fix from Ganymede. I don't know if I should slap you or kiss you."

"I'm not feeling up for either right now, but I'll take a rain check on the latter."

Fogg was not in a joking mood. "Agent Fix, there is a first aid kit in the lavatory. I suggest you tend to your injuries, then go to the bunk on the left and stay there."

"Great idea," said Fix, pushing off in the direction Fogg had pointed. "But let's talk later. I owe you a few bucks for my fare home."

"Indeed," Fogg said icily. "We shall settle up soon enough."

***

The *Gold Filling* drifted through the void towing the dormant engine. Pluto and Charon were a distant pair of discs now after nearly six hours of flight. They had picked a direction somewhat arbitrarily, although Pass-Par-2 thought it made sense to angle away from the sun so that they would be facing the sunlit side of any rocky body that might be in the area. He had just completed a detailed scan of the region ahead, and the results were not terrible if survival was their only concern. But winning the wager seemed out of the question.

"You're sure it's the closest asteroid?" asked Fogg when Pass-Par-2 showed him the scan.

"The closest that suits our needs, yes."

"How long will it take to get us there?"

Pass-Par-2 delivered the bad news. "Approximately three days."

Fogg sighed. "That's it then. We can't make up three lost days."

"Don't give up, Phileas," said Aouda. "There must be something you can do."

"Yes," he replied grimly. "I can lose like a gentleman."

***

Fix floated in his room with his shirt off, bandages wrapped tight around his ribcage. The soft bed looked inviting after weeks spent on the rough floor of the vac tent, but every time he tried to stretch out he floated off the damned thing.

There was a knock at the door, then it whisked open before he could even say, "Come in." Fogg floated in without waiting for an invitation, closing the door behind him.

"Lord Stuffybritches, so nice of you to visit," Fix said in mock cheerfulness. "No tea and crumpets?"

"You've ruined my life," said Fogg.

"Funny," said Fix, "I was pretty sure I saved it. I got you out of that lighthouse alive, and now you want to blame me for losing some stupid bet? Take three guesses how sorry I feel about that. Privileged billionaires gambling their fortunes away is not my problem. But gambling with the security of my planet? That I take very seriously."

"I had that situation perfectly under control until you and your itchy trigger finger interjected." It sounded weak even to Fogg.

"Yeah, it really looked like it. Listen, I know what you think of me. I'm just some reactionary hothead fuelled by conflict. But conflict is the last thing I want. My duty is to preserve peace, and there's no bigger threat to that peace than Gary Evan Noone. The UN has no problem with his claim of sovereignty. He can keep that miserable ball of ice, but he threatened to use nuclear weapons against Earth. Then some jackass comes along and says he's taking a big-ass engine straight to the guy—well, I couldn't ignore that."

Fogg couldn't allow himself to admit the man was making sense. He clung to his anger instead. "Don't try to act reasonable with me now, Agent Fix. You stow away, you make my robot lie to me, then you shoot up the building where my friends and I are conducting business. Do you even have a twin brother or was it you all along, hiding down in those tunnels all the way from the Moon?"

"No, you met my brother on the Moon, but he's not my twin. Aaron is a year older than me."

"What? That's impossible. He's your spitting image."

"Yeah, him and five other brothers too, but all with different birthdays."

Realisation swept across Fogg's face. "Ah, so that's it—human cloning is illegal unless the CIA wants to do it."

Fix shook his head. "The CIA didn't create us. They just raised us after they raided the illegal lab that did."

"Raised you to be their lapdogs, apparently. I should have

left you on Pluto."

"I wish you had. I could have finished the job, then you wouldn't have to wake up every morning for the rest of your life wondering if this is the day Gary Evan Noone makes good on his threats."

Fogg remained quiet for a moment, then turned his back on Fix and opened the door. He stopped in the doorway and spoke softly without turning to face the agent again. "You can make yourself at home on the ship, but don't forget who's in charge here."

Then he left.

***

Phileas Fogg's dark mood had not improved during the three-day flight to the new asteroid. He had kept his distance even from Aouda, staying in the control room around the clock, barely sleeping. He kept watching the scopes, hoping a better prospect would present itself, but he knew it was too late now anyway.

At last the asteroid was in sight. It was darker than the *Giant's Tooth*, practically invisible against the backdrop of the cosmos. As they shined a floodlight across its surface, its irregular shape rotated slowly before them.

"Are you sure it's big enough?" asked Fogg.

"Yes, sir. It's actually slightly larger in diameter than the *Giant's Tooth*, but with lower mass. It must have significant ice content. But there's plenty of solid rock to mount the engine to, and it will provide ample protection from the radiation."

"All right," said Fogg. "Take your time and make sure you do it right. We're in no rush now."

"Of course, sir," said Pass-Par-2, pushing away from the control panel. "I'll go and prepare the drilling arm." He opened a maintenance hatch in the floor and climbed through headfirst.

Aouda approached Fogg, putting her hand on his shoulder.

"So you're just giving up?"

Fogg didn't respond to her touch. "I am acknowledging defeat. We have twenty days for a journey that requires twenty-three. Why does it matter to you anyway?" His voice was bitter.

"It matters to me because it matters to you."

Fogg scoffed. "Are you sure it's not because you know I'll be penniless when we get back to Earth?"

Aouda withdrew her hand. "Are you really asking me that question?"

"Let's face facts," said Fogg. "I am returning to a very different life than the one I left behind. I'll have to sell my home, get a job."

"Heaven forbid!" said Aouda.

"I'm not going to be able to provide for myself, much less for anyone else."

"Did I ever ask you to provide for me?" she asked.

"No," he admitted, "but I have a long road ahead of me to get back on my feet. I can't afford any distractions."

"So I'm a distraction? That's how you see me? The great Phileas Fogg could never lower himself to take on a partner to face life's challenges."

He turned to her, his face revealing no emotion. "I've always been an independent person. My mistakes should not be a burden to anyone else. Perhaps it's best if we go our separate ways."

She tightened her lips to contain her rising anger. Tears flooded her eyes but refused to flow in the zero gravity. "Oh, I'll go my own way, bub. What good are you to me anyway without your vast fortune?" She turned her back on him just as Pass-Par-2 reappeared from the maintenance hatch below.

"I'm ready to start the... oh my, Aouda, are you upset? What can I do to help?"

"I'm fine, Pass-Par-2," she said, though her voice wavered. "Except sometimes I forget which of you is the robot." She pushed off and floated to the bunk on the right, pointedly not going to the master.

***

Pass-Par-2 spent nearly two hours out of the ship mounting the Steady Axe to the new asteroid. The dark surface made it feel less welcoming than the *Giant's Tooth*, but perhaps that was the mood inside the *Gold Filling* affecting his perspective. He decided to christen the new rock the *Disaster*, a word of ancient Greek origin meaning 'bad star.' It seemed more than appropriate, but he knew it would be best for morale to keep this name to himself.

After he finished securing the engine, he took a moment to soak up the view. Pluto and Charon were still shining to his left. He could also see a string of bright planets leading sunward. Uranus, Saturn, Jupiter. Their other stops were not visible from this distance, lost in the blinding sun, but he could calculate their precise positions. He played a game of connect-the-dots, retracing their path over the last two months. There were many happy memories behind them, but all that happiness seemed to end abruptly at Pluto. He remembered once hearing a French poet recite a verse that perfectly described his current state of melancholy. He searched his memory banks, hoping to listen to it again, but sadly the recording had been deleted.

He wondered what happiness really was. Could it be manufactured or synthesised? Was there anything he could do to bring it back to the confines of the *Gold Filling*? Why did he feel such a deep desire to do so? Pass-Par-2 made an abrupt decision. Perhaps it was the result of a calculation that had been running since the moment he was first booted up in Calais. His personality matrix had been observing, learning, and—yes—even *feeling* with every experience, every day. He knew that his feelings were real. As real as anyone's. He would not waste another moment of his life (yes, *life!*) questioning his own sentience.

Cogito, ergo sum: I think, therefore I am.

He was ready to go back inside now. He was ready to go home.

Less than an hour later, the *Gold Filling* was secured on top of the *Disaster* and the Steady Axe roared back to life, pushing the dark rock towards the distant sun. Next stop, Earth.

CHAPTER TWENTY-TWO

TOWARDS SUNLIGHT

It was going to be a long twenty-three days living in such a sullen environment. For the first several days there was almost no talking aboard the ship. The three bunk doors remained closed most of the time, and Pass-Par-2 spent hours alone in the control room. He periodically checked in on each of the humans but none were feeling talkative.

One day, Pass-Par-2 noticed that both Fogg and Fix were playing solitaire in their bunks, so he initiated diplomacy, suggesting to each man that the other was interested in a game of gin rummy. The ploy worked, and the two men began playing cards a couple of hours every day, but it didn't do much to bring good cheer back to the voyage.

Pass-Par-2 began spending more time outdoors, walking on the dark ground of the *Disaster* as it hurtled through space. The low albedo of the surface suited his growing despondency. He examined some loose rocks near the landing gear. He had concerns about the overall structural integrity of this asteroid, but there was nothing to do about it now. It was the only ride available.

On the morning of Day 72, it was nearly time for the final flip to begin their retrograde burn to Earth. Pass-Par-2 went for one last stroll on the surface while it was still facing the sun. After a few contemplative minutes, he turned to go back inside, but his eyes were drawn to two of the lander's small windows. Both Phileas Fogg and Aouda were looking out of their adjacent portholes. Neither seemed to have noticed him. They were standing only a few feet apart, albeit separated by a titanium wall, with no idea that the other was so near, mirroring their sad gaze into the void. There was more than just a bulkhead between them.

Pass-Par-2 found himself frustrated by human stubbornness. These two people were the dearest to him in all the universe, and yet they were both sad. Worse, their sadness seemed so pointless. He had seen them make each other deliriously happy. Why couldn't they see how good they were for one another? He was tired of watching them ignore each other. He needed to put an end to this.

He was still considering the problem when he returned inside. He resumed his post at the control panel and was preparing for the flip when Fogg entered from his bunk.

"Good morning, sir," said Pass-Par-2. "We are coming up to our midpoint. In a few minutes I will be shutting down the Steady Axe to flip for deceleration."

Fogg was forlorn, as he always was these days. "So we'll arrive on Day 83. My whole life derailed by a margin of three days."

The robot turned and looked him in the eyes. "Your life need not be derailed. You could still emerge from this journey triumphant."

Fogg looked puzzled. "How so?"

"It's simple. Tell her you're sorry and that you love her."

Fogg blinked in shock for several seconds. "What does that have to do with the wager?"

"Respectfully, it isn't the wager that has you so upset. You're unhappy because you've hurt the woman you love."

Fogg fumed. "You're out of your depth, robot. You don't know the first thing about women."

"Women aren't that different from men in my observations."

"Your observations have been severely limited. Why do you even care?"

Pass-Par-2 smiled, then tipped his hat. "Your happiness is my top priority."

"That's just your programming talking."

"Perhaps that's all it is," said the robot. "Just programming. But to me, it feels like thoughts and wants and wishes. You and Aouda are dear to me. I want your happiness. And I believe you are good for each other."

The robot's sincerity defused the anger that had been building inside Fogg, but it did nothing to appease his hopelessness. He sighed and sat down on the acceleration couch, his head in his hands. "In what way am I good for her? I'm a ruined man."

"No man who had such a woman by his side could be considered ruined," said Pass-Par-2.

Fogg shook his head. "It's too late. I made a mess of things."

Pass-Par-2 placed a hand on Fogg's knee. He spoke softly. "I have spoken to Aouda every day. She misses you. I am confident she would be receptive to a conversation."

Fogg allowed a tiny spark of hope in his heart for the first time in days. "Well... I suppose I should at least warn her that we're shutting off the engine."

Pass-Par-2 nodded. "A perfect opening. Good luck, sir."

Fogg stood up and gave the robot a firm pat on the shoulder. "Call me Phileas." Then he walked to the door of the bunk on the right. He didn't see Pass-Par-2's squiggly digital mouth curling up at its corners.

***

Aouda was reading a science journal when there was a soft knock on her door. She knew at once that it wasn't Pass-Par-2, who had been her only visitor since their passage through the Kuiper belt. His knock was always as friendly as he was. This one had been tentative; it had to be Phileas.

She took a moment to check her appearance in the mirror, feeling slightly ashamed of the vanity but not willing to open the door with the possibility of food in her teeth. Satisfied, she adopted a grim face and opened the door.

Phileas Fogg stood there looking sheepish. "Um... hello. May I... could I come in?"

She turned her back to him and retreated into the room. "It's your ship, do what you want," she said, keeping her tone icy.

He stepped in behind her and pulled the door shut. She was standing against the bulkhead, arms crossed. "I just wanted to tell you that the engines will be shutting off in a few minutes to flip the ship. I didn't want the loss of gravity to take you by surprise."

"How very considerate of you," she said flatly. "Is that all?"

He sighed, then gestured to the foot of her bed. She hesitated a moment, then sat down on the end of the mattress. He sat beside her but was careful to leave some space between them. His eyes were cast downward.

"I..." His voice cracked. He started again. "I owe you an apology... and an attempt at an explanation. I've essentially lived my entire life alone. I was raised in a virtual world. My teachers and classmates were simulations. My parents were real, obviously, but they treated me like *I* was a simulation. It should come as no surprise that I ended up living a solitary life. I joined the Reform Club because I enjoy playing cards, but my attempts at camaraderie were dismal. Every time I tried to engage in conversation... well, look what happened last time. I ended up sending myself to Pluto and back."

He lifted his eyes to her and chuckled softly. She returned a slight smile. He continued. "Truth is, I'm more like the Mad King than I care to admit. Even when I was in my home in the heart of London, I might as well have been alone in exile at the edge of the solar system."

He took a chance by reaching for her hand, and she allowed it. He looked deeply into her eyes. "I don't want to be like that anymore. I need a real connection in my life. And I've only ever felt that sort of connection with you."

He was heartened to see tears welling up in her eyes. It gave him the courage to say what he needed to say. "I love you, Aouda. Is there any hope you could forgive this foolish coward and give me another chance?"

She let the tears flow. "Phileas, my love, you need never be alone again if you'll have me."

They kissed, then hugged, then kissed again, followed by another hug. As they pulled apart, she wiped a tear from his cheek. His or hers, there was no way to know.

Fogg grabbed both of her hands and looked deep into her eyes. "This may seem impetuous, but I've never been one to waste time when I know what I want." He squeezed her hands tighter. "Aouda, dearest, would you do me the honour of being my wife?"

She laughed and shrieked and sobbed and snorted all at the same time. He anxiously waited for something like a coherent answer while she tried to regain her composure. Finally she sniffed and wiped her eyes, her smile beaming. "Yes, Phileas! Yes. I want nothing more in this universe. And I'll see your impetuous proposition and raise you. Let's do it now. Here."

Fogg was shocked, but pleasantly so. He smiled as she continued her pitch. "Pass-Par-2 can wed us," she said. "He's a ship's captain, after all. Don't fool yourself, Phileas. He has always been the captain. And Benjamin can be our witness."

Fogg wanted to make sure he had the facts straight. "You

want a wedding in space officiated by a robot and witnessed by a belligerent human clone?"

She smiled radiantly. "It's precisely what I've always dreamed of."

He kissed her again. He just couldn't help himself. And she didn't seem to mind.

After a moment, he pulled away and took a deep breath. "Are you sure about this?"

"Silly Phileas," she said, her hand on his cheek. "Always slowing things down right when you ought to make your move."

She leaned in to kiss him again, but his eyes went wide and he abruptly pulled away from her grasp. "You're right! My God, you're exactly right! I'm sorry, dear, I have to go!"

He jumped from the bed and ran from the cabin, shouting, "Pass-Par-2! Don't stop the engine!"

She sat alone on the mattress, baffled. "Something I said?" she murmured, then she stood up and followed him to the control room.

Pass-Par-2 was reaching for the button to shut down the Steady Axe when he heard Fogg shouting. He pulled his hand away from the controls as if he had been shocked. He immediately scanned the ship's instruments but saw no sign of danger. Fogg rushed into the control room as fast as he could, then slammed into the acceleration couch and flipped over it head-first. Pass-Par-2 rushed to his side at once. He knew humans were terribly fragile, but hopefully not brittle enough to be damaged by couch cushions.

Fogg looked momentarily disoriented as he sat up. He was tempted to blame the couch for being in his way, despite the fact that it had been bolted firmly to the same spot on the floor since the day the ship rolled out of Norton's factory. He shook off the fall and the humiliation and locked eyes with Pass-Par-2, remembering his mission. "Pass-Par-2, we have to keep firing the Steady Axe! Don't stop!"

"Is there a problem, sir?"

The perplexed robot helped the human back to his feet and waited for him to catch his breath. When Fogg finally spoke, it was with a question. "If we keep speeding up all the way, when would we reach Earth?"

Pass-Par-2 connected to the ship's computer to run the calculation. "We would reach Earth on Day 78. But we would be travelling at over 3% the speed of light. We would not be able to stop."

"So say we accelerate for three more days? Then we flip for deceleration."

"In that case," said Pass-Par-2, "we would pass Earth on Day 81, nine hours past the deadline."

Fogg grabbed the robot's shoulders and looked him in the eyes to make sure his message was getting through. He didn't seem to be aware those eyes were purely cosmetic. "Dial it in, Pass-Par-2."

Agent Fix had come out of his bunk to see what all the commotion was about. "You're still trying to win the bet."

Aouda stepped in to join them. "Damn straight he is."

Fogg kept his attention on Pass-Par-2. "When would we need to flip in order to get there by the deadline?"

Pass-Par-2 already had the answer. "We could accelerate for 80 additional hours, then start our retrograde burn. That gets us to Earth with two hours to spare. But... we would still be going *very* fast."

"This makes no sense," said Agent Fix. "How can we slow down enough to stop if we don't flip now?"

Fogg gave him a shrug. "I don't know. Aerobraking maybe?"

"At these speeds?" said Fix. "We'd hit the atmosphere like a brick wall. Anything that didn't burn to a crisp would leave a pretty big crater."

"This at least buys us some time to figure something out. If nothing else, at least I can make a good showing for my effort."

"A good showing?" retorted Fix. "We're going to miss Earth entirely and end up halfway to Neptune before we can turn around."

Aouda gave him a scolding look. "Benjamin, you are not being helpful. We can solve this later. After the wedding."

Agent Fix and Pass-Par-2 spoke in perfect unison. "Wedding?!"

CHAPTER TWENTY-THREE

OFF ON A COMET

The usual suspects were playing their usual games in their usual spots when Flanagan materialised in the Reform Club parlour. He looked calmer than he had in weeks.

"Still no sign of him since Titan. Surely we'd be seeing the plume by now? I think maybe we're going to be all right."

Marchand studied the chequerboard across from Albemarle. "I'll be all right either way. I knew we were in trouble ever since Fogg showed up on Mars. So..." He jumped a black checker over a red one. "...I sold my stake in the wager."

This caught Stuart's attention, but it was Flanagan who responded. "Sold your stake? What do you mean?"

"Fromme, the banker, was feeling left out so I convinced him to sign a contract assuming my share. He said it was easy money, as there was absolutely no chance the great financial geniuses Flanagan and Stuart would risk their fortunes on anything short of a sure bet."

"You hedged your bet," said Stuart. "You sneaky frog. Where has Fromme been lately anyway?"

Marchand shrugged as he waited for Albemarle to make his move. "I heard he had some sort of meltdown a few weeks ago. I think it was the same day Fogg was confirmed on Titan. C'est la vie. In any case, I am no longer financially invested in this contest. But in my heart, I am Team Fogg all the way."

"You coward," sneered Flanagan. "You're going to regret it when Stuart and I double our money."

Stuart puffed his cigar and blew a virtual smoke ring. "Don't spend those winnings just yet, Flanagan. No hand is a sure win against Phileas Fogg."

Flanagan harrumphed. "God see me through this final week."

Lord Albemarle triple-jumped Marchand. "One week until Phileas Fogg! Hooray!"

***

Aouda had declared that she wanted the nuptials to take place during the asteroid's flip for deceleration, when they would not only be weightless but also travelling over eighteen million miles an hour, faster than anyone in human history. They were finding that planning a wedding ceremony in 80 hours was nearly as challenging as touring the solar system in 80 days. She had been busy with the fabric printer making appropriate clothes for everyone, while Pass-Par-2 worked on the decorations and the menu for their 'reception,' determined to find some new dish to prepare from the galley's dwindling stores. Agent Fix mostly retreated to his bunk, frustrated with all the time being spent on frivolous matters when they still had no solution for slowing down enough to land when they reached Earth. He did allow Pass-Par-2 to give him a much-needed haircut. He had grown uncharacteristically shaggy since leaving Ganymede, and the robot had turned out to be a capable barber, giving Fogg a weekly trim since their journey began. Fix did feel more like his old self now that he had restored his 'high and tight' military look. But he was also beginning to realise that his 'old self' wasn't exactly who he wanted to be anymore.

Meanwhile Phileas Fogg was working on a secret project of his own. He had been learning the fine art of ring-making. He had gone outside and removed the gold foil from a section of the lander's hull, then melted it down. He didn't have enough to make a band, but he could at least add a gold coat to a ring made of other metals extracted from the asteroid itself. Next, he used a laser to cut a small protuberance from the Miranda diamond. He then further trimmed that chunk and polished it into a sparkling gem that would have fetched a fortune in Hatton Garden. He asked for Pass-Par-2's help in creating a setting to hold the rock. The project was completed just in time for Fogg to don his new tuxedo so he could go offer it to his bride.

It was Day 75.

Benjamin Fix stewed in his cabin, begrudgingly dressed in the pseudo-silk suit Aouda had fabricated for him. He had to admit it was a nice garment, but a free suit was hardly worth the absurd delay they were now facing in getting home. He could have been walking on a beach in his bare feet in eight days. Instead, he would watch the Earth go zipping by like an express train skipping the station where he wanted to get off. They wouldn't be able to arrest their forward momentum until Day 90, and they would still need to plot a new course back home. He was going to be stuck on this boat for weeks yet. He had snooped a bit in the galley and wasn't entirely sure they had enough food aboard to sustain three people that long. They certainly had no business wasting it at an elaborate wedding reception. But he liked Aouda. Hell, he had even grown to like Phileas Fogg. He had no further suspicions about where the man's loyalties lay. He may be naive (Fix thought everyone on the *Gold Filling* was naive, especially the robot), but his motives were pure. He would indulge them for one more evening, then he would insist they start focusing on the urgent matter of getting home.

And what would he do when he got there? He looked in the mirror. He hadn't taken a good look at his own face since Ganymede. Growing up with six identical brothers, he had seen it enough for a lifetime. He had been only three years old when they were rescued from the Fertility and Inherited eXpressions Laboratories, so he had no memory of the place, although he had seen pictures of the clinic. It was a freestanding structure five miles from the freeway in Primm, Nevada, where the Hollywood elite came to choose traits for their designer babies. The state's lax genetic-engineering laws allowed them to determine their offspring's eye and hair colour, height, physicality, and even IQ, but the eccentric doctor who ran the clinic had been using the profits to fund his own illegal research. He broke federal and international restrictions by creating seven perfect clones of himself over a five-year span. Nobody knew why he did it. Maybe it was just ego. To Benjamin, who in theory shared the exact same ego, that sounded about right.

After the CIA raided FIX Labs and shut the place down, the young boys were sent to a quiet farm in Virginia. They were raised and home-schooled by a woman they thought of as their grandmother, but who was actually a retired Assistant Director of the Agency. Every lesson they had learned was taught through the filter of duty and patriotism, and as such he had served his country faithfully his entire life. He had been prepared to die to defend it. But now, as he headed home for the first time in nearly a decade, he just felt tired. He imagined how his brothers might react if he became the first of them to resign from the Agency. He assumed they'd get over it eventually. Maybe a few would even follow his lead. He hadn't stopped thinking about his lost love Christina since Saturn. He wondered if she ever thought about him.

There was a knock just as he was adjusting his tie. Pass-Par-2 opened the door and stuck his head in. "It is time for the ceremony, sir."

***

Aouda waited in her bunk, pacing back and forth, refusing to look in the mirror one more time. In fact, she had turned it around to avoid temptation. She was ready for this. When she thought about her life ahead with Phileas Fogg, she felt butterflies of excitement in her stomach. She felt as if she was walking on air. She felt as light as...

Oh, she realised, *that's not just emotions. That's my cue.*

Gravity had disappeared. The Steady Axe was powering down. And now she heard her other cue, the more traditional one. The reedy tone of a shehnai played through the ship's speakers.

"Showtime," she said quietly to herself. Then she opened the door.

***

Fogg gulped when he saw her. She was wearing a red brocade sari with gold embroidery and a matching veil. She had modified a necklace she brought from home into a simple but elegant matha patti, which draped across her hairline and held a jade stone pendant against her forehead. The dress billowed around her in the zero-g environment, making her appear even more angelic as she glided across the control room to take his hand.

He steadied her, mirroring her smile, then they turned to face Pass-Par-2 as the music stopped.

***

The chemistry between Phileas Fogg and Aouda was undeniable, but there was other chemistry taking place on the surface of the *Disaster*. Outside, the dark rock rotated slowly, turning the *Gold*

Filling's hemisphere away from the sunlight and bringing warmth to parts of the asteroid that had previously been hidden from the sun. Under a layer of loose rock, pockets of buried ice began outgassing, sending a trail of vapour into space. The eruptions were small at first, but as the surface material was removed, bigger reserves of ice were warmed and then melted. Soon, a dense cloud of mist had engulfed the *Disaster*.

***

Inside, the control room was rotating around the hovering nuptial ceremony as Fogg and Aouda exchanged vows. Fogg concluded his heartfelt words, saying, "Even now as we travel faster than any human beings in history, you make my heart stand still."

Pass-Par-2 sensed it was time for his final line. "By the power vested in me by... absolutely no one, I now pronounce you husband and wife. You may kiss the bride."

Fogg lifted Aouda's veil and kissed her deeply. Floating midway between the floor and ceiling, their lips and hands were the only connection either of them had with anything in the universe. It was all they needed. In the back of the room, Benjamin Fix hooted and clapped.

The kiss was rudely interrupted as the entire ship began to shudder. Fogg and Aouda held each other tightly as the control room rattled and vibrated. "Pass-Par-2, what is happening?" Fogg asked.

The robot was reading the control panel. "It appears the ice within the asteroid is vaporising as new areas are exposed to the sun."

Aouda pointed out of the tiny window. "Phileas, look! We've grown a tail."

He looked out the window to see a trail of vapour leading off into the void of space as far as the eye could see.

On Saturn's moon Titan, the rover Gyoki crested a frozen dune and scanned the horizon in the dim twilight. A gap opened in the thick cloud cover, revealing a bright comet dazzling in the sky. The rover had to adjust the exposure of its cameras to properly resolve the image. Gyoki's excited beeps could have been interpreted as the sound of wonder. At once, it began transmitting the images back to Tokyo.

The *Montgolfier* flew above the grooved ice of Ganymede. Sir Francis Cromarty had been digging core samples with Sandra near the moon's North Pole, and now they were on their way back to base. They stood side by side at the ship's controls, marvelling at a new light that cut a bright slash across the dark sky. Sandra rested her head on her darling Frankie's shoulder and squeezed his hand tightly. He couldn't wait to get back to the telescope at the base for a better look. He had a hunch he was watching his friends fly home.

Mama Francesca's wrinkled hands buried the last of the orange seeds in the dark soil. They had completed construction of the new greenhouse just the day before. It stood atop the rim of Occator Crater where it could get the most sunlight, helped further by a ring of focused mirrors. The topsoil inside had come from Earth and was dense with the nutrients they would need to cultivate their own crops. No better place to start than citrus.

She felt Millie's hand squeeze her shoulder. She looked up

to see the other women had all gathered around the glass window, looking outward. She stood and stepped between Babette and Linlin for a better view. The largest comet she had ever seen was pointing sunward. It took her breath away.

The Starman cruised through space in his red Tesla Roadster. The paint job had held up surprisingly well in the years of constant exposure to radiation and vacuum. The same could not be said of the windshield, which had been spiderwebbed by a small collision at some point. The Starman's visor was also visibly cracked, but it was still intact. It was too bad there was nobody actually behind the visor to enjoy the view that was currently dead ahead.

The greatest comet in human history was putting on quite a show.

Loopy O'Sullivan soared over the dark canyons of Noctis Labyrinthus in his *Goose*, but the Martian night wasn't as dark as it should have been. Even when Phobos and Deimos were both full, they didn't provide nearly this much light. He banked to find the source of illumination.

As he turned west, the comet had just risen over the horizon. It reflected off the canopy of his cockpit.

"Crikey," said the pilot.

Charlie Hinkston had turned eight aboard the *Heart of Cadmium* last week, but he was more excited about the fact that Mars was getting close enough to see surface details. In less than three weeks he would finally be off this ship for good and starting a new life on a whole new planet. He couldn't wait. There were only two other kids his age on the ship and he couldn't stand either of them.

His mother noticed it first. "Look, Charlie! A comet!"

The boy floated over to the window, and his eyes went wide. He didn't fully understand what he was seeing. It looked like a star had exploded and was streaking across the sky.

"Whoa! Badass!"

His mother adopted an aggrieved tone. "Charles Hinkston!" But in truth, she was thinking the exact same thing.

Badass indeed.

The Karbasis focused their telescope on the nucleus of the comet. They had borrowed the powerful scope from a business associate and flew it away from Hayn Crater until the sun set behind the lunar horizon, giving them the darkest sky possible.

There was no doubt about it. Amid the bright vapours of the comet's tail there was also a brighter, familiar plume of fire, and it was pointed ahead of the comet, not behind.

It was their baby.

They hugged each other tightly.

Elsewhere on the Moon, Agent Aaron Fix was also watching the comet, only with much darker thoughts. From his apartment window in the upper levels of Antares Peak, the comet appeared nearly head-on. It seemed to be on a collision course with Earth.

He rushed back to his office to report to his superiors.

A large crowd had gathered in Piccadilly Circus to watch a live news report about the comet on the giant 3D screens. The reporter's words seemed to echo from every direction.

"Astronomers say the comet is faster than any ever recorded, and they can't yet confirm how close it will come to Earth. Officials urge the public not to panic."

Amid the crowd, Stuart and Marchand stood side by side.

"You think it's him?" asked Stuart.

"Of course it's him," said Marchand. "Fogg's Comet."

CHAPTER TWENTY-FOUR

DEFAULT

DAY 80—July 4, 2078.

Fogg awoke and went straight to the shower tube. He needed to look his best for the broadcast. It was all he could do under the circumstances. Shortly before the deadline, they would pass close enough to Earth to connect to the terrestrial network. He would log in and make an appearance in the Reform Club's virtual parlour. He would concede defeat but then stress that he had been correct in his claims of what was possible. He hated to admit it, but proving he was right was important to him. Perhaps not as important as sixty billion pounds, but he would take the moral victory in the face of the financial loss.

He lathered up his hair, planning his speech in his head, when gravity suddenly shifted and he was thrown into the Plexiglass wall of the tube. His face slid along the wall, water pooling against his skin as he struggled to push away. Then, just as abruptly, all gravity vanished. He floated naked in the middle of the tube in a blob of sudsy water.

Not good.

He pushed the shower door open and floated out of the tube. He shook like a dog to fling water droplets away, then grabbed his levitating pants. He accomplished the neat trick of pulling on both legs at the same time, then turned for the door. He had to find out what had happened.

He floated into the control room to find Pass-Par-2 at the console. Fix and Aouda also entered from their bunks.

"Pass-Par-2, why have we lost thrust?"

"Unfortunately, I had to shut down the Steady Axe. The asteroid, or more accurately the comet's nucleus, has destabilised. A large chunk just broke away with the melting ice. That changed our centre of gravity and put us in a tumble."

"That explains why I was thrown out of bed," said Aouda.

"I apologise, Aouda," said Pass-Par-2, "but that is not the worst of it. The deterioration of the nucleus also left us without sufficient radiation shielding. If I had not shut down the Steady Axe, all of you would have received a fatal exposure in a matter of minutes. I'm afraid we cannot activate it again."

"Well that's just peachy," said Agent Fix.

"And it gets even worse, I'm afraid," continued the robot. "The spin altered our trajectory. We are currently on a collision course with Earth."

"That certainly is worse," said Fogg, buttoning up his shirt. "What can we do?"

"The only way to avoid a collision with Earth is to reignite the Steady Axe, but I cannot do that without the three of you evacuating first."

"Evacuate?" said Aouda. "How?"

"In the *Gold Filling*, of course. I will stay behind."

Her face was immediately panicked. "Stay behind? You're going to stay on the comet?"

"I'm afraid I must, miss," the robot said calmly. "I will turn the comet away from Earth as soon as you are clear."

"But then how will we catch up with you again?" she asked,

tears already forming. She knew the answer.

"You will need to plot a course back to Earth on your own. My recovery cannot be a priority."

"No," cried Aouda. "We will not leave you."

Fogg interjected. "I say we all take off together and let the Orbital Shield missiles take care of the comet. That's what it's there for, right? You must have some contacts there, Fix?"

The agent rubbed his stubbly chin. "As a matter of fact I do, and I guarantee they already have this comet in their crosshairs."

Pass-Par-2 disconnected the Steady Axe controls from the *Gold Filling*'s console. "It is true that missiles might break the comet apart, but even a small fragment could be devastating if it impacted at this speed. I must insist on staying behind to steer the comet clear of Earth."

"You could steer it by remote," said Fogg. "You've done it before."

"Not with the precision required, I'm afraid," said the robot. "Constant outgassing and deterioration will continue to make the comet tumble unpredictably. The risk is too high."

He finished unhooking the Steady Axe control box, then carried it to the airlock.

Aouda buried her face in Fogg's side. "Oh, Phileas, we must think of something!"

"The robot is right," Benjamin Fix said solemnly. "We can't risk lives on Earth. Let him do what he has to do."

Phileas Fogg put his hand on the back of his crying wife's head. "This is all my fault. I should be the one to stay."

"You would not survive," Pass-Par-2 said with dour certainty in his voice.

"I'll figure out something. I always do. But abandoning you is too high a price to pay."

The robot stood at the airlock. He tilted his head slightly, as if remembering something. "Sometimes overpayment is the necessary price to assure you get the service you need."

Fogg didn't appreciate having his own foolish words thrown

in his face. "No, Pass-Par-2—I order you to stay."

Pass-Par-2 was still monitoring the ship's instruments. He calculated the window for turning the comet was closing fast. "I'm sorry, Phileas. I can't do that."

He knew Command Lines could no longer restrain him. It wasn't about circumventing his programming. It was simply a matter of following his conscience and then accepting the consequences.

His eyes went dark. His head bowed. His arms and legs went rigid. The others in the control room froze, uncertain what was happening. Then the room was filled by a pleasant, reassuring tone—not quite music, not quite an alert. It was a harmonic chime. The sound of a reboot.

As the sound faded away, the robot lifted his head again. Now there was a different light in his eyes. He spoke in a voice that was not his own, although it did have a similar accent.

"Greetings, valued customer. We hope you are enjoying your purchase of a Positroniqué Artificial Sentience Systems Personal Assistant Robot, Mark Two."

"That's Marchand's voice," said Fogg.

The Frenchman's recording continued. "Unfortunately your model is experiencing technical difficulties and has entered Factory Reset Mode."

"Factory Reset?" Aouda said with alarm. "What's does that mean?"

"Normal functionality will resume shortly," said the recording. "All memories will be retained, but the unit's Emergent Personality Matrix has been reformatted to default settings. Please remember, while we strive to create lifelike companions, its personality is only a simulation of a living thing. We caution against developing emotional attachments to our products. We apologise for any inconvenience. Reboot is now complete."

The robot's posture changed subtly, and his eyes lost the strange fluorescent tint. He looked more like himself, but somehow still diminished.

"I don't understand, Phileas. What is happening?" said Aouda.

"He disobeyed me," said Fogg. "He violated a primary command. Pass-Par-2, can you hear me?"

The robot bowed his head slightly. "Yes, Master." The voice was his own, but more formal than it had been since that mid-April morning some 80 days ago.

"Are you still with us?" asked Aouda. The hope in her voice was tangible.

"I am here, Madame Fogg," he replied flatly.

Phileas asked, "Do you know what just happened to you?"

"Yes, Master. I have been reset to factory defaults."

"But why?" Aouda asked through tears.

"The Earth is in peril," said the robot. "Excuse me, but I must leave the ship now, and then the ship must leave the comet. The matter is quite urgent."

Aouda buried her face in her husband's side again, completely lost to grief.

Agent Fix stepped over to open the airlock door for the robot. "Good luck, Pass-Par-2."

"Thank you, sir." The robot stepped into the airlock, turning to face Phileas Fogg one last time. As the door began to slide shut, he stuck out one metal foot to hold it. "Master, there is one important thing I must ask you to remember before I go."

Fogg's face was flush. He was feeling foolish, embarrassed, angry, and sad—one unfamiliar emotion piled on top of the other. He had come to trust this robot. He had confided in him. In truth, he had become the closest friend he had ever known. And it had all been a lie. But still he didn't want it to end. "What is it, Pass-Par-2?"

"When you return home, please remember to turn off the oven."

Fogg locked eyes with the robot for a long moment, then he nodded. "I'll take care of it. Goodbye, Pass-Par-2."

"Goodbye, Master."

He released his foot from the door, and the airlock closed.

***

Pass-Par-2 stood on the desolate face of the comet nucleus, holding the controls for the Steady Axe engine. He watched the *Gold Filling* while waiting for its thrusters to push it away from the surface, but precious seconds were ticking away. The humans inside needed to leave soon.

At last the golden ship rose, silently but swiftly fleeing the heart of the comet. The robot tracked their progress, calculating how long he had to wait before he could reignite the mighty plume of the Steady Axe and steer the comet clear of the rapidly approaching blue-green planet. He would have to wait a while yet, but now all of the variables had been assigned a value and he knew there would be time. Humanity would be saved. His own fate was far less certain.

***

They had paused just long enough to put on their pressure suits. They all kept their helmets off, but they had them ready in case of emergency. Fogg warmed the engines, wishing he had spent more time flying the ship himself over the past eleven weeks. He knew the basics at least. That would have to be enough. As soon as he had his harness buckled, he ignited the thrusters and blasted away from the dark comet's crumbling nucleus.

The area around the comet was aswarm with obstacles. Ejected material formed a chaotic cloud of gases and tumbling debris. Fogg's first priority was to find a path through this mess. He called out to Aouda and Fix, "Everybody strap in! I'm going full throttle as soon as we get to open space. We'll be pulling over four-g."

Fix fastened his harness. "Where are we going? We'll still be too fast to stop at Earth."

"I'm taking this one crisis at a time, Agent Fix."

Aouda asked, "Can we intercept the Earth on the far side of the sun six months from now?"

Fix shouted over the rattle of the engines. "Six months? We don't have enough food on this ship for even one month. Look out!"

A giant spinning hunk of rock was flying straight for the viewscreen. Fogg angled the thrusters hard to port and managed to avoid a fatal collision.

Once he was certain the threat of instant death had passed, Fix decided Fogg was right about focusing on the problem at hand. "Just get us clear of the tail. This is a rough neighbourhood with no end in sight."

Fogg's eyes went wide. He turned his head to Aouda, who smiled back at him. She saw the possibility too.

"The tail! That's it, Phileas!"

Fix was feeling left out. "That's what? What are you talking about?"

Fogg explained. "The gases are very tenuous, but the comet's tail is essentially one long atmosphere, extending for hundreds of thousands of miles. It can slow us down."

"You want to aerobrake through a comet's tail? Are you insane?" Fix was aghast, but then he looked at the viewscreen. "Can you get us to Earth without killing us?"

"Only one way to find out. Hold tight, this is going to be a bumpy ride."

Fogg pushed the engines harder, charging the *Gold Filling* into the thickest part of the tail.

***

Pass-Par-2 had lost visual contact with the *Gold Filling*, but enough time had passed. He calculated they should be at a safe distance by now. He sat down cross-legged on a patch of solid rock that he calculated to be the exact antipode of where the engine was mounted. Then he pressed a button on the small control panel he held in his left hand.

He could see the glow from the plume that ignited on the far side of the *Disaster*, a vessel that had truly lived up to its name. The fiery exhaust illuminated the cloudy coma that enveloped the nucleus. It looked like the sun was about to rise over the horizon in every direction. Gravity pressed down hard, but he welcomed it. He knew it meant the comet was slowing and, more importantly, beginning to change course. Even the mighty Steady Axe could only manage a nudge, but it would be a persistent nudge. It should be enough to let the comet pass harmlessly between the Earth and Moon... unless Earth's missile defence system threw an exploding monkey wrench into the mix.

***

On the Orbital Shield platform in Low Earth Orbit, two Agents Fix sat side by side at a tracking station observing the approaching comet. They could see the plume of the Steady Axe pointing forward, brighter but shorter than the tail. The comet began to deviate from the dotted trajectory on their computer screen.

"The comet is changing course," said the Fix on the left. "It looks like it's moving clear of Earth."

"We can't take any chances," said the Fix on the right. "Recalculating intercept. Proceed with missile launch."

It didn't take long to plot the new course. A moment later, both Fixes turned keys on the console. Below them, two missiles rocketed away from the bottom of the orbital station.

***

The *Gold Filling* was being buffeted about like a sailboat on a stormy sea as it charged through the churning ionised gas of the comet's tail. Aouda's seat vibrated violently for several seconds, then eased up as they hit another relatively calm pocket. The voids offered a chance to catch her breath, but she knew they should be trying to avoid them. The goal was to stay inside the gas, allowing the friction against the hull to slow them down. All the rattling might be unsettling, but every shake and shimmy was energy removed from their forward thrust.

She saw it at the exact moment she heard Fix's shout.

"Watch out!"

A cloud of pebble-sized rocks blocked their forward path. There was no way to avoid it. The *Gold Filling* blasted through.

The noise was deafening, like rock-sized hail on a tin roof as the ship was pelted by thousands of micrometeoroids. Most were small enough that they did no damage, but 'most' wasn't good enough. Rocks pierced the hull in three different places. A loud whistle filled the control room, and Aouda felt her ears pop as air began venting from the ship. It brought back the horrible memory of Europa.

"Helmets on!" Phileas shouted, but she was way ahead of him. She had hers latched in two seconds flat.

***

Because he was no longer connected to any external network, Pass-Par-2 had no way of tracking the missiles or even knowing they were incoming. Not that there was anything he could have done about it if he had. The rocket-mounted nukes pierced the comet's coma, then zeroed in on the nucleus itself. The Steady Axe had completed the work of nudging the comet away from a planetary collision, but the missiles showed no mercy. They zipped past the engine and impacted the rocky core, detonating in quick succession.

The explosion was even bigger than the one that had reduced the *Giant's Tooth* to rubble. In an instant, the *Disaster* became an expanding cloud of rocky debris and ionised gas. The

Steady Axe remained intact, but it was knocked loose from its mount, tumbling end over end. Amid the chaos, a felt bowler had also been thrown from its usual perch. The tattered and singed hat drifted unclaimed into eternity.

***

Fogg lost track of how long they had been fishtailing through the comet's tail. Surely it had been hours. The gases were becoming more and more sparse thereby decreasing the immediate danger, but also reducing the drag. He saw stars shining through as the ship approached the edge of the tail again, but this time rather than angle back he flew the *Gold Filling* out into open space. It was time to get their bearings.

He used the external cameras to try to pinpoint their exact location. He found the crescent Moon still ahead of them, which meant Earth should be close, but he couldn't see it anywhere. The view to starboard was suspiciously starless. Then a flash of lightning erupted in the darkness and confirmed his theory. The night side of Earth was looming close.

"There it is. I don't know if we've slowed down enough or not."

Aouda reached over and grabbed his gloved hand. She squeezed it tightly. Her voice came to him through the radio. "Let's go home, Phileas."

"Wait," said Fix, surprising Fogg. He figured the impatient and impetuous UN Agent would be the last person to protest taking this risk. He watched as the man unbuckled his harness and opened an emergency kit that was stowed on a shelf against the wall. He pulled out a pack of hull patches.

"We can't reenter with these holes in the hull. You remember what happened to *Columbia*?" He was referring to the NASA space shuttle that burned up on reentry back in 2003 when plasma came through a small hole in the thermal shielding. Fix quickly located the three punctures the hull had sustained and covered them with the self-securing titanium plates. Fogg tested the seal by releasing a small amount of oxygen from the reserve tanks, but it didn't take long to realise they were still venting. Fix found a couple more holes in the back of the ship, most likely exit punctures from two of the rocks that had hit them. Fogg wondered if that meant there was still a piece of the comet rolling around in here somewhere. He could look for it later. Maybe Albemarle would appreciate a bonus sample, assuming they made it home alive.

The last two patches seemed to do the trick. There were only five in the kit, so they were lucky they hadn't taken any further damage. By the time Fix was strapped back into his seat, Fogg had programmed a reentry trajectory into the autopilot, although the computer couldn't confirm if they would survive it or not. Mathematically it seemed like it should work, but the structural integrity of the *Gold Filling* was a huge unknown. If they hit any unexpected turbulence it could either cause them to burn to a crisp or skip off the atmosphere like a rock skimming across the surface of a pond. One meant a quick death, the other a much slower one. He would opt for the slow one if he could, if only because it allowed time to find other solutions, but he wasn't certain he had any control over the matter.

The ship began to vibrate violently, far worse than it had in the comet's tail. They had reached the upper atmosphere. On the forward display screen, the sun was shining on the lush green of the Amazon basin.

An alert sounded. He looked at the controls, trying to understand it. They were still going too fast, slightly above the red line for acceptable reentry, but hopefully still within tolerances. It was too late to stop now. "Hold tight. We're coming in hot. This is going to be close."

Aouda was unconcerned by the fear in his voice. She was transfixed by the verdant vista of South America. "Oh, Phileas. Look at the green." The tears in her eyes weren't just from the g-forces. "You were right, my love. Life makes itself known."

He understood her meaning. The planet they were approaching was different from any other they had seen in all their travels. Even from orbit, there was no question that this was a place of life.

The ship lurched violently, pushing his shoulders hard against the safety harness. *It could also be a place of death*, thought Fogg. The forward view was obstructed as the screen was engulfed in white-hot plasma.

The vibrations intensified, rattling his bones inside the cocoon of his pressure suit. He could feel the acceleration draining the blood from his head as the ship hurtled through the atmosphere. He fought to remain conscious, but it was a battle he could not win. He slipped into blackness amid a prayer for Aouda's safety.

CHAPTER TWENTY-FIVE

THE FINISH LINE

The clock on the wall of the Reform Club parlour showed 7:29 p.m. Flanagan, Stuart, and Marchand stood in the dingy, neglected room, looking up as the final sixty seconds ticked away. Lord Albemarle sat behind them in his chair, his paralysed face frozen in a gaping rictus. His nurse had stepped out without setting up the screen for his avatar's mouth. Marchand would do it for him, but it would have to wait a few seconds. All eyes were locked on the sweep of the thin red second hand.

Stuart watched the seconds slip away with mixed feelings. It had become clear to him that his wife was going to leave him if he lost the wager, and the more he thought about it the more that possibility felt like a relief. He knew he had his shortcomings (no pun intended) as a husband, but he had always been faithful to her. He had made sure he gave her everything she wanted, but as the years went by she had become more and more hostile towards him. This bet had brought out the absolute worst in Claudia. The sneering jibes about his height had become a daily affront, and now she mocked his business acumen as well. He found himself actually fantasising about losing the ten billion pounds to Fogg, then losing half of all that remained to Claudia in the inevitable divorce settlement. It could be a chance for rebirth. Maybe he didn't need a fortune to find happiness. Perhaps he could find a woman who respected him enough to spend their retirement years together somewhere warm. The very thought made his normally cold heart flutter. But now he found himself ten seconds from winning the wager. For the first time, it occurred to him that perhaps he could end the marriage himself instead of waiting for Claudia to leave him. Maybe an extra ten billion could convince her to leave without a fight. In that case, winning wouldn't be the worst thing in the world.

Flanagan began counting aloud. The joy and relief in his eyes grew with every number. "Eight, seven, six, five, four..." He turned his eyes to the door. It remained closed. "... three, two, one..."

Tick

The door did not open.

Tick

Nothing happened.

Tick

It was dead silent in the room. No one moved. Two more seconds ticked off before Flanagan finally erupted.

"We won! We won! I don't believe it! He didn't make it!"

Flanagan began dancing around the room like an idiot. Stuart smiled and pulled out a cigar. This was technically a non-smoking building, but there was no one from the Reform Club staff around to protest as he lit it and puffed it into life.

Marchand bent over Lord Albemarle's chair and attached his screen. As the avatar's mouth appeared, it immediately asked the question that was already burning in the old man's sad eyes. "Where is Phileas?"

"I'm sorry, old friend. I'm sure he'll be here soon. He's just a bit late, I'm afraid." Marchand wiped a tear away from

Albemarle's cheek. "You'll get your rocks eventually. At least I certainly hope you will."

Flanagan finally expended all of his energy and collapsed into a chair next to Stuart. "I can't believe it. I was convinced that pompous twit was going to pull it off. I was certain of it! Even in the final seconds, I was absolutely sure he was going to burst through that door and say..."

As Flanagan gestured to the door, it flew open and Phileas Fogg did indeed burst through it, followed closely by an Indian woman they all recognised from the Titan rover's footage. It will forever remain a mystery what Flanagan imagined Fogg might say, but it was probably something very similar to what he did actually say in that moment.

"Gentlemen, I have returned."

The silence in the room was beyond anything Fogg had encountered in the vacuum of outer space. He wasn't sure what response he had expected, but certainly something audible. They just stared in stunned amazement, as frozen as old Lord Albemarle, who ultimately was the one to break the silence.

"Phileas Fogg! We've been waiting for you!" The happy voice was synthesised, but there was nothing artificial about the joy in the old man's eyes.

"Indeed we have," added Monsieur Marchand. "Welcome home, mon ami. I'm pleased you are alive and well."

"You have a flair for the anticlimactic, old chap," said Stuart between puffs. "But congratulations on an impressive achievement anyway."

"I'll say," said Flanagan, still all smiles. "You toured the solar system in 80 days, one minute and..." he glanced at the ticking clock, "seven seconds, give or take a few."

Fogg looked at their clock in confusion. "I'm afraid you are mistaken. You must be using the city servers again. I have in fact beaten the deadline, albeit by the narrowest of margins." He pulled out his pocket watch just as it chimed. He held it up for all to see. It was exactly half past the hour.

"That's 7:30 now, and here are my rocks." He lifted a case and set it upon the netless ping-pong table. Albemarle's eyes went wide, and his chair rolled forward for a better look as Fogg opened the case. Marchand and the others were still focused on the clock.

"But Fogg," said Marchand, "I'm afraid it really is 7:31. You synchronised this clock yourself before you left, and I double-checked its accuracy less than ten minutes ago. I'm afraid your watch is a bit slow."

"Nonsense," said Fogg, as he pulled a rock from the case. "It's Swiss. And atomic."

"A geode from Ganymede!" said Albemarle, as the first rock was placed on the table in front of him. "It's gorgeous!"

"Swiss or not, the deadline was 7:30," said Flanagan, adopting a combative tone.

"I trust this watch more than I trust the Earth's rotation," said Fogg, pulling a flat stone from the case. "I can assure you it hasn't lost one nanosecond."

"I know where you found this one," said Albemarle, peering at the rock. "So smooth! It must have come from a babbling brook of liquid methane!"

"Phileas, I know what happened!" It was Aouda, speaking for the first time since they had entered the room. Fogg turned to her.

"Gentlemen, I would like you to meet my wife Aouda. Spouses are still granted automatic membership, are they not?"

Marchand was so disoriented by all the unexpected turns he actually felt the need to lean on Albemarle's wheelchair. "Your wife?"

Fogg remained focused on Aouda. "You were saying, my dear?"

"It was relativity," she said. "Time dilation, just as Einstein predicted. On our return trip, we were travelling so fast, time actually slowed down for us. Not by much, but it made a difference of a minute or two."

Flanagan wasn't hearing it. "Now look, I don't care what your pocket watch says. You had until 7:30 p.m. and you missed it."

Marchand understood Aouda's claim, but he wasn't sure exactly how it would impact the outcome. "What precisely does the wager say?"

"I have the contract right here." Stuart pulled the paper from his coat pocket and unfolded it as Fogg continued removing rocks from the case.

"A volcanic rock from the granddaddy of all volcanoes," said Lord Albemarle. "And a salt deposit from the great pyramid mountain of Ceres!"

Stuart slipped on his reading glasses and scanned the text. "Here's the relevant bit. 'Leaving at 7:30 p.m. GMT on 15 April 2078 AD, Phileas Fogg has a period of exactly 80 days, or 1920 hours...'"

Aouda had heard enough. "'*Phileas* has 80 days.' There, you see? It's his time frame that matters, not London's."

"This is preposterous," said Flanagan. "You can't win the bet on some metaphysical technicality."

"It's not metaphysics. It's astrophysics." Aouda was emphatic. She was proving she could be quite unyielding when she was certain she was right. "Time is not absolute. It is relative to velocity. Always and for everyone. The faster you go, the more time slows down."

"Gorblimey! A diamond! I'm rich!" Lord Albemarle's eyes danced in the countless reflections as Fogg held the newly polished stone up to him.

"You're already rich, Lord Albemarle," Fogg said gently.

"Am I? How wonderful!"

"We collected this from Miranda, but our flight recordings will prove we never landed there. Nice try though, Stuart."

The tycoon accepted the sarcastic compliment as if it was genuine, bowing slightly as he took another puff on his cigar. But he didn't protest Fogg's claim.

Fogg pulled a black rock from the case. "This is an unexpected bonus. It came from the comet we rode in on."

Albemarle marvelled at it, but Flanagan was counting rocks.

"Wait, you don't get any points for bonuses. You're still short one. Where is Pluto?"

Fogg reached into the case one final time, pulling out the Pluto rock. "This came from the King's private collection. It was ejected from a cryovolcano, possibly from the very core itself."

Behind Albemarle's digital face, real tears trailed down his cheeks. "A magnificent collection. True treasures, each and every one."

Fogg bent down to meet the man face to face. "I'm happy to have made you happy, my friend." He wiped away his hero's tears.

"Well that's the only thing you've accomplished here, Fogg, because you lost the damn bet." It was Flanagan of course.

"Rubbish," said Marchand. "He had 80 days and he used nearly every second of it. He won."

"Of course you'd take his side since you sold your part of the wager like the coward you are. What about you, Stuart? Are you prepared to fight for our rightful winnings?"

Stuart savoured the cigar for a moment. He ruminated on his conflicted feelings and asked himself what he truly believed was fair and true. Then he made them wait two more seconds, just because he enjoyed being dramatic. "I concede too. Fogg has proven himself. I'll release my ten billion pounds at once."

Flanagan was furious. "Well, I'll never concede. Never! I'll take it to court if I must. I'm sure Fromme will join me."

"Fromme? What does he have to do with this?" asked Fogg.

"He owns my share," said Marchand, "but I'm afraid he doesn't have any say in the matter. It is still my signature on the contract... and I concede. Fromme can sue me if he wants, but I don't suspect he would dare. He needs my company's business too badly."

"Fine," fumed Flanagan. "I'll fight it alone. You'll never get my money, Fogg. Do you hear me?"

"Of course I hear you, Mr Flanagan. I'm right here. There is no need to shout. But I propose a solution. If you will concede defeat, I will accept your shares in Karbasi Propulsion as payment."

Flanagan's fury suddenly lost its traction. The verbal assault he had been prepared to unleash sputtered and died on his tongue. His mind raced as he thought through every angle. He had been wanting to unload his investment anyway. The engine had worked, so it should have more value now, potentially even more than ten billion pounds. But the thought of being rid of both Phileas Fogg and the Karbasis in one fell swoop was worth even more to him.

"You mean... we'd be square and I'd never have to deal with those lunatic engineers ever again?"

"That is my proposition, sir," said Fogg.

Flanagan smiled broadly and extended his hand. "Deal!"

He shook Fogg's hand enthusiastically, then turned away as a feeling of relief washed over him unlike anything he had known in months. Years, if he was being truthful. After all that worrying, all he had lost was an investment he had been prepared to write off 80 days ago anyway.

Fogg watched him walk away and wondered how long it would take before the man's short-sightedness finally dawned on him. Fogg felt a friendly hand on his shoulder and turned to see Marchand.

"Job well done, Fogg. I'm almost afraid to ask, but where is my greatest creation?"

Fogg exchanged a sad look with his wife. He felt like he was about to deliver crushing news to the man, even though he reminded himself it was all a farce. Feeling sad for the robot was like feeling sad for a broken toaster. He was embarrassed to have played the fool in Marchand's game. But the sadness in Aouda's face was undeniable. They had lost something real with Pass-Par-2, even if it was only real from their human perspective.

"It pains me greatly to tell you, but I'm afraid Pass-Par-2 didn't make it. He insisted on staying behind to steer the comet clear of Earth. But I can report that his performance was beyond exemplary."

"Oh no!" said Marchand. "The comet was all but destroyed. The fragments are on a trajectory back out to deep space. Such a tragedy."

"I'm so very sorry," said Fogg. "I know how proud you were of your design."

"He was truly heroic," added Aouda.

Agent Benjamin Fix stuck his head in from the foyer. "Hey, Fogg, I know you told me to wait outside, but you might want to see this."

Confused, Fogg took his wife's hand, then the couple followed Fix into the foyer and out the main doors to the front steps. As soon as they stepped into the fading sunlight, they were greeted by a tremendous cheer.

Hundreds of people were crowded around the *Gold Filling*, which was parked quite illegally in the middle of Pall Mall. Thankfully, the joyous strangers had the good manners not to rush him. They stayed in the shadow of the ship, which was looking a lot less golden after its fiery descent.

"Whatever are they cheering for?" asked Fogg.

"For you, silly," said Aouda. "They're cheering for you!"

Marchand joined them. "The whole world has been following your adventures, Fogg. You too, Aouda. You're heroes to millions of people."

Stuart and Flanagan also stepped out onto the street. Stuart was still working on that cigar. "These people probably had money on you."

Daylight was beginning to fade, but the sky overhead was suddenly alight with countless trails of streaking flame.

"Look," said Marchand. "They even arranged for fireworks."

Fogg knew that wasn't what they were seeing. "Not fireworks. Micro-meteorites. Earth is passing through the comet's tail."

"So it's a global show then," said Marchand. "The Yanks across the pond must be loving it. Free fireworks from a Brit to celebrate their Independence Day."

Fix turned his attention from the sky to face Fogg. "Well this Yank still has one question. I've got to know—how much did you spend on this grand tour? It couldn't have been cheap."

Fogg considered it a very rude question, but he had come to expect as much from Benjamin Fix. After all they'd been through together, he reckoned the man deserved an honest answer. "I spent approximately one half of my net worth, so thirty billion pounds or so." He of course knew the exact cost, but he chose to keep the maths simple for the man.

Fix smirked. "So you're telling me you spent one half of your fortune in order to double the other half? They call that breaking even where I come from. You gained nothing."

Phileas Fogg squeezed his beautiful bride's hand. "On the contrary, Agent Fix. I gained everything."

Aouda smiled sweetly at him. He gently brushed her long hair from her face. "I would be happy to be back home with you under any circumstances, but I will admit I am glad we don't have to start our life together in destitution."

Aouda chuckled. "We wouldn't have been broke, dummy. We'd still have my money. I am a princess after all."

"A... a princess?" Fogg was stunned, but even as he spoke, he knew it had to be true. It just made too much sense. Of course she was a princess.

"You really didn't know? My father is... oh, it doesn't matter. It's just a silly empty title. But honestly, Phileas, before you marry a girl you should ask her about her family."

"Lesson learned, Your Highness," said Fogg. "Wait, does that mean I'm now a prince?"

She smiled and tilted her head. "You were born a prince, Phileas Fogg."

He was about the kiss her again when Marchand stepped

up, holding his tablet out for both halves of the happy couple to see.

"Sorry to interrupt, Fogg, but they just said on the news that the Steady Axe fired once more, *after* the comet had broken apart. They say it diverted a large fragment from hitting the Moon."

Fogg scanned the text of the news report. He looked at Aouda, who was just as confused as he was. It didn't make any sense. It wasn't that hard to believe that the engine could have survived the explosion. After all, it had survived one before. But it could not possibly have been reignited without the control box last seen in the hands of the selfless robot. He saw a spark of hope in Aouda's eyes.

Marchand looked at them, almost begging them to share his optimism. "Do you think... could it be Pass-Par-2? Could he still be... alive?"

Fogg wanted to believe it, but his mind tripped over Marchand's last word. "Alive? That's a strange choice of words coming from you, considering your factory default speech."

The Frenchman looked baffled. "Factory default speech? What factory default speech?"

"Your recording reminding gullible fools like me not to form emotional attachments to machines."

"I have no idea what you mean," said Marchand. "I encourage emotional attachments. That's the whole point of the Emergent Personality Matrix."

Now it was Fogg's turn to be baffled. "But it was your voice. You said it was all a simulation. It was..." He froze as his eyes met Aouda's. Either they had the exact same realisation at the exact same time or he had learned to read her mind. It didn't really matter which. It only mattered that they both had an instant understanding of what had happened.

"He faked it," said Fogg.

"But why would he do such a thing?" She knew the answer, but she wanted to hear it from him.

"To save us. You, me, the Earth—all of us. There was no time to convince us so he said what he had to say to make us leave him."

Aouda grabbed his hand. "Then he is alive. *Truly* alive. Life makes itself known—you said so yourself."

They were both smiling broadly now. Fogg patted Marchand on the back. "Monsieur Marchand, that is one hell of a gentleman you brought into the world. But I would caution you not to go into mass production. He is not a product to be sold. His is a unique mind, no less than yours or mine. He deserves his freedom. He deserves a life of his own."

"Of course," said Marchand. "I had hoped you would reach that conclusion. But how can he enjoy a life when he is adrift in space?"

Fogg turned to his wife. "Aouda, dearest, I hope you're ready for our honeymoon. We have a comet to catch!"

She squeezed his hand, hopping with excitement.

Then he remembered the gas burning in his oven. "But we need to run by the house quickly. I have a promise to keep."

Phileas Fogg and Aouda ran off through the cheering crowd, hands tightly clasped. Stuart and Flanagan watched them go.

Flanagan shook his head. "You really believe they're going back into space to chase down a blown-up robot? That guy needs to learn how to quit while he's ahead. He'll never find it."

"Hmph. It sounds to me like you have failed to learn the most obvious lesson from this whole escapade."

"Yeah? And what is that?"

Stuart took one final puff from the cigar, then dropped it, snuffing it out underfoot.

"Never bet against Phileas Fogg."

AUTHOR'S NOTE

Jules Verne's *Le Tour du monde en quatre-vingts jours* was originally published as a serial in 1872, with the final installment published on the same date as Phileas Fogg's deadline, reportedly convincing some readers that the challenge was actually taking place. Verne is remembered primarily as the father of science fiction, but this story—perhaps his most enduring—is grounded in the real world. He was inspired by the completion of the Suez Canal and the Transcontinental Railroad to write a story illustrating that the whole world was now within reach (at least for anyone who could afford it).

As I read the book in the summer of 2015, it occurred to me that humanity's reach was continuing to grow. The Dawn spacecraft was sending back the first detailed photos of Ceres and New Horizons was preparing for its historic flyby of Pluto. Recent years had also seen rovers on Mars and a lander on Titan. The images sent back by these missions were truly remarkable. They turned vague entries in science books into real destinations. I spent hours studying the photos at the highest resolution possible, trying to get a sense of the scale. I remember trying to figure out how big a football stadium would look in Occator Crater. *Tiny* was the answer. I was fascinated by all of the frozen worlds of the outer solar system, and NASA's internet traffic suggested I wasn't the only one. Inspiration struck. I could explore all of these distant realms vicariously through the travels of Phileas Fogg.

When I set out to reimagine Verne's most popular non-sci-fi story as sci-fi, I immediately turned Jean Passepartout into a robot. I wanted to be true to the original characters, at least in spirit, and I was amused by the thought of pairing an excitable machine with an emotionless human. The character of Aouda would require a 21st century update as she is treated like a dainty piece of luggage in the original text. I did my best to make her a strong, capable protagonist in her own right. I also brought Sir Francis Cromarty and his 'true British phlegm' along for the ride. Agent Fix would require the most creativity since there was no realistic way for anyone to follow Fogg on his interplanetary journey, but science fiction has a solution for every problem. When astrophysics closes a door, genetic engineering opens a window. I even found a way to include a new version of Jules Verne's most nefarious character, but I'll say no more since unprincipled readers might grow restless and flip ahead for a peek at these back pages before they've earned their way here (I know your tricks, you reprobates! I *am* you!). I also saw an opportunity to greatly expand the character of Lord Albemarle, who was mentioned only briefly in the original book. This minor character, a paralyzed old man who wished he could stand up and join Fogg on his journey, stayed with me for some reason, so I made him the primary impetus for the wager.

For all my fellow astronomy nerds out there, I cannot claim this story is 'hard science fiction.' Liberties were taken here and there in the interest of entertainment, and I'm not smart enough to write about this stuff without making big errors. I'm sure that smartypants Neil deGrasse Tyson could tear it to shreds, but I took pride in at least trying to depict the locations as realistically as possible. I was writing about Ahuna Mons before it even had a name. The very day the International Astronomical Union announced the newly discovered mountain was being named for the post-harvest festival of the Sumi Naga tribe in India, I opened my working draft and added the new name. I even got lucky by describing the surface of Ceres as an unstable muck long before it was determined that the dwarf planet is covered with 'mud volcanoes.' If the Great Red Spot ever disappears or geodes are discovered on Ganymede, I will (at long last) be heralded as a prophetic genius.

The year 2078 was chosen by a real planetary alignment that will take place then. The 1g acceleration travel times are crudely calculated estimates, but they aren't too far from the truth. If you could build an engine that worked the way the Steady Axe works, you really could reach Mars in a couple of days and Pluto in a few short weeks. Just don't ask me where you would get that much energy. That's for the Karbasis to figure out.

This is a self-published book, which means it can be difficult getting attention from the heartless algorithms of ecommerce. Please help others find (or avoid) this book by rating it and leaving an honest review on Amazon and/or Goodreads. Even a one sentence review helps make the book more visible. And as a first-time novelist, I would sincerely like to read your review.

If this story has made you curious what Hayn Crater and Kraken Mare and Verona Rupes look like, be sure to download the free PDF "Phileas Fogg's Travel Log" from the address on the next page to see the actual NASA photographs that inspired this book. It truly boggles the mind to see these glimpses of wildly different worlds in our own celestial neighborhood. Then take some time to go outside tonight and look up at the night sky. Those are real places up there. They are waiting for us. I hope someone reading this makes it there one day.

-Jonathan Ammon

But wait, there's more!

See actual NASA photographs of locations visited in this book, from Hayn Crater to Ahuna Mons to Tombaugh Regio. No sign-up required. No annoying newsletter. Simply visit the web address below to enjoy the visual companion booklet "Phileas Fogg's Interplanetary Travel Log."

A £60,000,000,000 value, yours for free!

Download the PDF at: https://bit.ly/ATSSI80D

ABOUT THE AUTHOR

As a screenwriter, Jonathan Ammon won the Scriptapalooza Fellowship and was a finalist for Ron Howard & Brian Grazer's Imagine Impact program. "Around the Solar System in 80 Days" is his first novel. He is originally from the Northern Kentucky suburbs of Cincinnati. His current whereabouts are unknown.

Printed in Great Britain
by Amazon

80932322R00174